The Fragility
of Light

The Fragility of Light

A NOVEL

HEATHER S. LONCZAK, PhD

Ivy Lane Press

Original Title: The Fragility of Light
First edition: March, 2024
© 2023, Heather S. Lonczak
© 2023, Ivy Lane Press
www.HeathersLonczakAuthor.com

Hardcover ISBN: 979-8-9896481-4-6 (Amazon KDP, Hardcover)
Paperback ISBN: 979-8-9896481-5-3 (Amazon KDP, Paperback)
Kindle ISBN: 979-8-9896481-6-0 (Amzon KDP, Kindle)

Hardcover ISBN: 979-8-9896481-0-8 (IngramSpark Edition, Digital Cloth™ Cover)
Paperback ISBN: 978-1-7353625-9-5 (IngramSpark Edition)
Ebook ISBN: 979-8-9896481-1-5 (IngramSpark Edition)

LCCN: 2023923304

Printed by Lightning Source
For sales and distribution reach out to: INGRAM or ipage

For the invisible ones.

When light pushes away the darkness,
eventually another darkness shall come.
When the darkness itself is transformed into light,
it is a light that no darkness can oppose.

-Rabbi Menachem Mendel Schneerson, adapted by Tzvi Freeman

I am terrified by this dark thing
That sleeps in me;
All day I feel its soft, feathery turnings, its malignity.

-Sylvia Plath

Prologue

As my body slowly comes to, my mind remains submerged beneath the weight of itself. The fingers on my right hand ache as I flex and squeeze them. I don't have to look; I know my fingernails will be black with charcoal. And that it will be smudged across my body, even darkening my face. The house will be similarly swathed in the wreckage of my emotional entropy. There will be piles and piles of drawings. As if, at some level, I knew I'd need to stock up—the fall was coming.

Like so many mornings before, I'm dead weight—barely mobile, paralyzed by despair. An invasive, sickening despair that sits somewhere at the base of my throat, spreading its tendrils throughout my bloodstream and organs—rendering me defenseless against a crushing sense of hopelessness.

I gradually open my eyes, noticing the expected carnage throughout the room. The floor is covered with clothing and shoes, plates and cups are littered about the dresser and nightstand, and charcoal is smeared across the sheets. As I turn my body toward the door, the bed creaks ever so slightly. My eyelids feel inexplicably heavy and, as I begin to let them close, I hear her.

She's always there, listening and watching. *She always knows.*

"Mama," she whispers softly, ever careful with her broken mother.

"Yes, my angel?" I croak, barely audible.

I hear the door squeak as she opens it further. I hear tiptoed footsteps move across the hardwood. I hear dishes being rearranged on the nightstand. I feel soft, slightly sticky fingers touch my face, lightly caress my cheek.

"I brought you a scone," she says, her little girl voice infiltrating my sickness, reminding me of my absolute failure as a mother. As tears begin to fall from the corners of my eyes, tiny fingers wipe them away.

"Don't cry, Mama."

I look at my perfect girl. Her dark curls are tangled and wild, and she's wearing her favorite pink princess nightgown. Her green eyes seem impossibly big, impossibly sad. I notice that she, too, bears the familiar black markings across her arms and forehead. I watch her thick black lashes move up and down as she watches me, hoping to God I'll act like a mother today. She's so beautiful, my darling girl. As I look at her, I imagine who she might become. Will she be an artist like me? Or perhaps something more serious like her father? Will she experience pure happiness—that which comes without cost or penalty? Like a thousand times before, I pray to a God I don't believe in—please let her not be like me.

As the darkness secures its grasp, these thoughts of my beloved girl hold the sickness at bay—if only for a moment. Just long enough to keep me above the surface, with the steady rhythm of my heart reminding me that I'm still here. And with the feathery touch on my cheek reminding me of why I must stay.

Chapter 1 ❧ Sunny

I often dream of my mother's dead eyes. There is that familiar falling sensation before I am abruptly plunged back into the conscious world. I used to startle myself out of bed, sometimes landing face down on the floor. My husband had comforted me at the beginning. But eventually my night terrors and odd continence were but another aspect of our unspoken pact—an acceptance of the increasing bounds of normalcy.

Those dreams, which had appeared in various forms throughout my life, intensified as I reached adulthood. When the world shut off, the nights became my bitter nemesis—leaving me face-to-face with my torments. While my memories of my mother remained vague and shadowy—a blur of constant motion and color—I could always sense her there in the corner of my mind. To me, she was an enigma—an unearthly presence I could neither grasp nor release. I also found it difficult to disentangle my recollections of her from those of my father. Perhaps in my yearning to know her, I had desperately coveted his memories too.

When I was a little girl, my father's impenetrable love for my mother was always there—behind his every expression, his every movement. I recall him taking her hand and softly kissing each finger as his eyes never left hers. And gently twisting around strands of her lustrous black hair. And laughing as they danced in the living room, her stockinged feet spinning gracefully on the floor. When we went places without her, he often pointed out her favorite songs or foods. And later, once she'd left us, if he saw a woman who resembled her, I would secretly watch his eyes follow her. The longing on his face during those moments flooded my mind with despair. His was a chasm I could not fill.

My dad remarried when I was thirteen. By then, references to my mother had disappeared from his tongue as he focused on his new wife. His new family. He met Linda at Whole Foods of all places (only my charismatic dad could pull that off). She was a kindergarten teacher with a petite frame and shoulder-length wispy blonde hair. She wore almost no makeup and was pretty in a crunchy sort of way. She was soft-spoken, but had a quiet strength about her.

I did my best to dislike Linda—she had taken my father away, after all. I was pouty and insolent, refusing to accept her presence—and she was *always* around. As a teenager, I remember her trying to hug me as I either recoiled or stood rigid as a board. Sometimes she brought me little gifts like stuffed animals or craft supplies. Yet I always resented her; I resented that she monopolized my dad, I resented her pretense of liking me, I resented her long skirts and unpainted toenails, and I resented her soft, feathery voice. Thinking back now, she really didn't do anything wrong except that she was not my mother. My mother was all swirling lights and music; Linda was as bland as boiled eggs.

As I got older, I often looked for traces of my mother in the things she loved, like quartz crystals in rose and amethyst, old sequoia trees, and flowers—she so adored flowers. I recall my father bringing home fragrant bouquets that made her squeal with delight as she breathed in their scent. She always displayed the bouquets on the dining room table after arranging them in a cranberry crystal vase I was not allowed to touch. Lilies were her favorite and, despite the headaches they caused my dad, he bought them anyway. He didn't tell her about the headaches—he was unselfish that way. But I knew. The scent of lilies has always muddled my mind with vague, disjointed images I don't fully understand, but also with an aching need for my mother—that much is undeniable.

It was my mother's love of flowers that often propelled me toward the Farmers' Market during that period of blissful ignorance when I was newly married—when the future seemed feasible. After leaving my office in the evening, I was drawn to the overflowing baskets of vibrant Japanese eggplants, kaleidoscope carrots with the stems attached, and glossy bell peppers in deep red and yellow. And the heady scent of sun-warmed tomatoes still clinging to the vine that reminded me of my grandfather. I would make my way toward Viktor, the stout middle-aged flower vendor who always spotted me from afar, saying, "How is my beautiful Sunshine today?" with a Slavic accent. I was usually too shy to speak more than a few words to him and would blush each time he offered me a single pink rose.

I would head toward home, gazing up at the dingy Citibank clocktower—forever stuck at 2:47—before inhaling the intoxicating sweetness of my favorite European bakery. I purchased muffins there nearly every morning, sometimes giving one to the homeless woman on the corner. Occasionally I also indulged in a soft pretzel or a decadent cinnamon roll I could never finish. The scent of the bakery would be replaced by a nicotine cloud that invariably hovered over the Whistlestop Pub—a favorite hangout of my coworkers that I had never entered. As I dodged the cigarette smoke along with leering eyes of businessmen leaving for the day, I would quicken my pace. Once I passed the small law office with its peeling yellow paint and rickety porch swing, I would sprint up the stairs toward my front porch—unconsciously counting each step—my heart fluttering in anticipation of seeing my beautiful husband, Joshua.

Months later, my mind would often return to that period of innocence, that irreplicable respite just before the storm.

Joshua and I met as juniors at San Diego State University. I could have gone to a better college—maybe even Ivy League, as I had been an honor student my entire life and particularly excelled in English and literature. But SDSU was close to my family, which would make it easy to check in on my grandparents after class. I'd also been jogging near the campus for years and was in love with the white Spanish Mission-style buildings encircled by palm trees. Despite my father's misgivings, I had dreamed of going to SDSU and didn't bother to apply anywhere else. It was my one act of underachievement, and I never regretted it.

I had always been bookish and shy, something of a loner—and college was no different. Other students likely found me standoffish and aloof—story of my life. Guys would approach me from time to time, only to be quickly discouraged by my lack of responsiveness. I didn't much care. Even after learning I was a bit nearsighted freshman year, I rarely wore glasses outside of class—I appreciated the blur; it was like an artificial boundary between me and everyone else. And although my self-constructed fortresses seemed to make everything easier, it was a tradeoff. In truth, I craved being around people. I wanted to go to parties and reveal some semblance of myself. But I just couldn't seem to get to the other side.

Unlike other guys, Joshua didn't give up on me. I often saw him glancing at me during the spring of my junior year, quickly looking away when discovered. In the afternoons, students gravitated toward the outside campus—throwing a frisbee or chatting with friends. Sometimes I studied on the lawn with my best friend, Elizabeth. But more often, I sat alone either drawing or reading a book. There were several weeks when I caught Joshua looking my way at least once a day as he walked by. Unlike me, he was never without an entourage of college buddies. I didn't think much of him at the time; he blended in with the rest of them. Plus, I figured he was just another admirer who would be unimpressed once he got closer, moving on to the next one soon enough.

One particularly sunny afternoon, he decided to approach me. I was sitting beneath a magnolia tree on my dad's gray NYU sweatshirt, reading *Lolita*. I was lost in the book when he said hello, causing me to nearly jump out of my skin.

"Oh no, I'm *so* sorry! I didn't mean to scare you. I just wanted to introduce myself." I squinted up at him, the sun in my eyes.

"That's okay, it's easy to do."

This moment is, according to Joshua, the most pivotable one in our relationship. He told me later that once he saw my watery blue-green eyes, he knew he was done for.

"My name is Joshua. I believe you're in English 302 with me. Sylvia?"

"It's Sunny. I go by Sunny."

"Nice to meet you, Sunny. That's a perfect name for you," he flirted.

Here's the part where I always seemed to fuck up. I didn't know what to say next and my mind was spinning as I searched for something clever. I didn't want to reveal myself as an imposter, but I was at a loss. So I just sat there mutely, like a damned imbecile.

"What are you reading?"

Okay, this is familiar territory. I can answer this question. "*Lolita*, you know, by Nabakov."

"I've heard of that book. Isn't he a pedophile?"

I shrugged. "There's more to it than that."

"What class is that for?"

"It's not. I'm reading it on my own. It's one of my favorites. The way he writes is like, I don't know…poetry washing over me." *Oh God, did I just say that?* "I've read it three times so far."

"Can I see it?"

I handed him the worn copy. He read the first lines: "'Lolita, light of my life, fire of my loins. My sin, my soul. Lo-lee-ta: the tip of the tongue taking a trip of three steps down the palate to tap, at three, on the teeth. Lo Lee. Ta.'

"Okay, now I'm definitely intrigued. But are you sure he isn't a pedo?" he asked, handing the book back to me.

"You just need to read it yourself." Having forgotten my sunglasses that day, I blocked the sun with my hand while looking up at him. I could feel the dull beginnings of a headache.

"Well, then I will!" he said, smiling.

I'll never forget the first time I saw Joshua smile. His face changed entirely. It's not that he had perfect teeth; they were pretty, but not completely straight and one front tooth was slightly chipped in the corner—it was the joy his face morphed into when he smiled. What I thought was a smug little frat boy face immediately dissolved into something else altogether. His face was earnest, his smile complete, all the way to his eyes.

Joshua had the type of handsomeness that sneaks up on you. With his brown hair and average height, he could blend into a group. But his eyes sparkled with intelligence and his engaging personality made people feel significant. He even had me believing he truly wanted to read *Lolita* because *I* recommended it. I suppose I finally noticed him on this day too.

Joshua slowly crept his way inside my heart. He walked me home from class, holding my sweaty hand and, like something from a 1950s postcard, sometimes even carrying my books. He wrote love notes and slid them under my apartment door or left them on my windshield. He was resolute in his persistence, not at all deterred by my reticence. He didn't believe me when I said I was shy, insisting it was impossible—that I was far too beautiful. It was a naïve phrase that would normally annoy me, but not with Joshua. And even though it took some time for me to trust him, I found myself actually *wanting to*. That was a first.

After a few weeks of walking home and studying together, we went to a college bar with live music. Joshua knew the door guy, who didn't ask for ID. I drank sweet pear cider and felt myself loosening up. I had little experience with alcohol, mostly because my dad had repeatedly warned me of its dangers. More than that though, I feared losing control; control was *everything*. But I remember how my face tingled and my inhibitions dissolved as that cider took hold of me. I was funny and sarcastic, perhaps even sexy. Joshua leaned over the filthy wooden table and kissed me. Our first kiss. It was soft and gentle, and tasted sweet—leaving me wanting more. We continued to drink and found ourselves dancing and making out. *Publicly* making out—and I didn't even care. I was buzzing—soaring far above my usual self-doubt and disquietude. And I remember thinking, *Oh, this boy, this man, how I want him.*

19

And so began our love story. It was a love that would be tested and stretched, teetering on the edges of rationality. Yet never lacking.

I wasn't a virgin when I met Joshua, but I'd never "made love" either. I was used to boys pushing their tongues down my throat, tasting their stale beer breath as they urgently shoved their erections against me. Guiding my head downward, roughly grabbing at my crotch, squeezing my breasts too hard. Leaving angry marks on my neck. This was the "love making" of adolescent boys, and I hated it.

I was seventeen the first time I had sex. I didn't know the boy well; in fact, I'd only met him that night. Slutty though it was, I just wanted to get it over with. Feeling ashamed of my lack of experience, I wanted to sleep with someone I'd never see again. The sex was quick, but painful. Even worse—it was humiliating. And there was the blood, *so much blood*. I figured there was yet something else wrong with me. When he finished, I lay there crying and shaking uncontrollably. But at least I was no longer a virgin.

With Joshua, I understood what the great poets were talking about. My heart fluttered at the thought of seeing him. My stomach ached at the thought of losing him. I'd never known this type of pain; it was beautiful in its own way. Lord Byron's haunting words swirled feverishly in my brain:

> *When we two parted*
> *In silence and tears,*
> *Half broken-hearted*
> *To sever for years,*
> *Pale grew thy cheek and cold,*
> *Colder thy kiss;*
> *Truly that hour foretold*
> *Sorrow to this …*

I could not lose him.

The first time Joshua and I had sex was in my college apartment. It was a small studio overlooking Point Loma. After living in the dorms during my first year at SDSU, then with roommates until I was a junior, I was thrilled to have a place all for myself. It had dark wood floors, a modern kitchen all in white, and was furnished with a desk and queen-sized bed.

We waited for weeks before sleeping together because we wanted it to be right. Morrissey was singing as we sat on my bed drinking cheap champagne.

Our connection that night was almost feral, yet deeply human. We explored each other's every crevice, freckle, and imperfection. We were insatiable. When he was inside me, our eyes never left each other.

We touched souls, Joshua and me.

Our hunger for each other never subsided, it only showed itself in different ways. As we got closer, I gradually exposed more pieces of myself. No guy had ever really known me, and I didn't want to scare him off. I was convinced there was a deep ugliness about me and would need to tread carefully.

And yet somehow Joshua found me entirely lovable—either not noticing or not concerned with my endless stream of defects and eccentricities. He didn't comment when I picked my cuticles until they bled, leaving a morbid scattering of flesh across my lap. He didn't judge my profound sense of inadequacy and awkwardness at parties. He didn't see me lie wide awake for hours after a social interaction, harshly evaluating my every move, my every word. And he didn't know about my mother, or the counting, or my grandparents—or *any* of it. Not yet. He sensed a worthiness in me that I didn't, and I was petrified by what would happen once the veil was lifted.

Chapter 2 ❧ Sunny

We got engaged during our senior year. Joshua dragged me to a college basketball game, saying his buddy was a star player. I'm still not sure how he convinced me to go, I hated the whole scene: organized sports, hard benches, and crowds—the trifecta of irritation. Unlike football, which I especially loathed, at least basketball games were quick. This helped me to cope with the smell of beer, the drunk girl sitting to my left, and the loudmouthed idiots kicking the seat behind me. At halftime, Joshua left his seat for the bathroom; a perfect opportunity for me to take out the paperback I'd stashed in my purse. Five minutes later, I heard his voice on the loudspeaker.

What the fuck?

"Um…good evening, everyone." The crowd became quiet. "I won't take up much time, I just have a quick question for my girl."

Oh. My. God. What is he doing? I could feel my heart in my stomach. I thought I actually might vomit or pass out. I sank down in my seat as I heard my name and saw everyone looking at me. Joshua was on a big screen, getting down on one knee. The crowd became eerily quiet.

"My Beautiful Sunshine, my Sylvia Marie Zielinski, I've loved you since the first time we met. And I'll love you until the day I die. Please say you will spend forever with me and be my wife. Will you marry me?"

All eyes were on me, but I couldn't speak. I nodded my head.

"Is that a 'yes?'" he asked.

"YES!" I said as loud as I could muster before sinking back down again.

The crowd exploded. The drunk girl spilled beer on me and I didn't even care. Being with Joshua was like that. His love was intoxicating and I couldn't imagine life without him.

We both graduated in June of 2001, a little more than a year after we met. I double-majored in English Literature and Fine Arts, and Joshua majored in Business. We didn't sit together during the graduation ceremony, as we marched in alphabetical order (Fitzpatrick and Zielinski were worlds apart). Our families waited patiently up in the stands. I was magna cum laude, whereas Joshua slipped through with a 2.6 GPA. He was considerably less disciplined than I, content with mediocrity if it meant he could go to parties and smoke weed. Nonetheless, he received far greater applause than I when his name was called. My family was proud to be sure, especially my father who bragged about me at every opportunity. But they were soft-spoken and chose their words carefully. They couldn't compete with a rowdy gang of fraternity brothers yelling, "Fitz, Fitz, Fitz…!"

Our families gathered awkwardly after the ceremony. Joshua's parents lived in Indiana, so it was my first time meeting them. I was edgy as hell, wiping my sweaty hands on my robe and picking off my purple nail polish. At least my stepmother, Linda, stayed home with my half-siblings (Maddy and Spencer, five-year-old twins), knowing the lengthy commencement would've been too much for them. Their presence would only have added to my agitation.

Joshua's parents were kind enough, both of them hugging me lightly when introduced. His mom, Debbie, was of average height and maybe sixty pounds overweight. She wore her light brown hair in a bob with gray strands loosely framing her face. She was likely pretty at one time, but seemed to have given up on herself. Joshua's father, Rick, was tall with a straggly brown-gray beard and a receding hairline. He was friendly in a pure sort of way, whereas Debbie's kindness carried an undercurrent of judgment. Joshua also had two teenage brothers, Michael and Pete, who stood around nudging and poking at each other, paying little attention to much else.

My dad, who was tall and slender with dark wavy hair, gold-rimmed glasses and a neatly trimmed goatee, dodged Joshua's handshake, instead going in for a hug. Next, he greeted Debbie and Rick amicably, shaking each of their hands. I felt proud as I watched my warm, handsome father. Unlike me, he was a great conversationalist who could mix with most types of people. After introducing himself, he presented my grandparents to the group. They were hanging in the back, unsure how to act. They were not native English speakers, nor did they like crowds. He encouraged them to move forward and they shook hands with each of the adults.

My grandparents had met Joshua several times when we stopped by after class, but they often seemed tired, so we never stayed long—even as they fussed around the kitchen trying to feed us. Plus, I'd always felt protective of my grandparents, introducing them to few people outside my family. But now that I was soon to be married, I was finally ready to share these two remarkable people with my future husband. My babcia, whom I had called Baba since I was a baby, gave Joshua a kiss on each cheek, which amused me—I'd never seen him blush before. But my grandfather, Papa, went with a vigorous handshake. Then, still holding Joshua's hand, he said, "You know, Joshua, or *Yehoshua*, is a special name in Hebrew with origins the same as Jesus. It means 'the lord is my salvation.' Yehoshua was a brave leader of the Israelites. Quite a namesake, no?" This comment made Joshua blush even further, leaving him at a loss for words. From then on, Papa always referred to Joshua as "Yehoshua," which Joshua accepted with pride. On that special day—as always—my grandparents radiated kindness and gentility mixed with an unspeakable sadness in the backs of their eyes.

It was a big deal for Baba and Papa to attend my graduation. They rarely went anywhere besides the grocery store, nor did they mix with people other than their immediate family and the Polish friends they made after coming to America. I was so honored that they came to this noisy, unfiltered event. Baba had gone to the salon or beauty parlor, as she called it, earlier in the day. Her thinning hair, which she'd been dying blonde for as long as I could remember, was helmeted perfectly in place—not a strand breaking free despite a moderately windy day. Her nails were painted dark burgundy and she wore several beautiful rings.

My baba had been a beautiful woman and, even in her late 70s, had never stopped caring about her appearance. She wore a bit too much makeup, a red silk blouse, and black jeans. Baba was tiny, weighing no more than ninety-five pounds. She was probably only five foot two, although I'd rarely seen her without heels. But after a recent fall, my father and I had finally convinced her to relinquish her stilettos. Today she wore a low-heeled, black ankle boot. Flats were simply out of the question and we respected her feelings too much to push the issue.

Papa wore jeans and a blue cashmere sweater that accentuated his eyes. He was around five foot five, and slender like Baba. He wore black-rimmed glasses that contrasted with his thick white hair. As I watched these two people—*my people*—I felt a lump in my throat. *God, how I loved them.* But I also felt a stab of pain, as they both seemed impossibly frail. Trying not to worry, I instead focused on the eventful day and how much I knew they would love my future husband—how could they not?

During lunch we sat at a large round table at an upscale seafood restaurant. Being a vegetarian, I'd selected the place for everyone else. Our table was on a garden patio dripping with lavender clematis. The place was known for its clam chowder—which Papa devoured. My general memory of the meal is blurry, as I was painfully nervous around Joshua's family. I wondered if they would like me or think I was a freak. Or if they would think I was good enough for their beloved son, their firstborn. Not likely.

I nibbled on my salad and did my best to respond to Debbie's barrage of questions about my career plans. Maybe she was just being friendly, but it didn't feel good. I picked at my cuticles under the table until they hurt. When Joshua squeezed my hand, I tried to wipe my bloody fingers in my napkin hoping he wouldn't notice. I was relieved when he changed the subject.

Baba, who was most interested in the wedding, had several questions: "Where will it be? What type of flowers will you have? Have you looked at dresses?" My mild-mannered grandmother became animated when she talked about my wedding. I'd never seen her like this before and it warmed my heart. I needed to get more into the wedding planning, if only for her sake.

"More importantly," interrupted Papa, "have you two kids learned to dance?"

My grandparents adored dancing—as in old-school stuff like waltzes and the foxtrot. They were quite a hit back in the 60s, as they often reminded me. I told them we hadn't made any wedding plans just yet, but promised we would take dance lessons. This also caused Joshua to squeeze my hand under the table; I would need to wear him down before he set foot in a dance class. I'm not sure what our fathers were talking about throughout the meal, and Joshua's brothers wordlessly scarfed down their burgers while either staring at me or freaking out as an occasional bee zoomed over their plates. They were gangly pubescent boys sorely lacking in table manners and general etiquette; I didn't like them much. I was so glad for the meal to end; mixing my family with others felt wrong. They were mine alone; no one else could possibly understand them.

That summer, Joshua and I moved into my family home. It took a fair amount of persuading for my dad to allow Joshua to live there too, but he eventually gave in. I reasoned that the arrangement would save money, but that was not my true motivation—I was simply too lovesick to imagine living separate from Joshua. The white Dutch Colonial had plenty of space, including five bedrooms, four bathrooms and a half-acre of land in the back. Before they were married, Linda decorated the house in granny chic—

subjecting much of it to loud floral wallpaper and matching upholstery. She deviated a bit in the living room, which, although it did contain floor-length curtains displaying large red poppies, there was also red-striped wallpaper and a large velvet couch in the same deep crimson as the poppies. I quietly referred to that room as "redrum," since it reminded me of the scene from *The Shining* when blood poured through the hotel's haunted walls. But, consistent with her general theme, my room was originally decorated with a pink canopy bed and matching floral wallpaper. Elizabeth said the house looked like a Laura Ashley wet dream—I didn't disagree. But I guess it was cozy, in a gaudy sort of way.

When Linda became pregnant during my junior year in high school, my bedroom was moved to the basement. I actually preferred this arrangement since the downstairs offered more privacy and, as an added bonus, it had yet to be assaulted with Linda's floral vomit. The basement contained two bedrooms, a bathroom with a shower, and a decent sized rec room with a large leather couch and TV. I happily left my canopy bed and matching furniture upstairs for Maddy to use when she was older, opting instead for a simple double bed, white dresser, and oak bookshelf. Since the walls in my new room were all white, Linda occasionally offered up her decorating skills, to which I politely declined.

My room was nonetheless drenched in childhood memories. My most treasured possession was an antique mahogany jewelry box my dad brought me from Italy when I was six. It sat in the middle of my dresser and I often opened it, watching the white swan dance in circles to "Lara's Theme" from *Dr. Zhivago*. Inside the box was a red lipstick of my mother's, my favorite pieces of jewelry, and a folded up note on which she'd drawn beautiful tulips encircling the words, "I love you, my angel." I'd found the note in my lunchbox when I was in kindergarten and managed to hold onto it ever since. There was also a good-sized collection of costume jewelry and dress-up clothes in an old brass trunk at the foot of the bed, a stack of my childhood drawings under the bed, a pile of stuffed animals that dominated the end of the bed (or, lately, the floor), and various knickknacks, little toys and plastic crap throughout the room I didn't have the heart to throw away. The bookshelf overflowed with my favorite childhood books and classic literature I read during high school.

The second bedroom, which was down the hall, also functioned as a small gym. Along with a twin-sized bed, the room contained a treadmill, a large red exercise ball, a bench, and numerous weights. This was meant to be Joshua's room, but of course we only slept in mine. My dad didn't want to know about our sleeping arrangements and didn't ask.

The best part of my dad's house was the backyard cottage where Baba and Papa lived. It was an adorable little house with two small bedrooms and a bathroom with a surprisingly large jacuzzi tub where I occasionally took bubble baths as a teenager. It also had an old-fashioned-looking (but modern) kitchen with a black and white tile floor and a 1950s deco kitchen table. The family room was inviting and comfortable with a loveseat and Baba's easy chair. I had to give my dad (and maybe even Linda) credit for choosing this house in part because it included such an ideal place for my grandparents.

Baba and Papa seemed content in their little home. Baba enjoyed the light-filled kitchen, and Papa appreciated the backyard fruit trees and majestic live oak that the twins often climbed. Baba also cultivated a garden with plenty of herbs, carrots, cabbage, cucumbers, and other vegetables. But my grandparents never wanted to be burdensome or intrusive when it came to my dad and his new wife, rarely coming to the main house without being invited. Plus they continually attempted to pay rent—which my father never accepted—and babysat the kids several times a month. Honestly, Linda won the lottery with those in-laws.

I loved having my grandparents close during the summer after graduation. I checked in on them several times a week, often finding them gardening, cooking, or reading; and they were always delighted to see me. Sometimes I helped Papa pull weeds as he patiently described how to tend to his various plants; or I hung out with Baba as she prepared dinner or worked on her needlepoint. I remember those days with a painful, unyielding regret—if only I had taken better advantage of that time with my grandparents. *If only.*

Regardless of whether I was in the house or the backyard, Sparky—the terrier-mutt my dad and Linda adopted while I was at college—was always nearby. He had big, trusting brown eyes and often cocked his head to the side when being spoken to, which gave him the appearance of an empathetic listener. His soft white and brown coat smelled oddly of corn chips and, with his endless stores of energy, his little feet rarely stayed in one place.

Occasionally, when they were feeling up to it, my grandparents and I went on short walks around the neighborhood with Sparky pulling us along. Although they (especially Baba) weren't crazy about dogs, they always welcomed him as best they could. But I adored that little guy! He followed me everywhere, either wanting to play or curl up in my lap when I was reading or watching TV. He revealed a deep longing in me to be around animals, which I brought up with Joshua one muggy evening as we lay naked in bed—the sheets twisted around us.

"When we have our own place," I said, gently running my fingers along his chest, "I want six cats and at least two dogs—one little one, like Sparky, and maybe a pit bull or Labrador. Rescues of course. And a bunny. No—*two* bunnies, they must have a friend…"

Joshua turned to me, mocking an appalled expression. "Take it easy, Dr. Doolittle! Let's just focus on finding a home and getting married."

I looked at him with my saddest eyes.

"Okay, one, that's *one*, cat!" he gave in, expectedly. *Ha! Triumph.*

But of course we needed to get our lives in order before expanding our family. I received a job offer a few weeks after graduating and would be starting in August. It was for a medium-sized, well-established publishing company that was only a short drive from the house. It was the perfect job for me and, although I was excited, I was already overwrought with anxiety. I'd never done well with change, not to mention being around new people who would be evaluating my performance. But I'd always dreamed of becoming a book publisher and already consumed books like water. So, what better job than to read for a living? Of course, as the company's grunt, I would be doing nothing but editing for a low salary as I worked my way up. But I was fine with that.

Joshua, on the other hand, was pounding the pavement in search of a job. He sat at my father's computer in the kitchen feverishly typing cover letter after cover letter—each one edited by me. Sometimes I heard him sneak upstairs in the middle of the night to check his email. He was terribly anxious about finding work. But I knew he'd find something and instead tried to focus my thoughts on the wedding.

The date would be August 31st, less than three months away. Everyone told us it was too last-minute and that we should wait a year. We didn't care; we loved each other and were ready for the next big step in our relationship. But I was no bridezilla; I just wanted a meaningful ceremony with our families.

I did what was expected of me. I registered at Williams Sonoma, choosing delicate china and overpriced kitchen gadgets I knew I'd never use. I asked Elizabeth to be my maid of honor and enlisted a few not-so-close high school friends to fill in the bridesmaid slots. And I went to try on wedding dresses with Elizabeth, Babcia, Linda and Maddy. I decided on my third dress with conviction. It was a straight ivory gown with spaghetti straps and a generous slit up the side. And it was made with the most intricate Alençon lace in the bodice. It was perfect. Baba snatched it away in her little hands, along with the lace veil I picked out, and headed to the cashier before I saw the price.

We decided to get married at the beach where we'd shared so many memories. This idea was met with some disappointment by Debbie, who firmly believed in church weddings. But Joshua and I were not religious and I didn't believe in having a phony ceremony just to please others. Besides, I was technically Jewish and Joshua was a lapsed Catholic with little respect for organized religion. So we stood our ground knowing we'd regret it otherwise. Plus, we were saving our parents some money by marrying at the beach. We did, however, give in a little by choosing a local pastor to officiate with a mix of Christian and Jewish scripture. This got Debbie off our backs for the time being.

The ceremony was to be followed by a reception at Joshua's fraternity house—a stately Tudor that we'd managed to rent for the evening. The house had somehow remained classy and beautiful despite its generations of rowdy, bibulous inhabitants. But it was definitely dirty, so my father planned to hire a deep cleaning service in the days before the wedding. I would decorate the house with pink wisteria and white freesia (mostly for the heavenly scent), and my wedding bouquets would include cream-colored roses with hot pink tips. I wished I could've had lilies for my mother, but she loved roses too. My bridesmaids would wear short but classy pink cocktail dresses which Debbie would later describe as revealing and inappropriate. As I was quickly learning, Debbie was a fuddy-duddy who could put a negative twist on just about anything. I was forever grateful that she lived two thousand miles away—the stress of planning a wedding *and* starting a new job would've been unmanageable with her icy blue eyes looking down on me.

Chapter 3 ❧ Sunny

Knowing how much my life would be changing in the weeks ahead, I tried to calm myself by going on long jogs around the neighborhood or at the beach. Or sometimes I tried to read by the pool as Sparky snoozed in the sun. But as soon as he got too hot, he'd throw himself into the pool with abandon before shaking his wet fur all over me and my books. And, unless they were napping or at their gymnastics class, Spencer and Maddy were usually around—their bottomless need for attention putting an abrupt end to any attempts at relaxation.

The kids were fraternal twins with identical white-blonde hair, big brown eyes, and skin so fair it was almost translucent. Linda was forever applying sunscreen to their flailing limbs as they whined nonstop. As a teenager, I was prepared to despise these children. I was disgusted when I learned that Linda was pregnant, and quietly referred to the unborn babies as "The Replacements." When I first saw them at the hospital, I was surprised by my response. They were pruny-looking creatures with red blotchy skin and no hair whatsoever. To me, they looked like miniature old men who smelled bad and never stopped screaming. I began to address Spencer as "Winston" and Maddy as "Churchill," until my dad made me stop. But I was strangely captivated by them—often holding one or the other, bouncing about like a crackhead in my desperate attempts to shut them up.

As the kids got older, their personality differences became more apparent. Maddy was always ready to play; she could go for hours. She would bring boxes of doll furniture out on the grass and we would create what she called "setups"—which were sprawling households for her collection of trolls and Smurfs. She was a strong-minded little girl who was not afraid to voice her opinions. If I gave a troll the wrong voice or decorated the room incorrectly, she would immediately let me know. But she was also sweet, with a soft sing-song voice and gentle touch. Maddy had been obsessed with me since she was two, constantly wanting me to play with her, tell her a story, or do something artsy. It was equal parts endearing and annoying.

Spencer was generally quieter than Maddy, except when he was upset. Spencer's tantrums were legendary, they could be heard for blocks. Fortunately, at age five, they were rare, but Maddy still knew how to push his buttons. He was a physical kid who loved to play sports, have pretend sword fights, and jump in the pool—preferably dragging me in with him.

The kids were beside themselves with happiness when they learned that both me *and* Joshua would be living back home over the summer. Maddy appointed herself as the recreation director, reciting a long list of obligatory activities—each of which sounded excessively tiring and/or messy. She and Spencer would often fight over me and argue about whether to build setups or go swimming. And if they caught sight of Joshua, they would immediately descend upon him like locusts, pulling him toward the backyard for one of their interminable games of hide-and-seek.

The twins were like different children altogether when they were with my grandparents. They were not only civilized, but obedient and pleasant. Perhaps they were either sensitive to their grandparents' relative frailty or Baba and Papa had a calming effect on them, I wasn't sure. But one thing was obvious: my grandparents were totally besotted with their grandchildren from day one. When they were colicky newborns, Papa had a special way of holding one in his arms while gliding around the room—it quieted them every time. Baba would sit in Linda's rocking chair with a baby in her lap as she sang softly in Polish. They never seemed to cry when she did this, their little eyes either glued to hers or unable to stay open as they drifted off to sleep. As the kids got a little older, it was sweet to watch them interact with their grandparents, who were eternally kind and patient—perhaps in the same way their own long-lost parents and grandparents had been with them.

As she got older, Maddy often clung to Baba. When I visited my grandparents over the summer, I'd sometimes find her in the cottage either watching Baba cook or helping to roll out dough for pierogi, which were stuffed with farmer's cheese, potatoes, mushrooms, or cabbage, and served with a generous side of sour cream. Maddy especially loved it when Baba made cookies, sneaking mouthfuls of dough when she thought no one was looking. Baba was definitely an exceptional cook and she relished having

Joshua and me home to cook for. "Eat, eat," she would say, looking at me, "you're no bigger than a matzah!"

I had missed Baba's cooking while I was at college, especially her borscht, which tasted like home. And, after being introduced to Baba's cabbage rolls, which were stuffed with meat and drizzled with tomato sauce, Joshua couldn't get enough of them. Although Papa was a less experienced cook who preferred gardening, he was known for his karpatka—a delicate cream-filled pastry that he learned how to make from watching his mother more than fifty years before. Sometimes if Joshua or I had a craving for karpatka, we would send one of the kids over to the cottage with a written message, such as: "We love you, Papa! Can you *please* make karpatka? XOXO." Our tactic usually worked, but, even when it didn't, it always made Papa laugh.

Linda and my father were decent enough cooks, although they were inconsistent. Linda, who was vegan, made delicious salads, hearty soups, and homemade bread. Unfortunately however, she'd recently learned how to make inedible fake meat patties, or "cow pies," as Joshua and I secretly called them, and falafel balls that were dry enough to choke a camel. If I was sitting outside, she would sometimes bring these out to me for lunch. Eventually, I made myself scarce around lunchtime or sneaked the dry fare to Sparky or the squirrels. My dad's culinary expertise was mostly limited to grilling chicken, veggies, and seafood. Living with a vegan *and* a vegetarian—much to his chagrin— my father was considerate about at least keeping red meat out of our meals. Although I knew Joshua snuck the occasional burger, especially when he stopped for a beer after one of his job interviews.

Joshua was so consumed with finding a job that I ended up doing all of the wedding preparation myself. He gave me a list of attendees and groomsmen, for whom I ordered black tuxes with pink bowties. His tux would be white with the same pink bowtie. When it came to choosing invitations, I poured through a stack of invitation books I'd checked out from the store. Every time I thought I'd picked one, I changed my mind. After two weeks of this, it was starting to consume me. I asked Joshua to help me choose, but he said he trusted my judgment. This annoyed me to no end.

One night I sat in the basement rec room until 5:00 a.m. looking at invitation books, when I broke out in tears. "I can't do this," I told Joshua, standing over the bed.

"Huh?" he said groggily.

When I repeated myself, he looked a little alarmed. "Can't do what?" he asked cautiously.

"I can't pick out the invitations, there are too many!" Now I was sobbing.

He let out a sigh of relief. "Come on to bed. You go to sleep while I look through the books."

Grateful, I collapsed into bed with my soggy roll of toilet paper in hand. In the morning, Joshua had picked his favorite from my top twenty list. We both agreed on the invitations, and I promised to stop looking at the books and make the order. Later that day, I noticed he'd returned the books to the store. I felt like this should've bothered me, but it was actually a weight off my chest.

I had around one hundred invitations to send, which were mostly to Joshua's friends and family. My side of the guest list was relatively small, including a handful of friends, a great aunt and uncle, and a few cousins. My dad and Linda added some names too. But the bulk of my family, which would have been large on my father's side, was wiped out during the Holocaust, leaving few descendants. As I looked at the two lists next to each other—Joshua's easily five times longer than mine—I felt that loss more keenly than ever, causing me to catch my breath. I felt an overwhelming surge of sadness when I considered the weight of this unmistakable void for my father and grandparents. That evening, I hugged all three of them tightly as they looked at me with puzzled expressions.

My mother's side of the family was small too, but for other reasons I didn't fully understand. I did have one grandmother: Sylvia. She was my namesake, although she went by 'Sylvie'. But she was in a nursing home of some sort and certainly wouldn't have come even if I invited her. I'd only spoken to her a few times in the past ten years. She had outlived her latest husband (there had been multiple) and her second husband—my grandfather, took off long before I was born. I never met him and had little interest in doing so.

Grandma Sylvie was an odd woman who had mostly kept to herself over the years. Growing up, we only visited her on rare occasions and it never went well. She lived in a small wrangler just outside Las Vegas. I remember it as being crowded with boxes, magazines, and cats—*so many cats*. The house smelled of mothballs and urine—two scents that still conjure up her image and make me want to retch. Grandma Sylvie was sometimes nice, offering me butterscotch candies that were nearly as old as she was and occasionally sending me a twenty-dollar bill for my birthday. But she was unpredictable— sometimes a little spacy and other times off-the-charts bizarre. During our last visit when I was only seven, she was vile toward me, insisting that I'd been sent to spy on her. Then she turned on my father, screaming, "You too! Get out of my house, traitors! Get out!" as spittle formed on the edges of her mouth and her eyes darted back and forth. I had nightmares about that scene for months thereafter.

Grandma Sylvie would not be invited to the wedding.

I consolidated the wedding list, compiled addresses, and researched the best way to write wedding envelopes. I was disgusted by the antiquated sexism suggested online, as there was no way I would be addressing any female by her husband's name. In fact, I decided to avoid the use of "Mrs." altogether—even though I knew this would annoy Debbie and some of the older guests. Once I was sure of the list, I decided to alphabetize it by the woman's first name. Then I changed my mind and alphabetized it by the woman's last name. I went back and forth with this, becoming increasingly frustrated. Joshua reminded me that this made no difference. But I didn't care.

I decided to address the envelopes myself using calligraphy. I didn't know how to do calligraphy, but I was an artist, so how hard could it be? I bought a calligraphy book and a special pen, and practiced for hours. When I eventually wrote my first envelope, it looked terrible. I tossed it away and tried again. And again. And again. Eventually, I only had half as many envelopes as invitations. When Joshua came home after the third day of this, the wadded-up envelopes lay all around my bedroom as I sat on my bed staring at the wall.

"What's up, my love?"

"I suck at calligraphy," I said in monotone.

Joshua laughed.

"What the hell is so funny?"

"Whoa, easy there! You don't need to *write* them; we can make labels on the computer using a script font. It will look great! Don't worry."

"But that's so impersonal. I want them to be special and perfect."

"No one is judging our wedding invitation envelopes, honey. Trust me," he said comfortingly while rubbing my back.

Joshua ended up ordering more envelopes and purchasing labels, which I typed out over the next few days. He was wise enough to order three times more than we needed. When I had my final stacks of labeled invitations, I alphabetized them again—several times, before adding stamps. Then I counted them and was sure someone was missing. I went back to my list and couldn't figure it out. Math was not my forte, but something had to be off. When I counted them the fourth time, I realized that I had made an extra label for the same person. When I finally took them to the post office, I felt only slightly better. I was sure I wrote them incorrectly or missed someone, which I worried about for days. But I kept it to myself.

About a week later, after I'd calmed down about the invitations, I was outside reading when Joshua rushed over. "I got a job, I got a job!" he chanted, pulling me up from my chair and swinging me around. He had been hired as a financial analyst at a tech company in Tula Vista. The job sounded mind-numbingly dull, but he was ecstatic. We were both relieved, as we were desperate to find a place to live, pay off our debt, and get on with our lives.

Like mine, Joshua's new job started in August, giving us several more weeks to enjoy our time off. We decided to make the most of it and explore the area like tourists. We visited the zoo, went to a waterslide park, hiked in the desert, went whale watching (which made both of us seasick), and spent two days at Joshua Tree National Park. We also enjoyed several restaurants, including sketchy dives and a 5-star French restaurant where we celebrated my 23rd birthday early, since it occurred during the week my job started. That period was filled with beautiful moments I wished I could bottle up forever.

July ended far too quickly and I could feel myself growing increasingly anxious about my job, which started before Joshua's. I'd been sorting through my wardrobe for a month and, on my final weekend of unemployment, I decided nothing would work and went shopping for new clothes. On the eve of my first day, I laid out an above-the-knee black skirt, black wedge shoes, and a silky pink blouse. Consumed with worry, I barely slept that night and, at one point, found myself short of breath and sitting straight up at the foot of the bed after an unintelligible, but disturbing dream about my mother.

I got up early the next morning feeling agitated and nauseous. As I sat up in bed, I took deep breaths and tried to calm myself down. It didn't help. With shaky hands, I managed to style my hair in a loose bun and apply my makeup, which I kept light. I started pitting out as soon as I got dressed, my blouse feeling damp against my skin, and was too nauseated to eat breakfast. Joshua said I looked both beautiful and professional.

"Thanks. But I didn't hear any airplanes today, Joshua," I sat on the end of the bed and gazed out the window.

He looked baffled.

Exasperated, I said, "It's *always* a good day when I hear airplanes in the morning. Today: Nada. I'm doomed."

He shook his head and tried not to smile. "You will be brilliant, you always are."

Once Joshua kissed me and reminded me again of my worthiness, I grabbed my purse and plodded upstairs. Fortunately, I was early enough to avoid the rest of my family—I had no stomach for well-wishes and platitudes. When I heard the kids arguing upstairs, I flew out the kitchen door. I would grab a coffee on the way.

When I arrived at the publishing company, my boss, Emily Blackburn, came to the waiting room to greet me. She was tall and thin, with black-rimmed glasses that were too large for her bird-like face. She dressed like an old-time librarian, but was likely in her 30s or 40s, I wasn't sure. But she greeted me kindly before showing me around and introducing me to everyone. I must have met fifteen people, but I couldn't recall a single name.

She sat me down in a bland little office—a windowless space near the employee kitchen—and gave me a stack of papers to read, most of which were about the company and its policies. I also read a grammar and punctuation manual, but I already knew most of it. As I sat reading, I calmed down a bit. I kept reminding myself that I was perfectly suited for the job and that they truly wanted me there. When 6 p.m. rolled around, I practically ran out of the building. But I was glad to have managed my first day without making an ass of myself.

Joshua was excited about starting work the following week. He looked so handsome on his first day, wearing khaki pants and a button-up blue shirt. He ate a big breakfast, gave me a kiss, and was out the door by 7:30 a.m. As I got ready for work that morning, I found myself irritated with him for being so chill about something that literally made me shake. Then I decided I was jealous, which evolved into self-ridicule for being an insecure loser. These ruminations occupied my mind for a little while, but were replaced with despondency as I drove to work. *Why was everything so damned hard for me?*

By mid-August, I had mellowed out a great deal. My boss was pleased with my work, which wasn't too difficult. The company was in a slow spell, so my workload was relatively small. I also ran errands or ordered office supplies, but this low-level work didn't bother me at the time—it was a nice distraction. My main issue was the weekly staff meetings. The meetings made me so anxious that I ruminated about them for hours beforehand and then sat there with sweaty palms, not saying much of anything, and feeling like an idiot.

By the third week, I went to my general practitioner who prescribed Xanax. I took half a pill before the meetings and this helped considerably. I could answer all questions directed at me with an acceptable level of competence. Although the combination of the Xanax and stress never failed to give me a splitting headache. Fortunately, the meetings were toward the end of the day on Thursdays, so I was able to go home shortly thereafter and lie down. Eventually, Joshua called them my 'Thursday Headaches,' and was always there to rub my head when he came home.

Joshua liked his job well enough. The work was interesting and manageable, but the hours were a bit long—he never came home before 7:00 p.m. There was one co-worker he described as an "arrogant douche," but he liked the rest of his team.

On the weekends, Joshua and I looked for a new place to live and took care of final wedding touches. While the wedding plans were in good shape, I felt increasingly keyed up as the day got closer. I was worried that *something* would go wrong, but I didn't know what. I was especially concerned about my grandparents—I wondered if they'd be okay with all of the people and noise. And I worried that I would trip or pass out or say something stupid to Joshua's friends or family. I worried about *everything*.

I continued jogging, which eased some of my tension. I threw on my running clothes as soon as I got home from work and ran five miles every day (except Thursdays, when I had headaches). Eventually, I found that if I didn't run the same amount every time, I became convinced that something terrible would happen to my grandparents. After all, they had been through so much in their lives and all I had to do was run a lousy five miles. Any excuse not to run was simply pathetic.

Late one night as I was lying in bed, I became concerned that the different running route I'd taken after work that day was slightly shorter than my usual one. As I went over it again and again, I just wasn't convinced that I had run the full five miles. I thought I might've been short by about an eighth of a mile.

Damn it! Why did I have to change my routine! I knew I had no choice but to redo my run, otherwise I'd never sleep—or something far worse would happen. So I quietly snuck out of bed, got dressed, and headed out the door. When I returned at 4:20 a.m., Joshua, who was sitting upstairs in the dark kitchen, scared the shit out of me.

"Where have you been? I was worried sick," he asked with a mix of concern and anger that I had never seen in him.

I was still out of breath and didn't answer.

"Oh my God. You've been *running*! At this hour? Are you crazy? Do you know how dangerous that is?" He was really upset.

"Well, I didn't do a full run earlier and so, I …" My words drifted off into nothingness.

Joshua calmed down and held me. "Honey, you don't need to do all of this running, you are perfect the way you are. In fact, you're actually too thin. And it's not safe to run in the middle of the night. Please promise me you won't do that again. And please just relax."

Normally someone telling me to "just relax" had a disastrous outcome. Joshua *really* didn't understand, but I was too tired to argue. I mumbled "okay," knowing that I'd be more careful about my routes so no more middle-of-the-night runs would be required. Although I did kind of enjoy the darkness and solitude.

Joshua and I found a condo in mid-August. It was close to my office and less than six miles from my dad's house. We could only afford it because my father co-signed on the loan and Joshua's parents helped with the down payment. It was a light, airy townhouse with a deck overlooking a nearby park. The master bedroom was huge and had a connecting bathroom with textured slate tiles in green, white and copper, along with a gorgeous clawfoot tub with silver lion paw feet—a major selling point for me. We signed the papers and planned to move after our wedding.

Joshua was really excited about our new place and I felt pretty good about it too. I loved the idea of walking to and from work. But I couldn't fully enjoy our new purchase until after the wedding, which was looming ahead perilously, causing one of my eyes to twitch. I kept anticipating something awful happening despite my family's assurances that everything would be fine. I *so* wished I could believe them; but, at this point, I just wanted to get it over with.

Chapter 4 ❧ Sunny

On the day of the wedding, I awoke with a start at 6 a.m. When I realized what day it was, a knot immediately formed in my throat. At my insistence, Joshua had stayed with a friend that night. I thought it would make the day more special and, in all honesty, I didn't want him around when I was getting ready. I sure was glad he didn't see me at that moment. I ran to the bathroom and dry-heaved several times before lying back down. I needed to get a grip—I'd never get through the day like this. I tried desperately to go back to sleep, to no avail. I tried reading, but I couldn't concentrate. I tried to watch TV, but only stared at the screen numbly. When I finally trudged upstairs at 9:30, my dad was in the kitchen.

"Good morning, pumpkin!" he said lovingly. He was wearing blue Adidas pants and a white T-shirt, and was drinking coffee from the "World's Greatest Dad" mug either Maddy or Spencer had given him.

"Hello, Dad," I answered in barely a whisper. I hadn't looked in the mirror, but I was still in my nightgown and I'm sure my hair was a disaster.

"What is it, honey?" he asked.

"Oh, you know, it's my anxiety. I'm really scared," I said before yawning.

He gave me a big hug and held me at arm's length. "Joshua is a great guy and you two are so compatible. You have a wonderful future ahead of you. Don't worry!"

"It's not *that*, Dad, I know Joshua is great. It's the *wedding!* I don't want to mess it up."

"Sweetheart, how can you mess it up? Just put on your beautiful dress and walk toward Joshua. I'll hold your hand all the way there. You will be the most enviable bride anyone's ever seen. And everyone attending the wedding loves you very much."

"Joshua's friends and family don't love me. They don't know me. What if I say something stupid or throw up? God, Dad, I feel so sick." At this point, I started to cry. He held me for a few more minutes before making me a cup of tea and some toast as I sat with my head on the kitchen table.

"I want you to drink your tea, I made it just the way you like it. And have a few bites of toast. Then you're going to sit outside and take some deep breaths. Maybe do some yoga."

"Dad, I hate yoga."

"Okay, okay, never mind the yoga. Would you like me to have Elizabeth come over?"

"No, thank you. I'll see her at 3:00."

I took my food outside and managed to gulp down most of the tea and one piece of toast. Shortly thereafter, I heard Linda directing the children back inside the house, which I appreciated. Even Sparky was giving me space. I felt less nauseous, but I was still in a wretched state. In the end, I took a whole Xanax and rested in my room until Elizabeth showed up.

Elizabeth had been my friend since elementary school, she knew me as well as anyone. She and I were both 5'8", but she was substantially larger. She had reddish-auburn hair that bounced like a mess of corkscrews, and lightly freckled ivory skin. She was rarely without a sarcastic gleam in her eye and a ready retort. In many ways, she was my polar opposite: Outgoing, confident, hilarious, and strong. When Elizabeth showed up, everyone knew it. She had a real presence about her. I felt more myself around Elizabeth than I did around my family or even Joshua. With her, I didn't need to hide who I was, which was a relief.

When she entered the house, I heard her from the basement. Her clogs clomped along the floor and I heard her chatting it up with my dad. My friends' parents had always petrified me, I don't know how she did it. Then I heard her clomping down the stairs singing the familiar "Sunshine on my shoulder makes me happy…" She came into my room and I felt instantly better; I knew she had my back (of course, the medication and nap didn't hurt either). For three hours, she helped me get ready as we joked about all sorts of things. I was shaking, but able to function well enough. Fortunately, I'd had my short nails painted pink the day before and, since I'd been consciously limiting my cuticle destruction to only one sad finger, my hands looked better than they had in months. My dad brought down a sandwich that I couldn't eat, but I managed to drink a couple glasses of water. Elizabeth was amazing with cosmetics. She helped me apply false eyelashes and cat-like eyeliner, along with the rest of my makeup. We decided to put up some of my hair because she said it would accentuate my cheekbones. Then she made sure each of my dark curls hung down my back just right. And lastly, she added a gorgeous antique rhinestone barrette on the top of my head.

"You are stunning, my dear. Absolutely stunning," she said as she stood back to take a look at me.

I looked in the mirror and decided I really did look pretty. *Thank God for Elizabeth.* When I slipped into the dress, she said, "Damn, are you skinny! I'm jealous, but still… Have you been eating *at all?*"

"Yeah, I mean, maybe not the last two weeks. I've just been really anxious about the wedding."

She just nodded her head. The dress fit okay, although a bit baggy. "Well, at least it leaves plenty of room for cake!" She laughed. "Not that you'll actually eat any."

I put on my bejeweled Christian Louboutin stiletto pumps, which glittered in the light. Joshua didn't know about the shoes, they were a bit of a splurge. But, as I looked at them now, I felt no guilt whatsoever—they were exquisite. Elizabeth said they were the ultimate glass slipper. I stood in front of the mirror as Elizbeth adjusted my veil.

"I suppose you'll do," she said.

While chunks of my wedding day have remained nebulous or totally inaccessible, there are other bits that have been indelibly cemented into my brain. My father's reaction when I emerged from the basement is one of them. He inhaled audibly and his eyes teared up. My heart hurt for him.

"Your mom would be so proud," he kvelled, trying to subtly wipe his eyes. He looked dapper in a black tux with a gray yarmulke pinned to his dark curls.

He said all of the things a bride needs to hear, giving me the sense that everything *might just be okay.* Babcia and Papa, who were waiting for me in the kitchen, had reactions that also moved me. Papa was wearing a gray pinstriped suit complete with a vest and white handkerchief. Either the suit was old, but incredibly well cared for, or he managed to find something vintage. His black yarmulke was slightly crooked and I reached over to adjust it. He looked adorable. With his hands resting on my shoulders, he said I was as beautiful as his Chana on their wedding day, which was no small compliment.

Baba took me aside and said she had something for me. She was wearing an off-white sequin dress that fell just below her knees. The sleeves were short and she accented her arms with cream-colored gloves that went almost up to her elbows. Her outfit, which reminded me of something from Gatsby, fit perfectly with Papa's look. She obviously just had her blonde hair set, as not even a hurricane could touch it. Her makeup had been carefully applied, and her dangly sapphire earrings complemented her blue eyes. As we sat beside each other on the *redrum* sofa, she opened an ancient-looking jewelry box and pulled out a gold necklace with a Star of David pendant. I'd seen this before—Babcia had worn it for years.

"But, Baba, that's your beautiful necklace from your Mama. It was with you during the war. I can't take that," I said, trying desperately not to cry and ruin my makeup.

"You *must* take it, my darling. I've been saving it for you, you see. My mama, your prababcia, would insist that you have it. I'm so proud of you, my sweet girl. And you needed something old, no?"

"Thank you so much, Baba. I love you," I said, hugging her. Then she helped me lift my hair as I attached the necklace. That moment is forever etched in my heart.

My father helped me into his SUV, followed by Linda, my grandparents, and the kids. Maddy looked adorable in a pink chiffon dress and Spencer was wearing a tiny white suit with a pink hanky. As my dad started the car, I began to freak out.

"Oh no! Where's my purse? Do we have the rings? My stomach hurts! Where are my extra shoes?"

My family assured me that everything was taken care of and not to worry. My dad asked everyone in the back to be calm and quiet, and turned on classical music as he held my sweaty hand. "It's going to be perfect," he whispered.

We decided to get married at a gorgeous beach in La Jolla that had a rocky bluff sitting right over crashing blue waves. Joshua and I used to come here for picnics when we were dating, so it was special. It was a public park, but fortunately, Uncle Fredrick (Linda's younger brother) arrived at our wedding location in the morning to commandeer our spot. I'm not sure how he did it, but he saved it for the entire day. When we pulled up at 7:00, I gasped. A large crowd had gathered near the top of the bluff. I saw the groomsmen lolling about and looking so handsome. I saw more of Joshua's friends and a few distant relatives. Then I noticed that both the wooden stairway leading up to the lookout and the railing surrounding it had been adorned with beautiful pink lilies. The scent hit me hard when I emerged from the car. I was taken aback.

"Oh, Dad! But your headaches…" I said, trying not to cry.

"We're outside, sweetheart—it will be fine. Besides, I'd take a thousand headaches for you!"

Another perfect moment.

I hugged him closely and we headed toward the crowd to take a few pictures before the ceremony. Joshua, who was at a nearby hotel with Randy, his best man, had been instructed to arrive five minutes before the ceremony, at 7:25. Various people came up to me, smothering me with embarrassing compliments. In a swirl of pink, I saw Elizabeth, along with my bridesmaids, Vanessa and Kim. They looked gorgeous.

Debbie and Rick, who had mercifully stayed at a hotel, immediately came over to me. Rick kissed my cheek and said I was stunning; whereas Debbie gave me a quick hug before commenting, "My, but you're skinny!" And with a dry laugh, she added, "I hope this isn't a reflection of your cooking!"

I stood there stiffly, unsure of what to say. But, fortunately, Elizabeth gently pulled me away, mumbling "Stupid bitch," under her breath.

We took awkward family photos for about fifteen minutes when someone said, "It's time," which caused me to catch my breath. *Oh my God, can I actually do this?* I was escorted behind my dad's car as Joshua arrived and everyone quieted down. My dad held my hand. Then I heard the sound of the conch, signaling the start of the ceremony. I saw Joshua in the distance, his face radiating happiness. I could see the bridesmaids and groomsmen following him as they made their way up the stairs. I heard a collective "Aww" as I saw Spencer and Maddy heading upward with Linda holding their hands. Maddy was tossing rose petals along the way.

"This is us," said my dad. "I love you so much, my beautiful *tournesol.*"

We headed toward the path as all eyes were on us. My arm was interlaced with my father's and I had a death grip on his forearm. We moved slowly up the stairs. When Joshua saw me, his face immediately changed from a smile to a look of awe. He wiped his eyes. Joshua's reaction was another of those moments I hold within me always.

I heard an airplane overhead and looked toward the cloudless blue sky. Then I was somehow up there, in the sky, with the seagulls. I had always envied those birds, but today I was one of them. I remember hearing the pastor talk about marriage and what it meant. He said a lot of other things too, but they are lost to me now. I could hear Joshua repeating his vows as he barely stifled a cry. I heard myself whisper mine too. I saw myself circling around Joshua. I heard the crowd laugh at something. I heard waves crashing and the occasional sound of a car. I heard a baby cry. I saw a young couple surrounded by loving people dressed in their finest. The scene below me was magical, such a lucky couple! Joshua stomped on a wine glass, which startled me back to him, back to our wedding. We kissed and the pastor said, "Mazel tov!" And just like that, we were married.

My father had rented a white convertible Bentley to take Joshua and me to the reception. I knew about the car, but it was a surprise for Joshua, who had a thing for the classics. Joshua was speechless when he saw it, moving his hand very lightly along the side of the car as if it was too fragile to touch. How I loved my father for this gesture. The driver opened our doors and, once Joshua helped me into the car, Elizabeth reached in covering my hair with a scarf. When the doors shut, everything was finally still. Joshua was staring at me.

"You take my breath away," he said. "I love you forever."

How did I ever find this man? "I love you too, my sweet Joshua."

The fraternity house had never looked better. The lawn was immaculate and there was an arch with wisteria winding through it just in front of the entrance. We sat in the car for several moments as we watched people go inside. Joshua made a few wisecracks about some of his friends' clothing choices, as well as his great Auntie Bernadette's ridiculously tall, feathered organza hat.

"Oh, tally ho, do you fancy my purple fascinator? I had my cockatiel stuffed for the occasion!" he said in a perfectly terrible British accent.

"That's *so* not a fascinator, you doofus," I teased halfheartedly, my queasiness and apprehension increasing rapidly as we made our way toward the house.

I'm told the reception was one hell of a party. There was a band and plenty of champagne and dancing. The evening was chaotic for me, but a few things come to mind. First, there was the stupid receiving line that Debbie had insisted on. It was old-fashioned and unnecessary—just another way for my mother-in-law to torment me. I guess Debbie didn't know about my social anxiety; but still, this was the last thing I needed. Joshua was first in the line followed by me, my dad, Linda, Rick, and Debbie. Each time a person approached, I tensed. I decided to just copy Joshua, who generally said things like "Thank you so much. Great to see you. Thank you for coming." And so on. But the guests were different with me. They all wanted to hug or kiss me, which I hated. I mean, who even *were* some of these people? Plus, my words became garbled and I often forgot what Joshua had just said. When I saw an ancient-looking couple gingerly heading our way, something inside me snapped.

"I can't," I said to no one in particular.

And, with that, I left the receiving line and headed further inside. *Fuck it! This is my wedding and I don't have to do this.* I heard Joshua say something in the background, followed by Debbie—who was far louder than her son.

"What on earth! How rude. Go get her, Josh!" she insisted.

I turned back and gave Joshua a non-subtle gesture to stay there, and walked toward the champagne. When Joshua found me later, I was hiding behind my friends while enjoying a fantastic buzz. He looked at me with bemusement and I just shrugged. But I allowed him to lead me toward the dance floor, waiting as he made small talk with at least six people along the way. The band stopped playing and I heard The Stones' "Wild Horses" reverberating over the sound of the crowd. This was our dance, our very nontraditional wedding waltz. Joshua and I had practiced it a hundred times and were ready. I *so* wanted to make Papa proud. I believe we danced well; Joshua didn't step on my expensive shoes and I saw Papa beaming from across the room. But mostly, we held each other and whispered loving words. We gave each other compliments and reiterated how lucky each of us was. We kissed softly as we moved together, knowing it would take far more than wild horses for us to stop loving each other.

When it was time to cut the cake, I felt even more buzzed thanks to the champagne I'd been grabbing from tables throughout the night. I had minimal interest in cake and rarely ate it—especially white cake. I was more of an ice cream person. But tradition is tradition, so there I was standing in front of a 4-tier wedding cake that cost more than my first car. I was feeling good though, just going with it. We cut the cake and fed each other dainty pieces. It was a sweet moment that was abruptly shattered when one of Joshua's friends yelled, "Lame! Come on, Fitz, you can do better than that. Give her a *real* bite!"

I saw Joshua take the bait as he grabbed a huge piece of cake and moved his hand toward my face.

I thought he knew better than this.

I felt the wet, sticky frosting all around my lips. I felt it on my chin. I heard people laughing. A torrent of rage surged through me. *This was my special day. How dare they!* I bent toward the cake and, not even bothering to use the spatula, scooped up the entire top tier—including the waspy plastic couple on top.

"You think that's funny, *motherfucker?*" I screamed before hurling the cake toward the crowd. I then marched out the back door of the house where I promptly puked all over the lawn. At some point, I was tucked into an upstairs bed where I slept as the party continued.

And that was my wedding day.

Chapter 5 ∽ Joshua

Sunny changed me forever. I was a naïve college junior when I met her. I'd enjoyed college life, probably too much thanks to the endless fraternity parties. Having grown up in Indiana, I fully planned to go to school as far away from home as possible. I'd had enough of the Indiana winters, which didn't even include ski slopes. And, while I loved my family, my mother could be overbearing. She monitored my every move and always had something to say about any girls I brought home (which were few). My father was less involved with my everyday life, with the exception of academics—where he expected the best from me but rarely received it. There were endless fights when I failed a test or received a C or worse in a class. I'll never forget the time I got caught skipping classes. It was the spring of my junior year in high school and my friends and I decided to bypass our afternoon classes and drink beer at the lake instead. I got away with this for several glorious weeks until the school called my mom. I hid in my room until my father came home that evening. I could hear them talking downstairs followed by my father's familiar heavy footsteps on the stairs. Then he really laid into me.

"What the hell are you thinking, Josh? Your mother and I work hard so you can have a great life. Look at this room? You are not wanting for a damn thing!"

I looked at him blankly, unsure of the relationship between my bedroom and my truancy. *Whatever.*

"You know the guy who dances around holding a sign in front of Quick Lube? Well, that's exactly where you're headed. And I've seen you dance…"

At this, I chuckled.

"Oh, it's *so* not funny! You *will* get it together if you want any privileges whatsoever. Do you hear me?" He was getting louder.

"Jesus, Dad, get a grip. I didn't commit a felony."

"Is that right, young man? As far as I'm concerned, you have. And, by the way, you're grounded for two weeks. That means no parties and no driving anywhere other than to and from school. And no allowance either, got it?"

"Fine!" I blurted, like a spoiled child. After he left the room, I muttered, "fucking asshole" and slammed the door.

So, yeah, I wanted to get far away from my parents and I'd always dreamed of living in California. I wanted to go to parties, meet girls, and have fun. I wanted to go to the beach and maybe learn to surf. Those were my lofty aspirations. I applied to several California colleges, but I was only accepted by one—which also happened to be a major party school. My parents weren't thrilled, but since I'd managed to make SDSU my only option, what could they do?

I joined the Greek system because I didn't know a soul at SDSU and I figured a house full of instant brothers would make life easier. Plus, I imagined living in a fraternity would be a blast; I'd seen the movies. Randy, my best friend from home who moved to Lemon Grove, CA, just after high school, thought fraternities were for spineless assholes who thought they were better than everyone else. I didn't care. I was thrilled to be out of Indiana and ready for a new adventure.

I was accepted into several decent fraternities, but, stupidly, I chose the one known for excessive partying. The house was a large brown and white Tudor made of wood and stucco. It had an enormous front porch where guys drank beer on old couches while ogling the passing females. Not surprisingly, pledge week was miserable—I'd never been around so much alcohol, not to mention the constant pressure to chug it as quickly as possible. I tried adding water to my cups when no one was looking, but still ended up with several hangovers that felt like death. Plus, as pledges, we were treated like servants, or "squids," as they called us. We were required to clean the house each day and basically wait on the older guys. Scrubbing toilets that have been consistently disrespected by disgusting guys is a special kind of torture I wouldn't wish on anyone—it made me retch nearly as much as the booze. And there was the day we had to run through the cafeteria at noon wearing nothing but adult diapers. It was that incident that had me wondering if perhaps Randy was right—maybe I was turning into a mindless frat boy loser. But I was in too deep at that point and had no other friends, so I stuck with it. Plus, I knew my time would come to be at the top of the food chain.

I quickly became popular in my house. Along with the guys finding me funny, I loved to party, so of course I fit right in. Every week we held keggers that left the place in shambles. In the beginning, I relished the freedom that came with dancing unabashedly as beer clouded my inhibitions and loud music fed my angsty 18-year-old brain. Plus, it was exciting to be around so many attractive girls. Our sister sorority was across the street and we held numerous combined parties, often with themes such as Hawaiian, 1980s, and of course toga. I dated a couple girls from that house, but it never amounted to anything. There was a girl named Christy from a different sorority who had a mad crush on me. She partied as hard as any guy and had a particular talent for the upside-down beer bong; I'm not sure I ever saw that girl sober. She came to every party and always made a beeline straight for me, whispering sloppily in my ear with her hot, boozy breath. Not wanting to hurt her feelings, I did my best to dodge her. I just wasn't interested in party girls who lacked substance or were into me simply because of my fraternity. In fact, after two years of partying, I was feeling empty. Maybe I was finally growing up, I don't know. But I was drinking less and spending more time playing basketball, frisbee and tennis with the guys. I even hit the library now and then. Convinced there was no wife—or hell, even girlfriend—material at SDSU, I'd pretty much given up on finding love.

I was taking a required English class during my junior year. It involved a lot of essay writing—not my greatest skill. The professor was a cantankerous old man with a gift for monotonous gab. I often found myself daydreaming in class and trying desperately to keep my eyes open. There was a dark-haired girl who sat in the first row. I thought she must have been a brain because she was always early and took a ton of notes. Occasionally, she raised her hand and said something intelligent. I found myself watching her. Her dark, almost black, hair was incredibly thick and shiny. Sometimes it was springy with curls, other times it was straight—I preferred the former. I wanted to touch those curls. I imagined how they might smell. She usually wore glasses in class and, although it was hard to see her face clearly from my seat, she was pretty in a non-obvious sort of way. She never seemed to sit still, she was either taking feverish notes, picking at her fingers, or shaking one of her feet. Sometimes she managed a mixture of all three.

At first, she was a distraction from a painfully dull class. But eventually, I started to wonder about her—*where did she come from? What was she like?* She always left before me, so I watched her walk outside. She was tall, maybe only two inches shorter than me. Her legs were long and her body was thin, but she also seemed fit—like a dancer. She wore faded jeans that were never too tight. She didn't flaunt her sexuality, but rather, had a natural allure that was apparent regardless of her clothing. She moved like she had somewhere better to be, so she was always quickly lost in the crowd.

I started to notice her outside of class, either walking with her giant red-haired friend or sitting in the grass reading. On one occasion, I saw that she was sketching a nearby cherry tree in full blossom. *Wow*, I thought, *this girl is talented.* I was starting to feel stalkerish, so I decided I needed to talk to her. I'd probably lose interest at that point, or maybe she would be far too smart for me. But I had to do something.

One particularly hot day, I spotted her reading under a large pepper tree. *This was my opportunity.* I was strangely nervous to speak to her—*what was wrong with me?* She seemed lost in her book, as she didn't look up as I approached her. When I said "hello," I startled the hell out of her. *Way to go, Fitz, really smooth.* I couldn't tell if she was annoyed by my interruption; she was hard to read. But she set down her book and looked up at me. The sun was in her eyes, so she squinted a little. *Oh, but those eyes!* They were bluish-green or greenish-blue, I wasn't sure. But they were startling there in the sunlight. When she spoke, her voice was soft, almost timid. She was reading classic literature *for enjoyment*—huh? She was so out of my league. And "Sunny," really? She could not have had a more befitting name. There was something special about this girl that I couldn't put my finger on. She was gorgeous for sure, but she was more than that. When she gave me her phone number, I walked away with butterflies in my chest. I must've had one hell of a stupid grin on my face for the rest of the day.

Who was this girl?

Knowing I was with someone exceptional whom I likely didn't deserve, I treaded carefully with Sunny. I kept her away from my fraternity brothers as much as possible—I wouldn't tolerate any wisecracks about her. I walked her to class and took her to the beach, holding her hand as our naked feet sank into the warm sand. She was incredibly shy, which I didn't understand. How could someone like me have more confidence than this beauty? But her shyness was sort of charming. I had become used to girls who tried to impress me with their overdone makeup, skimpy clothes, and shameless flirting. They were garish and just way too much. Sunny was a rare gem that you could only glimpse a little of at a time. She never tried to accentuate who she was, but rather seemed almost to hide it.

Over time, I saw more and more of Sunny as she gradually emerged from her armor. I couldn't believe how much she was hiding within herself—she was sweetly sarcastic and could be hilarious. She was also a dork, occasionally so absorbed in her thoughts that she tripped or bumped into something. She danced around her apartment when she thought no one was looking. She sang, pretty horribly, in the shower. She both startled and blushed easily. She had tiny freckles across her perfectly straight nose. Her fingers were long and elegant, with short nails that were always polished, but with cuticles that were rough and often bandaged. She was self-depreciating and didn't seem to know her worth. She was so damn smart that sometimes I didn't know what she was talking about. She had a playful grin, but was stingy with her full smile. I was addicted to that smile.

It didn't take long to notice Sunny's kind and gentle soul, especially when it came to animals and nature. Her convictions sometimes outweighed her fears. She once confided in me that she snuck into the psychology building and freed a handful of rats outside. She was terrified of spiders but refused to kill them. She didn't eat animals—an idea that was foreign to me and I knew would appall my mother. And, when it came to the few people she allowed into her heart, she loved with ferocious intensity. She was like a vibrant sunrise peeking through a cloudy sky. She was warmth, light, comfort, and dazzling beauty. She made me dizzy with wanting her. And she made me want to be a better man.

Chapter 6 ❧ Sunny

I wasn't sure I'd ever escape the emotional torment of my wedding. As it was, I critiqued myself after all social interactions—even when I performed fairly well. Debbie was perplexed by my behavior, but I think someone—either Joshua or Rick—told her to let it go, as she never brought up the debacle. But I always sensed her disapproval of me, even as I heard Joshua speaking with her on the phone. I was growing to resent my mother-in-law and I feared she knew the horrible things I thought about her.

It turned out that my cake hurl landed on Randy's forehead. I liked Randy and felt bad about this—I had been aiming for someone else. Fortunately, Randy had a great sense of humor. When I saw him two weeks later, he greeted me with, "What's up, Slugger?" A nickname that stuck, and which made me feel slightly less awful about my behavior. And of course, there were running jokes among Joshua's friends during the first months after our marriage. Such as when we attended another wedding shortly after ours and one of the guys looked at me and announced, "Uh oh, there's cake on the table, everyone take cover!" I only found this mildly amusing, but I knew I deserved it. I still wasn't sure what happened to me that day. Joshua blamed it on the champagne and my dad blamed it on the stress. But had I known the perilous course my life would soon be taking, I'd have gladly taken those playful jabs over the pained expressions and awkward silences that eventually took their place.

The worst part was that I'd disappointed my father and grandparents. The day after the wedding, my dad hugged me and asked me if I was okay. He wasn't mad at me, but had a worried look in his eyes. Papa didn't mention the incident, but Babcia talked to me about it after our two-day honeymoon in Vegas (we planned to take a real honeymoon once we saved some money). She was warm and gentle, telling me it was "but a pebble in the grand scheme of life." Baba knew how profoundly I carried shame; she knew I would allow this event to torment me endlessly. Baba was there when I cried for days after stuttering during a school presentation when I was twelve. She was there that same year when I came home from school in tears after tripping in the school cafeteria and dropping my tray in front of everyone. She was there when I overheard girls in the high school bathroom calling me a "stuck-up bitch." She was there when I was frightened, shy, embarrassed, and ashamed. Her slight and fragile shoulders held me up like an oak tree in a storm. When she spoke to me about the reception, she held me as I cried softly, saying, "We are all flawed, my darling. But our, how you say…mess-ups. Our mess-ups do not define who we are inside, we must choose to be happy. It is a great mitzvah, happiness—you know?" I knew my baba was right, but mitzvah or not, happiness had often eluded me. I didn't know how to forgive myself.

I'd never had a drinking problem, but I certainly drank more than I should have during my reception. But I had no choice. The people, the rules, the noise, the *overwhelming attention on me*—it was all just too much. When Joshua shoved that damned cake into my face, I saw red. I felt an anger that I'd never experienced before. Venom consumed me until I could not contain it. The explosion was without control, absolutely nothing could have stopped it—this is what bothers me the most. What if I was some kind of freak who blew up at the worst possible moment? I decided to limit my future alcohol use to no more than two drinks at a time. I'd never acted that way before, so the booze must have played a role. I also tried to simply forget the reception, not even bothering to look at our wedding photos. I had Joshua—the rest didn't matter. This is what I told myself.

My greatest fear was that Joshua would regret marrying me. After all, I'd made a total ass of myself in front of his family and friends. They were probably placing bets on how long we'd stay married. I worried that he would stop loving me. But my beautiful Joshua did not give up on me. The day after the wedding, I woke up feeling disgraceful. With my tongue stuck to the roof of my mouth and my head throbbing, we drove home very early. I sat quietly in the car, submerged in my shame, until I finally muttered, "I'm *so* sorry for being such a fool. I'm disgusted with myself. I hope you still love me."

"Wild horses," was all he said.

Joshua tiptoed around me for the next couple weeks, choosing his words carefully. But eventually, we were back to normal. Our condo was amazing and I enjoyed decorating it. Elizabeth and I would go to garage sales and consignment shops where we found all sorts of boho chic furniture, rugs and knickknacks. My favorite was a French Empire chandelier that was dripping with Swarovski crystals. It was likely worth thousands, but I found it at a junk store for $200. Joshua had a few pieces of furniture he attempted to incorporate into our décor, which included a stained beanbag chair, a huge black metal desk, an upright bar with vinyl barstools, and the classic "dogs playing poker" portrait. It was such stereotypical guy stuff. The desk and the beanbag chair were nonnegotiable, they were *out*. We also donated the barstools and bought new ones. The bar was retro and cool, so we kept it. And the picture had some sort of sentiment to it, so we kept that too (although I had it framed). We purchased a queen-sized bed, a light blue velvet couch, and several wooden bookshelves for my book collection. Although he sighed heavily when he saw the enormous pile of boxes containing books that needed to be lugged inside, Joshua carried each box without protest. He was, however, curious as to why I had such a large collection of books by Jewish Holocaust writers such as Primo Levi, Imre Kertész, Simon Wiesenthal, Elie Wiesel, Shlomo Venezia, and Sara Nomberg-Przytyk; but we didn't really talk about it. Papa gave us a beautiful brass mezuzah, which I kissed and hung on our doorpost.

But the absolute best thing we acquired, hands down, was our new kitty. We found him at an animal shelter, which was a dangerous place for me—I wanted every last one of those poor creatures. But when I felt a little orange paw touch my shin through a cage, I knew I had found my baby. We named him Chester. He was two years old with soft orange fur and enormous green eyes. Joshua had never had a cat before, but was immediately smitten. Chester played fetch and was always there at the door when I came home from work. Sometimes we put a harness on him and walked him around the complex where he loved to roll around in the sun and eat grass. Joshua said he was a dog in disguise. While Chester loved Joshua too, that kitty was *all mine*. He followed me around and slept on my pillow every night (walking over Joshua's head to get there). He, somewhat painfully, made biscuits on my belly and lulled me to sleep with his gravely motor. I was so overcome with love for Chester that, from the moment I brought him home, I was terrified about the day he would leave me. For I knew all good things were temporary—held together by the slightest gossamer strand.

Less than two weeks after getting married, that delicate thread came apart in an instant. I had finally gotten into a routine and was no longer ruminating over the wedding fiasco every minute of the day. Joshua and I were happy and I was feeling pretty stable in my life. Then I woke up one sunny Tuesday morning to planes crashing into the World Trade Center. Joshua and I sat glued to the television in disbelief. That evening, I spoke with my dad, who had lived in NYC for several years and had friends who worked in one of the towers—he was frantic. Over the next week, he was greatly relieved to learn that his friends were safe. But I couldn't bounce back from it. I broke down when I saw images of people jumping from those burning buildings. No matter how I tried, I couldn't get those falling bodies out of my head. Plus, along with the horrors I continually envisaged, now I had to worry about terrorists destroying American buildings. And, at that point, I'd sworn off ever flying again. So much for seeing the world. I was fraught with anxiety and had zero energy or motivation, so I called in sick at work.

The 9/11 terrorist attack also touched my omnipresent sense of not belonging anywhere. I've always been an anachronist; that is, a person out of place in history. So much of my reading takes me back to earlier periods in American and European life before cell phones, nuclear weapons, and the internet. I have yearned to live in the 1920s, brazenly wearing a short flapper dress and holding a glass of whiskey in one hand and a cigarette in the other. Or in a shtetl in the Polish countryside at a time when my large Jewish family could live freely, without fear of persecution. Sometimes this fantasy takes me out of the shtetl and into Berlin, where I proceed to execute that evil fascist shitbag thereby altering the course of history. The terrorist attack exacerbated these deep-seated yearnings, yearnings that can never be realized and are thus a great source of frustration and melancholy for me. I would always be stuck in this body, in this place. And so, I moped around the condo for a good week after 9/11 before venturing back to work. On my second morning out, I noticed a man whistling as he walked toward a bus stop. I wanted to scream at him: "How dare you whistle so soon after 9/11! What the hell is wrong with you?" And I would have too, except that I was running late. The tragedy consumed me, invading my thoughts and dreams for months—far longer than it seemed to affect my family. But this was par for the course.

Despite the impact of 9/11 and my various anxieties, those first months of marriage were still the best time of my life. My job no longer stressed me out, except for the Thursday meetings, which I still dreaded. My workload gradually increased and I found I was able to keep up. I was editing book drafts for much of my day, but I also spent time researching content to make sure it was accurate or realistic. I also sent out a fair number of rejection letters, my least favorite task. My boss quickly realized that I had a solid grasp of punctuation and grammar, and grew to trust my work. I also worked at a fast pace, for which I received many accolades (and the occasional glare from a coworker). But mostly, I sat alone in my quiet little office poring over the one thing that gave me solace: letters on a page. Sometimes my coworkers went out for beers after work or ate together in the office kitchen, but I always made excuses and set off on my own. I would have liked to make new friends, but I just didn't know how. So, I hid away in my puny office shielded by a familiar cocoon of words.

Joshua and I got into a groove. I was always home first, so I played with Chester and headed out for a run. Once I had dinner started, Joshua came home. The anticipation of seeing Joshua each evening remained intense; I still missed him anytime we separated. We continued to kiss and touch each other at every chance, "christening" each room in our townhome. Joshua especially loved to have sex in the shower, while I preferred the living room couch. He often nudged me with his erection first thing in the morning, which, on weekdays, I typically dodged by flying out of bed to get ready for work. He was insatiable.

We weren't rich and had to be careful about our spending. But our cozy, loving home made me feel safe. And the more I was around Joshua, the more I realized I'd made the best choice in my life in marrying him. His kind-heartedness and affection continued to grow over time. Joshua was endlessly attracted to me. If I got dressed up to go out, he would whistle at me and bombard me with compliments. He never tired of looking at me. There were times when I was in a T-shirt with no makeup and I caught him gazing at me with so much love and admiration it brought tears to my eyes. He was especially besotted with my legs—much appreciating my short skirts and heels. He claimed to be enchanted by my eyes and often spent hours running his fingers through my hair. He made me feel like the most gorgeous, desirable woman in the world. He wasn't a jealous or insecure man, but sometimes, when other men looked at me just a few seconds too long, I could sense his discomfort. But he wasn't possessive, mostly he was proud to have such a coveted wife. While Joshua did have his flaws, such as messiness and general impatience with people (besides me), he was a good man—a true catch, whom I loved down to my bones. He and Chester were my sanctuary.

When we weren't playing house, Joshua and I spent a lot of time at the beach. He was learning how to surf while I would go for jogs on the sand. Afterward, we would run into the waves together, splashing like kids and floating together like the newlyweds we were. We went on hikes with Joshua carrying lunches of baguettes, smoked Gouda, fresh berries, and sometimes even champagne. We explored the area, visiting posh neighborhoods. We loved San Diego and dreamed of owning a beautiful stucco house with a swimming pool in La Jolla. We imagined our future together, with Joshua deciding we should have three kids: Two boys for him to teach sports and a little girl for him to spoil rotten. I reminded him he could teach our daughter sports too. Although I indulged him, I did not see myself having three kids. One *might* be okay, but, beyond that, I was good with a house full of cats, dogs and books. These were areas I could handle. Children felt like murky water, with far too many unknowns hiding in the crevices.

We spent a lot of time with my family. There were regular gatherings at my dad's house which usually included my grandparents too. Joshua would swim with the kids for hours, leaving them exhausted by bedtime, which made Linda love him all the more. I would sit with my grandparents, making sure they were okay and learning about Baba's garden or what Papa's chess-playing buddies were up to. Of course, like most old people, they also kept me abreast of their latest health challenges. Baba's hip had been bothering her for some time and I noticed her slight grimace when she sat down. She was doted on by Papa, as well as everyone else in the family, which, despite her protests, I think she secretly loved. She was our queen and Papa especially made sure she knew it.

Although my grandparents didn't speak much about religion, they still practiced shabbat (which they called "Shabbos"). They also ate kosher, but they had never been especially strict about my food. They were progressive that way—wanting me to make my own decisions about religion as I got older. Joshua and I attended Shabbos at my dad's house twice a month on Saturdays. Baba and Papa would prepare the traditional Shabbos foods the night before. These dinners helped me to grieve 9/11, as for several months, my father said a special prayer for the victims and their families. Joshua was visibly uncomfortable with Shabbos at the beginning. He had nothing against Judaism, it was just totally foreign to him. But he grew accustomed to Shabbos and even began to crave challah and Baba's savory cholent stew. Joshua was touched by the ritual candle lighting and storytelling that took place at every Shabbos, and it wasn't long until he greeted his hosts with "Gut Shabbos" like the rest of us. While I wasn't particularly religious, several Jewish customs such as Shabbos held a special meaning for me. Joshua and I celebrated both Hanukkah and Christmas, or "Chrismukkah," as we playfully called it. I'd always adored Hanukkah and had an ornate silver menorah a distant relative sent as a wedding gift. Christmas was familiar to me as well, since my mother was not Jewish and, when she was in a good mood, went all out when it came to gifts. She also insisted upon the largest fir tree in the lot, which we covered with expensive designer ornaments. The shallowness of this annoyed my father, who preferred sentimental decorations.

Unlike my mom, I favored a small, potted tree that we could plant outside after the holidays. I had zero interest in watching a living thing dry out and die in my living room. I didn't want to weigh down the little tree, so a strand of tiny white lights and some small wooden nutcrackers was plenty. And since Chester delighted in batting at the ornaments until they fell off, I was glad they weren't fragile. We only placed a few gifts under the tree that year, as I remained more attracted to Jewish holidays. Shabbos, Hanukkah, and Rosh Hashanah connected me to my lost ancestors while further anchoring me to the people I loved most in the world. When Baba covered her eyes and lit the candles during Shabbos, I always felt a little choked up.

When I thought of my grandparents, I was overcome with a mix of protectiveness, respect, love, and a panic deep in my stomach about the prospect of losing them; how would I possibly manage? They had held me close and given me comfort during my darkest days. My mother died when I was eight. I was at school when the principal collected me from my classroom. Papa and Baba were waiting in her office with ashen faces and teary eyes.

"Come here, my darling," said Baba, "We need to talk to you." Baba's voice broke as she held me.

"Your mama has been in an accident," continued Papa. "She has gone to heaven."

The rest of the conversation is lost to me, as is the remainder of that day. I recall something about a car accident, though the details are hazy. But my worst fear had been realized: My beautiful mama was gone. She wasn't perfect, my mama. But she was my everything. Sometimes she would disappear for weeks at a time, with my father telling me she needed to "go rest for a while." I didn't understand why she was so tired and I deeply missed her during those absences. There were also times when she became furious with my father for days on end. I would hear them in their bedroom, her screaming and him trying to calm her and pleading with her to lower her voice. I remember wondering what my father had done to make her so upset.

I tried not to listen to their fights, but it was hard not to. My father was always trying to get her to take her medicine. At the time, this made me angry with him. *I hated taking medicine too! Why couldn't he just leave her alone?* She wasn't sick as far as I could tell. They would fight about me a great deal, usually with my dad criticizing something she did, or didn't do. Like the times she didn't pick me up from school or was incredibly late—this really pissed him off. I didn't understand it either, plus it was embarrassing.

I recall one occasion when she didn't show up until the janitor arrived. I sat in the lunchroom pretending to color while the vice principal made frantic calls. Eventually, my father appeared, apologizing profusely. *God, was that humiliating.* No one ever told me why she hadn't picked me up. Even worse was the day she came to the school in a frenzied state—throwing herself into the front reception area like a crazed peacock. She was wearing a brightly colored dress and had charcoal all over her arms, hands and face. She looked absurd. On top of it, she was loud, extremely talkative, and way too enthusiastic. I heard her as I was approaching the front of the school with my backpack: "Isn't it a gorgeous day! Where's my girl? Oh, Sunny? Sunshine? Where are you?" I stopped in my tracks. There were at least five kids out there, every one of them seeing and hearing the spectacle that was my mother. I knew it would only get worse, so I practically ran out of the school toward her car. I refused to speak to her for the rest of the day. At some point thereafter, a babysitter began picking me up from school each day, which was fine by me.

My parents also fought about money. Having lost her beloved gallery job long ago, Mama was chronically unemployed. But this didn't bother her. She was always trying to persuade my dad that her art would make them "filthy rich" sometime soon. My dad didn't buy it. She was talented, but her drawings didn't exactly attract mainstream collectors. They were dreary and depressing, and it was difficult to discern their meaning. She was such a colorful person; I didn't understand why she only used black charcoal and never drew anything pretty. Yet, she always had "people" whom she knew would buy her art at a hefty price. These "buyers" had told her so time and time again. I never met such people, but I thought they were unreliable and not to be trusted.

Making matters worse, Mama had a spending issue. I recall her taking me to the expensive toy store downtown and buying me anything I wanted. Once, I came home with a giant stuffed giraffe whose head nearly touched my bedroom ceiling. Sometimes there were so many packages of toys for me, and clothes and shoes for her, that the bags barely fit in the car. We would always hide our stash before Dad came home, but the giraffe was a garish symbol of her excess that couldn't be missed. *Damn, did he hate that thing.* When the credit card bills arrived, he knew everything she'd been up to anyway. I felt so guilty about the money, I stopped playing with most of my new toys.

They also fought about my general care, like my meals, clothing, and homework. They fought about her going out with friends and coming home late into the night. And they fought about how she didn't take care of herself. She constantly skipped meals—remaining frightfully thin—and had terrible sleeping habits. As always with these fights, she was loud, but my father's voice remained calm despite his pain and frustration. He would try to shush her, but it never worked. I wanted to make myself disappear at those times.

But, when Mama was sad, I missed the fighting. I wanted her back in any capacity—loud, garish, embarrassing, vulgar—whatever. We never knew when the switch would happen, but it was plainly apparent the moment it did. As every drop of her magic disintegrated, she would take to her bed. It was like a dazzling cityscape snuffed out by nimbostratus clouds. When she was a ghost, she only just existed. She slept, watched TV or took lingering baths that scared the shit out of us. And she cried so much, I wondered how she had so many tears. I thought they should have dried up. She stopped looking like Mama during those times; she was gaunt and bleary—barely there.

When I tried to speak to her during her blue days, her answers were brief and without feeling. I know she *tried* to say the right thing—desperate to pull out meaningful words from somewhere deep inside her. But they were out of reach. When she called me "Sunshine," it hurt more than her silence. Sometimes she became hostile when my dad tried to help her, calling him names I didn't know the meaning of. She was never as angry toward me, but this may have been because my dad and grandparents were so effective in shielding me. She also didn't trust certain people, including Baba. And she had disturbing conversations with someone who must've said terrible things because she was always telling him or her to "Stop!" "Shut up!" or "Go away!" But whenever I peeked through the door crack, she was all alone. She looked miserable as she covered her ears and rocked back and forth.

I recall her believing that my kind-hearted little baba could read her mind and was sending someone to kill her. Of course, I wasn't supposed to hear this, but I had been eavesdropping again. I sure wish I hadn't. I recall storming into the room bawling, asking what she was talking about. It was that evening that my dad took me aside and told me that my dear mama was ill. But that her illness was inside her head, making her do and say things she couldn't control. That it wasn't her fault. And that Babcia most certainly wasn't trying to harm her. That was a crucial day, as it helped me to better understand my mother. I was relieved both that Babcia wasn't involved and that there was a reason for

Mama's bizarre behaviors. Yet, I also worried that this sickness could kill her. I was thoroughly confused.

The absolute worst part about those dark days was when she had had enough. Of course, no one told me about her suicidality, but I knew. I knew because I had my ear to the door when I heard her say things like "Just let me die," or "Please, I've had enough, let me go," or "I'm a piece of shit, you're better off without me." I always heard the soft murmurings of my father trying to placate and comfort her, and the two of them crying. How I wanted to run in and shake her out of it! I wanted to bust Mama out of this awful shadow person.

Her wish to die was somewhat predictable, occurring after weeks of shopping sprees and wild behavior, but before her lengthy absences. My father would not let her die. He would pack up her suitcase while she sobbed and begged him not to. After a while, he stopped attempting to dress her, he had learned the futility of it. He simply put a jacket or sweater around her, shoved some slippers on her feet, and practically dragged her out to the car.

And then she was gone.

As Mama disappeared in the distance, my grandparents were always right there. They would envelop me in their arms, wiping away my tears. They made comforting foods, like mac 'n cheese or chicken soup with matzah balls. In the evenings, they took me downstairs and tucked me into their bed. I guess Papa slept on the couch, since I only recall sleeping next to Baba. I normally loved staying down there with them, but not so much when my mother was taken away. At those times, I only wanted Mama.

When I was missing her, I remembered my other mama, the one my father and I so cherished. The one who danced gracefully through the house like a fairy, with her flowery skirts flowing to music as she spun me in circles. The one who would share her art supplies and build masterpieces with me, which often resulted in my father coming home to a house buried in paint and glitter. The one who told me elaborate adventure stories that left me mesmerized and inhabited my dreams. The one who played with me at the park for hours and who let me help prepare extravagant dinners for the five of us. The one who taught me how to sew fancy outfits for my stuffed animals. The one who still entranced my father as they danced or held each other. The one who filled me with wonder and curiosity, and made me yearn for more of her.

Mama loved books and I recall piles of them throughout the house. Sometimes my dad would cuss after tripping on one. But I loved her books too; they transported me to different places and captured my imagination. I recall a thick book of nursery rhymes with Old Mother Goose on the cover. I was crazy about that book and, when Mama was in a good mood, I often asked her to read it to me. My favorite rhyme was by Henry Wadsworth Longfellow:

> *There was a little girl, who wore a little hood,*
> *And a curl down the middle of her forehead.*
> *When she was good, she was very, very good,*
> *But when she was bad, she was horrid.*

Mama would touch my curls and emphasize that I could be both good *and* horrid. In my naïve little mind, I believed Longfellow wrote the poem specifically about me. Although, even at such a young age, I also believed I was far more horrid than good. But I didn't tell Mama this.

When Mama died, my world lost its beauty. My soul lost its light. Those days are a blur of confusion, unyielding pain, and panic. I would only sleep in her bed, smelling her hair on the pillow as I sobbed until my head ached. When my father wasn't looking, I collected my favorite pieces of her clothing, along with her perfume, reddest lipstick, and most sparkly jewelry, and hid them under my bed; I had to keep them safe. I recall grownups acting oddly around me during that time. My parents' friends whom I did not know would often hug me or stroke my hair, which I couldn't stand. They all looked at me with the most tortured expressions; I'd never known such pity. My mother's memorial was a shitshow thanks to Grandma Sylvie making an appearance. A small number of friends and family gathered at a quaint little chapel my mama had always adored, mostly because of its exquisite garden of pale pink roses. Each adult talked about how they knew my mom and what she meant to them. They were loving sentiments. I remember words like funny, talented, beautiful, generous, passionate, charismatic, and one-of-a-kind. Although one person spoke of her "demons," which offended me—my mama was no demon!

As I sat listening to these strangers sniffle and speak about my beautiful mama, Grandma Sylvie showed up and sucked the air out of the room. She seemed wild to me, with unkempt wiry gray hair, wrinkled, dirty clothing, and a booming voice. She entered with an equally disheveled old man, on whom she was leaning. She interrupted someone's speech with a guttural wail that sounded unhuman. As everyone turned to look at her, she flew into the room like a torpedo, throwing herself into a large, framed photo of Mama that was leaning against the pulpit. She then rocked back and forth on her knees wailing "My baby, my baby!" again and again until either she or I was removed from the room—I don't recall which. I often wish I could somehow excise that memory from my consciousness for good—it haunts me every fucking day.

My father was never the same either. Up to that point, my mother had been chaos and my father had been stability. When her fiery passion engulfed the room, it was my father who dampened the flames. When she didn't come home, it was he who found her. When she sobbed, it was he who held her. It was almost as if she charged him with energy—both good and bad; but, without that charge, he became empty, dead inside. He always tried to pretend like he was fine, calling me "Pumpkin" and attempting to play with me. But I could sense the emptiness of it. He was going through the motions, but it wasn't working. The glint in his eye was gone and his face looked older somehow. He didn't laugh and his smiles were only replicas of what they once were. He was drinking too much and, though he tried to hide it, I could smell the beer on his breath. He slept a lot, and, sometimes, late at night, I heard him crying. This made me want to bury myself in my pillows. To me, his sobs were yet another stabbing echo that could never be unheard. He would play the same sentimental songs over and over. In particular, "Ain't No Sunshine When She's Gone" by Bill Withers was on repeat so many times I can't bear to listen to it today. Baba came upstairs every day to cook dinner and check on me. But, one day, both Baba and Papa showed up and said I was going to stay with them for a while.

Chapter 7 ～ Peter

My eldest daughter was unexpected. Her mother was supposed to be getting a contraceptive shot each month but had apparently missed a few doses. I loved children, but I knew my wife, Gracie, couldn't take care of a baby. She could barely take care of herself. I met Gracie at an L.A. bar. I was a young lawyer having martinis with a coworker when in walked the sexiest woman I'd ever seen. She was tall with a blunt bob of straight dark hair that exposed her elegant neck. She wore a short dress or skirt and had legs that went on forever. As she approached the bar and asked for a double shot of whiskey, neat (an odd drink for a beautiful woman, I thought), I noticed her large green eyes and succulent red lips. Of course, I wasn't the only one looking at her. She had her pick of any guy in the place; but, for whatever reason, her eyes landed on mine.

"Cat got your tongue?" she said playfully. I must have deserted my coworker because the rest of that evening was all about Gracie. She was gorgeous; but more than that, she had a presence, an energy, which was undeniable. When she asked me about myself, she responded as if I was thoroughly fascinating (which I wasn't). In fact, she had a love of life that astounded me and made me feel like I'd been wearing blinders up to that point. Her laughter was contagious, and she was both smart and funny.

Gracie pulled me into her light and we drank, talked and danced until the bar closed. Then we went to my place. Before Gracie, I'd had girlfriends, but they were child's play compared to this exotic creature. We made love all night and I soon realized I was desperately besotted with her. She took over my thoughts day and night. I was consumed by her and just couldn't get enough. It seems, at least according to my friends, that I'd lost sight of myself.

They said I was "thinking with the wrong brain." I was an intelligent man and a decent lawyer, but I had zero sense when it came to her. I wanted only to be with her, regardless of any warning signs along the way.

I had moved to L.A. from New York City two years earlier. Along with receiving a much-wanted job offer, I had always craved sunshine and was tired of the chaos and expense of NYC. My parents, who had lived through more horrors than I could comprehend, were also having a difficult time dealing with New York winters. Their years of nearly freezing to death in Poland were enough for them to never see another snowflake. So, the three of us packed up and set out for LA. We rented a house in Encino and my parents reconnected with some old friends from Europe. The sun did each of them good, as they enjoyed daily walks and gardening. My life was good: I had a great job, my parents were content, and the daily dose of sunshine felt incredible.

I was the only attorney at my firm who lived with his parents, but I didn't care. Mama and Tata had emigrated to the United States in the late 1940s after surviving the Holocaust. My great uncle, Ezra, sponsored them, offering up his little Brooklyn apartment without a second thought. My parents arrived with nothing but a tiny suitcase and their immigration cards. And, while they spoke four languages between them, English was not one of them. They were both sickly thin and ill-equipped for the confusion, noise, and crowds that awaited them. But they also possessed a startling amount of perseverance.

My tata immediately began working at the same factory as my uncle, where he spent long days on the factory floor sorting auto parts and, eventually, building car engines. My father would have much preferred an academic job, for he loved books and never tired of learning and teaching others about the world. But he never complained. Mama helped her sister-in-law with chores and eventually started working at a nearby café where she cleaned and did dishes. To others, their lives must have seemed incredibly hard, as they were in a strange country where they couldn't communicate and had low-paying jobs that were beneath their abilities. But, to them, their daily lives were not only manageable, but were blessings. For the first time in more than a decade, Tata and Mama were *free*. And until one loses their freedom—especially in such a barbaric and mechanized way—I suppose it's impossible to know its worth. But my parents knew and they instilled in me a gratitude to which my peers could never relate.

Being a child of Holocaust survivors is something that is difficult to put into words. They didn't speak much about what happened to them; yet, it was always there, looming around us like a suffocating cloud. I knew they spoke to each other about it in Polish or Yiddish. But they spoke in whispers and, while I had absorbed a great deal of both languages, this topic was their own. I believe they wanted to protect me from what they had endured. But their losses were ever apparent, particularly since they both had almost no living relatives between them despite coming from large families. My mother had somehow smuggled a necklace along with two very worn photos of her immediate family in the hem of her coat. I have no idea how she pulled this off, having lost everything else and knowing the punishment if caught. But the pictures were more valuable to her than diamonds. Those photos, which were framed and displayed in the living room, contained more than ten other people, including my maternal grandparents, six aunts and uncles, and several cousins—*all of them* murdered by the Germans. I often stared into those faces, wondering what they were like—what their dreams may have been. I considered the horrors they experienced, feeling inadequate in my ignorance. One photo showed a baby and two young children, no more than five years old. When I looked at them, my heart hurt. What happened to those innocent souls, I wondered. What kind of a God would allow this?

While my parents tried their best to shield me from their horrors during the war, this was an impossible feat. When I later learned about intergenerational trauma, I realized it had sunk its oppressive teeth into me long ago. Their experiences had fundamentally changed them, as well as their perceptions of the world. Mama wanted nothing more than to embrace being American. To her, America symbolized the antithesis of war-torn Poland and the Nazi regime. There was freedom, of course; but America also meant safety, choices, open spaces, and other "luxuries." She changed the spelling of her name from "Chana" to "Hanna," and she took English-speaking classes in the evenings. She learned how to make American food such as hamburgers, although she always retreated back to familiar Polish dishes. She enrolled me in T-ball and then softball, attending every game. She was determined to be the perfect American mother and housewife whose child blended in with other kids. At the time, her overzealousness annoyed me. But, thinking of it now, my heart aches for her. She would have given her life to ensure that my childhood was the polar opposite of hers, and that none of her pain would spill over onto me.

Despite their best efforts, my parents were vastly different than those of my classmates. Their thick accents were a dead giveaway. Their way of speaking so embarrassed me that I rarely brought friends home. I was also petrified that they would see Mama's tattoo, despite her constant attempts to keep it covered. And while I loved my parents' traditional cooking, I worried that the aroma of cabbage and beets would stick to my clothing, accompanying me to school.

Having endured starvation, both of my parents had an unusual relationship with food. There was always an overabundance of it in our household. My mama kept the cupboards stocked with enough canned and boxed food to feed a family of ten. Any time we consumed even one item, she or my father would rush off to the store to get a replacement. They never wasted food, to them this was a mortal sin. Fortunately, I was not a picky eater; but I do recall several occasions when I sat at the table all evening as I refused to eat peas or some other detested food set before me.

My mama was incredibly overprotective. While other kids in the neighborhood simply went outside to play, she wouldn't allow this. She had to know where I was and with whom *at all times*. When I think of the terrifying places her imagination must have taken her, I feel guilty for being such a brat as she hovered over me. I had often begged my parents for a little brother, or hell, even a sister. Anything to take off some of the pressure and give me a trusted confidant who could share in my suffering. At first, they said they were working on it, but eventually they were silent and gloomy when I asked. So, I gave up. Both of my parents did their best to hide their inner pain, but sometimes their eyes would look lost as their minds wandered to some unfathomable place. Mama spaced out like this more than Tata, and I especially recall her doing so while washing the dishes. Her hands would continue to go through the motions as she stared blankly out the kitchen window, not even noticing her beloved sparrows.

My tata was at work until early evening, so his impact on me was relatively less than was Mama's. But he did his best to separate me from his anxieties, playing catch with me every weekend and always reminding me how much he loved me. But his torment often showed itself, particularly in his dreams. Hearing my tata scream in Polish or Yiddish during the night was just a regular part of life. Sometimes I tried to listen to his words, but all I understood was "Mama, Mama, *no!*" There were times when he flew out of bed in a panic, and others when he seemed to be digging in his sleep. Mama also had nightmares, but she wasn't as loud. She tossed and turned, often waking up drenched in sweat. Sometimes she moved her mouth, as if she were eating.

I recall having a friend sleep over when I was around ten and, when I woke the next morning, he was gone. Tata had one of his nightmares, which scared the daylights out of my friend—who walked four blocks home at 2 a.m. I slept through the whole thing. The hell that awaited my parents when they slipped into unconsciousness was but another slap in the face by the Nazi pigs who wouldn't even allow them the solace of sleep so many decades later. The war and the systematic genocide of Europe's Jews by the Germans was forever implanted within the minds and hearts of my beautiful parents. It was something only those who were there could even begin to comprehend. I thank God they had each other, for, between them, was a private world of shared trauma and understanding.

I tried to learn more about what happened to my parents when I was around eleven. But any time I broached the subject with Tata, he just said, "It's best to forget." But of course, I knew he couldn't. When the subject came up, he looked so despairing—more like haunted—that I didn't have the heart to ask again. Mama was more forthcoming about her experiences during the war. The conversation commenced when I asked her about the tattoo on her forearm. Back in those days, few people had tattoos, and certainly not Jewish mothers in America. The tattoo was grossly out of place on her delicate arm. At first, she said something dismissive about a phone number, but did not elaborate. But I was smarter than this. And I'd heard a little about the Holocaust on the news and at school.

When I asked her if it was from a concentration camp, she sighed deeply and said, "Yes, my aniołku [angel], that is true." It was on that day that she told me the most about her past. I have revisited that conversation a thousand times, trying to remember her every word. She described how she was born and raised in a picturesque town in Southern Poland called "Dąbrowa Górnicza," or "Old-Dąbrowa." She said her town was on two rivers and she had wonderful memories of splashing in the cool water on summer days. She described the thick oak forests and how, even now, the familiar scent of oak reminded her of childhood. Her town was near Będzin, where a number of her family members also lived. She smiled when she spoke of Będzin and its breathtaking Walzin castle. She told me her father, my "dziadek," was a family doctor who was beloved in the town because of his kind nature and vast medical knowledge. "My tata was my hero, you see," she said. "He cared deeply for his patients, no matter who they were—Jew or gentile. When someone called on him late in the night, he always grabbed his doctor kit and ran out the door. Sometimes he came home so tired he could barely sit through dinner. The townspeople loved my tata, often dropping off vegetables or fruit from their gardens, or delicious desserts to show their gratitude. Some of our neighbors were so poor, food was all they could offer as payment. But he always helped them no matter what. He made me so proud, my tata. I wanted to be a doctor just like him one day."

She also talked about her mother and sisters, telling me how close they were. "My mama, your babcia, was slim and beautiful with dark blonde hair. She was a strong person and was strict with me and my sisters, but also very loving. She was a wonderful cook and we all loved helping her in the kitchen—especially when she made bread and sweet pastries. She had passion, my mama. How she loved music! She and Tata owned several record albums and would dance with us girls as Bach filled the room. My little sisters, Rachela and Ida, who were only babies when the war began, were so full of life! They adored animals and were often outside playing with the goat and kitties. Ida, the younger one, followed me everywhere. She bothered me so much at the time! Oh, but if only she could have lived, I would never complain about her again…"

Poor Mama. I vividly recall her speaking about her little sisters. There was a mix of love, pain, and guilt in her voice that I'd never heard before. I started to worry that maybe I should not have brought up the topic—damning myself for my infernal curiosity. But she kept on, just a little longer.

"We were so happy, Piotr, but we didn't know how happy we were until everything was taken from us. Remember that lesson Piotr, always be thankful for what you have! We were a large family, with more than thirty aunties, uncles, and cousins. Our home was busy, always with family or neighbors coming and going. We enjoyed many weddings and holidays together. Until Hitler came to power and it all changed, that is. The Nazis broke my tata down bit by bit. They told him he could no longer treat non-Jewish patients—of which he had many. They destroyed his office, breaking windows and painting "Juden" across the front. They…"

Her voice trailed off, her hand trembled. "They murdered them all, my beautiful Mama and baby sisters died in Auschwitz. They took our tata away. And the rest, they fled to Warsaw and… I'm sorry, my darling, I can't talk about this anymore now. But, you see, this is why I have this awful tattoo on my arm, they took everything from me—even my name. This is why all of these people, *our* people," she said referring to the familiar photo, "are no longer here. This is because of the Nazi murderers."

On that day, my mother told me more than she ever had about her past. Her face almost lit up when she described her pre-war life. It sounded idyllic. But she could not reflect on her childhood without the darkness of what happened later seeping in and destroying her happiness. There was a black cloud over *all* of her childhood memories. I wanted to cry at the injustice of it. I had so many more questions, but I could see that it took a great deal out of her, so I refrained from asking. I'm not sure that she had ever talked about what happened to her with anyone else other than my father until that day. I still didn't know what had happened to Tata, but he seemed even more fragile than Mama, so I wasn't going to burden him with questions. At least now I understood about the tattoo, as well as many of their strange and overprotective behaviors. While my parents would continue to embarrass me, it was now tempered with a new sense of compassion for the unimaginable memories that plagued them.

Chapter 8 ∽ Peter

I'm not sure what it is about me that made me so attracted to Gracie, in spite of the red flags that must've been everywhere. Maybe because she was so different than my parents, who were reserved and chose each word carefully. Gracie was unfiltered, like a wild animal. She also wasn't Jewish, about which I had mixed emotions. I'd dated very few Gentiles in my life and, from an attraction standpoint, I didn't really care. But there was a part of me that felt a responsibility to carry on my Jewish culture after all that my people had endured. And I didn't want to disappoint my parents. But I pushed those feelings aside and appreciated Gracie's charisma and disregard for what others thought, which was refreshing. Or maybe I was just lonely.

Gracie was visiting friends in LA when we met, but she actually lived in San Diego where she worked at an art gallery. She was a talented artist, creating charcoal sketches that were both disturbing and beautiful at the same time. She gave me a tour of her place of work when we were first dating and I couldn't take my eyes off her sketches, most of which were in the workshop in the back of the building. The gallery was stunning and had a decent collection of scenic watercolor pieces I could not afford. One of Gracie's sketches was displayed on the back wall of the gallery. It was simply labeled 'Circles,' and consisted of a woman with wild, wavy hair who appeared to be spinning around. She had somehow captured this movement, along with the model's crazed eyes. I'd never seen anything like it. "This is incredible," I said. "Who is it?"

"Oh, that's good old Mom," she answered. "She wouldn't sit still while I sketched, so I gave up. My boss, Jeremey—he owns this place—just loves it."

"I can see why. You are not only beautiful, but talented too!" This earned me an enthusiastic and rather sloppy kiss.

Gracie took over my life in record time. On Fridays, I would head to San Diego to spend the weekend with her, first making sure my parents had everything they needed. They were pretty quiet about Gracie, having met her only twice. Tata said she was pretty and Mama just described her as bouncy, of all things. But I knew my parents well. Although they would not speak ill of someone unless it was fully warranted, I sensed their disapproval. And they knew she wasn't Jewish. I wasn't too worried though, I figured she would grow on them eventually.

Gracie made me forget my worries; she was all-consuming. Her apartment was a bit of a disaster. It was a large studio with a Murphy bed that never made its way back into the wall when I was around. She had a ton of clothes, which were often strewn about the place along with loads of charcoal pencils and paints, empty or half-done canvasses, shoes, makeup, dirty dishes, and books. At the time, I thought she was eclectic—far too artistic to waste time on house cleaning. The current me would've seen her as a slob, a quality I loathe. But I was an idiot, so there you go. Over time, shlepping back and forth became too much and we talked about moving in together. I found a lower-paying position at a San Diego firm and we rented a house about a mile away. The house was large enough for my parents to live in the fully finished basement. Fortunately, it was far nicer than our LA home. It even had a large, sunny backyard where they could garden. But, they were more than dubious about the prospect of me quitting my job and moving in with Gracie.

"I don't think this is wise, Piotr," said my mom when I gave her the news. "You have a good job that you worked so hard for. You don't really know this woman. You aren't even married."

"I proposed to her last week."

"Oh, Piotr, please slow down. I am worried."

But, of course, I did not listen, moron that I was. And so, we all moved into a cozy bungalow on, ironically, Easy Street. We eloped in Vegas soon after moving and were excited to start our lives together. We enjoyed a honeymoon period, which involved a lot of sex, pretentious restaurants, and local art galleries. I kept telling myself, "You see, Peter, everything is fine. She's a wonderful woman, if not a bit eccentric. She will mellow with time."

Gradually, our home started to look like her old apartment. She seemed incapable of getting dressed without going through her entire wardrobe, which she rarely put away afterward. Sometimes she got inspired by her art and was up all night sketching madly in the kitchen. I couldn't understand how she could get zero sleep and go to work the next day, but she said she didn't need sleep, that it was overrated. I picked up after her and made excuses about her behavior to my parents, who mostly stayed downstairs. She managed to go to work every day at 2 pm, but there were occasions when she didn't come home until after midnight—two hours after her shift ended. When I questioned her, she said she was schmoozing with local artists in order to help her career. One night she came home dead drunk at 3 am. She gave me the same excuse, but I was pretty pissed off by then.

There were other times, however, when she was lovely. She often made delicious, healthy meals that the four of us enjoyed on our garden patio. We would go for long walks together on the beach and she could be incredibly affectionate and loving toward me. When it came to Gracie, I was torn. I was a ridiculous stereotype. The hedonistic side of me simply ignored her flaws and odd behaviors, wanting only the excitement and beauty she brought to my life. But the sensible side of me kept whispering in the back of my mind, "Something's wrong. Get out while you can!" But I pushed my intuition away; I was married after all—it was too late. As someone who had litigated divorce cases, I had zero interest in being on the other side of the desk and was determined to make this work. And besides, I desperately loved my wife.

Before I met Gracie, I wanted kids—not a lot, maybe just one or two. I had clichéd visions of roughhousing with my son and knowing the gentle love of an adoring little girl. But I was petrified of procreating with Gracie, I just didn't trust her to be a responsible parent. I also wondered about her genes, especially since her mother wasn't exactly normal either. She said she didn't want any children, so I wasn't particularly worried. I didn't discuss any of this with my parents, who were biased given their absolute desperation for grandchildren. They had wanted many children themselves; but, as it turned out, my mother's body had been so ravaged by her time in the camps that on the rare occasions that she conceived, the pregnancies always resulted in devastating miscarriages. I felt guilty, especially being their only child, but I refused to change my mind about having kids. At the beginning of my relationship with Gracie, I was open to the idea, but this quickly dissipated.

Gracie wasn't just messy and energetic, she was at times disheveled and chaotic. She reminded me of a mix between Pig Pen and a whirling dervish, spinning out of control and leaving a disaster in her wake. Sometimes she would speak a mile a minute, almost desperate to get out as many words as possible—her brain working much faster than her mouth. Perhaps worst of all, she had no concept whatsoever that she was behaving strangely. If I brought anything to her attention, she would minimize her behavior and place the emphasis on me, saying things like, "Oh, Peter, you're such a fuddy-duddy. Just lighten up and have fun for once in your life." At first, her words almost worked, as they made me wonder if I had inherited my parents' reserved and overly cautious nature. But later I could see that something was not right with my Gracie.

We'd been married nearly a year when things got drastically worse. Gracie had been staying up all night most nights, either drawing or writing hastily in her innumerable notebooks. Once, when I peeked into the spare room to see what she was doing, I saw her writing frantically while having an animated and decidedly unfriendly conversation with someone. I wondered who was in our house at 3 am, but no one was there. She ate very little and had dark shadows under her eyes. One day, Mama ran into Gracie in the yard and was taken aback by her appearance. Mama came to me later saying she was terribly worried about Gracie and that she seemed to be quite ill. Mama thought she had cancer; but, in all honesty, cancer would have been easier to manage than the true culprit.

Gracie was also spending a great deal of money on art supplies, clothes, gifts, and even some rather expensive paintings and sculptures. Our credit cards were nearly at their limit. When I mentioned this, her head spun. "This is *my* money, too, Peter! Don't be such a cheap bastard," she screamed, throwing a ceramic plate across the kitchen as a final touch.

Soon after that incident, Gracie went to bed and refused to get up.

Darkness overtook my vivacious wife like nothing I'd ever seen before. Not only did she not get up—which meant she didn't go to work—but everything about her seemed to be in slow motion. If she did speak, it was in a monotone whisper. She moved like a snail, which seemed to take tremendous effort. She was a woman who took pride in her appearance, but had stopped caring. She wore no makeup and didn't bother to comb her hair. Worse yet, she didn't bathe and was starting to smell. Of course, I asked her what was wrong and what I could do to help, but she only said she was done, and rolled over toward the wall to cry. I tried desperately to get her to go to a psychiatrist, but she immediately became agitated and said shrinks were not to be trusted and would "turn her in"—whatever that meant. After several weeks of this, things only got worse. I heard her throwing up one afternoon and God damn if she wasn't pregnant.

The first half of Gracie's pregnancy was the gloomiest part of my life up to that point. For the first two months, she refused to go to the doctor. But she continued to vomit—which was most unlike her, and her breasts got bigger. She was also peeing a great deal. I convinced my doctor to make a house call. Gracie would not allow him to fully examine her, but he asked a lot of questions and took a blood sample—which confirmed my fears. When she learned of the test results, Gracie barely cared. "Oh great, just what I need," was all she said. The doctor also asked her about her depression symptoms and provided a referral to a psychiatrist, but Gracie was adamant in her distain for anyone in the mental health field. For about a month after the pregnancy was confirmed, Gracie talked about either killing herself or getting an abortion, but she simply didn't have the energy or wherewithal to do either. At least in this instance, I was grateful for her avolition, as, along with my love for Gracie, I already felt an attachment to the poor little soul trapped within her precarious womb.

Like me, my parents were conflicted about the pregnancy. Sometimes I noticed Mama's face light up when we talked about it, other times she only sighed with worry. My parents and I developed an unspoken pact—we would welcome this baby with love and enthusiasm, but we also would do our damnedest to protect him or her from Gracie. For a solid six months, Gracie lounged about in bed or on the couch. She barely said a word, floating about like a phantom. Sometimes she stared at the TV, but nothing seemed to register with her. Even her books and art held no interest. Our greatest challenge was getting Gracie to eat. We prepared her most coveted foods, always asking if she had any cravings. Mama made her favorite types of pierogi and I placed takeout foods in front of her, but she barely touched any of them and was losing weight. We were petrified for the baby. After numerous threats of hospitalization, Gracie finally forced down several bites of every meal. Fortunately, she also drank milk and took her folate. I began to fall behind at work because I was so consumed with Gracie and the baby. I thank God for my parents, who took over Gracie's care, thus preventing me from getting fired. Mama said she had seen women whose bodies were ravaged by hunger and brutality secretly give birth to beautiful babies while in Auschwitz, which was sadly reassuring. Of course, those innocent beings never stood a chance.

At around the six-month point of the pregnancy, there was a dramatic shift in my wife. When I woke up at dawn to get ready for work, Gracie was not in bed, which was highly unusual at that time. She wasn't on the couch either. I found her in the nursery covered in purple paint.

"Um, what are you doing, Gracie?"

"I'm flying to the moooooooon!" she said dramatically. "What does it look like I'm doing? I'm *nesting!*" she added with a twirl, which caused paint to splatter across the floor.

"At 6 am?"

"Is it six already? How does it look? I just love purple! Do you like it? I'm almost done, just one wall left. I also want to buy a rug. And what do you think of a mural on this wall? I could paint fairies, animals, or maybe dinosaurs. I kinda wish I knew the baby's gender. Do you think we should find out? Oh, and we need some curtains too. And blinds, it's way too light in here at night. I also want to refinish the dresser. We need a changing table too. We should go shopping this weekend. Will you go with me? I think we—"

"Slow down, sweetheart. So, you've been at this all night, huh? You seem to be feeling much better."

"I feel *fabulous!*"

"That's great, honey. But how about taking a break? I'll make you something to eat and then you can rest."

"I'm almost done, I can't stop now. And I'm not one bit tired."

Here we go again, catapulting down the rollercoaster tracks, I thought to myself. I made Gracie some toast with peanut butter and a cup of decaf, imploring her to lay down when she finished painting. I warned my parents of her mood change and headed off to work.

At least now we didn't have to practically force-feed Gracie. She ate very well indeed, sending me out for watermelon and bean burritos almost daily. She had more of a glow about her and was back to her hilarious, vibrant self. Over the course of a week, Gracie not only painted a nature scene in the baby's room, but also wallpapered the bathroom, refinished a dresser, organized the kitchen cabinets, planted flowers outside the nursery window, and spent hours at the mall. She was also writing in her journals again and sketching. The nursery was amazing, though bordering on vulgar. But she racked up our credit cards again, spending more than twenty grand on baby stuff and God knows what else. And she was convinced she could see into people's souls, which is why her drawings were so much better than anyone else's.

She was out of control. *Again.*

Gracie's depression remained on the back burner for the rest of her pregnancy. We watched her like a hawk—we had no choice. I treated her like a child, which she greatly resented and had no trouble letting me know. I took her credit cards when she was asleep—this really pissed her off. I simply couldn't afford not to. If she continued to spend, we wouldn't be able to pay the mortgage or buy food. Perhaps even worse, I blackmailed and bribed her into resting. I was prepared to use any means necessary to keep our baby healthy and safe. I locked up her art supplies and only let her have them after she took a nap. When she wasn't interested in art, I threatened to call her mother if she didn't rest—boy, did that do the trick! If there was one thing that drove Gracie out of her mind, it was speaking with her mother. Honestly, the apple didn't fall far from the crazy tree; but Gracie only saw her mother as nuts, certainly not herself. She believed she was just fine. Or rather, she believed she was *amazing*, with enormous talent and unlimited energy. I don't know if Gracie actually took naps and she barely slept at night, but at least I got her to lie still for a couple of hours each day. My corrections-officer approach paid off, since, two days before her due date, Gracie went into labor and delivered Sylvia Marie—the most perfect little girl on the planet. I remember wishing she would stay tiny forever, safe from the harsh realities of the world.

Chapter 9 ❧ Sunny

Joshua and I fell into a comfortable routine. He got up before me and always set a large mug of coffee on my nightstand. He added just the right amount of milk and sugar—he knew me well. As I stepped out of my shower, Joshua would kiss me goodbye, say "I love you," and head out the door. He was inexplicably cheerful first thing in the morning; whereas I took some time to warm up. I had never been a morning person, but lately I'd been having nightmares that left me unable to go back to sleep. I hadn't slept well for as far back as I could remember, but waking up in a sweat—sometimes on the floor—was something new. My nightmares were vague, but there were always two consistent themes: My mother and sheer panic. These night terrors left me exhausted the next morning.

Despite my fatigue and lousy mood, I always tried to look my best for work and gave myself plenty of time. I often put my hair up, leaving dark spirals around my face, and I never went out without eye makeup and lipstick. Our office dress code was business casual. I usually wore silky dresses that landed above the knee, or blouses and skirts of the same length. I had an impressive shoe collection and generally went with a two- or three-inch heel. The endless compliments I received on my fashion choices fed my fragile ego. Once I was ready, I would squeeze my sweet Chester and kiss his cheeks repeatedly before taking off. Chester was my baby, I loved him so much and felt guilty for leaving him.

With pink Converse sneakers on my feet and my heels in hand, I kept up a brisk pace as I breathed in the sights and smells along the way to my building. I enjoyed walking to work, and soaked in the shared hustle and bustle of my neighbors as they started each new day. I often waved to Viktor, as he set up shop. And sometimes I stopped at a deli or bakery for a muffin. The walk was four blocks, which was just right. Sometimes I got distracted by my surroundings and would certainly have been late for work had the route been any longer. Each day I passed a homeless young woman on the same corner near a coffee shop. She was disheveled with dirty blonde hair and dark roots. Her miserable face was covered in red sores. Something about her tugged at my heart. I always gave her a bit of money or, if I didn't have any, I handed her my muffin. It was the least I could do.

The publishing company was in an old building with reddish bricks. It had ten floors, and the windows toward the top had boxes bursting with white geraniums. I loved the building's old-world charm. Although we were on the seventh floor, I never allowed myself to take the elevator—even if I was carrying heavy files or books. Instead, I jogged up the seven flights, counting each stair in my head (there were nighty-eight) until I reached my floor. Once I changed my shoes and caught my breath, I headed to my tiny office. Sometimes, if was feeling claustrophobic, I would take my work to the downstairs espresso shop, where I could sink into fat, cushiony chairs and loveseats. One of the baristas, a handsome guy named Stan, was unabashedly flirtatious toward me, always forming my latte foam into a heart. But, of course, my heart belonged only to Joshua.

I was pleased with my job. In contrast to her severe exterior, Emily was a decent enough boss. She gave me a big stack of work each day, which mostly involved editing in-press manuscripts. Determined to succeed, I dove into my work with fervor. Emily was consistently impressed by my efficiency—I could get through more documents in one day than any of the other junior staff, and my attention to detail was unparalleled. I really wanted to like Emily, but she was drab and without humor. I just couldn't connect with her. My other coworkers were kind and friendly. They made me feel welcome and invited me out to lunch or for drinks after work. But the prospect of socializing with them caused a lump in my throat and made me feel jittery. I wish I could've been myself and allowed these people to know me, but I just couldn't do it. It was true, I had very few friends—unlike Joshua, who had tons. And although this didn't really bother me, somewhere in the back of my mind, I wondered if my hermit-like nature was normal. Nonetheless, I politely refused their invitations until they finally stopped asking. I also brought my lunches from home, which served as a ready excuse to eat alone.

But I was not always able to hide myself from others. The blasted office birthday celebrations, which occurred about once a month, presented one such situation. Those events were insufferable. Our office manager, Melody, would set up the staff kitchen with a birthday banner and a large cake. Then a birthday card was passed around the office. Those cards gave me such anxiety! First of all, how many original ways are there to say, "Happy Birthday"? My coworkers added trite remarks like "Have a great day!" or "Glad to have you on the team!" Blah, blah, blah. Secondly, I worked at a damn publishing house, so any written word had to be *flawless*. With my chronic perfectionism and indecisiveness—which seemed to be worsening, signing these cards was a real struggle. Sometimes it took me over an hour. I finally started passing the cards along after pretending to sign them, which made me feel like a bit of a jerk.

The worst part of the office birthday parties was the cake. When cake time arrived, Melody would summon everyone to the kitchen. I don't know what happens to people in an office, but my coworkers dropped everything and sprinted toward the cake like so many starved rats. Elizabeth and I laughed about this. She said you could put a plate of turds in any office kitchen and they would disappear in twenty minutes. I didn't share in their gluttony. For one thing, with the exception of cheesecake, I can't stand cake—especially the ones Melody bought. They were cheap, store-bought monstrosities, which I didn't understand given the plethora of bakeries nearby. The first time this happened, I obediently shuffled along with the others. Predictably, once so-and-so blew out the candles, we all clapped as if the birthday person was a toddler. I choked down a few bites of cake; but then, as I struggled to make small talk, I felt myself go red with the embarrassment of forced pleasantries. A track ran through my head of things I might say, but nothing ever came out right. So, I shrank into myself as my inherent inability to fit in left me further isolated and ashamed. The second time I attended one of those celebrations, I was determined to not eat any of the wretched cake. When I politely refused, Melody, who was maybe twenty pounds overweight and had a Texas twang, said, "Don't tell me you're on a diet? Come on, Sunny, live a little!" What the hell did she care if I ate cake? Embarrassed, I took the cake and managed one small mouthful. But that was the last time. On subsequent birthdays, I hid in a toilet stall like a loser. And I vowed to be home sick when my day came.

While the dreaded Thursday meetings continued, I had gotten more comfortable with them and now I only took a quarter of a Xanax beforehand. Well, to be honest, I did take more if someone intimidating was attending, like Mr. Penterhaus—the company CEO and founder. He was an old British guy who looked like an aged John Lennon. Round glasses framed his deeply etched face, and his short hair, which was died a ridiculous orange-blonde, was parted on the side. He was both opinionated and pedantic, and seemed to make everyone nervous. I will never forget one particular meeting when he was present. I'd been with the company for a few months and it was a typical agenda where we went over questions and decisions regarding new manuscripts. I guess I was lost in my thoughts, as, when I heard my name, I noticed his steely blue eyes aimed right at me. As I tripped over my words, Mr. Penterhaus looked at me like I was no better than a gnat. *God, it was humiliating*. Feeling profoundly anxious, I watched him carefully, just in case I was called on again. As he spoke, I noticed that his teeth were straight but extremely yellow, which revolted me.

On this particular day, we were having a brown bag meeting and he was chomping away on a sandwich. As I watched him chew tuna salad with his yolk-colored chops, a wave of nausea overtook me. I thought I might actually puke, but managed to hold it down. But then, once Mr. Penterhaus finished his food, he began sucking his teeth. I mean *really sucking*, as if the world's fortunes were caught up in there! For whatever reason, that sucking, which no one else seemed to notice, grated the inside of my eardrums. It was intolerable and then, somehow, utterly hilarious.

As I watched the scene as if looking down at a movie, I saw the old man's lips pucker as he sucked air through piss-colored Chicklets. Then something horrible happened: I broke out in uncontrollable laughter. And not your garden-variety laughter. I'm talking about deep, rumbling laughter that reached my stomach, made my eyes leak, and made my bladder attempt the same. It would have been a marvelous moment of bliss, had I not been the only one laughing. And had it not been directed at the worst possible person. Emily asked me if I was okay, which really meant, "Shut the fuck up!" I just nodded my head and continued to shake while trying desperately to snuff out each chortle. Emily glared mightily and gestured for me to leave the room. Ever the object of grace, I left the table so abruptly, my chair fell backwards. Afterwards, I sat in my office cell and laughed for another fifteen minutes or so before Emily showed up. Her face was beet red, giving her more of a parrot face than her usual gullish look. *She was pissed!*

"Sunny! What on earth was that in there?"

I was speechless. What could I say? I didn't know why I acted like that. Either I was deeply flawed or the situation was indeed hilarious. I was thoroughly confused.

"Hellooo?? What in heavens were you thinking? You just disrespected *our CEO!*"

"I'm *so* sorry, Emily. It's just that he was sucking his teeth, which are just so yellow. And…"

"What are you talking about? So what if he was sucking his teeth, who cares! He's our *boss*. Don't you get that?"

"Yes, I'm really sorry. I haven't been feeling well lately. Maybe my sinus infection affected my brain?" I lied.

"Yeah, I doubt that. You need to write Mr. Penterhaus an apology right now. And I want to read it before you send it. And Sunny, don't ever act like that again."

I felt like a two-year-old being chastised for misbehaving. But of course, I deserved it. Not only was I puzzled as to why I did it, my lack of contrition was equally mystifying. Sure, the guy was stodgy and intimidating, but he was an old man and *I laughed in his face! Publicly!* I must've been having an off day—I was not this type of person. I had to find a way to control myself in the future. Maybe more Xanax? While I didn't fully trust myself to never do it again, I promised Emily I wouldn't and wrote an insincere but convincing message to Old Yeller.

What the fuck was wrong with me?

Chapter 10 ❧ Sunny

Despite my work challenges, I treasured those early days with Joshua. He was gregarious and likable, and so much fun to be around. Apparently, his coworkers thought so too, as he quickly established a group of work friends. Joshua also did well at his job. Along with being good at all things finance (an area that was foreign to me), he was amazing at presenting his work—even in front of large audiences. I found this astounding—I could never do it. Sometimes he would go out for a beer with coworkers after a challenging day, which meant he wasn't home until at least 9 pm. And on the rare occasions when he went out with his fraternity brothers, he was home even later. This annoyed me, but I kept myself entertained by drawing or reading with Chester purring in my lap.

I turned our spare bedroom into an office-studio, covering half of it with a tarp and setting up my easel and other supplies. Sometimes I took my supplies to the beach, but I didn't like the attention I usually attracted. Men seemed to think my artistic efforts provided a free ticket for lame pick-up lines like, "What are you working on there?" or "Wow, you're really good!" or, my personal favorite, "Can you draw *me?*" Occasionally, I brought Elizabeth with me—she had no difficulty discouraging admirers! Sometimes I found more private areas to draw or I resolved to work on our patio instead. I was in the middle of working on a set of animal scenes, which so far included Anna's Hummingbird, which I shot a picture of at my dad's house, a fox squirrel I saw at the park, and a seagull that was stealing my lunch as I picnicked at the beach with Joshua. I was excited about painting Chester and Sparky next.

Joshua was my own private fan club. He loved my work and his enthusiasm inspired me to keep going. The hummingbird piece was his favorite. Mine too, actually. Using colored pencils, I was able to capture the iridescent green plumage on her side, and the vibrant magenta that framed her face. Joshua, who was artistically challenged, was as perpetually astonished by my talent as I was by his unnerving ability to interact with all types of people with zero self-consciousness. If I didn't love him so much, I'd hate him. I would have taken his talents over mine in a heartbeat. He still managed to be home by 8:00 on most days, so we often enjoyed a late dinner together and either fell into bed out of passion, exhaustion, or a mix of both.

We started having dinner with my family more often after Baba twisted her ankle and hit her head when slipping on the stairs outside a store. We were all broken up by this. Poor Baba was obviously in pain, but was forever stoic. "Oh, stop your fussing! My goodness, this old body has been through far worse," she would say. But it didn't matter. Babcia was invaluable to our family, so we cooked for her, ran errands, and basically waited on her until she yelled at us to stop. She was so uncomfortable feeling like an object of pity. But I was growing increasingly worried about her. Her injury had left her temporarily immobile, yet even after she recovered, her lethargy continued. Baba was an active, outdoorsy person, but her garden was of little interest to her beyond staring at it out the window. She also refused to go for walks with me or Papa, and wasn't even excited about Hanukkah, which occurred a month or so after her accident. Instead, as Papa sadly observed, every day she sat in her favorite easy chair and watched TV.

Worst of all, Baba's sharpness was diminishing—she was losing words right and left, and sometimes even forgetting our names. For some reason, she had completely forgotten who Sparky was and had even become a little afraid of him. Sparky was all of ten pounds and had not an ounce of aggression in him. She and Papa had always been weird about dogs, never letting my dad get one and crossing the street to avoid them. As Holocaust survivors, their distress around dogs made sense, but Sparky? Really? It seemed that my beautiful grandmother's muddled mind was yet again being tormented by her wartime trauma. Why couldn't the dementia target her darkest memories and leave intact those that brought her peace? Life was so unjust.

When my seagull drawing was complete, I decided to dive back into my books. Maybe it was because of Baba, but I gravitated toward my Holocaust collection. Honestly, there is a part of me that was determined to suffer alongside Baba and Papa. If they were forced to remember their atrocities, the least I could do was to submerge my privileged mind into the same nightmarish subject. Although I'd read it maybe four times, I decided to reread *If This Is a Man* by Primo Levi. Levi was in Auschwitz for a year and his poignant memoir made me cry every time. As I explained to Joshua shortly after moving into the condo, my interest in Holocaust writings stemmed from growing up so close with my grandparents. Of course, I'm also a Jew, but not a very good one. I doubt I would be losing myself in this genre if not for my poor grandparents' personal hell, along with having lost so many extended relatives to the Nazis.

Everybody wanted to shelter me from what happened to my grandparents. My father rarely talked about their past, but after Mama died, he was in no emotional state to adequately monitor me. This was all up to Babcia and Papa. But what none of them understood was that despite the quiet and generally obedient nature I had back then, my curiosity was insatiable. I was nosy as hell. I had seen Baba's tattoo many times and my father gave me a vague explanation of what happened. I was also aware that, whatever had haunted them was still at it. Time had offered no relief. It was as if a malevolent seed had been implanted in both of their brains, with its sole purpose to prohibit them from ever knowing complete contentment or peace.

While they both had terrible dreams, Papa's were the worst. Or at least the loudest. Hearing one of his nightmares from across the house left me troubled for days. Plus, my grandparents were odd—there was a melancholy about them that they could not mask. They spoiled me like most grandparents, but in a different way. They bought me a few too many toys and could be permissive when it came to sweets, yet they also held me too close. I didn't have the freedoms of other kids on the block. They always worried about me. My father had told me how protective they were with him and now I understood.

By the age of ten, I was aware that they had been through something so horrible that it may have been impossible to fully articulate, much less comprehend. But I had such an overwhelming love for my grandparents, that if something catastrophic had happened to them, I *needed* to know. So, over time, I paid close attention—listening to their nightmares and hushed conversations, and snooping through their books and papers. When I was older, I would listen carefully when they were speaking Polish or Yiddish and attempt to translate it, which earned me a few tidbits of information. I also asked my dad a lot of questions. But the bulk of information I uncovered came straight from Baba. And, eventually, even Papa opened up too—but just a little bit.

One day when I was twelve, I came home from school in tears. Our class was studying history and, specifically, WWII. When the topic of the Holocaust came up, I knew my family had been affected by it. It was only briefly included as part of our coursework, but I wanted to know more, so I looked it up in the school library during lunch. The photos I saw stopped me in my tracks. The emaciated, ageless bodies clad in stripes horrified me like nothing I'd ever seen. When I saw the many Jewish victims from Poland, I slammed the book shut. After school, I was withdrawn and sullen. Baba tried to cheer me up while gently asking me what was wrong. I was never good at keeping my emotions inside and by the end of the day, I could hold it no longer. "Baba," I asked with tears beginning to fall, "what happened to you in the Holocaust?" I'll never forget her reaction. It was as if the heaviness she'd been carrying gave way. Her shoulders slumped and she bowed her head before answering.

"Oh my, I will need to sit down," she said with a deep sigh as she sat on the edge of my bed. "Okay, my dear, I will tell you what I can. The Germans came to Dąbrowa when I was fifteen, not much older than you. Before this, we were happy. My mama was loving and kind, she was a wonderful cook. My papa was a doctor, but he always made time for his four girls, as he called us—Mama, me, and my little sisters. Poor Papa, all of those girls and just him!" she added with a slight chuckle. "We had such fun, me and my sisters and cousins. And we got into mischief too!"

"Mischief? Really, Baba?" I couldn't imagine such a thing.

"Oh yes! We climbed trees and chased each other through our neighbor's corn fields. There was a pond not far from our house and we would sneak out in the early evening and look for frogs. My cousin Saul always found the most. When Mama was baking, my friends and I would grab a kolaczki or sweet roll when we thought she wasn't looking. Mama would shoo us outside with her broom! But she was never really angry."

I tried to picture my great grandmother. She sounded so very different than my own mother; how I wished I'd known her. "What happened to your mama?"

"Oh, she was taken from us. You see, the Nazi's came to our town in 1939 and everything changed. It was terrible, so terrible. They marched in and each day things got worse for our family and the other Jews. Of course, you know about the yellow stars."

I nodded my head.

"Yes, we had to sew them on our clothes or we would be..." her voice trailed off. "We just had to do it. Papa was a target of these awful men. They destroyed his clinic, they smashed the windows and told him to go home. My papa, he was a proud man. He was tall and elegant. But, after they came to our town, he seemed to shrink and become old overnight. We all thought it would end soon, that the British would help us. But it just kept on happening and got worse. So much worse."

I noticed that she was shaking. "Are you okay, Baba?"

She patted my hand. "Yes, my darling. I will tell you what I can for today. Papa was determined to continue his work as a doctor. He knew how much the townspeople needed him, especially his Jewish patients who had nowhere else to go. He went to his patients' homes, often without any pay at all. He was so kind, my papa.

"One cold, rainy day, as he was walking home, an older Jewish woman tripped in the street and fell to the ground. There were some Nazis nearby who were laughing. They thought it hilarious that an old Jewess had fallen down in a mud puddle, you see. But Tata of course went over to help her, how could he not? Oh, but this angered those awful men. They said to leave her, that she belonged there, in the street, covered in dirt. But he didn't listen and helped her up."

Baba stopped for a moment, closed her eyes, and shook her head gently, as if she was trying to rid herself of an image. I held her hand and she continued. "So, they beat him, they beat my tata until he too was there, in the mud. And they left him like that. Of course, no one helped him, for they saw what would happen if they did. When he finally came home much later (Mama had been worried sick), he was covered in a mix of blood and dried mud. He was limping and his face was swollen. We almost didn't recognize him."

"Oh, Baba!"

"We took care of him as best we could. Mama even stitched up a deep cut over his eyebrow as he explained how to do it. Mama wasn't good with blood, but she managed. Tata was in shock and rarely went out after that. Then, since the Nazi's were sending Jewish men away, we kept him hidden in the basement for as long as we could. But, one night, they stormed into the house, found him, and pulled him away by the arm as the rest of us cried and screamed. Mama desperately reached for his hand until one of those beasts hit it with his rifle. He broke Mama's finger! They took him away to a labor camp, you see. We never saw him again."

I felt horrible hearing this, my poor Baba. My tears had started to fall. "Baba, you can tell me about your mama later, it's okay."

"I think I will do that, my darling—I need to lay down now."

Baba left the room, but had the thoughtfulness to send in Papa to read me a story. Of course, I was way too old for stories, but she didn't want to pollute my dreams with all that she'd just told me. Her selflessness knew no bounds. I tried to listen to the childish story, but my heart and mind were somewhere else.

It was weeks later before Baba told me what happened to her mother. I didn't bring it up, though I wanted to know. She realized the story she told me was unfinished and that she needed to continue, no matter how painful. I think she wanted to spare my dreams this time, as she asked me to go for a walk with her one Sunday morning. I remember that it was a gorgeous day and we walked to the park. We made small talk until we reached a bench in the shade, where we both sat.

"I know I have held back on telling you about my life in Poland," she said as she gently patted my leg. "I wanted to spare you of the bad—no *terrible*—things that happened to me and the rest of our family. But you are as old as my sisters and cousins who experienced it, so I guess you are old enough to know. And they are *your* family too. So, I will tell you as much as my heart will allow," she said before blowing her nose with a tissue. She took a deep breath and continued.

"After Tata left, Mama was lost. They had been together since they were children, he was a part of her, you see. She became stronger eventually, but for a while I took over much of her work. Plus, she had a broken finger, so it made things much harder for her. Jews were not allowed to go to school anymore, so my sisters and I were home. I collected eggs, fed the chickens and the goat, helped Mama with dinner, and watched my sisters. We were all hoping to hear from Tata and only received one letter. He was in a labor camp that was a few hours away by train. His letter—well it was barely a letter—was short and did not sound like him. He wrote something like "My Dearest Dvora, I am working at Skarzysko-Kamienna labor camp. We are treated well. I miss you and the children. All my love, Benyamin." That was the gist of the letter. Tata was a lovely writer and would have said so much more to his beloved, if he could. And the writing was not like him; it was sloppy, you see. That letter made Mama more upset than not hearing from Tata at all; she knew he was not well and that the mail was censored.

"Things around town became more awful. Our food was rationed to half of what our Gentile neighbors received. Some Nazis took our beloved chickens one day. After that, we sold our goat to a kindly Gentile neighbor. At least we knew she would be treated well. There was so much bad news. Two of my uncles and an older cousin had all been sent to labor camps. Another cousin, Annah, who was the same age as me and was my best friend, was too stubborn to wear the star. She was blonde and pretty, and believed she could pass, you see. And she did pass, for a time. But one of our neighbors turned her in for a reward. This neighbor was always a friend; Tata had treated his elderly mother. And he turned on us like so many others! Well, the Nazis shot Annah right in front of her house with her mother watching."

Baba stopped for several moments, seeming to watch the crows overhead, and began again.

"We thought it was as bad as it could get, but oh, how wrong we were, my dear. They created a ghetto in Dąbrowa and forced all of the Jews to move there, plus many from neighboring towns. I had lived my whole life in our house; I had known no other home. The worst part was leaving our kitties! I know you love animals, Sunny—I do too. We had four cats, a mama and her three babies. One of them, Henri, was *my* kitty. He was gray with white stripes and he slept with me every night. Leaving Henri and the other kitties with our neighbor broke my heart into pieces."

For whatever reason, hearing about the cats made me cry instantly. I guess it was the most relatable part of Baba's story. I had always adored animals—especially cats, so I empathized with Baba, who was only a couple years older than me at the time. I quickly wiped away my tears, hoping they wouldn't cause Baba to stop talking.

Baba kissed my check and said, "My sweet girl, I know this is awful to hear. Shall I continue?"

"Yes, please keep going."

"After we gathered as many of our things as we could fit into the back of a wagon, we walked along the main street in the town with the rest of the Jews who'd been expelled from their homes to an area of only five or six streets. I vividly recall a girl I knew from school laugh and throw rocks at us. It was such a humiliation! Mama had carefully sewn all of her jewelry, along with the rest of our money, into the hems of my sisters' coats where she thought the Nazis would not look. Our new 'home' was a one-bedroom flat with a small kitchen and a dining room. This was meant for ten people! Can you imagine it? Me, Mama, two of my grandmothers, my grandfather, my sisters, my auntie, and her boys were all crammed into this tiny space. I don't know how we did it! And my poor grandparents, how sad and uncomfortable they must have been. But they did not complain.

"There was very little food, but Mama and my auntie did their best to make it last by cooking watery soups and something resembling bread. We were so hungry! I remember my sisters crying at night as their empty stomachs growled. There were children who snuck out of the ghetto under a hole in the barbed wire and came back with a little food like maybe an apple, piece of bread, or a couple of potatoes. One of my cousins, Calev, joined these boys in their adventures. He was a brave boy of only nine or ten. I don't think the adults really knew what he was up to, but they were so relieved to have a bit of food that they didn't ask many questions. But one day, Calev did not return. I think my Auntie lost her mind after this, she stopped cooking or doing much of anything. She gave up." Baba stopped for a moment, then continued.

"The ghetto was just horrible, Sunny. People starved and there was so much disease. There was no clean water or medicine. When my grandfather took ill, Mama went in search of a doctor, but never found one. He died in his sleep. We moved his body outside and it stayed there for the longest time. It was…" She stopped for a moment.

"I'm sorry, Baba," I said before giving her a sideways hug.

She continued speaking. "The only saving grace was that my dear grandfather did not live to see the rest of it. Eventually, we were told that the ghetto would be emptied and that all of us "lucky" Jews would be resettled somewhere better. A place where we could work and raise our families with other Jews. There were rumors that no such place existed and that we would be killed. But we didn't believe them. The Germans were cultured people after all. We couldn't believe they would murder thousands of innocent people, including children. Besides, why would they kill so many workers? It made no sense to us. We should have listened to our instincts, Sunny. Always listen to yourself when something doesn't feel right, yes?"

"Yes, Baba."

"One day in June, just before my nineteenth birthday, they herded all of us into a train. But not like when we rode on the train here. They put us in cattle cars, where horses and other animals are normally placed. There were so many of us in each car that it was hard to breathe. Plus, it was such a warm day, we thought we would suffocate. And the smell! People went to the bathroom in a bucket and someone vomited. It is impossible to describe that stench.

"The train sat still for quite some time before moving and often stopped along the way. When it reached its final destination, we'd been locked inside for hours and hours. The doors were thrown open and the light hurt our eyes. But much worse was the immediate yelling from the Nazi guards who had been waiting for us. 'Raus, Raus!!' they screamed at us. 'Out, Out! On the double!'

And they held these big dogs, you see. They were German shepherds, and they were growling and showing their sharp teeth as they tugged on their leashes. Those dogs really wanted to tear us apart! We jumped off the train, but it was really high up! My grandmothers had a hard time getting down and one of them hurt her ankle. But those horrible guards did not care, they just pushed her along with their weapons. And there were other people there too. How strange I thought they were! They were men, I think, in striped clothes. They were so thin and had no hair. I didn't understand who they were. They pushed us along, but much more gently than the guards."

I remembered the camp inmates I saw in the library book.

"Anyway, we were forced into two lines… Sunny, this will be the last part of the story. I will need to make it brief, okay? It is hard for me to say."

"It's okay, Baba. You can stop."

"Thank you, my darling. I will in a moment. So, they shoved us into the two lines. Me, Mama and my auntie went into one line, and my grandmothers were put in another line with the children. In fact, their line contained a lot of children, babies, and old people. I felt relieved that they would be going someplace where they could rest. My auntie began screaming that she wanted to be with her son. One of the strange people in stripes whispered for her to stay where she was. But she didn't care, she had already lost her husband and older son, you see. She continued to scream until one of the guards grabbed her and roughly threw her into the other line. Then I remember saying to Mama …" She wiped her nose and took a few breaths. "I…I said she should go over there too." Baba immediately inhaled as if startled. "I thought she would be safe there. She was so very tired. But I didn't know…I didn't know."

I got up and gave Baba a big hug, wiping away her tears. "I know you loved your Mama very much, Baba," I said gently.

"Yes, I did. But my beautiful mama, auntie, sisters and cousin all perished on that day. They were not in the good line, you see. So, I was all alone in this place I can only call Hell. An unspeakable place I endured for more than a year. And you know, during that time, I didn't see a single bird—I guess they knew to stay away. Maybe someday I will tell you about that, but this is enough for now."

And, with that, I took my beloved babcia's hand and we walked slowly back home. I was devastated for Baba and was also grieving the loss of my own family—the many loved ones I would never know. My heart felt heavier after that day; I don't think it ever got much lighter. What I learned explained a great deal about Baba and the inexplicable pain she felt, but it also left far more things yet unexplained, most notably, man's limitless cruelty. This, I will never understand.

Chapter 11 ❧ Sunny

Baba never told me much more about her tragic experiences during the war, but I learned more from other sources. As a teen, I spoke to my father a few times about what happened to my grandparents. Because he knew some Polish and Yiddish, he picked up on a lot from Baba's phone conversations with other Holocaust survivors. And he often understood what Baba and Papa were saying to each other in hushed whispers. From him, along with my Holocaust studies, I discovered more about Baba's story.

I learned that she was deported to Auschwitz along with her mom, sisters, and several other relatives. With the exception of herself, two cousins and an uncle, Baba's family was gassed upon arrival. The remainder of her extended family fled to Warsaw and were all murdered at Treblinka. Baba worked hard labor at Auschwitz and was wasting away from starvation and exhaustion, rapidly becoming a "Muselmann"—a walking skeleton with dead eyes and no will to live. One fortuitous day, she discovered a school friend who worked in the camp's sorting area, which contained all of the prisoners' stolen belongings. This area, which the inmates called Canada, was overflowing with piles upon piles of clothing, shoes, photographs, eyeglasses, jewelry, food, and cherished heirlooms of all kinds that had been stolen by the Germans. Baba got a job there too, which saved her life, as the work was indoors and far less strenuous than her prior labor assignment. She also found food and warm clothing among the victims' stolen possessions.

When the war was reaching its end, prisoners were ordered to leave Auschwitz. Terrified that anyone left behind would be killed, those who could walk gathered anything warm they could get their hands on. This often amounted to very little. As the infamous death march commenced, sixty-thousand concentration camp prisoners, mostly Jews, were forced to march toward Germany in freezing conditions, only stopping at night to sleep in barns, churches, or the open air. Each morning they were greeted with the bleak discovery of more dead comrades.

Baba was among those forced to march 35 miles to Wodzislaw, Poland. I can't imagine it. Going this distance during the dead of a Polish winter would have been torturous for a healthy person. But these prisoners were already sick, broken, starving and exhausted, and often without adequate clothing or boots. Some had no shoes at all. When prisoners fell or stopped to rest, they were shot. I painfully envisioned my beautiful grandmother among those wretched souls being prodded along a bloody trail littered with corpses.

Only a quarter of the prisoners survived the death march to Wodzislaw. Baba likely remained alive due to the warm coat and leather boots she'd retrieved from Canada. Along with 20,000 other prisoners, she boarded a death train to Dachau—the first of Hitler's concentration camps. As others have described, the train would have been a hellish nightmare for Baba and the other prisoners who travelled for around twelve days with nothing to protect them from the frigid temperatures. She would've been surrounded by dead bodies, which would've been thrown overboard to make more room for those still grasping for life.

At Dachau, Baba would've been among thousands of dead or dying emaciated bodies strewn about the camp. But even this would not have marked the end of her hellacious journey, as she ultimately ended up at a camp in Tegernsee, Germany—a six-day march from Dachau. Those who survived the march to Tegernsee were liberated shortly thereafter. And while she did somehow manage to survive one horror after another, Baba was in a dire state at liberation. She suffered from typhus and must have been nothing more than skin and bones, a mere shadow of her former self.

She stayed in a displaced person's (DP) camp run by the Americans for a short time before being moved to a hospital in Germany. This is what I know about my courageous grandmother. Only she can bear witness to the profound cruelty, humiliation and terror that took place in the ghetto and camps, as well as during the death march. But there is one thing I know about Baba, she never allowed the Nazis or their collaborators to steal her dignity— another factor likely contributing to her endurance.

Learning about Papa was far more challenging. He was already a reticent person and was even less inclined to talk about his most painful experiences. Like so many in his generation, there was a belief that the past should stay in the past. And people really wanted to move forward after WWII and try to forget it. Despite his best efforts, I believe Papa simply could not forget. The pain he endured was sketched within the fiber of his being. It was part of him.

Over the years, I learned, mostly from Baba, that Papa was from Krakow where he lived on a dairy farm with his four brothers and sisters (he was a middle child). His family was poor and more religious than Baba's. Papa's father, Akiva, was a learned man who often studied the Torah when he wasn't working. His family was large, with many extended relatives. Baba described them as a hardworking, close family. Having no photos of Papa's loved ones has always left me with an acute sense of emptiness. I have been robbed of all traces of my lost family.

The details I did learn about Papa's wartime experiences mostly came from repeated questions to my dad, combined with my own observations. What I discovered was horrific. The Nazis ordered Akiva to hand over nearly all of the milk produced on his dairy farm. With their meager rations, the milk was keeping the family alive. Akiva was accused of hiding milk and thus stealing from the Nazis.

One day, when Papa was out somewhere with his older brother Eli, they saw Nazis heading toward their farm. They hid, but were close enough to see their mother, father, brother, and sisters marched into the woods. They followed behind discreetly, ultimately witnessing something that changed them forever. For Papa's beloved parents and siblings, along with many more of the town's Jews, were made to dig a long trench. After being forced to remove their clothing, each man, woman and child was shot before falling into the grave they had dug themselves.

Learning of Papa and Eli helplessly watching their beloved family massacred in this way left me shaky and withdrawn. It is a horror I have dreamt about myself. When my father told me what happened, his voice caught. I don't think he had ever said it out loud. I have read about the murderous German Einsatzgruppen, how they coldheartedly engaged in mass shootings of innocents. And how they laughed while throwing Jewish babies in the air as target practice. So ghastly was this work that some of the Einsatzgruppen could only execute it while inebriated. Perhaps those few murderers did have some semblance of a soul, deeply submerged though it was. I don't know. When I asked my father about Papa's repeated nightmare where he is crying for his parents and digging in the bed sheets or the carpet, he and I both understood. For it was in this insentient state that Papa was desperately trying to dig out those he had loved most in the world. Night after night, poor, sweet Papa could not escape this agonizing loop.

According to my dad, Papa and Eli joined the resistance after their family was killed. Their bravery is astonishing. They blew up bridges and railroad tracks, stole weapons from the Nazis, and smuggled key information to the Russians. After months of sabotaging the German's war and genocide efforts, Eli was caught. I cannot bear to think of what they did to my heroic uncle before murdering him. I know that resistance fighters commonly hid cyanide capsules in their clothing in case they were discovered. God, how I hope my great uncle was not captured alive.

Papa also had a number of relatives who were sent to the Krakow ghetto, most of whom either died there or were murdered in the Belzec camp. Papa stayed with the resistance until the end of the war when he ended up in a DP camp in Germany. At that point, he must have been overwhelmed with exhaustion and desperation, as he had to face the realization of all that he had lost. Of more than forty relatives, only three of Papa's family members survived the war. Two of whom where an aunt and uncle who had fled to the United States in the 1930s. It was these two angels who sponsored Papa and Baba so they could move to New York.

My grandparents' wartime experiences have affected the deepest part of me. I have imagined what happened so many times, their past feels inexorably linked to mine. To me, both Baba and Papa have always symbolized the purest form of kindness, generosity and love. And, as I get older, the more I appreciate their astounding resiliency. Their slight statures were incongruous with the depth of strength within each of them. It is because of my grandparents that I often find myself looking at old people with a sense of curiosity. I wonder what trauma or obstacles they've faced in their lifetimes. And what valuable lessons might they impart to the rest of us. My own grandparents—whose hearts had been repeatedly shattered in the most unimaginable of ways—taught me more about love than anyone else in my life.

I did find one story about Papa's past that he would speak of. I'll never forget the day he opened up about what happened after liberation. It was my sixteenth birthday and we'd just enjoyed ice cream in the backyard. Papa wanted to show me the fruit trees he was close to harvesting, so we went for a little walk toward the edge of the property. Somehow the subject of me having a boyfriend came up and I asked Papa how he met Baba, and how he knew she was the one for him. This is the only time Papa's eyes danced with merriment when I asked him about his past.

"Oh, I knew your babcia was my great love the first moment I saw her," he said with a crooked smile.

"She must have been very beautiful."

"She was in a DP camp in Germany. I went there to rest up—I was weary to my bones. I saw Chana sitting up on a cot that had been moved outside so she could feel the sun on her face. She was but a sliver of a girl, Sunshine. She looked so young and so fragile, sitting there. Her hair was very short and her skin was blotchy. She looked terrible, truly terrible. But do not tell her I said this," he added with a wink.

"I promise."

"I went over to her, thinking maybe I could bring her some food or something. I thought she was a little girl, I couldn't tell. When I got close, I said hello. She must have been lost in thought, for she started a bit before looking up. When our eyes met, I was taken aback. Here she was, this tiny and desperately ill person with the most determined and beautiful blue eyes I'd ever seen. And when she spoke, she had an honesty and warmth about her that reminded me of my own mama. So, yes, Sunshine, she was very beautiful indeed."

Even thinking back on this conversation now, a shiver runs through me.

"But your babcia was extremely sick, she had a high fever and could barely walk. She was malnourished and weak. When the American soldiers were transporting her to a hospital, I carried her to the lorry. She weighed almost nothing, Sunshine. I remember thinking it was like carrying a pile of clothing, with no body underneath. She went to a hospital in Germany where they treated her for typhus, dysentery, malnutrition, and I don't recall what else. She was so near death. I visited her there every day for months. I brought her any books I could find, flowers, and love notes.

"And what I saw was a most miraculous transformation! This wasted body of hers gradually responded to treatment, fresh air, and, I like to think, love. Every day she was a little bit stronger until, finally, her body caught up with her mind. She became more, how do you say, *animated*. She was like a precious motyl—a butterfly."

Now I understood why Papa sometimes referred to Babcia as "his little motyl".

"Your baba started to become herself again. She was funny and so clever, just as she is now. We went for walks outside or read books under a tree. Sometimes I brought her little treats, which she could only eat in small amounts—so delicate was her system. There were many days that we cried together as we thought of our murdered loved ones. We told each other all about our parents and siblings; I started to feel like I knew her family.

"And we shared our dreams of a better life—of freedom. She wanted to go back to her town in Poland, to her home. She thought that, by some miracle, someone in her family might be there, waiting. And she wanted to collect photos, clothing and other items left behind. But we heard so many stories of Jews going back to homes that were no longer theirs. Even with the war over, we Jews were met with such hostility when we tried to retrieve what was stolen from us. So, she gave up on that idea. I was glad, since I didn't know how much more devastation her heart could withstand. The two of us had no one else, just each other. How blessed was I to find her—the love of my life. My beautiful motyl."

I cherished this love story. And I believe it is because of Baba and Papa that I have never settled for anyone who doesn't accept and adore me. Unlike other girls, I never pined away over disrespectful guys. I preferred my solitude over their arrogance. And despite suffering from serious deficits in confidence and self-worth, I have always resolved to save my heart for those who will treat it kindly. I credit this determination to the enduring example of unconditional love and acceptance modeled by my remarkable grandparents.

Chapter 12 ❧ Joshua

What can I say about life with Sunny? It certainly was never dull, nor predictable. It was always at its best when it was just the two of us. At the beginning of our marriage, I observed my talented and passionate wife emerge a little bit more each day from the protective veil she hid behind. I had known she was artistic, but her latest drawings blew my mind. She had an uncanny ability to capture the light in just the right way, and managed to bring every last detail to life. I thought her hummingbird drawing looked expensive and museum-worthy, but what did I know about art?

And when Sunny was content and relaxed, there was no other person I'd rather be around. She was witty and sometimes hysterical. She made me laugh without trying. Occasionally, with the right mood and music, Sunny could go to a different place altogether. I recall one evening when I came home late from work. I could hear Tori Amos blaring all the way outside. When I entered the condo, Sunny was dancing around the living room in a world that was all her own. She was wearing a silky white nightgown and had a nearly empty glass of red wine in her hand. I stood and watched her for several moments; God, she was beautiful—unintentionally beautiful. And she looked so free, as if she had been unburdened of the suitcase of anxieties she normally carried around. I could have watched her for hours. She was a lovely enigma I doubted I would ever fully understand.

Though she did her best to hide them, Sunny's various eccentricities were creeping out of the shadows. She depended upon sameness and stability—things had to be just so. It was like living with a Fabergé egg—a real one, encrusted with priceless jewels. That exquisite but fragile egg could so easily shatter if placed off balance. Sunny required balance. I remember back when we first moved into the condo. I came up behind her while she was cooking and listening to music, and gently kissed her neck. Sunny screamed and damn near jumped out of her skin! Then she yelled at me, "What the fuck, Joshua? Why would you do that to me?" I hadn't just startled her, I'd terrified her—adding more weight to the burden she already carried. I never did that again. Instead, I always made sure she heard me approaching. Eventually, I started "meowing" as I came near her—a tactic that was both ridiculous and effective. It wasn't exactly like walking on eggshells; it was more like walking on broken glass—moving with the perfect mix of caution and noise in order to avoid pain. When it came to my wife, I was very careful indeed—sticking to a routine and avoiding surprises at all costs.

If I noticed any of her more benign behaviors, such as counting and whispering to herself, I let them go. Nor did I mention anything about her books. I appreciate books myself, but Sunny took it to another level. She had hundreds of them. Despite having four large bookcases that were crammed full, there were piles of books throughout our home—even in the bathroom. She refused to get rid of any of them, saying that, once read, they had become a part of her. So, of course she could never part from them. Such was her logic. I worried that we'd need to rent storage space just for the books. Sunny certainly was a consummate bookworm. She went through a book in record speed and seemed to be in the middle of no less than three at all times. But I was most bothered by the way she became so completely lost in her books that nothing else seemed to matter. And lately, she was focused on her Holocaust collection—which sometimes left her unconsolably sad. I fully understood her desire to know more about her own history, but at what cost? But she was far too sensitive about anything related to the Holocaust or her grandparents for me to voice my concerns.

Interacting with other people represented the main challenge in our relationship. My wife was an amazing, beautiful woman—but she didn't see this in herself. She turned heads everywhere she went. It made me a bit jealous at times, but mostly I just felt lucky to be with her. If she knew how gorgeous she was, she didn't show it. I found Sunny's lack of self-confidence illogical—it was totally inconsistent with her many exceptional qualities. And it left her incredibly awkward around anyone new.

I first noticed the extent of her social anxiety when, after a month at my new job, we were invited to go to dinner with my boss, his wife, and a few coworkers. Sunny worried about this dinner for days, asking me a thousand questions to which I had no answers. On the day of the dinner, she pulled most of her wardrobe from the closet, trying on one outfit after another—never satisfied with any of them. When she was finally ready—and she looked fantastic—she said she might actually throw up. I didn't really believe her until she dry-heaved in the car on the way there. We parked outside the restaurant until she'd calmed down, causing us to arrive thirty minutes late.

During the meal, Sunny was of course polite, but also very quiet. She came across as aloof. But I knew her better than this. She was so incredibly self-conscious that I could almost hear the wheels turning in her brain as she painstakingly weighed *every single word* she might utter. And I saw the bloody napkin in her lap which she was pressing against the cuticles she'd torn off during the meal. That evening, as we lay in bed, my poor Sunny critiqued her dinner performance as if she'd been trying out for a Broadway play. She judged her behavior that evening as grossly inadequate—it was a part she clearly did not get, nor ever would. And she needed copious amounts of reassurance before she could finally fall asleep. I remember telling her she did just fine and that everyone liked her, but she didn't believe me.

"How do you know everyone liked me?" she asked, more than once.

"Because I could tell."

"Oh, so they didn't actually *say* they liked me, that's just your interpretation."

"No, they said you were nice."

"Who said that?"

"I don't remember, maybe Marcus."

"So, you aren't sure if it was Marcus."

"Sunny, you did great, stop worrying. Besides, it doesn't matter what other people think."

"Oh, I see. Then they *definitely* hated me."

And that's how it went.

I managed to keep her out of work events from then on. I suppose it was fortunate that my parents were far away. Sunny didn't trust anything about my mom. In fact, she thought my mom despised her. In all honesty, my mom was thoroughly perplexed by Sunny. The wedding cake incident shook her to the core. Apparently, my dad found my mom crying shortly afterward. She was convinced I'd made a horrible mistake in marrying such an unstable mess. My dad persuaded her to keep these feelings to herself. He thought the wedding was too stressful for Sunny and that she simply needed time to adjust to being married. He also blamed it on the champagne. My dad has always been the eternal optimist. But he got my mom to keep her mouth shut, for which I was grateful.

When my parents called on the phone, Sunny was always conveniently absent (no doubt hiding in case they wanted to speak to her). I only shared the best parts of our lives together, leaving out various other details. I didn't tell them about the mornings she refused to get out of bed because she didn't hear any airplanes in the sky. I didn't tell them about her extreme decision-making issues, such as her clothing challenges or the time she went to the drug store for toothpaste and came home hours later, empty-handed and in tears. There were too many types of toothpaste to pick one, she just couldn't do it. I didn't tell them that she was so frighteningly bonded to Chester that I doubted we'd ever be able to travel because she would not leave him overnight. I didn't tell them about the numerous times she awoke from nightmares either sitting straight up in bed or somehow landing on the floor, but always trembling and gasping for breath. And I didn't tell them about her odd relationship with books, her jumpiness, her social anxiety, or any of her other unusual behaviors. I wasn't just trying to spare my parents from worry, I truly believed Sunny would mellow over time. What was the point in upsetting them about behaviors that would eventually fade?

Despite it all, I adored my eccentric wife and had no regrets about marrying her. She brought more richness and color to my life than I'd ever experienced. She saw beauty in things I took for granted. A rainbow or sunset could bring her to tears. The way she moved and the ferocity with which she loved was unspeakably sexy. Her talent and intelligence amazed me every day. And she could be incredibly affectionate and loving. I'd never known a person with her degree of compassion—especially for animals, people in need, and, of course, her family.

Sunny's heart was always out there, on her sleeve, exposed to the world's endless injustices. She was like a delicate flower that could wilt with a slight change of wind. There was a sadness about her that must have been torturous to bear. I recall a song that was popular at the time, "She Will Be Loved" by Maroon 5. Well, that troubled girl with the broken smile, that was my Sunny. And I would be there to love her always—no matter what. There were times when I sat in my car listening to that damn song over and over again.

Despite her emotional obstacles, Sunny was highly competent in some areas. I was really proud of how well her job was going. Every morning she set out for work intent upon doing her absolute best. She didn't lack determination. Or intelligence, for that matter. I hadn't met anyone from her company, I guess they didn't have dinners or happy hours. But Sunny said her boss, Emily, was thrilled with how she was doing. Sometimes she brought manuscripts home on the weekends, even though she was ahead of schedule. My wife was the ultimate perfectionist and people pleaser—she craved approval and accolades. Most importantly, Sunny seemed happy enough with her job and, given her considerable editing skills, I'm sure they were thankful to have her. I only hoped she could keep her peculiarities at bay during the workday.

One of my favorite things about Sunny was how she adored her family. She was loyal to a fault. Sunny was like her own exclusive club. If you were fortunate enough to be accepted by her, she would love you with abandon. And she would love you forever—so intense was her loyalty. *God damn* was I glad to be part of that elite club. Sunny's grandparents were her anchor and it's no exaggeration to say she was obsessed with them. They had always been there for her, especially after her mother died. They were wonderful people and I loved them too. Our Shabbos meals had become so special to me. I was grateful to share in this custom with two such resilient and beautiful people.

I also experienced my first Hannukah that year, the last day of which was shared with the whole family. Papa proudly recited the blessings and, as was the custom with the Zielinski family, Babcia lit the freshly polished silver menorah. This was followed by joyous singing and the spinning of the dreidel, which Maddy and Spencer especially enjoyed. The children also received a small, but meaningful gift on each of those eight days.

Sunny and I also had a quiet Christmas celebration in our new home, but I could see that sharing the Jewish holidays with her family is what filled Sunny's heart. She had such a look of pride and admiration when her grandparents performed each sacred custom associated with the Holiday of Lights. These were among the invaluable experiences Sunny brought to my life, and I was a better person for knowing her grandparents.

But Sunny held them in such reverence that they could do no wrong. Even worse than this, she seemed dependent upon them for her very survival. She called and checked on them constantly. She bought Babcia a medical bracelet in case she fell down again. She offered to do all of their shopping (which they always refused). She monitored what they ate, the vitamins they took, and the amount of water they drank. And she didn't like them driving, so she was constantly offering to take them places. Honestly, she probably drove them a little nuts—but they never complained or got upset with her. I believe they loved her in much the same way. The relationship was a dysfunctional mix of adoration and suffocation.

Sunny's overbearingness toward her grandparents derived from her deep-seated terror that they would leave her one day. She was intent on them making it to one hundred. Of course, this perspective was wholly unrealistic and worried me a great deal. Who knows what physical toll their wartime experiences may have had on them? And Babcia's health had been really declining recently. Nonetheless, Sunny would not discuss anything pertaining to her grandparents' health, instead either sugarcoating the situation or becoming extremely upset.

One day I said, "It's important for you to accept the fact that your grandparents are getting old, they won't be here forever." She looked like I'd slapped her hard across the face. I'll never forget that expression. Then she quietly walked into the bedroom and sobbed all over Chester. I was really concerned about what would happen to Sunny when they died. Of course, I realized the integral part they played in her life and would do everything in my power to support her when that time came. Sunny had experienced enough painful transitions in her young life and I was hoping this would be the last big one for a while. And, once things had finally smoothed out, I thought she would be okay. This much I had to believe.

Chapter 13 ❧ Sunny

It happened on a cloudy day in January. It was a Thursday and I was preparing a list of questions for the upcoming meeting. It was just the in-house team, so I wasn't particularly nervous and didn't plan on taking any Xanax. I was caught up in my work and jumped when my desk phone buzzed. I picked it up.

"Hello, this is Sunny."

"Sweetheart, it's Dad." He didn't need to say much more, I knew something terrible had happened. He'd never called me at work before. And his voice sounded strange. A wave of panic seized me. I couldn't speak.

"Sunny, are you there?"

"Yeah, Dad," I whispered.

"It's Babcia, she's in the hospital."

I knew it, I just knew it. But it smacked me in the face just the same.

"What happened?" I was already in tears.

"She wasn't feeling well this morning. Her right arm was numb causing her to spill hot tea on herself. Then her speech became garbled."

"Are you saying she had a stroke? Is she okay? Where is she?" I was bordering on hysteria.

"Slow down. Yes, honey, she had a stroke. She's at the hospital downtown and is unconscious."

"What do you mean unconscious?"

"She's in a coma."

Oh God, it was actually happening. This was The Day. It was too much—I couldn't bear it. My father told me where Baba was staying and I hung up the phone. I started hyperventilating. I tried to catch my breath, then I grabbed

111

my purse and ran out of the office. Fuck the Thursday meeting, my world was collapsing.

I chewed half a Xanax in the cab on the way to the hospital and asked the driver to hurry up. He looked annoyed. Maybe I was just another passenger to him, but he didn't understand that nothing would ever be the same again if Baba wasn't okay. I must have been muttering to myself, as I noticed him looking at me in the rearview mirror.

"Please hurry," I again pleaded, although I wasn't entirely sure if I said it out loud or in my head. That distinction was becoming increasingly blurry lately. When we finally reached the hospital, I flew out of the cab forgetting to leave a tip. I heard the driver cussing in the background as I ran toward Baba.

When I reached her room, I saw Papa, my dad, Linda, and both of the children. Everyone was sitting quietly around Baba. Papa was closest to the bed, holding her hand. He looked pale and broken. He was staring at Baba with red eyes.

And I saw my beautiful Baba quietly lying there, seemingly oblivious to the nightmare surrounding her. She looked so very small—her body almost disappearing under the sheets. Her thin, blondish-gray hair framed the pillow. Papa must have done this, since it was the way she always slept. She was intubated and not wearing any makeup, as she had collapsed early in the day. I remember thinking how much this would bother her. But her red fingernails looked perfect as usual, although her fingers were swollen and the two rings she always wore looked constricting and uncomfortable. Her eyes were closed and she was breathing peacefully. A monitor was beeping continuously and she had an IV and various tubes and devices connected to her. There was a bag of urine just beneath her, which I covered with the blanket to preserve some level of dignity. My dad hugged me first and didn't let go for quite some time. I could tell he'd been crying. Then Linda gave me a hug and a kiss on the cheek. Papa just sat there, oblivious to anyone except his cherished wife.

I sat opposite Papa and laid my head gently on Baba's chest. Tears were rolling down my cheeks as I mumbled, "Baba, please don't die, please don't die, please don't die…" I felt my dad's hand on my back. I remember experiencing a strange sensation in that room. I felt somehow separate from myself, like I was floating around, observing everyone. My body felt fluid; I wasn't sure where it ended or where it began.

A doctor showed up at some point—it could have been hours or minutes later as far as I could tell. He was very tall and middle-aged with gray hair and kind eyes. I hated him. He said Baba, who must have looked to him like some ordinary old lady, was brain-dead. Yes, I hated him for the ease with which he uttered those unspeakable words. He didn't know who he was speaking of—he didn't know her heart and the agony it had endured. He didn't know anything, and I told him so.

My dad, Papa and I were crying softly as the doctor patiently described how Baba had experienced an unrecoverable stroke and was currently being kept alive by a machine. He expressed his condolences and asked if we would like to have a rabbi present. I remember wondering how he knew we were Jewish. Papa said yes about the rabbi before withdrawing back into himself. I remember watching my dad discuss something with the doctor before he left. And I remember Linda holding my dad for several minutes. I remember Joshua showing up and watching me closely. I was still floating until Joshua touched my shoulder and I was suddenly back on the ground in that wretched place with my dying baba.

I remember Papa whispering to Baba in Polish. I don't know what he was saying, but it went on for quite a while and involved a lot of tears. There were a few old people who showed up, I guess they had known my grandparents for a long time. And there was a young rabbi I'd never seen before. He was incredibly kind and gentle, offering words of solace. He sang the Mi Sheberakh prayer and had a strong voice that was inconsistent with his thin frame. He wasn't there very long. My father took me aside and said they would be removing the tube keeping my baba alive and didn't know how long she would live afterward. This made everything so very real. I didn't want to let her go yet—I wasn't ready. I wanted to speak to her alone.

My dad asked everyone to leave the room so I could be with Baba. I held her hand, caressing her soft skin. I rubbed Vaseline on her lips. I kissed her forehead and cheeks. And I said goodbye as best I could.

"Baba, it's me, Sunny. I love you so much, Baba—I want you to know that. When Mama died, I would have been completely lost if not for you and Papa. You have been through so much hell in your life and yet are the strongest person I've ever known. I don't want you to die, Baba. How will I function without you?" I couldn't stop the catch in my voice or the flood of tears.

"Thank you for being my baba *and* my mama. You helped me to see the good parts of myself and the beauty in life. You will be in a place without the pain of haunted memories—they can never hurt you again. I will miss you every moment, Baba. I love you."

I continued to hold her hand as I again rested my head very softly on her chest. I don't know how long I sat like this, but eventually I was guided into the hallway so that Papa could say goodbye. When Papa finally left the room—looking as broken and withered as a charred twig—we waited outside the door as a nurse disconnected my beautiful grandmother's life support. Afterward, we stayed with Baba for two days until she passed away. I didn't know what to expect when she left us. She and I were so close, I thought I would feel her spirit leave or that she might give me a signal or something. But she died with the same quiet dignity with which she lived. And the world somehow kept on moving even though Baba was gone from me forever.

The following day, we stood outside the Jewish Cemetery. My dad, or more so Linda, arranged things. The rest of us were too shaken to be of much help. Elizabeth was there, as well as various other friends of my dad and grandparents. There was a different rabbi, a much older man I'd seen during my very occasional visits to the synagogue. I imagined he could see right through me to what a horrible Jew I was, not to mention all of the terrible things I'd done in my life. I felt evil in his presence and couldn't make eye contact with him.

My father talked about Baba through his tears. He said how loving and kind she was, and how special she made his childhood. He thanked her for helping to raise me. He said some other things too, I don't remember. Papa said something in Polish. He wasn't crying, but he looked like he might collapse. Joshua and another man were holding him up. It was a beautiful day when we buried Baba. The sky was blue and there was a very slight breeze. After Papa finished speaking, a pair of brown and white striped Lark Sparrows circled us and landed on a nearby branch. Baba had adored birds her whole life and was especially fond of the sparrows that often visited her since moving to California. The two sparrows sat there quietly, as if they too were part of the funeral party. I watched them as the rabbi sang the Kaddish, and as the shovel was passed from one hand to another. Then they fluttered away just as suddenly as they arrived. As I watched them in the distance, I felt momentarily peaceful. "Thank you, Baba," I whispered.

Although my dad and I were not observant Jews, Papa still retained many of the Jewish customs from his childhood. He ripped his shirt collars and lit a candle for seven days. Because he would not do any work, he sat around his little cottage looking shattered and alone until my dad insisted that he come to the big house, at least during Shiva. Papa relented inasmuch as he came for dinner each evening and sat on the couch afterward. But he wanted to sleep in his own bed. We were all exceedingly worried about Papa. He was a lighthearted, cheerful person by nature and had a twinkle in his eye anytime he spoke with me or the twins. But this person before us was not Papa, he was just a shell. He barely spoke, but just sat quietly, staring into space. It was awful to see Papa like this. We tried to comfort him, but my father and I were so lost in our own grief, I don't think we had much to offer. I believe it was mostly Linda who took care of him, although Joshua also checked on him every day.

When I wasn't at my dad's house—where I too sat on the couch and stared into space—I lay around at home lost in my sadness. I had taken a week off work and Joshua was only working sporadically during that time. He didn't really know what to do with himself nor how to help us through our suffering. He wanted to fix things, but of course he couldn't. So, he spoke softly and offered too much affection. And he waited on me. He was constantly trying to get me to eat, which, after a while, became irritating. Food was the last thing on my mind. But he didn't know what else to do. I had an emptiness within me that no amount of food could even begin to fill. Elizabeth called often, but I didn't want to talk. My most important person in the world was gone. I was lost at sea with no anchor, and no ability to swim on my own. I became incapable of making the most basic decisions and couldn't keep track of my thoughts. I kept trying to remember all of Baba's wisdom—I didn't want to lose a single word. I started writing everything down like a fanatic, until Joshua gently took the pen from my hand. But I was so restless, I had to do something or I too would die. I remember pacing around the condo for hours, trying to sit down, only to bounce back up and pace some more. I remember Joshua crying at one point, I guess because I was such a mess. But, as bad as I was, Papa was far worse.

My dad drove me and Papa to the cemetery a few days after Baba died. We placed rocks on her headstone and then sat quietly in the sun. For the longest time, not a word was spoken, until Papa said, "When I met Chana, my world was over. I had lost my family, my home, everything. I thought I would never smile again. But this slight girl, nearly dead herself, she brought me back somehow. She saved me. I have no way to live without her." We offered Papa whatever comforting words we could muster, but he didn't hear them. He was just speaking out loud. He didn't want or need a response. He wasn't our Papa anymore. His light was gone and he had neither the will nor the ability to reignite it.

My sweet Papa stayed like this for two weeks, just sitting around with vacant eyes. He ate very little and only when asked, and stayed in his cottage sitting in Baba's favorite chair. He had always been a quiet person, but now he was practically mute. I recall questioning whether a person can actually die of a broken heart. My mind kept going back to my senior year of college when I read King Lear. It was my favorite Shakespeare play and I was always moved by how the king was so devastated by his grief that it ultimately killed him. Kind and gentle Papa—beloved husband, father, and grandfather, who lived a life of intense love despite all that had been taken from him—died in his sleep less than a month after Baba left us.

I guess I got the answer to my question.

Chapter 14 ⅗ Joshua

Having Papa and Babcia die so close together was disastrous. Sunny and Peter were still deeply mourning the loss of Babcia when Papa died. It was too much. Sunny went back to work a week after Babcia's death, though I doubt she did a decent job—she had zero concentration. She couldn't even get through a TV show without losing track of the plot. She was only back for two weeks when Papa passed away. To me, this wasn't surprising. When his wife died, Papa seemed to have truly lost his other half—an overused phrase that was, in this case, fitting. Babcia and Papa had been together for more than fifty years. They had clung to each other after losing their entire families and surviving one of the most disastrous events in human history. Together, they came to a strange country where neither knew the language. And, if that wasn't enough, they dealt with losing their daughter-in-law to a car accident and watching their only child, Peter, fall apart. Following this tragedy, they totally stepped up, playing a huge role in Sunny's upbringing for ten years. They did all of this together, as partners.

These are the things I've learned about this extraordinary pair. I also observed their love for each other firsthand. Their relationship was symbiotic. They seemed to understand each other's needs without words. When Babcia was hungry, Papa was there with food. When Papa was tired, Babcia was there with a blanket. I never once saw them argue or even become impatient with each other. They had the type of mutual respect one can only hope to emulate in a relationship. I fully understood why Sunny loved her grandparents the way she did, they were remarkable examples of strength and goodness. And I also understood why Papa could not live without the woman he so cherished.

Sunny and Peter were floored by Papa's death. Peter was weepy and sad when Babcia died; when Papa died, he was disconsolate for at least a week. I'd never seen a grown man cry so hard— it was just awful. When we went to the cemetery the second time, the flowers on Babcia's grave were still fresh. Papa's funeral felt surreal, like déjà vu. The same rabbi was present, along with most of the same people. But there was one old guy I hadn't seen before. He knew Papa during the war and worked with him in the Polish resistance. This man, who went by Sam, described Papa as heroic. I knew Papa was a good man, the salt of the earth. But I had no idea of his depth. Papa had apparently slept in the woods for two years, often moving from place to place while engaging in countless acts of sabotage against the Germans. He somehow managed to smuggle a number of Jews from the Krakow ghetto, transporting them to partisan groups hiding in the Wolski forest. He even broke into a Nazi command center, stealing medicines that were then used to save sick Jewish children. There was more too, so much more. And, after all of it, he lost his brother—another resistance fighter and hero.

As Sam spoke about Papa, Peter became a wreck. I don't think he had known the full extent of his father's courageousness. Maybe he regretted not learning more when Papa was alive? Sunny was less affected by this information. She was just as despondent as when Babcia died—but in more of a quiet way than Peter. She stood there at the funeral holding my hand and staring off into the distance. She didn't really cry but had such a pained expression. After the ceremony, she stood there, in front of the graves, for a good hour after everyone else had left. I tried to gently pull her away, but she seemed to be in another world. She had such a look of concentration, it was as if she could hear something no one else could. She eventually snapped out of it and moved robotically toward the car.

I don't know how any of us would have gotten through that terrible period without Linda. Sunny never had much to say about her stepmother. I know there was some animosity when she was a teenager and Linda tried to establish some rules. Growing up, Sunny had this strange idea that Linda didn't like her. She believed Linda wanted her to disappear so she could have Peter all to herself. I could not imagine this. More recently, Sunny had referred to Linda as passive-aggressive, but I never noticed this quality either. Linda was warm and friendly when we went to their home for dinner, and always made sure to have Sunny's favorite foods. She was also a wonderful mother to Maddy and Spencer, with far more patience than I would have had with them. Whatever it was about Linda that Sunny didn't like, I couldn't see it.

Personally, I think Sunny was harboring a childish resentment over having to share her father, but I certainly never mentioned this theory—I'm not an idiot. And I especially couldn't see any fault with Linda when Babcia and Papa died. After all, it was Linda who made the funeral arrangements—both times; it was Linda who opened up her home to mourners who came from out of town; it was Linda who prepared food and drinks over the course of that month; and it was Linda who held Peter's hand, rubbed his back, and basically nurtured him back to life. Linda also did her best to nurture Sunny, but, if Sunny was going to lean on someone, which she had great difficulty doing, that person was me. Yet, Linda was always there for her, without a hint of impatience or resentment. It was pretty obvious to me that Linda loved Sunny, despite Sunny's insistence on the contrary. I had great respect for Linda myself and Peter's love and admiration for her was obvious. I could also see how desperately he needed her.

While Peter was hard hit by the deaths of his parents, he seemed to experience a somewhat predictable grieving period. He was a mess, he stayed home from work, and then he went on with life—at least this was my impression. Sunny, as with everything, experienced grief in her own unique sort of way. Peter, Linda and I did our best to get her to lean on us, but Sunny seemed to withdraw further into herself. It was incredibly frustrating. Sometimes she would just sit on our bed staring out the window for the longest time. I would try to hold her, but she was stiff as a board. And she wouldn't talk to me about her feelings, she was totally closed off. At times, I'm not sure she could even hear me.

Sunny took more time off from work after Papa's funeral, for which I was grateful. She never could have functioned at her job in her zombie-like state. During those weeks, she lay around the condo not doing much of anything. I was working at home so that I could care for her, but she wouldn't let me. She refused to eat or drink anything other than a few bites of toast, coffee, broth, and water—that was about it. She was already thin, but was becoming bony. And despite her constant lethargy, she didn't seem to be sleeping. There were a few occasions when I got up in the middle of the night to pee and there was my Sunny, lying in bed with her eyes wide open, staring at the ceiling. It was unnerving.

My parents knew about the deaths and were very sympathetic. My mom wanted to come to San Diego to care for us, but when I mentioned this to Sunny, she sprang to life like she'd been defibrillated.

"What did you say, Joshua?" She was now sitting up on the couch.

"I just said my parents are worried about you and would like to help."

"I don't *need* their help. You'd better tell them *not* to come! You'd better tell Debbie *now!*" She was inches from my face, her breath smelled rancid.

"Jesus, Sunny, relax. It's fine, they aren't coming."

"Tell them!" She stomped her foot like a petulant child.

"Oh my God, Sunny. I'll call them later. But they aren't planning to come."

And then, following that pleasant exchange, Sunny collapsed back onto the couch where she quietly reverted into herself and her own thoughts—*God help her.*

My mom really wanted to help, but I told her it would only make things worse to have more people around, that Sunny was an introvert and needed to deal with things in her own way. This was, of course, a gross misrepresentation of the situation. I tried not to get pissed off since, despite Sunny's feelings, my mom has always been loving—wanting only the best for both me *and* Sunny. She was a bit hurt by not being able to help, so she sent us a giant food basket. It wasn't your typical unhealthy assortment of chocolate and wine; but rather, it contained a collection of items meticulously hand-picked by my mom. There was fresh and dried fruit, dark bread, Swiss and Gouda cheese, healthy soup mixes, pasta, tomato and Alfredo sauce, organic juice, marbled halva, and specialty vegetables like marinated asparagus and artichokes. Aside from being expensive, the basket included everything Sunny loved. It was beyond thoughtful.

I wish to hell I hadn't told Sunny the basket was from my mom.

When it arrived, Sunny was in the bedroom sleeping—or more likely just lying there staring blankly. I put the basket in the kitchen and made fettuccine Alfredo, one of Sunny's favorites. I took the plate to her and, when I retrieved it from the nightstand later, she'd actually eaten maybe a third of it. This is progress, I thought.

Later that evening when I was in my office catching up on work, I heard a crash. I found Sunny standing red-faced in the kitchen. She had thrown the basket on the floor and was furious.

"You made me food that *your mother* sent?" she asked through gritted teeth.

"It's just a food basket from *both* of my parents. It's all of your favorite things. What's the problem?"

"Only the small detail that your mom wants to kill me."

"What the fuck are you talking about?"

"Get this *shit* out of here! Oh my God, you already fed it to me!" she then ran to the bathroom and puked up the fettuccine. I couldn't believe it. I knew she was grieving and was not in her right mind, so I controlled my temper and gathered up the food. I placed it all in a large moving box and shoved it in a closet in my office. I figured we could eat it later, when Sunny was better. Or I could eat it myself when she wasn't looking. But this paranoia about my mom trying to kill her, this was over the top—even for Sunny.

Sunny continued to lay or sit around, often holding Chester close as she whispered to him. Thinking back to that time, she spoke far more to the cat than she did to me. And sometimes I heard her mumbling to herself like the homeless people downtown. She had zero interest in her art and didn't read or watch TV. Sometimes she would cry softly, but usually she showed minimal expression. It was extremely hard to carry on a conversation with her, but I continued to try.

"Sunny, how are you feeling today?"

"Like shit."

"Can I get you anything? Are you hungry?"

"No."

"Would you like to watch a movie with me?"

"No."

"I love you, Sunny."

"Okay."

That was the gist of it.

And then my acutely self-conscious wife stopped bathing. She just stayed in the same pair of sweats for two weeks or so, never taking a bath or washing her hair. Her skin was oily and breaking out, and she smelled bad. This was alarming, as it was so uncharacteristic of her. I ran a bubble bath and somehow coaxed her into the tub. I gently washed her back and hair, and helped her shave her legs. I helped her out of the tub and wrapped her in a towel. I held her like that for several minutes as I silently wept.

A couple of days after her bath, Sunny seemed to get a burst of energy. I was sound asleep when I heard some commotion in the other room. At first, I was afraid we were being robbed. But when I saw her empty place in the bed, I felt another, almost worse sort of panic. *Where the fuck was Sunny and what was she doing now?*

I found her in the living room wearing her nightshirt as she sorted through her books. She had taken tons of them from the bookshelves and was placing them in piles around the room. There must have been ten stacks of books in the living room. But when I looked around, I saw piles in every room.

"Sweetheart, what are you doing?" She ignored me. "Sunny, what are you doing?" I said a little louder.

"Organizing books."

"Okay, but why?"

"So I can be ready."

"Ready for what?" This question caused her to sigh with impatience, as if I should have known the answer. Plus, I was clearly distracting her from her work.

"For when they come."

"For when who comes?"

"Joshua, stop! I need to do this! I need to have my thoughts in order so I can be ready."

"Ready for what?"

Sunny's face turned beet red. She was getting heated and I didn't know why. "Leave me alone, Joshua!" Exasperated, she let out a big sigh and went back to her task.

I called Peter and we found a psychiatrist for her to see the following week.

Chapter 15 ❧ Sunny

I was swimming inside myself. Drowning. I could still see fragments of my life, but as I slipped deeper into the abyss, they were becoming increasingly out of reach. I was already half dead when Baba died, *but now Papa?* My dear sweet Papa, how could I possibly have lost him too? Everything was slipping out of my grasp. It started with a penetrating sadness, but then transformed into a heavy nothingness. All I wanted to do was sleep; yet sleep only taunted me—it would not come. My body hurt and was difficult to move. Food disgusted me. I was a worthless mound of nothingness. Only thoughts of the sweet relief of death brought me any semblance of peace.

Joshua was constantly prodding me along. "Eat this, drink that, get dressed, talk to me…" His commands were constant and would have been annoying had I been able to feel them. On the day of Papa's funeral, he helped me dress like I was an invalid. Off we went to the cemetery once again: *Take two.* Except last time, I felt raw and heartbroken; now I was muddled and empty. I heard the Kaddish, I heard the talking, I heard the shovels, and I heard the weeping—but it was vague and distorted. People kept hugging me, *so many people.* I wished they would stop. Then they were gone and it was just me amongst the dead. But it was not quiet. Rather, there was a cacophony of words coming from all directions in the graveyard. Men, women, and even children. They were restless and pleading with a similar message: *Hide, escape, run! It's not safe here, they're coming for you!*

I stood there, doing my best to hear them, to respect their words. I knew they were on my side and I was grateful. And I knew they were talking about the Nazis. I took in their warnings, doing my best to pay attention.

Jews aren't safe here. They will steal your name. They will make you sterile. They will rip out your hair. They will starve you. They will break you at Appellplatz. They will send you to Block 11. The orchestra will serenade you to your death. They will throw you down the stairs of death or send you up through the chimney. The train is coming. Run!

On and on it went, this ominous symphony of the dead. Then, all at once, it stopped. They had made their point. And they had inserted themselves into my head. I placed a rock on each of the two headstones and allowed Joshua to guide me home.

Back at the condo, I sank further down into the mud. But now it was far worse—for now I was being hunted. It is a desperate thing to feel paralyzed when powerful forces are after you. My mind was actively fantasizing about where my enemies were, when they were coming, what they would do to me, and how I could escape. My husband was somewhere around the periphery, teetering in the ether as he tried to reach me. I could hear him talking to my dad and others about me. And Chester, my baby, was there too. I clung to him. Elizabeth wanted to come over, but I told Joshua no, I didn't want to see anyone. She sent me flowers, wine, and homemade lasagna—which I'm sure Joshua enjoyed. There were moments of relative lucidity when I was aware that I had a body that needed certain things, like food. But when I ate, I felt evil—*how dare I eat when others are starving?* And it didn't help that Joshua had accidentally tried to poison me with that so-called Red Cross package from his horrible, awful mother! He didn't understand anything, he was so naïve.

I had to do something, but my body would not let me leave the condo.

One day, my mother was there, standing in the living room. She told me to collect my books, that they would save me. My beautiful mother, I wanted her to hold me—to touch me. But then she was gone. So, I started piling the books based on their protective powers, with the oldest on top and the thickest on the bottom. It was calming me down a little bit, this barrier. The books were like a lifeline out of the swamp.

Joshua was dressing and prodding me yet again. "We need to get you some help. You are not well, my love." He was right, of course. At some place deep within myself, I knew I was not well, not well at all. I was lost and in physical and emotional pain. And I was terrified, not only because I was losing myself, but also because *they* were after me. Joshua guided, or more like pushed, me outside. This was so dangerous! I looked everywhere—around corners, in passing windows, under cars. He put me in the seat, fastened the belt and locked the door. *When had I become a child?* We drove a short distance to an ugly gray building. There was a waiting room with the obligatory fish tank. I didn't touch anything. Someone said my name. There was a blonde woman, maybe in her thirties, in a light green office. There were cushiony chairs and toys in the corner. *Where was Joshua?* The woman smiled and I heard her in the distance.

"Hello, Sunny. My name is Dr. Fletcher. It's nice to meet you." She smiled even bigger. She had an expensive smile, but an average face. "Please make yourself comfortable," she gestured toward the empty chairs. I sat down. "Can I get you some water, coffee or tea?"

I shook my head. They were telling me not to take any drinks from her. *Don't trust her*, they said.

"I'm a psychiatrist specializing in mood disorders and trauma. I'd like to help you feel better. I'll need to collect some information from you, but before I start, please know that, unless you are in danger of hurting yourself or someone else, everything you tell me is completely confidential. Make sense?"

"Yeah."

"How are you feeling today, Sunny?"

I wasn't sure how much I should tell her. Even under torture, I needed to keep quiet.

"Okay." I kept my chin down as I picked at my cuticles.

"I'm so sorry to hear about your grandparents' deaths. This must be incredibly hard for you."

How the hell did she know about that? Oh fuck—she could see inside my head! I glared at her.

"I spoke with your husband this morning. He told me you've been having a hard time since they died. Can you tell me a little bit about what it's been like for you?"

"No." *Nosy bitch.*

"How have you been sleeping?"

"I don't."

"You don't sleep, not at all?"

I won't repeat myself to this traitor, this collaborator.

"How is your appetite?"

"Okay."

"Have you been eating?"

"Yeah."

"Have you had any thoughts about death or hurting yourself?"

Trick question. "No."

"Have you done anything to try to harm yourself?"

"Again, no."

And this is how it went. She asked her stupid questions and I didn't give in. She wouldn't get anything out of me—*I would not break.*

"Sunny, I believe you are extremely depressed. This is nothing to be ashamed of, it's a biochemical response to the stressors you've recently experienced."

Stressors? Really? Is that all my grandparents were?

"I'd like to start you on antidepressants as soon as possible. They will help to increase your serotonin, which will improve your mood, energy, ability to sleep, and appetite. Do you have any allergies to medicines?"

"No."

"The name of the medication is Paxil. It's a serotonin reuptake inhibitor and it's very safe. I'm going to start you on a low dose of twenty milligrams, which we will gradually increase once we see how you're doing. But I need you to be patient—it takes at least five weeks for the medicine to work. I'd like you to take it at night because it can be sedating, which might actually improve your sleep. Make sure you eat plenty of fiber too. Does this sound okay?"

"Yeah."

"I'd also like you to talk to a therapist. I have a colleague who specializes in depression and bereavement, I think he can really help you. Here's his card. Please call him tomorrow."

I took the card. *There was no way in hell I would meet with this man.*

She asked Joshua to come in and handed him the script. She repeated her spiel about the medicine and the therapist, giving Joshua his card too. I could hear Joshua and his pathetic enthusiasm.

"Yes, that sounds great. Will do. Thank you so much, doctor." *Kiss ass.*

Back in the car, Joshua said, "Honey, you are *very* depressed. It's not your fault. This happens to tons of people, especially when they deal with terrible losses. This medicine will help you to be yourself again. You will have more energy and be able to sleep. You can go back to work. You will feel so much better."

"Okay."

Of course, I didn't trust the blonde woman with the perfect teeth, but I had to get myself moving. I desperately needed energy. Plus, Joshua was my ally, so I knew he wouldn't suggest something that would kill me. But then again, maybe he wasn't in on the plan? I would take the medicine only until I could escape, then I would toss it. But I had no time to waste. The Gestapo was coming.

Chapter 16 ✤ Sunny

Each night I took the pills like the obedient wretch I had become. Joshua watched me take them as if I was a mental patient. *Was I a mental patient?* I half expected him to look under my tongue. But he didn't need to—I swallowed every pill. Yet, night after night, my body felt no better. I was exhausted and weak, and moved like a sloth. Despite my intense lethargy, I still managed to check the windows and locks numerous times a day. I also insisted that the home alarm be on at all times, which irritated Joshua. He accidentally set it off twice, which struck such panic in me that I hid in the closet. Chester hid too—he understood.

I had taken the pills for a week or so and was only feeling worse. I was even more tired than before, my body ached, and despite what that damned shrink had told me, my insomnia was worse. Plus, along with constant ruminations about my desperate need to hide, I'd started hearing ghastly male voices telling me I was worthless, less than garbage. One morning, I looked around the bedroom and noticed that my vision was blurry. I could see okay closeup, but the walls were fuzzy. Then, when I got up to go to the bathroom, I fainted.

Joshua, who was working at home that day, heard a thud and ran to the room. I could hear him panicking in the distance, "Oh my God, Sunny! Sunny? Wake up! Wake up!" I sat up. I was confused and had a pounding headache.

"What happened?"

"You fainted."

"My head hurts. She's trying to kill me. The beautiful beast wants me dead. The wall is blurry."

"Oh, Sunny." He sounded so sad, so lost. He was holding me. "It's just the new medicine. Maybe it doesn't agree with you. It takes time to find the right dose for each person. She's trying to *help* you." He escorted me to the bed and gave me a glass of water, which I drank—my mouth was so dry. "I'm going to go call her. Just lie here for a minute and yell if you need me. I love you." He kissed my cheek and left the room.

Later that morning, Joshua was back by my side. "You were sound asleep, that's good, honey. I talked to the doctor and she said Paxil wasn't a good fit for you. She prescribed something else for us to try. You will take this one in the mornings." He had the bottle in his hand. *When did he go to the drug store?* I looked at the bottle: Prozac.

It was so odd. Even though I was lost in a mess of voices, fear, pain, and distant sadness, hearing the word "Prozac" shocked a sliver of my being back to life. I recognized that word—who didn't? It meant something. Hadn't I read the book, *Prozac Nation?* Maybe I even had it here somewhere? So, on top of everything—losing my beautiful grandparents, being visited but then, yet again, left by my mother, being hunted by the Nazis—*on top of all of this,* I was crazy. Just fucking great. But I couldn't allow myself to be crazy, I had things to do and plans to make. So, I took the pill each day as Joshua looked at me like a sad puppy. Perhaps if I took the pills, at least Joshua would feel better. That was better than nothing.

As I lay around, mostly in bed, I noticed my vision was back to normal. I was nauseated and my mouth was still dry as hell, but I felt better than the prior week. I spent the majority of my time lost in my fantasies. Because Joshua would hound me to eat or move around when I was in my own mind, I pretended to read. This usually got him off my back and also gave him hope that I was getting better. One evening, my dad showed up. At this point I'd been on the new medication for about three weeks and my body was feeling slightly better. I was sitting in bed with Chester plotting my escape when I saw him in the doorway. I hadn't heard him come in.

"Hi, sweetheart," he said, looking at me like I was an alien.

"Hi, Dad."

"How are you feeling?"

"I don't know."

He came to the bed and held me for a long time. I felt sad, having him hold me like this. And I felt sorry for him, so, after a few moments, I held him back.

"I love you so much, my *tournesol.* You're going to get through this. Joshua says the new medicine is going well. And we are all here to support you. I know it's been terrible losing Babcia and Papa, it broke my heart too." He stopped for a moment, trying not to cry. "It's normal to be sad when losing those you love." *Why was everyone trying to convince me that I was normal? I was not normal. I was crazy. And evil.* "Joshua says there's a therapist you can talk to?"

"Yeah. I don't want to."

"But honey, it's very important to talk to someone, it will help you so much. Please just go see this guy, *please*."

"I don't know."

He talked to me for a while about different things: the kids, the weather, Sparky, his latest business trip. I tried to pay attention, but I needed to work on my plans—this was wasting precious time. He finally said he needed to go, but that Linda had sent over some dinners for us. *Ugh, stupid Linda, always sticking her nose in everything.* Then he hugged me and left the room. I knew that some unreachable part of myself loved him too. But right now, I needed him to leave.

After about a month of the medication, I began to feel different. I had more energy and was sleeping better. I was eating more of the food Joshua brought me, even the stuff Linda sent over. I was moving around the condo much more and could pay attention to the TV. I also sat through an entire movie with Joshua, even laughing once or twice. Upon looking in the mirror, I also realized that I had become thoroughly revolting. I didn't recognize myself. My hair was greasy and limp, I had zits on my forehead and chin, my legs and even my pits were hairy—which made me extremely ashamed. My toenails were long, my fingernails were dirty, my teeth were filmy, and I was thinner than I'd ever been (which I honestly didn't mind). *God, I was disgusting.* I wondered how Joshua could even look at me. I started bathing and grooming myself regularly and began to look like the old me.

As my body came back to life, my mind continued to do its own thing. I still knew I was being hunted; yet, at the same time, I also knew that I was Sunny, that Peter was my dad, that Joshua was my husband, and that I was an editor. That part of my mind wanted to feel better again and do something meaningful. I also wanted to go outside, talk to people, go shopping, and return to work. I missed my beloved words—reorganizing and making sense of them. I missed being needed and appreciated. So, I did my best to ignore the voices telling me I was a detestable person and a failure, and the thoughts telling me to run and hide, and decided to go back to work.

I was right about the pills making Joshua feel better. When he came home from work and found me with clean hair and clothes, makeup, and freshly painted nails, his face seemed to inflate from its former lassitude. He was virtually gleeful. "It's my girl!" he said, squeezing me and kissing my lips. "Damn, I've missed you! You look so beautiful! How do you feel?"

"I feel better. I'm sorry I was so disgusting and shitty to be around." I was appalled with myself.

"Don't say that! You could never be disgusting to me. You were depressed—you've been through a lot, it's okay. Wild horses, right?"

"Right."

"I love you so much!"

"I love you too."

Over the next couple of days, I continued to improve and was eager to get back to my job. I emailed Emily and told her I was feeling better. I was worried because I'd been out of work for almost two months. But she was actually nice, expressing her condolences about my grandparents. She said they were thrilled about having me back, that they'd missed me. *Missed me, really? They didn't even know me.* She said I could come back the following Monday, which was four days away.

For the first time in many weeks, I felt a little excited about something tangible. Joshua was happy too. That night, he made stir fry and we had a cautious little celebration about my return to the living. Of course, I didn't tell him that part of my mind remained otherwise occupied. I didn't want to spoil the mood. He mentioned the therapist again and I said I would see how I felt. I had no intention of going and did my best to convince him that it was no longer necessary. Eventually, he dropped it.

When Monday rolled around, I popped out of bed two hours early—not the least bit tired. I had laid out my outfit the night before: A short black dress, textured black tights, and a two-and-a-half inch t-strap pump—also black. The outfit was perfect, but needed some color. I added a crimson cardigan and matching lipstick. I was dressed and ready to go before Joshua got up.

"Wow, you look incredible!" he said through groggy eyes. "But aren't you a bit early?"

"Yeah, but I have a lot of work to catch up on. Besides, it's a beautiful day and I want to go outside."

"Okay, well, have an awesome day! Love you."

"Love you."

And off I went. I hadn't been outside in at least a week, and not by myself in more than a month. Though it was a fine April morning, it felt strange to be amongst the familiar surroundings. My legs were wobbly at first, but I kept walking. It was so early, even Viktor wasn't around. As I saw people heading to work, I felt anxious. I didn't want to be followed, so I sped up my pace, only briefly stopping to give the homeless woman five dollars. Then I practically sprinted to my building. Once inside, I counted my way up the stairs, headed to my cubbyhole, and closed the door with relief. Sweaty and slightly shaky, I got to work.

When Emily tapped on my office door, I jumped and said, "Come in".

"Hi Sunny, it's so great to see you! How are you doing?"

Why are people constantly asking me that? "I'm doing much better, thank you."

"Well, you certainly look great! I'm so sorry about your grandparents. I'm sure they meant a lot to you."

How would she know? Everything about Emily was pissing me off. "They did, thank you for the flowers."

"Of course. So, it looks like you've already been busy at work—wow!" She then told me about the various manuscripts I needed to work on and in what order, as well as some other office housekeeping. I stayed quiet and nodded my head. Then she reiterated how glad she was to see me and, thankfully, left.

Okay, Ms. Birdy, Wordy, Wordsmith, I muttered to myself after she closed the door. I was feeling inexplicably annoyed.

For three days, I kept my office door shut and edited manuscripts at record speed. I was thrilled with my progress. *I was an editing phenom! A champion of words!* When I wasn't looking at pages, I paced around the room—I was restless. All the while, I was muttering nonstop about a thousand different things. Fortunately, my office was a safehouse, so the fascists would not find me there. And my coworkers stayed away too, which was good—I thought I might bite their heads off if they bothered me.

I didn't concern myself with lunch, but just ate an apple or whatever I grabbed from home that morning. I couldn't risk going out, especially in broad daylight. I never left the office before 7 pm, when I replaced my heels with sneakers and ran home. Joshua and I ate together and then I went back to work on my art. He was ecstatic to see me both working *and* being creative once again. I produced more than thirty drawings over the course of a few days—mostly late at night. I wasn't sleeping. Only now, I didn't care—I no longer needed sleep. It was wonderful! One morning, after a couple of days of this, Joshua eyed me suspiciously.

"Honey, I woke up during the night and you weren't there. Were you working on your art?"

"Yep! I wasn't tired, so I decided to do some drawings of Chester, flowers, the tree outside the kitchen window, you, my mother, Sparky, a spider I saw in the bathtub, and a bunch of other stuff."

"Okay, well don't burn the candle at both ends, you need your rest—it's important."

Ugh. "Don't burn the candle at both ends?" What are you, 80? Leave me alone, Jesus. Despite my petulance, I promised to get more sleep and we both headed off to work.

When I hunkered down in my office on that third day—ready to do my word magic, I noticed a birthday card on my desk. *Oh fuck, not again. I don't have time for this nonsense.* I ignored the card and turned on my computer. When I opened my latest manuscript, the words on the screen started jumping out at me. It was both bizarre and fascinating. I decided to print the document, thinking it might help. It didn't. If anything, the words on the hard copy were even more active. As I stared at them, I realized they were trying to tell me something. *Of course! Duh.* I spent several hours that day crossing out the moving words. *Now I was getting somewhere.*

Emily had emailed me a copy of the next day's meeting agenda and asked if I had anything to add. I froze as I realized Penterhaus would be there— that Aryan fuckface. I knew he wanted me dead—this was a real problem. I couldn't let him see me. I worked on my code deciphering for the rest of the day, then raced toward home—eyes downcast. As I passed the market, I thought I heard Viktor say my name, but I didn't answer. I couldn't risk it—he could be an informant.

Joshua had to work late that day, so I grabbed a sandwich and created a compilation of Penterhaus sketches. He was already ugly, but my drawings captured his malevolence—his essence of pure evil. I drew him like a mix of Ichabod Crane and Freddy Kreuger. At least once I was dead, these images might implicate him.

When Joshua came home he started in about my need for rest again. He was a broken record. So, I went to bed at a reasonable time and pretended to sleep. All the while, I was plotting how to escape the Aryan pig and his Gestapo cronies. It was a lot to think about.

When I got to my office on Thursday morning, I continued to decode the dancing words. The message was starting to make sense: *Take Cover, Hide, Run, Schneller, Schneller!* When it was almost 4:00, I crawled under my desk.

There was no way in hell I'd be taken to a camp and worked to death. Or gassed. I heard a tap at my door, I didn't answer. I heard my phone ring and my email beep several times. Someone opened my door. I held my breath. They couldn't see me under there, crouched way in the back, behind my chair. They left.

Then I remembered the birthday card. I quickly grabbed it and a pen, and retreated to my hiding place. I realized the card would allow me to alert the others. It contained the standard drivel along with four or five written notes. I quickly scribbled my warning: *They're here. Penterhaus is Dr. Death. He wants to kill me. He will kill you. SZ.* I threw the card back on my desk. Then I waited.

Eventually, the halls outside were quiet and the room darkened. I heard my phone ringing and ringing and ringing. I carefully left my office, not making a sound. I dropped the card in the office mailbox and ran down the stairs. I slipped on the way, bracing my fall with my arm. It was bleeding. Then, making eye contact with no one, I ran home—only stopping to peek around corners and hide in a few doorways.

Joshua greeted me at the door. "Sunny, where the hell have you been? It's after 8:00. I was worried sick!"

I was out of breath. "Meeting day…worked late. A lot of papers…"

"Why didn't you answer your phone, I called you, like, seven times!"

"I…uh…I was in the conference room. More space."

"Right." He looked at me strangely. "Why are you all sweaty and what happened to your arm? It's bleeding!"

"Slipped on the stairs, it's fine. Jogged home." I caught my breath. "Just getting my exercise."

Joshua watched me closely all night. I took a two-hour bath just to avoid his suspicious gaze. The hot water hurt the abrasion on my arm. I could hear Joshua talking on the phone, but I couldn't make out the words. He knocked on the bathroom door twice. He wouldn't leave me alone, it was intolerable. I lay in bed pretending to read, then turned my back to him and stared at the wall. After about an hour, I got up to go to the bathroom. As I sat on the toilet, I stared at the distorted animal shapes I'd often seen in the wall tiles. After a few moments, they began to move about in a frenzy. The alligator was snapping his gummy jaws as a turtle danced in circles, garishly winking at me. I got up and paced until Joshua knocked on the door. He was driving me crazy. *Or wasn't I already crazy?* I went back to bed and continued to plot under the guise of sleep.

The next morning, I got up long before Joshua and slipped out the door. I didn't bother with my usual grooming—dressing in old jeans and a T-shirt. *Fuck the dress code. Other things were more important now.* I needed to decode the rest of my last manuscript, it was vitally important. I would risk my life to do it.

I worked for three hours. The phone rang several times, I ignored it. I had to pee so bad it was excruciating. But I couldn't risk leaving my office. I might have to use the garbage can. Joshua texted me, asking if I was at work. *Duh.* I replied with a yes, and got back to my mission. I heard a knock on my door. Startled, I said nothing and scampered under my desk like a deer mouse. Emily walked in, she was holding the birthday card and I saw her looking at one of the decoded manuscripts I left on the side table. My body was trembling. Papers were littered all over the floor and she bent down to pick one up. Then she saw me. She jumped.

"Oh my God, Sunny, what are you doing under there?"

"Shhhhhhhh…." *God, she was loud.*

"What's going on? I think we need to call someone."

"No! Don't call them! Please, Emily, don't call. Roll call. Call girl. Slut. I'm afraid." As she reached toward me, I low crawled across the room like a combat soldier. I hunched in the corner, pulling the chair in front of me. I was petrified.

"Emily, shut the door! Please, I'm so scared." I felt something warm between my thighs. I'd wet my pants. The voices chimed in: *You're trash. Just kill yourself.*

Her voice was gentle, "Sunny, I'm going to step out for a moment. It's okay, you're safe here. I will shut the door behind me. Everything is okay." And as my body shook uncontrollably, I watched her slowly back up and shut the door. I was not relieved. She was going to get *him*. I was dead.

Chapter 17 ❧ Joshua

I woke up on Thursday morning to an empty bed. My heart sank—where was Sunny? She seemed to be unravelling and I didn't want her to go to work. I told her this the night before and she ignored me. Now her purse and phone were gone—so, sure enough, that's where she was. She was so goddamn stubborn. I called her—no answer, of course. So, I left her a message stating that I wanted to come pick her up immediately. Again, no response. Unfortunately, I had a huge report due the next day, so I went to my office but planned to sneak out by 4:00 so I could go get her.

I didn't understand what was wrong with Sunny. Of course, I knew she was seriously depressed and I understood why. But sometimes her words made no sense and I often heard her muttering to herself. The thing with the books was mindboggling. Literally hundreds of books were piled everywhere, it was an obstacle course. Her rationale for the book stacking was nonsensical. And she was *so* moody. She would go from being mute and expressionless to speaking animatedly about several things at once. I was beginning to think she was manic-depressive, but I knew very little about mental illness. At least not yet.

At around 10:30 a.m., I got a call from Sunny's boss. She sounded frantic.

"Joshua, it's Emily Blackburn, Sunny's supervisor."

Oh shit, here it comes. "Yes, hello. How are you?"

"I'm fine. Listen, Joshua, Sunny's in bad shape. This morning I found an employee's birthday card with an extremely disturbing note written in it. Something about our CEO wanting to kill her. It had Sunny's initials next to it. Then there were bizarre manuscript pages all over her office. She had crossed out about every third word and, using different colored pens, scribbled random words in the margins. There were at least a hundred of these pages. But here's the worst part: when I entered her office, she was *under her desk*, Joshua."

"Oh my God."

"And she was shaking like a leaf. She was legitimately terrified that someone was trying to kill her. She also appears to have wet her pants. She's a mess, you need to come get her immediately. Otherwise, I will have to call 911. I'm terribly worried about her."

I felt sick. "Where is she now?"

"She's still in her office. She's afraid to come out."

"Okay, please watch the door and make sure she stays put. I'll be there in fifteen minutes."

This was the call I had been dreading. When the Prozac started working, I thought Sunny was getting better, but her illness just took on a different form. Crawling under her desk and wetting her pants *at work?* I was mortified for her. When she was back in her right mind, she would never allow herself to get past this. It was a disaster.

I had no idea what to do with Sunny. As my shit luck would have it, Peter had been out of town the past week, so he couldn't help. I considered picking up Linda, but that would likely exacerbate whatever was happening in Sunny's mind. I considered my options as I grabbed my stuff and left my office. I told the receptionist I had a family emergency. This wasn't a lie.

When I arrived at the publishing company building, I ran up the stairs where a woman resembling Popeye's Olive Oyl was waiting. Based on Sunny's description, this was definitely Emily. She looked grim, like this was the worst thing that ever happened to her. After a quick introduction, she walked me toward Sunny's office. People stared as we hurried down the hall. I asked Emily to keep our situation private, though it may have been too late. Once outside Sunny's office door, I told Emily I had it from there. I didn't need an audience.

Doing my best not to startle Sunny, I tapped lightly on the door and said her name. Of course, there was no answer. I opened the door just enough to squeeze through and shut it in Emily's face. I was floored by what was before me. Since I'd known her, Sunny was obsessively neat when it came to her workspace. Yet there were papers strewn about the room and, like at home, stacks of books had been placed haphazardly on the carpet. And she had scribbled all over one of the walls with a red Sharpie. There were words such as "run," "hide," and "Juden." Toward the top, she wrote "Arbeit Macht Frei," and I saw "Dr. Death" in multiple places. I couldn't imagine the hell entrapping her mind.

And there she was—my beautiful, intelligent wife—huddled in a ball in the far right corner. Her chin was tucked down and her head was hidden under her hands. She almost looked too small to be human. Her body was trembling and she was mumbling to herself. She had no shoes on. It looked like she'd thrown them at the door. And I could smell urine. *So, this is what insanity looks like.* I slowly approached her.

"Sweetheart, it's me. You're going to be okay," I said softly while crouched down in front of her.

"It's Penterhaus. Ticktock. Hickory dickory dock. I'm a hunted mouse. That Aryan is going to kill me." Sunny kept her face in her hands as she spoke; her voice was frantic.

"No, he's not. Sunny, we need to get you out of here."

"No! He's out there!" She abruptly lifted her face and I saw her wide, painfully tormented eyes dart from me to the door.

"There's no one out there who will hurt you."

"Yes, there is!!" Her eyes remained focused on the door.

"I will double-check." I left the room, closing the door behind me. Several people were peeking out of offices. *Fucking looky-loos.* I saw Emily down the hall. I approached her and conveyed my annoyance. "Emily, I need to get her out of here, but I can't have all of these people watching or she won't come out."

"Okay, I'll get rid of them."

I went back in the office. "Sunny, there's no one out there. We need to get you home. Don't you want to see Chester?" I was desperate.

"Chester molester. They will rape me. Is my kitty okay? Did they take him?"

"No, sweetie, Chester is just fine." I gradually coaxed her out of the corner. I put her shoes on her feet and wrapped my jacket around her waist to cover the pee stain. I grabbed her purse and, with my arm around her shoulder, I guided her toward the door.

She stuck her head out, moving it left and right multiple times as she checked the hallway. We slowly left the office. The place looked empty, yet I could feel gazes upon us. Sunny allowed me to move her along gingerly. I saw one person, a young woman wearing a tight, ill-fitting dress and black-rimmed glasses, peering at us from one of the rooms. Sunny gasped and stopped moving.

"Get back in your office and mind your own goddamn business," I snarled. The woman quickly disappeared. "It's okay, my love. She's gone. Come on, Chester's waiting." I hated myself for using Chester as bait. But what choice did I have?

When we got to the stairway, she ran all the way down. My car was right outside the door with a ticket on it. I put Sunny in the back, got in, and locked the doors. I could see her in the rearview mirror, rocking, shaking, and mumbling. I was at a loss about what to do, but I knew she was disastrously sick and that I couldn't care for her. I drove to the emergency room.

When the car stopped, Sunny looked up and saw that we were not home. "Joshua, what have you done? The collaborators have infiltrated this structure. There is a tectonic force. A Titanic force. I will drown! No!"

"Honey, this is the hospital. They will take care of you, help you feel better."

"*What!* Nobody *ever* leaves the hospital alive! No!" She was becoming hysterical.

I called the ER and asked what to do. After about five minutes, a mobile hospital unit pulled up beside us. There were two men, one in his twenties and the other much older. I got out and spoke to them as Sunny rocked herself in the backseat.

We could hear her screaming. "Noooo! Dr. Death is in there! They won't take me alive! Death inside. I'm shit inside." She dropped to the passenger side floor and pressed herself into a tight ball against the backseat. She reminded me of a frightened potato bug.

What then ensued will sit in the bottom of my stomach until the day I die. I was betraying the one person I loved above all others. I opened the car door and scooped her up off the floor as she screamed, "Noooooooo!" Fortunately, she stayed in a tight ball rather than struggling, as if she thought she could disappear into herself. I carried her to the back of the ambulance and laid her down on a stretcher. When she looked up and realized where she was, she began kicking and screaming. After they asked me her name, the older paramedic asked me to step out of the vehicle. But I could still hear them.

"Sunny, it's okay, we want to help you," said the older man, who had a slight New York accent. "I know you're frightened, I understand. We are going to take you somewhere safe. A place where you can rest." Sunny's agitation increased.

"No! They will kill me. Phenol to my heart. Heartbroken, dead. That killer of crazies and undesirables," she screamed. My poor Sunny, she was truly terrified. She let out a blood-curdling scream, and was bucking and kicking at the men like a crazed horse. At one point, she struck one of them in the face with her foot. Sunny called my name, but there was nothing I could do. For a brief second, we caught eyes. She looked at me with such profound agony and disappointment. I had deceived her.

Once they closed the door, I couldn't hear much other than muffled screaming. The younger paramedic stayed outside the ambulance and, as he walked toward the driver's side, asked me to meet them in the ER. It took me a little while to find parking in that maze of a hospital. After I parked, I allowed myself to cry for exactly five minutes before heading inside. And so marked my entry into the world of psych visits, shrinks, pills, evals, and insipid bureaucratic bullshit. Welcome to the hamster wheel.

After I checked in, they sent me to a room that was separate from the other ER patients. It had a large sliding glass door that allowed patients to be seen from the nurses' desk. I expected Sunny to be screaming, but she was laying on the bed rocking side to side while whispering her incoherent pleas. She barely looked at me, and was unconscious in about thirty minutes. She had restraints on her arms and legs.

I walked back to the lobby.

"Excuse me, but why the hell is my wife in restraints?"

A nurse looked up from behind the desk. She was wearing pink scrubs and appeared to be East Indian. Her hair was pulled back so tight, it looked painful. "Your wife was aggressive and out of control. It's a safety precaution."

She didn't have an Indian accent, but sounded more East Coast. She was all business, with no empathy. I could tell she'd been asked this question many times before.

"*Aggressive?* My wife wouldn't hurt a fly—literally. She's afraid for *her own* safety. This will only make things worse." I was leaning over the counter, trying to reason with this ice queen.

"Mr. …?" She looked at her notes. "Zielinski…"

"Fitzpatrick."

"Mr. Fitzpatrick, your wife kicked one of the paramedics in the face. Have you seen his cheek? She's floridly psychotic and likely to run out into the street. She could easily hurt herself."

Oh shit! I didn't know what to say, maybe she was right.

I sat next to Sunny and tried to get a hold of Peter on my cell. I thought he might be in London, or was it Sweden? I had no idea, much less the name of his hotel. Peter was old school—he scoffed at cell phones and vowed never to get one. But a cell phone could not have been more warranted than this moment—and I planned to tell him as much. Then I called Linda and filled her in. Fortunately, Peter would be landing at LAX in the next hour and Linda would send him here immediately. She was clearly upset and wanted to come to the hospital too, but I dissuaded her. Then I just sat and waited, and waited, and fucking waited some more. The walls in the room were a sickening puce and the air was so chilly that my fingers and toes were getting numb. Was this on purpose—freeze the mental patients back to sanity? One of the fluorescent lights flickered nonstop and I heard intermittent screams in the distance followed by a woman yelling, "Get it out! Get it out!" This was a special kind of hell.

I wanted to call Sunny's psychiatrist, but I couldn't remember her name. I'd left her card at home. *Where in the hell was the doctor?* I complained to Nurse Ratched in the lobby, but she said it was a busy day, that he'd be there shortly. He wasn't.

Fortunately, Sunny continued to sleep soundly. On top of whatever they gave her, she had to be exhausted. She hadn't had any decent sleep in weeks. After two hours of sitting in the only chair available—a cheap, plastic piece of crap—my ass was tingling and my back was starting to ache. I went for a brief walk outside and found a coffee cart where I bought a latte. Then I sat back down next to my wife. I remember wondering why hospitals, with their exorbitant fees, couldn't provide a decent chair for people in crisis. *Where was the damn doctor?* Didn't this qualify as urgent?

After *yet another hour,* he finally arrived.

"Good afternoon, Mr. Zielinski. I'm Dr. Morgan." He was of medium height with thick salt-and-pepper hair and a European accent of some sort. He wore a perfectly manicured gray beard. *Nice, Sigmund Freud himself.*

"It's Fitzpatrick," I said, getting up to shake his hand. *Why couldn't she have just taken my name?*

He was looking at a chart. "Yes, well, Sylvia has…"

"It's Sunny, my wife goes by Sunny." *Jesus Christ.*

"I'm batting a thousand here," he said dryly. "Your wife has had a psychotic episode." As he walked over to Sunny and listened to her heart, I caught the musky aroma of his aftershave.

"Has this ever happened before?"

"Which part?" I glanced out the window, wishing I could take Sunny away from this place, this terrible predicament.

"Has she ever been hospitalized for psychosis or any other psychiatric problem?"

"Not that I know of, but I seriously doubt it. I've known her for over two years, and nothing like this has ever happened."

He shuffled through his papers before looking up at me. "Have you noticed any delusional behavior, like the paranoia she exhibited today? Or maybe hallucinations?"

"Both of her grandparents died less than three months ago, she's been a wreck ever since."

"How so?"

"Oh God, let me see." I leaned against the wall and took a deep breath, knowing I had a lot to explain. "Well, she was so depressed after they died that she barely got out of bed or ate anything. I took her to a psychiatrist and she was prescribed antidepressants. I don't remember the name of the first one, but it made her worse. So, she switched to Prozac and has been on it ever since. She felt better with the Prozac. I thought she was almost back to her normal self. But then she started acting *extremely weird*—like stacking massive amounts of books all over our home. And talking to herself. Pacing. Oh, and saying words that make no sense. The worst part is her twisted idea that the Nazis are after her. I mean, she's fully convinced. She was hiding under her desk at work today. She was shaking with fear. When she wakes up, she'll probably call you Dr. Death."

"I've been called worse," he said with an air of indifference.

What could possibly be worse? I was starting to really dislike this guy.

"When did she start acting delusional, as in talking to herself and being afraid of Nazis?"

"Umm…Maybe about five weeks ago."

"Is she on any other meds besides the Prozac? Is she on birth control? And, what's the name of the prescribing physician?" His manner was gruff, without warmth.

"Not that I know of and I don't remember, I'll find out when I go home. She has an IUD."

"Any medical issues, such as diabetes or heart disease?'

"No, she's very healthy."

"Has she ever tried to kill or harm herself, or talked about doing so?"

"No, she's afraid of other people. But she says they won't take her alive— which terrifies me."

"That's understandable. Has she had any other symptoms of psychosis, depression or anything else unusual since you've known her?"

"Well, nothing like this. She's a very sensitive person, socially anxious and shy. But that's about it."

"Does she have a family history of mental illness? Schizophrenia?"

"You will need to talk to her dad about this. Her grandparents didn't have mental problems, at least not since I've known them. But I'm not sure about her mother—there may be something there. Sunny doesn't talk much about her mom, but she has nightmares about her. Her mom died when she was eight or nine. That's all I know."

"How did she die?"

"A car accident, I think. Oh, and Sunny's grandmother on her mom's side—she's *out of her mind*. I don't know if it's dementia or what, but apparently she acted like a lunatic at Sunny's mom's funeral. But Sunny hasn't seen her in years—likely because she's insane."

He then asked me several more questions about Sunny's health, and use of drugs and alcohol. He said she would most likely need an antipsychotic when she woke up. He also intended to transfer her to the psych unit on the sixth floor and to place her on a seventy-two-hour hold for her own safety. *Oh God, not the psych unit.* But I knew she was in no shape to go home.

I could see that he was distracted and ready to leave, but I had a burning question: "Doc, do you think she's schizophrenic?" *Please say "no." Wasn't that like the cancer of mental illness? The word struck terror in me.*

"I won't know until we evaluate her."

"When do people become schizophrenic—what age?"

"Generally, in the twenties."

Oh God. "But her grandparents just died—they basically raised her. Couldn't this just be like a grieving response or something?"

"It's hard to say at this point. Didn't you say the depression was better after the Prozac?"

"Yes."

"Sometimes stressors will kickstart psychosis in people with a predisposition for mental illness."

Oh God, no!

"They'll page me when she wakes up. In the meantime, please find her father. I need to run now."

"Thanks," I muttered before collapsing back into that fucking plastic chair.

Chapter 18 ❧ Peter

Losing my parents knocked the wind out of me. I was an only child; a child who was desperately wanted and never doubted it. My parents' love was boundless. I felt the unconditionality of it every day of my life, which infused me with self-confidence. Of course, their horrific wartime experiences were ever-present, like inoperable lesions in their shared consciousness. At times, their histories stabbed at my heart; but, with this pain, there was also a respect so intense that it made me want to be a better person. Without their enduring examples of courage and strength of will, I would never have graduated from an Ivy League college or made partner in a respected law firm. My parents believed in me with their every fiber, and I absorbed the full weight of their rosy prophecy. I had been privileged to spend over fifty years as Mama and Tata's son. This was not something I was prepared to lose—not yet. My sudden orphan status left me untethered.

I'm not sure how I would have emerged from that dismal place without my wife. In some ways, Linda reminded me of Mama. They were both softspoken and slight of frame, but with a surplus of emotional strength. If either was ever angry at me—which was rare, I knew I deserved it. And I also knew their spoken wrath was far worse than any physical punishment. Linda had tolerated a lot over the years, primarily because of Sunny. Sunny disliked Linda from Day One and nothing would change her mind. Linda was competing with a ghost—what could she do? And this ghost, which had been pieced together in a child's imagination, was an imposter. Sunny only saw the splendor and excitement that was her mother. She didn't see the revolving door of anguish, hollowness, and disappointment. Though I was grateful for this myopia, as we all did our best to shield Sunny from the worst parts of

Gracie, it didn't help Linda.

I never permitted Sunny to speak rudely to Linda, but she found other ways to express her angst—eye rolls and dramatic sighs were particular favorites. After a couple of years, Sunny managed to show Linda some respect, although it was tempered with apathy and indifference. However, when Linda became pregnant, Sunny, who was around seventeen, immediately regressed to the same impertinent attitude as when she'd first met Linda. She began referring to the unborn twins as "The Replacements," which I of course forbade. But I know she was still using this term amongst her friends. I told her repeatedly that she was irreplaceable. That she would always be my firstborn and that my love for her would never change. Nonetheless, whenever she came home, I often caught her looking at Linda like she was a leper. But at least she was quiet.

When Maddy and Spencer were born, Sunny's disposition quickly improved. My stubborn daughter would not admit it, but she was smitten with those babies. She often visited from college with a pile of picture books and never left the house without reading them at least two stories. Later, they would beg for Sunny to come over and read to them. She held them often as infants and I saw the way she looked at them. Sunny's love for the twins took the focus off of Linda. And, over time, I believe Sunny even came to admire Linda's mothering skills. Linda has always been an incredible mother. She has somehow managed the perfect balance between affection, kindness, firmness, and consistency. I have often marveled at Linda's parenting style, which appears to be instinctual.

Even more commendable, there was never a "my kid-your kid" attitude with Linda. Even if Sunny was being insolent, Linda expressed equal amounts of warmth toward all three children. Linda was not perfect, of course; every now and then the kids worked their way under her skin. Yet she still spoke with a mix of firmness and love that I tried, usually without success, to emulate. And her thoughtfulness and patience toward Sunny never wavered. If Linda wanted to cook something fancy for Maddy and Spencer on a day when Sunny was home, she would ask Sunny if she had a preference. She often picked up little gifts for Sunny at the store and invited her to family outings.

The twins were born in May of 1996. Sunny was home that summer, spending the bulk of her time reading in her bedroom or next to the pool. If it wasn't for Maddy and Spencer, I doubted we'd ever see Sunny without a book in her face. But she always spent at least an hour each day with them, and, despite her misgivings, ate dinner with us each evening. Sunny was finally coming around with Linda enough for me to relax a little bit and enjoy my family. Of course, this respite was brief, as whatever effect Mama and Tata's death had on me, for Sunny, it appeared insurmountable. Now, every bit of my grief had morphed into a sickening panic about what was happening with my deeply troubled daughter.

When Mama died, I honestly wasn't paying much attention to Sunny, so lost was I in my own pain. I do recall her crying a great deal, but the rest is a blur. When Tata died, I'd never wept so hard in my life—it was like the final nail in my heart. When I'd calmed down somewhat, I went to the condo one evening to drop off some food. Joshua wasn't home and Sunny didn't answer the door. I knew she was in there. "Sunny, sweetheart, it's Dad. Come on, open the door... Sunny? Come on, it's me."

Just as I was about to give up, she opened the door only slightly, keeping the chain on. She made sure it was me, and then removed it. When the door was fully open, I was shocked. Sunny was skinnier than ever. She was swimming in a pair of sweats that used to be snug on her. Her hair was so dirty I could smell the oil. And she had purple bags under her eyes. I'd seen my daughter go through countless heartaches in her short life, but this was probably the worst she'd ever looked. I set the food inside and gave Sunny a hug. She was bony and unresponsive.

I held her at arm's length. "Honey, what's going on? I know you're sad, but you need to take care of yourself. What have you been eating?"

"I don't know." Her voice was monotone as she backed away and looked at the floor.

"What can I do to help you?"

"Nothing."

"Oh, Sunny," I sighed. I warmed up the soup I brought and set it in front of her with some crackers and lemonade. "You need to eat this."

"Okay." She sat down heavily at the kitchen table. It took several seconds for her to fully lift up the spoon—as if it were made of uranium. Then she slowly stirred the vegetables in circles for at least a minute. The spoon made a clicking sound that was grating on me.

"Sunny, please just put it in your mouth." I was standing behind her, not wanting to show my frustration and fear.

"Okay." She took one bite and then, eventually, ate half of the soup before pushing it away. She didn't touch the crackers.

"Please drink your lemonade." Sunny adored lemonade—she called it her kryptonite. Any time she tried to eat healthier, lemonade was her one weakness.

"I can't. I'm tired. Thanks for the soup, Dad."

I recall leaning over the kitchen sink as I rinsed out the bowl. I felt so desperate I almost vomited. I put away the rest of the food I'd brought, tucked Sunny into bed with Chester, and left. I immediately called Joshua when I got to my office. We needed to do something ASAP.

As bad as Sunny appeared that afternoon, I tried to remain optimistic that this was all part of the grieving process. Didn't everyone grieve in their own way? And Sunny took everything harder than most people. If a news story made the rest of us sad, it had Sunny in tears. She could be pathologically sensitive at times. Even from an early age, I had to skip certain parts of her storybooks because they upset her and caused nightmares. And any social issues at school, such as feeling unliked by other girls or not getting invited to a sleepover, could put Sunny into a funk for days or even weeks. So, I relied on whatever evidence I could find to support my theory that Sunny was an overly sensitive girl grieving two profound losses. Any alternative explanations were unthinkable.

But what Joshua told me on the phone shattered any last scraps of hope. When he told me about the nature of her paranoia, I felt lightheaded. *Hadn't my parents suffered enough because of the Nazis? Hadn't we all suffered enough?* But now, here they were again, with their toxic venom trickling down to the next in line. It was heart-wrenching.

Even worse was the familiar maliciousness of Sunny's symptoms—this was no regular grieving response. As Joshua was describing her delusional behavior, I dropped the phone and sank to my knees. The realization was like a punch in the face—my *worst fear*, even more so than losing my parents—had been realized. The demons that haunted Gracie had re-emerged, hijacking my daughter's precious soul.

I knew mental illness was often heritable; I'd of course looked into this years ago. Both Gracie and her mother had severe psychiatric issues. Gracie didn't speak much about her mom, except to say she was "loony-tunes." Gracie was never one for insight. Unlike her mother, Gracie had been labeled with many diagnoses—too many. There was major depression with psychosis, bipolar disorder, schizophrenia, schizo-something-else, borderline personality, anxiety, PTSD, panic disorder, and histrionic personality—among others. I was forever confused as to which disorder or *disorders* Gracie actually had. I also noticed that anytime she went to a new facility, they just relied on her prior records—accurate or otherwise. I could see these damned labels following her from one door to the next. The myriad of medications and doses they gave her was equally puzzling.

While I never knew what or whom to believe when it came to Gracie, bipolar disorder seemed to stick more than the others. I absolutely did not want children with Gracie, as I had no illusions about her ability to take care of another human being. Plus, it was bad enough that Gracie insisted on passing along her mother's name to our child—which never made sense to me—but I was terrified that she would also pass along her madness. When Sunny made it through college with top honors, a close best friend, and a devoted boyfriend, I thought *just maybe* we had dodged the genetic bullet that destroyed Gracie. The thought of going through all of this again felt agonizing, beyond endurance. But, of course, *I had to*—for Sunny. Only this time, I would be better. I would not let it take my daughter.

Chapter 19 ∾ Peter

I'd just finished a trip to London where I was meeting with clients. I always loved visiting the UK and would have enjoyed it if not for the constant aching in my gut. Even though Sunny was apparently doing better on her new medication and had even gone back to work, I couldn't kick an awful premonition looming over me. I just knew the good news wouldn't last. And, sure enough, the moment I arrived home Thursday afternoon, Linda tearfully told me what happened. She also seemed pissed.

"Peter, enough with your 'I don't need a cell phone' bullshit! You're getting one and that's that!" She was right, as usual. I set my bags down and headed to the hospital. I knew exactly how to get there.

They sent me up to the sixth floor—the psych ward. Seems like it used to be on a different floor, but I wasn't sure. The room was small, with only one bed and a tiny bathroom. The floor, although very clean, was an ugly gray linoleum. There were no windows. The only source of light was the fluorescent fixture overhead. The bed was to the right of the door, with the bathroom on the opposite side. The extent of décor was a large Monet print over the bed with a cheap metal frame, and two green pleather chairs—one on each side of the bed. The room stank of bad breath and had a general miasma of hopelessness.

Joshua was slumped over a chair. I thought he was asleep, but he jumped when he heard the door close. He looked utterly miserable.

"Hi, Peter," he said, stretching his arms over his head. "She's been asleep for hours, but is starting to stir."

I saw my daughter in the bed. She looked so peaceful there, submerged in the serene illusion of sleep. I dreaded the inevitable torment lying in wait—

ready to pounce once she opened her eyes.

"They had her in restraints earlier. Is that even legal?"

"When?" I could feel my blood start to boil.

"When we first got here, down in the ER. They said she was dangerous and gravely ill. They took them off up here though."

"I don't know what the current laws are, but it sounds like…"

Sunny sighed, interrupting my thoughts.

"I'm going to page the doctor," said Joshua, leaving the room.

I looked at Sunny, lying there so helpless. She looked like a child to me. Her ivory skin was clear except for a few freckles across her nose and cheeks, and a dark curl was stuck to her forehead with sweat. Her long, thick lashes fluttered as she dreamed of God knows what. *Please let it be pleasant.* And she was lying in the same fetal position in which she had always slept. *My little girl.* As I picked up a chair and moved it closer to the bed, I heard her.

"Dad?" Her voice was weak, barely there.

I stood next to her and held her hands. "I'm here, sweetheart. I'm here."

"Am I dead?"

"No, honey. You're in the hospital." I should've used a different word.

"Oh no, no, no, no, no, no, no! *Not* the hospital! It's a one-way door. The door to hell. Hellhounds gnawing at me, eating my skin." She was screaming and writhing about, starting to get out of bed. *Maybe the restraints were a good idea after all?*

"Sunny, you're having bad thoughts, they aren't real. No one is after you, please lay back down." I did my best to remain calm while gently holding her on the bed.

"Let go, Dad! They will kill you too! Jew. Judan. Hide!"

At that point, Joshua, the doctor and two other hospital staff members came into the room. When Sunny saw the doctor, her agitation increased tenfold. She was petrified of him.

"It's Mengele! I told you!" Sunny leaped from the bed and shut herself in the bathroom before they could get to her.

The doctor spoke to her from the other side of the door. "Sunny, I'm Dr. Morgan. I can assure you that I am not Dr. Mengele. I understand you are upset and want to help you. No one here will hurt you." *Was this guy actually German?* You've got to be kidding.

"Go away, Dr. Death, you murderer. Killer. Killing fields. Blood in the rye." Her yelling was followed by a banging sound. "You won't take me alive. Only *I* decide my death. Death squad. Fighter squadrons overhead."

The doctor turned toward me and Joshua. "She's hitting her head on the wall. She needs an antipsychotic ASAP. I'll send in someone who might be less triggering. But she may need to be restrained again. Let's just see how it goes." And he was out the door.

I could hear more of the banging—it was torturous. I tried to open the door, but she'd barricaded it with her legs somehow. "Please, sweetheart, don't hurt yourself like that. Please stop." I wanted to cry. The banging didn't stop.

The doctor was replaced by a tall nurse who was built like a linebacker. She was maybe in her early forties with thick blonde hair pulled back in a clip. She reminded me of one of Gracie's first nurses, except with a kinder face. "Hi, I'm Maggie," she said to Joshua and me before moving toward the bathroom.

"Hi, Sunny, I'm your nurse, Maggie. I'm here to help you, can you please come out of the bathroom?"

"No, Dr. Death is there! Where. Where for art thou? *Get out!*" The headbanging continued.

"The doctor left, I promise. Can you please come out?"

Sunny peeked out the door, looking around the room. Then her eyes landed on the nurse. "Oh no, Beautiful Beast! Rabbit killer! Beast. Breast. Arrest. Where is the SS?" She slammed the door shut and commenced her headbanging.

Maggie looked at us and whispered, "I'm going to need backup. She is acutely psychotic and we need to give her an injection."

Oh my God, it's all happening again. Maybe I was the worst father in the world, but I couldn't watch. When two additional hospital staff headed toward the bathroom, I left the room like a coward. But, as I stood in the hall, I heard everything: Sunny's scream and mangled, but desperate, words. A scuffle. Maggie's fruitless attempts at consolation, "It's okay, Sunny. No one here is going to hurt you. We need to give you some medicine to make you feel better." The last sentence was followed by a scream of such intensity that it had everyone on the floor looking in our direction. Then it was quiet for a moment. I went back in the room and saw that Sunny was back on the bed, but not under the covers. The shitty hospital gown they gave her was completely open and off of one shoulder, one of her breasts was nearly exposed which Joshua immediately covered. Her legs were bare and looked thin, stubbly, and bruised. I pulled the covers over them. Sunny was still extremely agitated, twisting around in the bed, glaring at the hospital staff.

"We can't have you getting up right now, you will hurt yourself," said Maggie with a mix of compassion and authoritativeness. "I don't like using restraints, Sunny. Please stay on the bed and try to calm down."

Oh God, "try to calm down," really? Those were fighting words.

"*You* calm down, you malevolent beast. Beauty and the Beast. Beasty Boys. No boys allowed, get the fuck out!" screamed Sunny. The insults made me feel bad for Maggie, who was a big woman after all. But she didn't seem fazed by any of it—just another day at the office.

Maggie and a young male doctor stayed in the room as the medication took effect. Sunny's garbled diatribe of insults, warnings, and terrors continued for another twenty minutes or so, until it finally slowed down. Her body had also stilled and I was relieved that the restraints had not been used. She closed her eyes and slept while Joshua and I sat there feeling crushed. After an hour or so, Sunny started to awaken and Joshua went to find someone. Maggie came back with him.

"Sunny," said Maggie, "how are you feeling now?"

"My head hurts. When are they coming to kill me? Those killers, killjoys. The joint is swarming with murderers and rapists." Her voice was calmer, but her words no less alarming. Her eyes darted around the room with panic.

"I'm sure your head does hurt, you were hitting it against the wall. Why did you do that?"

"Mengele is death. Phenol to the heart. My heart. My hand. *My hand!*" Although exhausted, she was getting more agitated. But she couldn't keep her eyes open.

"That sounds truly terrifying, but no one murders patients here. I promise. I'm going to let you rest for a little while."

Maggie gestured for us to go in the hall. "Let's let her sleep some more. She's in a floridly psychotic state, but the antipsychotics should help over time. Meanwhile, Dr. Morgan is going to transfer her care to a different doctor."

"Well, does this one have a German accent and resemble Freud, or worse yet, Mengele?" asked Joshua wryly.

Maggie smiled. Something about her elicited trust. I liked her. "Well, he's black, if that helps?"

Joshua and I laughed—which was sorely needed. But we had no idea if this new doctor would feed into some other aspect of Sunny's delusion. Time would tell.

"At some point, I'm going to need to do some tests—we need a tox screen, a CT scan, and a full blood panel. Is she at any risk for STDs?"

"Of course not," said Joshua.

"Could she be pregnant?"

"No," he answered. The thought of Sunny getting pregnant sent a chill through me. This simply could not happen.

She mentioned the seventy-two-hour hold. "What happens after three days? Won't we need a 5250?" I asked. Joshua looked lost. "That's an involuntary fourteen-day hold," I added for his benefit.

"That's highly likely. As it sounds like you already know, there are specific requirements for a 5250. We will know more about whether it's warranted over the next day or so. In the meantime, both of you look exhausted. You don't need to watch her sleep. We can see everything from out there." She pointed toward the nurses' station. "And once Dr. Bensen takes over, he will want to speak with both of you. So, please go eat something, have a coffee, put your feet up. You can't help Sunny if you don't take care of yourselves."

Maybe my words stemmed from the relief of having someone else in charge, someone who seemed trustworthy, but I simply said, "Yes, ma'am."

Joshua and I then dragged ourselves out of that wretched place.

Chapter 20 ❧ Sunny

My first week in the hospital was nothing but a blur of confusion and fear. People were coming and going at all times as they planned their murderous plots. The Beautiful Beast was the worst, always pestering me for information or poking at my body. I couldn't escape her. *They* were often there too, laughing and belittling me at every opportunity. Like their incessant chanting when I tried to give one of the nurses a urine sample and peed all over my hand. *Dirty bitch. Disgusting dirty bitch. Bitch. Bitch. Bitch.*

I often woke to find Joshua or my dad sitting near my bed with pained expressions. Sometimes Joshua was asleep in an awkward position on one of the chairs. I remember feeling guilty seeing him there, all because of me. Mengele didn't show up anymore, but I wasn't consoled. I had a vague memory of yelling at him, which caused me to tremble uncontrollably. I was certain I would be punished—maybe even transferred to Block 11. And, although he was gone, I knew his accomplices were still lurking around, watching. Sometimes I woke up with a terrible sore throat, which a nurse said was from screaming. I slept a lot, but it brought no respite. My mother was usually waiting for me in my dreams—either moving around me in a maniacal dance or watching me with mascara-smudged eyes. Sometimes Grandma Sylvie was there too, howling wildly.

One morning after I'd been in the hospital for at least five days, I awoke feeling particularly keyed up and fearful. I sat up and pulled back the covers. The blonde nurse immediately appeared. "Ah, we're awake!" she said cheerfully.

"I don't know about *you*, but *I'm* only mildly awake. Where are my clothes? I want to go home."

"You haven't been discharged, Sunny. Please sit back down. We're doing everything we can to help you."

Still confused, I got back on the bed. "But...I...don't feel safe. That doctor wants to kill me."

"No one here is going to hurt you."

I remember feeling confused, drained, and completely powerless. I sat with my legs curled in front of me and leaned against the pillow. The nurse listened to my heart and looked at some papers she was holding. She was wearing tacky white scrubs covered in orange flowers, which was unflattering for her coloring. But she had the prettiest hazel eyes. I thought she might be okay. I remembered insulting her to the best of my ability.

"I'm sorry for calling you a beast. I thought you were someone else."

"Happens all the time, no worries. Let's just get you feeling better."

I felt so bad for how I'd treated this woman, she was obviously not even German. *Maybe she was part of the resistance? But wouldn't they have killed me by now if they wanted me dead? Maybe this place was okay—for now. Unless that evil doctor returned.* As I considered how I might escape, looking around the room for a way out, she spoke.

"How are you feeling this morning?"

"Confused. What's wrong with me, why am I here again?" I thought we might have already had this conversation, but I wasn't sure.

"Well, your husband brought you in last week because you were extremely upset and thought people were trying to hurt you." *Last week? How long have I been here?* "And you hadn't been eating or taking care of yourself. On the first night, you were hitting your head on the bathroom wall," she said while looking toward the bathroom.

I remembered some chaos in the bathroom and wanting to kill myself. But then a terrible realization hit me—*hard.* "So, you mean I'm here because you think I'm crazy? *Oh my God,* is this a *mental* hospital?" I knew I was in the hospital, but not as a mental patient. *They* hated the mentally ill; was I here as part of the Nazi euthanasia program? I began feeling restless and terrified. *Had I just been duped by this so-called nurse? Was she going to inject me with poison? Where was Joshua?* I didn't know what to do. I began biting what was left of my cuticles. They tasted awful for some reason.

"Sunny, everything is okay, you're safe here. This is not a mental hospital, but yes, you are on a psychiatric ward because your family is worried about you. I see that you're upset and I understand how scary this must be. We only want to help you feel better."

"Where's my husband?" *If this place was so safe, where was Joshua? Had they arrested him in order to get to me?*

"It's 5 a.m. Your husband and father have been here every day and I'm sure they will be here soon, don't worry." Her voice was soft, maternal. I could see why she had this job. She was either an excellent nurse or an even better spy. But I decided to believe her at least until I could speak to Joshua.

There was another morning around that time when I woke up to birds singing. As I lay there in that mostly quiet room, a tidal wave of revolting memories started crashing into me. When I thought of Dr. Death, Penterhaus's stupid, yellow-toothed mug appeared, and then, *No, no, no, no, no, no—my job!* I recalled the last couple of days at work when I was feeling invigorated, useful. I was deciphering important messages. But then I remembered hiding under my desk as Emily was looking at me. That look on her face was worse than anything. There was pity mixed with, I don't know, disgust? And, oh, God, the piss! *Did I actually wet my pants?* At this, I began to cry. *I must be a popular topic around the water cooler these days. They must be having some good laughs about crazy, pathetic, disgusting Sunny. Maybe they came up with a new name for me, like "Insaney" or, less creatively, "Nut Job."* I was horrified with myself. My career was *over*. As these thoughts weighed down on me, I felt myself crumble. I wept silently until my tears dried up and my headache returned. All I could think about was the human waste I had become.

As I fluctuated between sleep and desperate, shame-filled moments of wakefulness, I heard some activity in the room.

"Sweetheart, it's okay." My dad was here.

"Daddy," I said, before breaking down again.

"Shhhh, I know, I know," he soothed. "Let me get you some tissues." He gently wiped my nose just as he had when I was a baby.

"Dad, I did something awful at work." I was speaking through my tearful hiccups. "They think I'm crazy. I'm so humiliated." *Did he know the details of my disgrace? Of what an embarrassing daughter I had become?*

"They don't matter. You were frightened at work, so Joshua came to get you. Don't worry about them, let's just focus on getting you back in shape."

"But I'm scared. They're still coming for me—I'm sure of it." I was still trembling, but hid my hands under the sheet.

"No one is coming for you, you're having mixed-up thoughts."

That conversation was interrupted by Dr. Bensen entering the room. I'd met him earlier during my stay and he checked back in regularly, asking me tons of questions and looking at me like I was a most intriguing specimen.

On this day, I noticed that he was quite handsome. He wore a white coat, and both his shoes and glasses looked expensive. He was slender and not especially tall. I couldn't have guessed his age, but he wasn't old. He seemed serious until he spoke, causing his face to become more animated and friendly.

"Hello, Sunny," he said with a smile while shaking my hand. He had gorgeous white teeth, I wondered how he kept them so white.

A weak hello was all I could muster as I wiped snot on my sleeve. I didn't belong in the presence of this elegant man. He greeted my dad before turning back to me.

"You seem much more alert today. How are you feeling?" He was looking right into my eyes, which caused me to turn away.

"Tired and depressed," I mumbled.

He looked at me empathetically. "I'm sorry, I know you've been through it. We're going to get to the bottom of this." He looked at his watch. "It's still early, so how about if you have some breakfast and then I'd like to come back and chat with you. Maybe in an hour, does that sound good?"

"Are you going to kill me?"

He was oddly nonplussed by my question. "No, I'm not. Nor is anyone else in this hospital. But I can't vouch for the food," he added with a grin.

I eyed him suspiciously. He didn't seem like a killer. "Yeah, okay."

He set up a time to speak with my dad later that day and turned back to me. "I'll see you shortly, young lady," he said before flashing that dazzling smile.

Once Dr. Bensen left, shame again encircled me and the tears started to flow. My dad held me for a while as I wept. He stroked my hair and told me I would be okay. I wanted to believe him. But I also felt that he simply didn't understand. He didn't know they were after me. He didn't hear the dire warnings from my comrades in the cemetery. And there were voices telling me I was stupid and disgusting. My mind was like a circus of chaos—my fears and desires swirled around madly, trying to make sense of the senseless.

The handsome doctor was right about the hospital food. No one told them I was nearly vegan and they brought in a tray containing runny scrambled eggs, sausage, buttered toast, and coffee. The smell alone was nauseating. My dad removed the offending items, leaving the coffee and toast—on which I only nibbled. The coffee was undrinkable. *Was it that ersatz crap from the camps?*

Dr. Bensen returned in less than an hour. My dad kissed me and said he'd see me later. I didn't want him to leave and pleaded with him to stay, desperately grasping his hands.

"Sunny, I'll be back in a couple of hours. You're safe here. I love you." Then he kissed my hand before removing its grasp on his arm. And he was gone.

The doctor moved one of the ugly vinyl chairs so that it was facing me, and took a seat. "So, how was breakfast?"

"Putrid."

He smiled. "I'm sorry. But I can assure you our medical skills outweigh our culinary ones." He opened a notepad and set it on his lap. "I've met with you a couple of times and I'm glad to see that the medications are starting to work. Do you remember speaking with me?"

"Kind of. I remember a lot of questions and thinking you might want me dead like the others."

"Yes, we spoke about that. But today your speech is making far more sense and you seem less agitated. I think it would be a good time for me to learn more about you, is that okay? Just answer as best you can, no pressure."

I shrugged.

"Can you tell me a little bit about your childhood, what was it like growing up?"

I told him about my grandparents, how they mostly raised me after my mom died.

"How old were you when she died?"

"Eight." I began picking a scab off my elbow. Thinking about my mom always had this effect on me.

"How did she die?"

"A car accident."

"That must have been terribly sad for you. What was your mom like?"

"She was fun, always playing with me and buying me stuff. But she was…" I couldn't think of the word. "She was unpredictable, her presence was, I don't know…fleeting."

"What do you mean?"

"Sometimes she was there, reading me stories and doing art projects with me. And other times, she was sad and just stayed in her room. I always seemed to be missing her."

"What was your dad doing when she was sad?"

"He would try to talk to her. They fought a lot, I could hear them even though my dad tried to whisper. But he was always upsetting her. When it got really bad, my dad took her away."

"Where to?"

"To a hospital, I think. To get better."

"Who took care of you when she was gone?"

"My grandparents, Baba and Papa." I couldn't help it, I started to cry. The kind doctor handed me a tissue.

"Sounds like your grandparents were wonderful people."

I nodded.

"Can you tell me more about what's been going on over the past six months? When did you start feeling sad or afraid?"

"After Baba and Papa died, one right after the other."

He expressed more sympathy. I must've looked utterly pathetic. He asked me tons of questions about my mood, sleep, appetite, etc. while taking notes. He was trying to determine if I was depressed after losing my favorite people on earth—how could I not be? Then he asked me about *them*—the ones who wanted me dead.

"When did you begin believing that Nazis were trying to kill you?"

"The spirits gave me the information. They wanted to warn me."

"When we chatted a few days ago, you mentioned spirits from the Jewish cemetery. Is this what you mean?"

"Yes, it's the survivors, they wanted to warn me, they…" *Shut up, you stupid bitch!*

"Sunny? Did you just hear something that I didn't?"

I nodded my head. *Shut the fuck up!*

"Are they frightening you?"

I nodded again. I couldn't talk about the voices or the Nazis anymore, I was terrified. They were chanting urgently: *Shut up, bitch. Shut up, bitch. Shut up, bitch. Shut up, bitch. Shut up, bitch.*

The doctor was looking at me strangely. I must have been some sight—one crazy, deranged girl. "Sunny, are you aware that it's 2002? There are no Nazis anymore."

"I know the year, but they came back for me. Because I'm bad."

"Sometimes when people go through trauma, like losing your grandparents, it can trigger other things in the mind. Like hearing voices others don't hear and experiencing false beliefs. This is called psychosis. Do you think it's possible that your beliefs about the Nazis might not actually be real?"

"I…I don't know. Maybe. But…" *Shut the fuck up!* I curled up in a ball and rocked back and forth. The circus was in full force.

"I'm so sorry you're going through this, Sunny. I want to help you clear your thoughts. We have you on Haldol, which is an antipsychotic medicine. I spoke to you about this earlier and you agreed to take it, do you remember?"

I nodded my head.

"It's already helping. And we've continued with the same dose of Prozac you were taking before."

"Is it poison?" I wanted to believe him, but I wasn't fully convinced.

"No, Sunny. It's medicine, it will help you." *Bullshit. Stupid bitch.* "I know you're scared and the voices are harassing you, it will help with that too. I'd like you to stay in the hospital for up to fourteen days. Do you remember me speaking to you about this?"

"Not really." I was appalled by the prospect of being there so long.

"Your seventy-two-hour stay was extended to fourteen days because it's critical for your health and safety. The paperwork is over there," he added, gesturing to a small table in the corner.

"Fourteen days is too long! Chester needs me." *Crazy bitch. Crazy bitch.*

"Well, you've already been here five days, and you may not need to stay for a full two weeks. And Joshua has mentioned that Chester is just fine. I'm going to ask you to trust me."

How have I been here five days already? I was so confused. I really wanted to trust him. And at this point, I would do anything to make them stop their ceaseless torment.

"Can you really make them stop?"

"The voices?"

I nodded.

"Yes. It will take more time, since the medication needs to build up. But antipsychotics are very effective in reducing or eliminating hallucinations."

This sounded hopeful. "Alright." *Stupid gullible bitch. You're dead.*

The doctor left after shaking my hand warmly, as if I wasn't worthless. Within minutes, a young nurse with acne came in and gave me my medicine. Maybe it was the realization of how long I'd be held there or the vitriolic voices telling me the medicine would kill me, but those pills stuck in my throat like dry chicken, causing me to throw up on my bed. But the nurse gave me another dose, which I kept down as she watched. As the voices grew softer and I felt myself recede into the background, I mumbled, "I shut my eyes and all the world drops dead."[1] I barely heard the nurse leave as I

---

[1] From *Mad Girl's Love Song* by Sylvia Plath.

collapsed into sleep—my only respite from the inferno my life had become.

In the days that followed, my thoughts slowed down and were no longer strangling my mind. I started to notice different things, like the near-constant talking and sometimes yelling from outside my room. I also became aware of the pain in my body. I had continuous headaches and could barely turn my neck. And I was always desperately thirsty. The nurses encouraged me to go for a walk outside my room, which did not interest me since I was still worried that *they* were out there. On one occasion, I gave in and poked my head out the door only to see a young, skinny patient with a black mohawk rapidly pacing back and forth down the hall while talking to himself. The guy, who couldn't have been more than twenty, was covered in tattoos—including on his neck and forehead. He stopped in his tracks and looked at me with crazed eyes. That was more than enough. I immediately shut the door and got back in bed.

As my jumbled thoughts came more into focus, I began remembering things, like the person I used to be. The girl who laughed and danced, and went to work every day. The girl with dreams and passions. The girl with a beautiful home and a loving husband. Those thoughts hurt more than the nightmares and vituperation of my enemies. For they were fraught with disillusionment about the person I thought I was, and the future I had imagined. And even though my mind was becoming less hazy, I knew something wasn't right in that hospital. I knew I was still in danger. Where was Joshua? I needed to get out of there.

Chapter 21 ❧ Peter

After leaving Sunny at the hospital on that first horrible night, I headed back home. I didn't realize the amount of weight I was carrying until I came through my front door and it all poured out. It was very late, but Linda came downstairs and gently guided me to the sofa. She made some chamomile tea and brought each of us a cup before sitting down next to me. I'd felt like such an emotional disaster around my wife lately, but I couldn't contain myself—Linda held me as I cried yet again. Over the years, I had done my best to suppress the pain I went through with Gracie, but I could see now that this was no longer an option. Sunny's psychological state had reopened old wounds—wounds that were deeper than I had realized. That night, I filled in Linda on Sunny's situation, but also shared more about Gracie than I ever had before. The ghost she'd been living with was finally resurfacing, but she handled it well.

"I knew Gracie was messed up, but I had no idea," she said with a mix of concern and astonishment. "I always wondered why you never talked about her. Now I understand."

"It was a horrible time, I just wanted to forget it. But life doesn't work that way, everything just seems to come right back up." I held my throat as I said this, as if I could push the memories back down. Then I told her more about how Gracie was unable to care for Sunny.

About the time she left her at school until the place closed. And the time she lost her in a department store during one of her shopping sprees.

"Oh my God, Peter," she said as a tear ran down her cheek.

Linda was such a gift, the polar opposite of Gracie. She didn't care about superficialities like designer clothes and expensive jewelry. She barely wore any makeup and had crow's feet in the corners of her eyes. But she was inexplicably beautiful in such a different way. She was profoundly kind and emotionally solid. I knew I could always lean on her one-hundred-pound frame. I silently wiped her tear.

"This makes me understand Sunny more—why she's so anxious and oversensitive. And why she's always pushed me away. Seems like a defense mechanism—a way to save herself from being hurt by another mother figure." She was contemplating this idea as she sipped her tea.

"Wow, I never thought of it like that."

"Losing a mother at such a young age is a tragedy I can't even fathom. And now, to lose Babcia—her second mother." She shook her head as she exhaled. "I just can't imagine how that would be for Maddy and Spencer." She wiped away another tear.

"I know. The children are the reason I take care of myself, why I go to the gym and take those damned fish oil pills you give me."

Linda smiled wistfully. "I've seen what losing Gracie—and now also her grandparents—has done to Sunny. I can't let that happen again."

She reached up and touched my hair, running her fingers through the back of it. A tender gesture that comforted me and, on a better day, would have made me amorous.

"The hell you went through being married to her, it's just awful, Peter. And now, with Sunny's psychological issues. I just keep thinking of what it would be like if Spencer or Maddy inherited such an illness. I'm so very sorry, my love." Her empathy astounded me.

As my eyelids became heavy, Linda held my hand and led me to our bed where I fell into an exhausted, but fitful sleep.

I awoke the next morning with a throbbing dehydration headache. My body felt heavy and my neck had a kink in it. But I managed to take a migraine pill, shower, and have some coffee. Then I cleared my work schedule for the next few days and headed back to the hospital. I'm not sure how I missed it before, but the second I walked through the hospital door, I breathed in the all-too-familiar scent from so many years before. That unmistakable smell of sickness and despair mixed with cleaning products that caused a bit of my coffee to come back up. But I took a deep breath and marched forward.

During her first several days in the hospital, Sunny was like a wild animal. She was mistrustful of everyone, especially the staff—whom she regularly insulted. In some ways, she reminded me of a combat soldier, constantly looking over her shoulder and startling at the slightest noise. There was one particularly upsetting occasion when I found her hiding under the bed. And she often froze as if hearing something no one else could. I wondered what the voices were saying to punish my innocent girl.

Her hair was both greasy and frizzy, and her eyes lacked the familiar humanness that was Sunny. Perhaps worst of all, she made no sense. Her sentences were strung together in meaningless, and often chilling, ways. The way she resembled Gracie during her times of madness was jarring enough. But even Gracie was able to organize her words. After Dr. Bensen attended a hearing requesting that Sunny's seventy-two-hour hold be extended to fourteen days, Joshua and I both breathed a sigh a relief. She *needed* to be there.

One morning, on Sunny's fifth or sixth day in the hospital, I arrived early and read the newspaper while she slept. I recall how angelic she looked as she slept soundly on her back, with her beautiful locks fanned out across the pillow and her arms folded over her chest. I was taken aback by her corpse-like positioning, particularly since she looked so much like her mother at that moment. I sat with her for about an hour when she began to stir. It was so much easier to watch her sleep, to see her at peace. She awoke with only a second of blissful ignorance, before reality showed itself. Sunny was immediately drowning in shame over her behavior at work. As a father, it was both heartbreaking and frustrating to watch—I didn't know what to say to help her. Perhaps there was nothing I could say at that moment. I tried to comfort my daughter as best I could before leaving her with Dr. Bensen.

I liked Dr. Bensen and felt Sunny was in good hands with him. Earlier during her stay, I met with him for an appointment I dreaded, but knew was necessary. I took the stairs down to his office, which was on the third floor. Entering Dr. Bensen's office was like stepping into a different universe from the stifling hospital environment. The large office contained a wooden desk with a worn leather couch opposite it. Most of the floor was covered with an exquisite oriental rug with geometric patterns in burgundy, blue and beige. It reminded me of the rug in my home office. There was an open window above the desk that mostly overlooked a parking lot, but at least there was one palm tree in the distance. The hospital smell was replaced with fresh air mixed with the masculine scent of leather. Bookshelves dominated three of the walls and were filled with books down to the last millimeter. Dr. Bensen was clearly a well-read guy who appeared to be highly precise. His numerous books were neatly arranged—not a single one seemed out of place. The wall without books contained multiple framed degrees, awards, and certificates—including a medical degree from Yale. Sunny would call this an ego wall. There were also several African masks hung above the diplomas and there was a crystal vase on the desk holding a fresh bouquet of tulips. Dr. Bensen exuded a rare mix of competence, expertise, and refinement. He gestured me toward the couch and asked if I would like something to drink, which I declined.

He pulled his chair in front of the desk so he was facing me. He had a yellow pad in his lap. "How are you doing?" His brown eyes peered into me.

I sighed heavily as I sat there, slumped over. "Not so great."

"I know, I understand. The good news is that Sunny agreed to take Haldol, which is an antipsychotic. This will help with her delusions, disorganized thinking, and hallucinations," he said, pushing his glasses up a little. He crossed one of his legs and I noticed that his black socks had little pugs all over them, which endeared him to me that much more.

"Oh God," I said while rubbing my still aching temples.

"We will continue to evaluate her and see how she responds to the medication. I had a lengthy conversation with Joshua yesterday. I understand that much of her illness began after the death of her grandparents, right?" He took a pen out of his lab coat pocket.

"Yes, both of my parents recently died. She was extremely close to and protective of them. It has done a number on me and the rest of the family, but Sunny seems to be uniquely devastated by it."

"I agree. I'm terribly sorry for your loss, this must be incredibly difficult for you." He must've made this statement a million times in his career, yet it still conveyed sincerity.

"Thank you. It's been rough."

"Do you know why Sunny's delusions are so focused on Nazis?"

"Yes, my parents were both Holocaust survivors. We tried to keep the details of their experiences from Sunny as she was growing up, but she was a bright, curious child—not much got past her. And when she was older, she began learning about the Holocaust on her own; she has countless books about it. A lot like this," I added, looking around the room. "And she's a bookworm, so the books aren't just for show—she devours them."

He wrote furiously before stopping to look up. I noticed he was lefthanded. "Well, that certainly explains a lot. The other thing I'd like to speak with you about is Sunny's mother. What was her name?"

"Gracie." *Here we go.* Speaking of Gracie made my breath catch. I rubbed my sweaty palms on my pants. I realized one of my feet was shaking, which I immediately stopped.

"Was Gracie mentally ill?"

"Gracie was the poster child for mental illness. She was a trainwreck."

"What were her symptoms?"

"Oh, well, let's see. She'd be up all night doing her art and sometimes talking to people who weren't there. She would go shopping and easily spend $10,000 in one week on toys, clothes, jewelry and God knows what else. She was generally unable to care for Sunny. She'd arrive late to pick her up from school, or not arrive at all. She'd forget to feed and bathe her. It felt like Sunny was just a playmate for Gracie—her mothering skills were minimal. Things were the worst when Gracie was depressed. She wouldn't get out of bed for days or weeks at a time, barely ate anything, and wanted to kill herself. This was when I drove her to the hospital."

"Yes, Sunny mentioned that her mother was often hospitalized. Do you know her diagnoses?"

"Well, she had a bunch of them, they were pretty inept with Gracie—giving her one diagnosis after another. It drove me nuts. Some doctors thought she was schizophrenic, others thought she was bipolar. And there were additional diagnoses too. It seemed like each time she was hospitalized, they simply rebranded her with the latest label in her chart."

"I'm sorry to hear that. Unfortunately, psychiatric diagnoses often follow patients, which is why we need to be careful when it comes to evaluation. Gracie was your wife, so *you* are the expert on her more than anyone. Which diagnoses do you feel were the most accurate?"

"Based on my reading, I believe bipolar fits her best. When she took her lithium, she definitely calmed down—but I would not say she was ever normal. And getting her to actually take her medication was a constant battle."

"That's helpful, thank you. Is there anyone else in Sunny's family with mental illness?"

I let out a big sigh and readjusted my sore back. "Oh yes, Gracie's mother is batshit crazy. Sorry, I mean, she's really sick. Gracie didn't really like talking about her and they had lost contact over the years. But she told me her mother could never hold down a job and would disappear for weeks at a time. She had bizarre delusions, like that the neighborhood crows were spying on her and sending data to the government. Gracie said she often yelled at the crows in front of the neighbors, which was mortifying. And there was a full year when she apparently left home and lived on the streets, leaving Gracie and her father distraught. He divorced her around that time.

"Oh, and she told me about one occasion when her mother thought someone was after her. She packed up her car with as much stuff from the house as she could, put Gracie in the back seat, and left town. Gracie's father was frantic—he and the police were searching everywhere. After a week or so, they found Gracie—who couldn't have been more than five, sitting alone in a bus station. Her mother dumped her there, thinking it would be safer. This memory really tormented Gracie. Apparently, she hadn't been fed for a few days when they found her and was covered in bug bites. And the poor thing was convinced that her mother was dead. I don't think Gracie saw much of her mother after that."

"Are Gracie's parents still alive?"

"Her father died of a heart attack when Gracie was in her 20s. But, as of the time of Gracie's death, her mom was alive and well—although, not actually *well*—and living in Las Vegas. She's very sick. But I don't know her diagnosis."

Dr. Bensen finished up a few more notes and set down his pen. "It does seem that there are some genetic factors playing a role here. Have you talked to Sunny about her mother?"

I stared out the window for a moment before looking back at him. Lately, I had been feeling terribly ashamed of my reticence when it came to Gracie. Hadn't I learned anything from living with my parents? Suppressing painful memories was not effective for anyone. And Sunny deserved better. "Honestly, not as much as I should have. I guess I tried to bury it and spare both myself and Sunny from the details."

"I understand your reasoning. But when children don't understand a situation, they will often fill in the blanks on their own. I think going to family counseling would be of great benefit to both of you once Sunny is stabilized."

"Yes, I agree."

"Has Sunny asked about the details of her mother's death?"

"Oddly enough, no." I rubbed at my temples as I felt the familiar weight of Gracie pulling me down.

"I can see how painful it is for you to talk about Gracie. Is it possible that Sunny hasn't asked because she doesn't want to hurt you?"

Okay, that was a punch in the gut. Was my weakness so obvious that my own daughter couldn't talk to me? "Yeah, that's possible." I lowered my head. I could feel my pits sweating as shame swirled around me.

"I'm not here to judge you, Mr. Zielinski. I understand your motives, I'm just trying to learn more about what happened. It seems like you haven't talked about it much, but you can practice on me. Can you tell me what happened to Gracie?"

Oh God, I so didn't want to go there. I rubbed my temples some more and took a deep breath. Then I told this man whom I barely knew what happened on the worst day of my life. By the time I finished, I was shaking and I felt a knot in my throat. Dr. Bensen said something sympathetic, which I barely heard, and offered me some water. But I just wanted to get the hell out of there. He could tell I was ready to leave, but he wasn't done with me. I came back to the present moment and tried to listen through the heavy brume that was enveloping me.

"There's a terrific psychologist I'd like you to contact. She does both family and individual counseling. I've known her for years. She specializes in psychotic disorders, depression, and grieving."

He placed a card in my clammy hand. He inspired confidence and I was grateful for someone to lean on. "Thank you, doctor. I'm just so terrified for my daughter."

"I know. And I can see that you're a devoted father. There have been great improvements in psychiatric medications over the years. Sunny is in good hands here and we will do our best to assess her and find an accurate diagnosis. Given how sick she's been, it would likely be in her best interest to stay in the hospital for a couple of weeks. Joshua is in agreement. How does it sound to you?"

"Oh, I know it needs to be done, but she'll hate it." I imagined having to fight with Sunny about staying in the hospital for even a couple of days and was grateful Dr. Bensen was taking the lead.

"She might, but she's also suffering a great deal. Once she starts to experience some relief from the voices, she may decide it's not so bad here. I also wanted to mention that, since this is her first psychotic episode, we are in a good position to reduce the likelihood of additional ones. It's often the case that the more psychotic episodes a patient has, the worse the prognosis. This being said, there is no cure for bipolar disorder or psychotic disorders such as schizophrenia. But we can manage their symptoms in such a way that the patient can still enjoy a meaningful, productive life. Sunny is an intelligent woman with a strong support system, which will certainly work in her favor."

"What do you think is wrong with her, doctor?"

"I'd like to do some additional assessments before I come to a conclusion."

"Are you leaning toward schizophrenia?"

"Based on what I know thus far, it does seem to fit. But the jury is still out."

So, there it was. Schiz-o-phren-i-a. Five sickening syllables with the potential to destroy my little girl. I felt completely defeated as I left Dr. Bensen's office.

I went to the bathroom and splashed water on my face before heading back to Sunny's room. When I entered, she was lying in bed with her eyes closed and Joshua was sitting in a chair close to her as he gently rubbed her head. I felt like an intruder, seeing them in this private moment. I also felt choked up since it was abundantly clear how much he loved her. I'd always cared for Joshua, but I had no idea of the degree of his depth and loyalty. He was a good man and I loved him like a son.

I didn't want to disturb Sunny, so I gestured for Joshua to go out in the hall. As we stood there, I noticed that he was a bit of a wreck. He hadn't shaved and his eyes were red and puffy. I gave him a brief hug.

"Any word from the doctor?" he asked me.

"I was just with him, he's still doing his assessments. He's a good guy, I really like him."

"I hope so. I'm scared, Peter. I've never seen anyone like this." He was close to tears.

"I know."

"Did the doctor say what's wrong with her?"

Should I say it? Or should I allow my distraught son-in-law a few more hours of innocence before the final blow? "No, he doesn't know yet."

And with that, we said goodbye and walked in different directions—each of us agonizing over what our next torment might be.

Chapter 22 ❧ Sunny

I loathed being in the hospital. I had always been a private person, but in this place, I lay helplessly exposed in my ugly nakedness—surrounded by glass walls and relentless eyes. Even the confines of my mind could not escape the constant intrusions. And, along with the endless questions, there were medical tests that revealed the inner workings of my brain and heart. I understood the need to rule out tumors, epilepsy, and so many other things—but was there nothing I could keep for myself? And I was sick as hell of being poked and prodded.

On the other hand, the doctor was right, the medication eventually started clearing my thoughts. Those malicious voices that had taunted me every day for weeks had finally backed down. I'd always lacked confidence; so, when *they* reaffirmed my long-held self-perception of worthlessness, my psyche buckled in on me. How is a fragile ego supposed to bear being called a stupid bitch every hour of every day? I was becoming so accustomed to those voices that, when they finally ceased, I remained vigilant. I thought they were toying with me—staying quiet as they plotted their next attack. But when they continued to stand down for hours at a time, I remembered the privilege of having my mind to myself. It was a monumental relief when that aspect of my living nightmare finally quelled. It made me wonder if there might be a speck of belief somewhere within me that I wasn't entirely useless, that I deserved some peace.

Although the demonic chorus was on intermission, my sense of being hunted had not dissipated. To my mind, the voices were adversarial, but the cemetery spirits were not. Rather, they were benevolent ancestors with devastating premonitions. How could I simply disregard them? Part of my brain knew it was totally illogical that Nazis were after me in the 21st century in San Diego, California. But the other part of my brain was not concerned with logic and still believed I was in grave danger. There was this ineffable sense that everyone who didn't believe—the doctors, my family, my coworkers—was unenlightened. That this righteous presence seeking to protect me was beyond their ability to comprehend. I knew they would never get it and their persistent doubts further cemented this conviction. So, I stopped talking about the warnings and, when pressed, I told people what they wanted to hear.

I knew my life was still at risk and I was losing confidence that the hospital was a safe place. I had stayed still too long. Eventually the SS would come for me and there would be no place to hide. They would murder me right here in my hospital bed. *I needed to get out of here.* Once I was within the comfortable confines of my home with both Joshua and Chester close by, I would plan my next steps.

I thought I had been in the hospital for weeks and was floored when Dr. Bensen told me it had only been eight days—how could that be? But the next thing he told me was infinitely worse. I had just finished picking at my dinner when he showed up. Both my dad and Joshua had left for a few hours.

"Still enjoying the food, I see?" he said as he took a seat to my left. He seemed more serious than usual, which made me nervous. He crossed his legs and looked at me in his intense way.

"Still as nasty as ever." I moved the mostly uneaten tray to the side and pushed my hair out of my face. I wished I'd put on some makeup that morning.

He gave only a slight smile. "I've spoken at length with your husband and father, and have finished my assessments."

"Okay, so, what's the damage?"

"That's not a word I would use, Sunny," he said, pushing up his glasses. "I believe, considering your symptom presentation, such as the voices and your confused thinking, your family history of mental illness, your response to the medication, and your age, that we are looking at schizophrenia."

This could *not* be what he just said, *it just couldn't.* I was horrified. I had always been a somatic person—forever worried about receiving a grim diagnosis. Once, when I had a mole removed, I was certain the doctor was going to tell me I was dying of melanoma. Though Dr. Bensen's proposed diagnosis took me by surprise, it too felt like a death sentence. I didn't believe him; there was no way I was schizophrenic. It was absurd.

"Bullshit." I sat up in the bed and glared at him.

"I know it's a tough thing to hear, but there are treatments that will greatly help you. I know—"

"Bullshit!" I repeated, more loudly. I wanted to sound angry, offended by his impertinence. But, yet again, my emotions let me down and I began to cry. He handed me a hanky I was afraid to use. I was trying to speak through my tears, often losing my breath. "This can't…I can't be *that*." *I couldn't even say it.* "I have plans. I went to…to college." I finally used the hanky to wipe my eyes. "I'm magna…cum laude, you know. I'm going to be a …a publish…er. And Joshua…" That was it, I had lost my words, I was now sobbing.

He gently patted my back as he waited for me to calm down. I wished he would stop looking at me. "Sunny, this diagnosis has nothing to do with intelligence or achievement. You likely inherited a disposition for it, which is certainly not your fault. But please understand, you are very young and you've only just gotten sick. This means your prognosis is good. We will continue to watch your medications, making sure you have the right type and dose for your symptoms. I'm referring you to a psychologist I'd like you to start seeing when you go home. You have a team of people here to support you. We all want to alleviate your suffering."

As I felt myself sinking into a bottomless chasm, I heard *them*, in the distance, just once: *Crazy stupid bitch.* "I want to go home."

The doctor talked to me a little longer about treatment and other things that did not register. He wanted me to stay several more days in the hospital, until the following Monday. I wasn't pleased with this; I still didn't feel safe and wanted out *now*. Then he told me he'd be back later to discuss next steps. He gave me another fatherly pat on the back and left. He forgot his hanky, which I immediately used to blow my nose. So, either everyone *thought I was crazy* or I actually *was crazy*—which one was worse, I did not know.

Once I'd finished crying, I sat in bed and ruminated about my future—or what there was of it. I thought about the homeless woman near my office—the woman for whom I'd felt such compassion. She sat there each day surrounded by her own filth. She smelled of urine and cigarettes. She held a sign that said, "Homeless mother, please help." I never saw her with any children. Maybe she didn't have any, but knew the words would elicit sympathy. It didn't matter. Her existence seemed to be one of unrelenting misery.

The most striking thing about that woman was the blankness in her eyes. She never made eye contact with me, only mumbled a barely audible thank you when I gave her food or money. Even the effort of looking at another person was too much for her. Like Thorndike's cats, learned helplessness had set in and she'd given up on trying to change her predicament. In this relationship, *I* was the privileged one—the woman with the college education, the great job, and the doting husband. *I* was the one doing a good deed by handing her my pocket change. I was meant to be pitying *her*. This had been my unstated social position in this exchange.

Until now.

If Dr. Bensen was right, someday—maybe even soon, I would be just like her: alone, hungry, terrified, and vacant. And, to the bulk of passersby, invisible. I would be chronically unemployed and broke. Joshua and the rest of my family would abandon me. I would be childless, my womb barren. Maybe I'd become a drug addict. I would be forever abused by forces beyond my control until ultimately my eyes would no longer focus and my body would rot from the inside out. This would be my destiny.

I was lost in my dire prophesizing when I heard the door open. It was Joshua carrying magazines and a bouquet of red daffodils in a vase. I'd been given a lot of flowers over the years, but *this* reason really took the cake. He didn't notice my crestfallen state, which said a lot about what he'd become used to. I could barely speak as *that word* swirled around in my head like a tornado. It was all I could think of. Yet, I could not tell Joshua—I just couldn't say it. And I didn't believe it anyway, so why upset him further? So, instead, I pretended to watch TV with him for a couple of hours, and finally feigned sleep. I wanted to be alone; keeping the secret was draining. I felt him kiss my forehead before he tiptoed out the door.

I woke the next morning consumed with the horror of my diagnosis and the days to come. Shortly after 9 a.m., my dad showed up. He looked a little flushed. He must've run up the stairs; that's something he and I had in common. He was wearing jeans and a dark gray Nike hoodie that matched the dark circles under his eyes. His face was stubbly, but he was freshly showered and smelled good. He greeted me with a kiss on the head and sat down next to me. I tried to sound friendly, but I couldn't hide my inner turmoil.

"Are you okay? You look a little off."

"You mean beyond being a mental patient?"

He sighed. His breath smelled like coffee. "Have you spoken anymore with Dr. Bensen?"

"Unfortunately, yes. Dad, he thinks I'm *schizophrenic*." I wanted to cry some more, but I was all dried up. So, I just looked at him dejectedly. "Can you even believe that?"

"I don't know, Sunny. You've been really sick. On top of your beliefs about people trying to kill you, you haven't been taking care of yourself. You stopped eating and are bone thin. You were in another world—no one could reach you. And you threatened to kill yourself. So, yes, I think there is some weight to what the doctor is saying."

Oh great, not him too. "But I feel a lot better now, the medicine is working. I think I just lost it because of Baba and Papa. I was really depressed," I said, trying to sound convincing. He looked at me with such overbearing sadness in that moment. He couldn't fix me and he knew it. "And I wasn't trying to kill myself."

"Sunny, what happened with you is not a regular way to grieve. This is… something else. And it requires treatment so you can get back to yourself again. I will do everything in my power to help you get there."

"But, Dad, I don't *want* to be schizophrenic! This is the worst thing I could imagine and I refuse to believe it!" A few lingering tears leaked from my desiccated eyes.

"Trust me, I don't want you to be either, honey." He was holding my right hand in both of his. His eyes were glossy and he looked suddenly older. "But we'll get through it together, as a family."

"I want to go home, but he won't let me leave until Monday!"

"That's only a few more days, honey. But once he discharges you, you need to be *very* diligent about his treatment recommendations at home."

"I know that and I will. I promise." I was ready to beg.

My dad left shortly thereafter. Joshua stopped in at lunchtime, bringing me a Caprese sandwich and a latte. He looked spent, with unwashed hair and wrinkly clothes. He kissed me on the lips and I noticed his breath was stale. My poor Joshua, he wasn't handling this well.

"Hi, honey," he said, handing me the sandwich and taking a seat next to me. He was sipping from coffee in a to-go cup.

"Hi. Thank you so much." I glanced in the bag, but I wasn't hungry. "I'll eat it later."

"Okay, as long as you actually *do* eat it." He gave me his best stern expression.

"I will, it smells delicious."

"How are you feeling today?"

"Good. I'm going home Monday."

He was about to take another sip of coffee when he froze halfway. "What do you mean?"

"Just what I said, Dr. Bensen is discharging me this Monday."

"Are you ready to come home, Sunny? I mean, you were pretty far gone and I—"

I interrupted. "You don't want me to come home?" Tears began stinging my eyes.

"No, no, no, honey, that's not it. I'm just worried about you. As you know, work is insane, I mean, out of control right now. I've already taken a week off at the worst possible time. I can't be home to watch you."

"First of all, you can say 'insane,' geez. Let's not alter our vocabulary because of this. And second, 'watch me?' I'm not a baby, Joshua." I managed not to cry, but I could feel a slight shakiness in my voice. I was sitting straight up in the bed doing my best to look as strong as a crazed woman in a hospital gown possibly could.

"Of course, I know that. You've been sick and I would worry about you just the same if you had a medical condition. I'm concerned about your health. Please don't be upset, I love you so very much." He stood up so that he was standing as close as he could to me and gently ran one hand through my hair. Then he held my hand. It was too much, more tears appeared, which he immediately wiped away. "Please don't cry, Sunny. We'll get through this, I promise."

Good luck with that promise. "Okay." I wiped my nose with my arm and he handed me a tissue from the nightstand.

"Skootch over," he said, nudging my shoulder. He climbed onto the bed next to me and I rested my head on his shoulder while we watched reruns of *The King of Queens*. It would have been a lovely moment if not for, well, everything.

A while later, he looked at his watch. "Oh shoot, I need to go speak with Dr. Bensen. Will you be okay for a while? I can come back afterward."

"That's okay, I'm really tired and you look like you are too."

"Gee, thanks!" he said with feigned indignation.

"You know what I mean." I didn't have the energy for playful conversation. I wanted to be alone; keeping information from Joshua felt awful. I was also worried about both him and Chester. "Please go home straight afterward and take care of my baby. I'm sure he's lonely as hell. And I know you're behind at work and the condo is probably a mess. So come back on Sunday, I'll be fine."

"But are you sure I can't bring you some food? What will you eat tomorrow?"

"It's okay, my dad brings me a bag of food every time he visits—he's trying to fatten me up."

He gave me a little smile. "Okay, I'll head home after my appointment. I'll give Chester extra cuddles for you and will call you tomorrow. I love you, Sunny." He kissed my cheek and the top of my head.

"Back at ya." After he left, I tried to eat the sandwich, but mostly picked at it, only eating the bread. Joshua's visit left me feeling worse, if that was even possible. It seemed he didn't want me home. How much more could my heart handle? I still felt desperately frightened about being in the hospital. I was wide awake for hours that evening, contemplating every potential catastrophe that awaited me. I was restless and laden with anxiety. I tried everything to fall asleep, even counting the ceiling tiles. Eventually, a merciful nurse saw my agony and gave me a sleeping pill. If only I could get more of those pills, I could muddle my way through life in a semiconscious state at least until *they* finally left me alone.

I spent Saturday reading *Angela's Ashes* for the third time. I'd had to beg my father to bring it, since he thought it would depress me. What a laugh, as if a book could make me feel worse about my predicament. Joshua called on Saturday afternoon and my dad brought me pizza at dinnertime—which made the nurses jealous. Spencer had a soccer game, so he didn't stay long, which was fine. The hospital banter was getting old. I fell asleep in the middle of the night with the book on my chest.

I woke up late the next morning. Although my head was groggy, it was nice to sleep deeply, without dreams. I obediently took my medicine and was still drinking my coffee when Dr. Bensen showed up. He was relatively informal, wearing Levi's and a light blue cashmere sweater under his white coat. When he sat down, I noticed his white Air Jordan shoes. He was hipper than I thought.

"Good afternoon, how are you doing?"

"Same as last time you asked."

He responded with his psychiatry textbook expressions of empathy, which always began with, "I know this is hard," or something along those lines. Then he opened his legal pad and asked me another fifty-plus questions. He wanted to know about the voices. I told them they had stopped, which was 98% true. He asked me about visions, which thankfully, I hadn't had in days. And he asked me a lot of strange questions, mostly about my tormentors: Did I still think they or anyone else was taking special notice of me or trying to hurt me? Did I see messages in songs, signs or other people's clothing? Did I think I had special powers? Did I believe thoughts had been put into or taken out of my head? Did I believe someone had tried to poison me or tamper with my food? Did I still feel unsafe? And on and on and on. I lied about many of these questions. I had to or I'd never get out of that godforsaken place.

He also asked me a lot about my mood and whether I wanted to hurt myself. I said "no" to these questions as well, although I wasn't really sure how I felt. If I *had* to kill myself, that's what I'd do. But of course, I'd rather not.

After maybe an hour of questions, he confirmed that he was prepared to discharge me on Monday *under certain conditions*. Then he got very serious. "Sunny, I need your assurance that you will take your mental health seriously. What happened to you these past months is not healthy or sustainable. You absolutely *must* take your medication as prescribed, *no matter what*. The more episodes you have like this one, the harder it will be to stay well. I will continue to be your psychiatrist and we will likely need to tweak your meds from time to time, so I want to see you every other week as an outpatient. But I also expect open communication in-between visits. And you need to go to therapy at least twice a week. Do you agree to take your medication, attend your outpatient visits, and keep open communication with me?"

I said I did, but honestly, I would've promised anything at that point.

He said he would get to work on discharging me the following afternoon, but that he also needed to speak to Joshua and my dad about the treatment plan. He shook my hand and said he'd check back in a bit later.

Once he left, I breathed out my relief. Maybe I *was* crazy and needed help, but at least I would no longer be stuck in this place like a trapped animal.

Chapter 23 ❧ Joshua

The past weeks had thrown my world into a reckless orbit, dropping me in a place I no longer recognized. It seemed like just yesterday that I was enjoying life as a newlywed and looking forward to sharing the future with my dream girl. Sunny and I had been so happy together. And our compatibility was obvious—she with her quiet brilliance, compassion, and reserved nature; and me with my boorish, unintellectual gregariousness. Each of our strengths offset the other's limitations. And we still had a surplus of chemistry. Cliché though it was, I pictured myself growing old with Sunny. Although I'd never been sure about kids, Sunny was the only person I could picture as the mother of my children.

If I couldn't have Sunny, I'd have no one.

Sunny had become a part of me. When she felt pain or fear, I hurt too. Of course, I sympathized with other family and friends, but this was different. It was such a deep connection that I both relied on it, yet also feared it. It was like an addiction. So, when she became depressed after the deaths of Babcia and Papa, I grieved along with her. When she lost sight of reality, I would have given my life to strangle the demons within her. Images of her cowering in the corner of her office, flailing in the back of the car, and throwing herself against the wall of the hospital bathroom ran through my mind like some perverse movie reel. While she was in the hospital, I developed an eye twitch and could barely concentrate on anything. I tried numbing myself with whiskey when I came home in the evenings, but it only made me more emotional and gave me a hangover. Even Chester was lost without Sunny, wandering from room to room looking for her or waiting by the door in the evenings. I held and petted him as much as I could, but I was no replacement for her. I never realized how easy my life had been until now, and I wasn't sure I had the emotional resilience to handle all of this. Sunny was the strong one, not me.

Friends and family tried to help, but I didn't want to deal with them. Elizabeth had become frantic when she hadn't heard back from Sunny for over a month. She dropped by the condo a few times when no one was home and left notes. When Sunny was first hospitalized, I was vegging on the couch one evening when my cell rang. I thought it might be the hospital, but it was Elizabeth. The two had been best friends for ages, so Elizabeth's concern came from a place of love. I knew Sunny wouldn't have wanted me to tell Elizabeth what was happening, but she was family. And besides, I needed someone to talk to. We chatted for around forty-five minutes, with Elizabeth clearly crying as I filled her in.

"Oh no, Joshua, this is terrible," she said, as her voice cracked. "You know, Sunny has always sort of functioned on a different plane than the rest of us. Sometimes I feel like an evil person because I'm not as affected by things as she is. I can't tell you how many cats and dogs she insisted on bringing home because she thought they were lost. When she couldn't find their homes and had no way to keep them, she always broke down. When my dad died, Sunny was at least as distraught as me. And she has always seen beauty in things I don't notice, like an unusual cloud or a tiny buttercup growing out of concrete. But she can be incredibly strange too, which is why I'm not totally surprised by all of this."

"I know. She's a force of nature that I'll never understand," I said as I stretched, trying to release the tension in my neck.

"There was one time during freshman year when I woke up in our dorm room and couldn't find her. Eventually someone tapped on the door, telling me Sunny was sleeping outside on the front porch. When I went downstairs, that's exactly where I found her—curled up in the fetal position, fast asleep in front of the door. When I woke her, she mumbled something about passing out after drinking too much. Joshua, I was with her all evening, she barely drank anything. It made no sense. But I pushed it out of my mind, thinking there must be a reasonable explanation. And finals week was always a disastrous time for Sunny. She would study day and night, barely stopping to go to the bathroom. She was always convinced she'd bombed every test or assignment, pacing the room and running herself ragged until grades were out. Yet, hers were always excellent, top of the class. I never could understand her lack of confidence and self-consciousness. Everywhere we went, she was coveted by guys and girls alike. No number of compliments could make her believe she was pretty or even, I don't know, worthy. It almost seemed pathological."

We talked like this for a while until Elizabeth said she wanted to visit Sunny at the hospital. But I told her this would not help, that Sunny was not in her right mind. And, once she was, she would be livid with me for allowing Elizabeth to see her that way. She finally conceded and said she'd wait until Sunny was back home.

Randy and some of my other friends also sensed that things weren't going well, as I'd missed several of our regular poker games. I didn't even watch the basketball championships with them for the first time in years. But I told them I was just overwhelmed at work, which they seemed to accept.

Then there was my mother. Ever since the wedding, she firmly believed that something was seriously wrong with Sunny. Sadly, she was right. My mom was incredibly perceptive and could read into my voice on the phone that I wasn't okay. Of course, I didn't tell her the details, only that Sunny was still having a tough time grieving the loss of her grandparents. She didn't believe me and wanted to fly to California to help. My mom was well-meaning, but her "help" would only have caused a precarious situation to completely crumble. She just had a way of saying the wrong things. Like telling me Sunny had a perfect life and that there was simply no reason for her to be unhappy. I was no expert on mental illness, but even I knew it was way more complex than this. I could shrug off a lot of my mom's words, but Sunny could not. Even on a good day, my mom could set her off like no one else. My mom and I argued back and forth about Sunny's situation during several phone calls until she really pissed me off and I finally told her to back off. She was hurt by this, which only added more guilt to my overflowing pile of emotional shit. Sunny just *had* to get better—this was no way for any of us to live. And I was hopelessly lost without her.

Over the past weeks I was starting to believe my wife was mentally ill, but I had foolishly hoped it was part of her mourning process. I think, deep down, I must've known that wasn't true. Surely, I couldn't be that stupid? When I went to see Sunny on Friday, she looked better and was making a lot more sense, but she still wasn't even close to being herself. She was distrustful, distracted, and, I don't know, just off. When she told me she would be leaving the hospital in three days, I didn't know whether it was true or merely part of her delusion. Then a disconcerting thought crossed my mind: is this how the rest of our lives would be, with me never knowing what was real and what was illusory? It was a chilling predicament.

I spoke with Dr. Bensen a few times, telling him everything I could think of about Sunny's recent behavior, as well as her personality traits since I'd known her. I also explained as much as I could about Sunny's relationship with her grandparents and the devastating impact losing them had on her. Peter must have filled him in on the rest. It was my meeting with Dr. Bensen on Friday that shook me to the core. Sunny was correct, she would be discharged on Monday. She was stabilized and no longer suicidal or gravely ill. While I missed her down to my bones, I was terrified about having Sunny home just now. I was behind at work and would be pulling 12-hour days, so I wouldn't be able to keep an eye on her. She adamantly refused to stay with Peter, only wanting to be back in her own home with me and Chester.

As I was still reeling from Sunny's discharge date, Dr. Bensen hit me with another bombshell: Sunny's diagnosis. I knew very little about schizophrenia, yet the word sent terror down my spine. I remember a distant relative on my mother's side, Aunt Fanny, who was rumored to have schizophrenia. I don't know the accuracy of the diagnosis, but the woman was as crazy as a loon. She believed the Catholics were taking over the world and sent postcards riddled with barely comprehensible threats and blasphemy to the Pope every week for twenty years. Apparently, she died in an institution somewhere back east. This was my introduction to schizophrenia.

Unlike Sunny, I wasn't an avid reader and certainly didn't watch the dramatic chick flicks she enjoyed. I had always been a guy's guy, instead preferring the superficiality of sports and action movies. So ignorant was I about schizophrenia, that I immediately thought Sunny had multiple personalities. I imagined her switching from sexy, flirty Sunny; to withdrawn, aloof Sunny; to Sunny as a three-year-old—the mere idea of this was horrifying.

I recall sitting on Dr. Bensen's leather couch stunned into silence after he gave me the diagnosis. I was speechless and he didn't try to fill the void. He patiently waited for me to say something.

"What does this mean, Doctor?" I said softly, after I finally caught my breath.

Dr. Bensen explained the disorder, noting that it was not the same as a dissociative disorder—which used to be called multiple personality disorder. He knew just what I had been thinking. Okay, so she wasn't Sybil, but the rest of it, *my God*. Hallucinations, delusions, flat affect, inappropriate behavior, social withdrawal, depression, paranoia, disordered speech, agitation, etc. There were so many perfectly awful descriptors and, what was infinitely worse,

Sunny fit *every single one of them.*

I was further disturbed when I learned that she had already been told the diagnosis, but didn't share it with me—even when I sat with her at length. I mentioned this to the doctor and he said it was common for patients receiving such a diagnosis to experience shame and disbelief. And he talked about the stigma—he sure was right about that. I guess her reticence to tell me made sense, but it still hurt. I was her husband, her soulmate—we needed to confide in one another. But I decided to forget about my ego and focus on my wife.

The doctor told me about Sunny's medication and therapy schedule. He thought the meds were working and I believed him. But how the hell could I make sure she continued to take them? And how would I get her to her various appointments multiple times a week? It was all so daunting. He suggested having someone check in on her each day until she was functioning better. He tried to make me feel better, telling me about pharmaceutical and treatment advances, Sunny's supportive family, etc. I appreciated the effort and maybe it provided me with a speck of belief that I couldn't yet detect; but nonetheless, I left that meeting like a battered zombie.

I was terrified of having Sunny home so soon. The timing couldn't be worse. My company was in the middle of an audit and we were desperately trying to seduce a huge client. I hadn't had my job very long and needed to be in top form—which I wasn't. So, I tried to appear competent, even though inside I was a massive clusterfuck. Fortunately, my coworkers covered for me and I was still getting things done, but my work situation was tenuous. I managed to get multiple days off while Sunny was hospitalized, as well as the Monday she was discharged. But, while I hated to leave her on the following Tuesday, we had clients visiting from out of the country. I would do my best to come home early, but any more than that would be pushing it. Peter and I took Dr. Bensen's advice and hired a home health aide. Damn would this piss her off, but I knew it was a good idea—the *only* idea. Fortunately, Peter offered to pay for it. I sure couldn't afford it.

Since Sunny would be home on Monday, I needed to clean the condo. I planned to clean on Saturday, but Dr. Bensen's meeting left me too hollowed out to do much of anything. I was glad Sunny sent me home until Sunday, I didn't want to face her. Instead, I went home, cried, and then stared blankly at the TV with Chester in my lap. I awoke with the same cloud that had been smothering me for days. My wife, my *schizophrenic* wife, was coming home. She would be in *my* care. *Holy shit.* I'd never been so stressed in my life. After two strong cups of coffee, I cleaned the house in a mindless frenzy—pushing down the mental shit spiraling endlessly in my head. First, I needed to deal with her books. I wasn't sure how she'd take it, but I put them away—likely in all of the wrong places. I cleaned the litter box and did three days' worth of crusty dishes. Then I vacuumed and did the laundry.

As I was putting away Sunny's socks and underwear in the dresser, I saw something shiny in the back corner. I stopped in my tracks. Beneath Sunny's silk lingerie was the extremely sharp Henckels meat cleaver we received for our wedding. *Holy shit! What the fuck was she thinking? Was this for protection or something else? And why didn't I notice it missing?* I set the knife aside and worked my way through each and every one of Sunny's drawers, as well as under the bed and between the mattresses.

Then I ventured into the master closet, which didn't look any different than usual. There was a black backpack high on the shelf, which I pulled down. It was heavy. Inside I found Sunny's running shoes, some black clothing, two bottles of water, a moldy baguette, and a rotten apple. There were two objects in a side pocket: a Christian bible (huh?) and a pocketknife. I felt something in a zipped side pocket and pulled out a pink satin bag. Inside, there were two diamond earrings, the ruby ring Sunny inherited from Babcia, a sapphire pendant, and the diamond Michele watch Peter gave Sunny for her birthday last summer. *Jesus. What was she planning?* Sunny treasured that jewelry—was she intending to sell it?

There was also a pile of about eight blue notebooks in the back of the closet which appeared to be brand new. I leafed through them and found that they were entirely blank until I got to the last one. The first two pages of that notebook made me gasp. They were completely covered with black writing. But, instead of Sunny's usual feminine script, the words were written in all in caps. This was the first paragraph:

THE HORRID GIRL WHORE HIDES INSIDE AND OUTSIDE. MANHUNT AND EXPERIMENTS. RABBITS. SEEN AND NOT SEEN. WE LEAN AND WAVER AT APPELL. WE DO NOT FALL. OR FALL FOR LIES. WARNINGS FIRED AND ALL WILL BE PUNISHED. THEY ARE HERE, THEY NEVER LEFT. GO LEFT FOR DEATH. OLD YOUNG WEAK COMMUNIST GAY JEW SELECTION: DEATH. NACHT UND NEBEL. WE ARE NOT SHEEP. GALLOWS AWAIT AND I RUN AND I RUN AND I RUN …

What the actual fuck? The second page was much the same. Plus, on both pages, she had drawn long, branch-like limbs twisting around the margins like some sort of deranged ivy. And there was a tiny ghoulish sketch of an old man on the bottom of the second page. Dumbfounded, I reread the pages three times. So, this was the concert inside Sunny's head. *My poor love.*

Seeing her demented thoughts in print was bloodcurdling. How could I have been so oblivious to the madness germinating right under my nose? A flood of shame and sadness washed through me as I sat on the carpet and stared at my incriminating discovery. I put the jewelry back in Sunny's jewelry box, ripped out the bizarre pages and locked both them and the knives—along with our other two sharp ones—in the back of my desk. Then I immediately left Dr. Bensen a message about what I'd found before heading back to the psychiatric ward.

Chapter 24 ❧ Sunny

When Joshua came to visit me around noon on Sunday—the second-to-last day of my imprisonment, he looked especially out of sorts. He was wearing sweats, hadn't shaved in a couple of days, and had a distracted look to him. *This is happening, I'm finally pushing him over the edge.* With few words passed between us, we played cards until Dr. Bensen showed up.

Again, I sent Joshua home for the night, telling him my dad would be visiting soon. This wasn't necessarily true, I didn't know when or if my dad would be coming. But I was getting increasingly frightened of the toll this was taking on my husband, with his squeaky clean childhood and general naiveté. My first instinct was to shelter him from my true self.

"How is the patient today?" said the doctor, sitting to my left with his usual pad and pen. He was dressed in khaki pants that were perfectly creased down the front and a striped, blue button-down shirt with the top of a T-shirt peeking out underneath. He wasn't wearing his white coat.

"Alright. Glad to go home."

"I bet. And how is your mood?"

"I don't feel depressed and I slept well last night." He asked me more of the usual depression questions pertaining to appetite, concentration, thoughts of death, etc. I denied each of them. I honestly didn't feel depressed—that would've required me to actually feel *something*. And I told him I wasn't suicidal, which must have pleased him. Suicidality always made so much work for doctors. I wasn't sure about the other symptoms; time would tell.

"Sunny, why did you have a meat cleaver hidden in your dresser and a pocketknife in your closet?"

I was not expecting that. *Dammit, Joshua!* I remembered the pocketknife;

I had purchased it during college to keep in my purse when walking at night. I'd never used it. A week or two earlier, when *they* were coming for me at any moment, I put it in my backpack, along with enough food and water to survive for a week. I told him this.

"And the jewelry?"

Oh shit, I'd forgotten about that. "I guess, in case I ran out of money," I said. I was planning to sew them into my clothes, which I left out. "I…um… didn't have much cash, so I threw that stuff in. I would never sell it though."

"Do you feel like you need the survival backpack now?"

"No."

"And the cleaver?" I was mixed up about that. I only recalled pacing around late one night, consumed with terror. As Joshua slept, I checked the locks and looked out the windows repeatedly. When I heard something outside, I thought *they* had arrived to arrest me. I grabbed the biggest, sharpest knife in the kitchen and crouched behind a chair until dawn. I must have hidden the knife away before Joshua got up, but I didn't remember.

"I just was having a bad night. I was scared about a sound I heard outside."

"As part of your delusion about the Nazis?"

"Yeah."

"Not to hurt yourself?"

"Oh God, no." *Seriously? A meat cleaver would never be my modus operandi.*

Then he went into the tinfoil hat questions with more detail, mostly wanting to know about my tormentors. I said what was necessary to go home—I would learn how to play this game. I knew *they* were still out there, plotting. This was but a cease-fire, nothing more. But I said I wasn't afraid and that the voices had thankfully stopped.

Ugh, those voices—my mortal nemeses. Why did they despise me so? I didn't understand them, they weren't even connected with the Gestapo. Their sole purpose was to destroy my mind and drive me to total despair. They were my primary reason for taking the meds. I could not exist in their company; my walls were too unstable. A couple of hours after Dr. Bensen left, my dad showed up bringing homemade minestrone. We sat together eating and watching the news until around 10 p.m.

Dr. Bensen went over my discharge summary the next morning, reiterating the importance of taking my medicine and going to therapy. He had increased the Haldol a couple of days before and I felt better. *They* were still quiet, although I had a sense that they were only temporarily muted. While I was less terrified about my enemies, every now and then I was struck by a deep sense of panic. But I didn't mention this to Dr. Bensen and promised to follow his advice. I thought I might actually give it a go, since doing nothing hadn't worked and I was tired of being miserable. Once he left, I tried to distract myself from my worries by watching TV and applying my makeup. Although my face looked okay, my hands appeared to have gone through a cheese grater. I had gnawed through every single cuticle over the past few days, leaving multiple open wounds. I tried to stop myself from inflicting further damage and leafed through a trashy magazine as I waited for Joshua.

When Joshua arrived at a little after 1:00, he kissed me, handed me some clothes, and asked me if I was ready to get out of there. I could see that he was trying to appear calm and friendly, but there was an edge lurking behind his words. He was a lousy actor.

"Joshua, why did you tell Dr. Bensen about the knives and the backpack?" I felt strangely violated.

He exhaled loudly. "Because I was worried. I didn't know what you were thinking, Sunny."

"Hmm." Neither did I. I couldn't decide if I should be pissed off or not. My life had become a kaleidoscope of confusion.

"Anyway, you're coming home today, isn't that great news?" He gave me a hollow smile.

Yeah right. "I am doing better now, Joshua. Things will be good," I said, trying to persuade both of us as I tied my shoes.

"I know, honey." I could see the love in his eyes combined with the uncertainty of living with a lunatic. I would have to show him I wasn't too far gone, that I was serious about my recovery.

When we went outside, it was a gorgeous day. Birds were chirping happily and vibrant red and orange tulips decorated the front of a building across the street. They reminded me that I really needed to get better. How could I waste away in a hospital when there was nature to behold? I breathed in the fresh air, but felt disoriented. Being hidden away had knocked me off kilter. We drove home, mostly in silence, as I gazed out the window.

Once home, Chester was waiting for me just inside the door. Oh God, was I glad to see his furry orange face, which I kissed and kissed until he started to squirm. I was so relieved to be back in my home, surrounded by the things that brought me comfort. The place was clean, although I saw that my books were out of place on the shelves, rather than neatly displayed how I liked them. Some were even upside down.

"Why are my books messed up?" I asked, as I moved them around.

"I didn't want you to trip over them, so I put them away. I'm sorry, I didn't know your organization system."

"Put them away?"

"Well, yeah. You had them in piles in every room."

"Oh." I suddenly remembered my frantic book piling, although I couldn't think of the reasoning behind it. But it was fucked up. "I'm sorry."

"Come here," he said reaching for me. As we stood hugging in the living room, he said, "It's okay, we'll get through this. I love you forever." He was more than I ever deserved. Unable to speak, I just held him close, breathing in his scent.

Over the course of that first week home, I approached life slowly, trying to get my bearings. I was tiptoeing on frozen water, trying not to slip through—for now I had a sense of what lurked below. Joshua was patient and accommodating—overly so. I wondered when he would tease me or chase me around for sex like he used to. I was like a preemie no one could touch as I precariously held onto life. I didn't like it. I wanted the old Joshua back.

While I was hospitalized, Joshua and my dad had become my program managers—setting up my therapy appointments, writing down my medication schedule, and hiring a babysitter to watch me. This was what my life had become—I was a 23-year-old toddler who would choke on marbles if not constantly watched. I wondered when he would be childproofing the kitchen and removing the glass coffee table.

I would be seeing Dr. Bensen every other Monday at 2:00 at his office, which, thankfully, was not in the hospital. On Tuesdays and Thursdays at noon, I would see my new therapist, a woman named Gretchen Turner. These requirements were reasonable, *but* they had also hired someone named Tiffany who, beginning tomorrow, would be coming by the condo every damn day to check on me and drive me to appointments. This, I knew, would be my undoing. I could drive myself and what was she going to do at home—stare at me while I did banal things like bathing and eating lunch? Would she be wiping my ass too? But I acquiesced, deciding to cooperate for a couple weeks, showing I didn't need a caregiver. Then I'd fire her.

My schedule had been typed up into a table and taped to the refrigerator. There was no way Joshua did this, it had Linda written all over it. But I didn't ask.

On my first evening home, Joshua ordered Thai food and we sat on the couch and watched *Six Feet Under*, just like normal. Afterward, I took a long bath with Chester perched near the tub mesmerized by the water. Then I sat on the edge of the bed in my nightshirt feeling lost. Joshua sat next to me.

"It's going to be okay, you know." He pulled a wet strand of hair off of my forehead.

"How do you know?"

"Because you're the strongest, most brilliant person I've ever met. And you are surrounded by people who will do anything for you. And I *need* you, Sunny." His voice cracked. This broke my heart still further.

"I'm so sorr—"

"Don't. Do *not* apologize. This is not your fault, schizophrenia is an illness."

Oh no, not on those lips, please don't say that word! I immediately tensed up.

He put his arm around me. "Look, Dr. Bensen is fantastic, you have a new therapist who sounds great, and your meds are doing their job. And, most importantly, you have *me*." He gave me that devilish smile of his, which reminded me of why I fell in love with him in the first place.

"And Chester, too," I added, as my beloved kitty made biscuits on my pillow.

"*Especially*, Chester. He's actually the one who set up your schedule and cleaned the house."

"I knew it." I smiled for the first time all evening. "I love you so much, Joshua." And I did, more than I could express at that moment.

"Me too, Slugger."

Waking up at home on Tuesday with no job felt painfully empty. Joshua left for work early, leaving me alone with my ruminations. I could barely think about my old job, the shame of it leveled any remaining traces of dignity. Who even was I if not an editor? I decided to go through the motions—*behaving my way to success*, as I had heard on a talk show. I made the bed, drank coffee, primped, and wrote a grocery list. Joshua said Elizabeth desperately wanted to see me, so I texted her and set up a time to meet later in the week. My dad called around 10:00 and I told him I was feeling much better, though I wasn't feeling much of anything. When I hung up, I saw my schedule and remembered that Tiffany was coming. And so began my next level of degradation.

I was sitting in the family room watching the news when I heard a very light tap at the door. *Oh yippy, she's here.* I took my time getting there. When I opened the door, I saw a tiny, impossibly young-looking, Asian girl wearing khaki pants and a blue, short-sleeved shirt. She looked like a Blockbuster employee. Her shiny black hair had a bob cut and she was wearing ugly plastic glasses. Whatever I'd imagined a "Tiffany" to look like, this wasn't it.

"Hello," I said without enthusiasm.

"Hi, I'm Tiffany, your home health aide." Her voice was timid.

"I'm aware." I gestured for her to come in. She was carrying a black doctor's bag; I wondered what she thought she'd be doing with it.

I sat back down on the couch and she followed me. "Have a seat," I offered, gesturing to a chair. "There's fresh coffee in the kitchen."

"Thank you, but I'm okay." She sat on the floral wingback chair to the left of the couch. "How are you doing today?"

"I'm good."

"I'm supposed to check your vitals," she said while opening her black bag. *Okay, I can handle vitals.* I shrugged as she came over and took my pulse. She also took my temperature and checked my blood pressure. "Everything looks fine." She wrote down the results in a small white binder. *No shit, I'm a mental case, not a cardiac patient.*

As she was carrying out her tasks, I got a better look at her. Her face was nondescript, except that one of her eyes seemed out of synch, focusing inward toward her nose. *So, my babysitter has a lazy eye—seriously? This was the person charged with protecting me from myself?*

"I also need to check your meds, where do you keep them?"

What? Ugh! "On my nightstand," I replied, rolling my eyes.

I heard her messing with the two bottles in the other room. Was she actually counting them? I hoped she at least washed her hands.

"Are you ready to go to your appointment?" she asked, returning to the family room.

"It's not for forty-five minutes." I knew the clinic was only ten minutes away.

She looked at her watch. "Okay. What are you watching?"

"Nothing much." *Holy shit this is awkward.* I wondered if this was how each day would be from now on.

She opened her binder and pretended to look busy. Chester came into the room and stopped in front of her. She looked at him but didn't say a word or even reach down to pet him. *What was wrong with this girl?* I called Chester over and he lay in my lap.

At exactly 11:40, she said, "I think we need to go now."

I looked at her, quickly averting my gaze from her wonky eye, instead focusing on her forehead. I thought about arguing with her but decided not to bother. I turned off the TV, grabbed my purse, and headed out the door with Tiffany plodding close behind.

She drove a green Subaru, which was extremely clean on the inside and smelled strongly of a dangling Tweety air freshener that was sure to give me a headache. She adjusted her mirrors for a good fifteen seconds and slowly backed out of the parking lot. She must've studied the directions, since she knew exactly where she was going. But it became immediately apparent that she was an abysmal driver. She consistently drove 10-15 miles below the speed limit. She stopped at a light that had only just turned yellow, causing us to wait unnecessarily at a long intersection. My aggravation was brewing and I could see she was also annoying the drivers behind her. Without exaggeration, she drove worse than Babcia—who had often held up traffic and was regularly flipped off, which she thankfully never noticed. By the time we got to the office, we were almost late and my left temple was starting to throb.

The mental health clinic was located in a modern white building. Inside was a large waiting room with a saltwater fish tank, standard ugly waiting room chairs, and a corner with toys—including a large wooden abacus-type thing that must've been a breeding ground for bacteria. There were around eight people waiting and I wondered about the demons plaguing each of them. They all sat silently, either looking through magazines or messing with their phones. The guy nearest me was in his twenties, pockmarked, and smelled like an ashtray. His hair was greasy and he looked like he just rolled out of bed. The speed at which one of his feet shook reminded me of a hummingbird wing. I sat down and Tiffany checked me in like I was mentally incompetent.

Almost immediately, a middle-aged woman came out and said my name. She had straight dark hair that was parted down the middle and fell just below her shoulders. There were quite a few gray strands framing her face and colorful earrings dangled from her ears. She was wearing a white button-down shirt, black pants, and a low black heel. She was tall with gorgeous tan skin and fine lines etched in her slender face. I thought she might be Native American, which was confirmed upon entering her office.

Above a metal desk hung a large print of beautiful young Native dancers dressed in beaded regalia and feather headpieces. On another wall, next to a small window, there was a black and white print of a wolf, with a dream catcher below its chin. And there was a framed poem or prayer by Chief Oren Anegada displayed next to the door. I wanted to read it, but couldn't quite see the words. The walls were painted a pale yellow—likely meant to soothe the unhinged. The office's three chairs were worn, but comfortable, and there was a sage green rug covering most of the dark wood flooring. I sat down and Dr. Turner took a seat next to me, rather than behind her desk.

We exchanged pleasantries, with the doctor shaking my hand warmly. She had a motherly way about her. We talked about my hospitalization and the events leading up to it—all of the usual fun stuff happening lately.

"Well, you've sure had a lot going on. How are you doing today?"

I sighed deeply, like a tire deflating.

"You seem troubled—how do you feel?"

"I'm starting to despise that question. I'm constantly being asked it and, maybe it sounds stupid, but I just *don't know* how I feel. I guess, at this moment, I feel a combination of confusion and annoyance."

"Okay, let's start with the annoyance. What's annoying you?"

"Oh, just the fact that I'm such an emotional disaster that my dad and husband hired a babysitter to watch me who looks about twelve, has a lazy eye, and drives like an eighty-year-old."

She smiled and I could see the mirth in her eyes. "Well, that certainly *does* sound annoying. Why do you think they did that?"

"Because they think I will do something crazy."

"And, if they indeed think that, why would they go to the expense and trouble to hire a caregiver?"

"Because they're worried about me."

"They must really love you."

"Yeah."

"And you mentioned feeling confused. Can you tell me more about that?"

"It's just …everything. Dr. Bensen says I'm *schizophrenic*, but I can't get my head around it. I don't see how it can be true. It feels like the end of my life." I looked down at the green rug. I noticed a gum wrapper under one of the chairs.

"A label like that is a big pill to swallow. What is it about schizophrenia that's the most scary to you?"

"It's not who I am."

"Who are you?"

"I'm an editor, a bookworm, an artist. I am always trying to educate myself. I got straight A's in college. I have goals. And I want to be a good daughter and wife. I don't want to be a blubbering psychopath." I wiped away a few tears. I really didn't want to cry, *dammit*.

"Let's unpack what you just said. First, where did you get the idea that you are a blubbering psychopath?"

"Well, I lost my job because I went crazy at work. I heard voices and was doing all sorts of weird things."

"That sounds like a person struggling with mental illness. And I'm looking right at you, I see a lovely young woman—not a blubbering psychopath. Do you know the definition of a psychopath?"

"I mean, not specifically."

"It's not really a word we use in psychiatry, but is generally associated with someone who lacks empathy, like a sociopath. I've only known you for twenty minutes, but, even during this brief amount of time, I can see you are a sensitive person who carries a lot of remorse. Does that sound about right?"

"My dad says I carry guilt like a second skin."

"Okay, so do you think you might be able to drop the psychopath label?"

"Yeah. But I just don't want to be crazy."

"I understand. Let's think about the rest of your statement: You have goals, you're an editor, you want to be a good wife and daughter, you're a bookworm, and you're an artist. Who says you can't still be those things?"

"It's just that the schizophrenics I've known of are unable to function, like a woman near my office. I've just always pictured them within the snake pits of Bedlam."

"That's a common association. There's is a great deal of stereotyping and stigma when it comes to mental illness. Hollywood hasn't helped. You just said, 'the schizophrenics you've known of.' What about those you haven't—the countless mentally ill people you've come across in your life but didn't realize it? What if I told you there are people from all walks of life, who appear as functional as anyone else, managing their mental illnesses? And, in doing so, pursuing their goals and enjoying their lives?"

"That would be better, I guess."

"It's the people *not* doing well who stand out the most. And how a person responds to and deals with mental illness, including schizophrenia, is highly individualized—no two people will have the same experience. You are *here*, Sunny. You're already taking the right steps toward getting better. Having a psychiatric diagnosis *and* being the successful person you want to be, are not mutually exclusive. One of our goals in therapy will be to help you with your internalized stigma, which doesn't help self-worth and can create a barrier to recovery. Another goal will be to help you accept your illness *and* do the things that bring you meaning and happiness."

"Okay." *This woman might just be alright.* She made me feel calmer and less like an outcast. I still didn't want the diagnosis, but I liked the rest of what she said. She gave me two homework assignments. The first was to write down five to ten things that make me feel alive and to see how many I could engage in before our next meeting. For the second assignment, she handed me a *Goal Form* requiring me to list my short-, medium-, and long-term goals. I took the paper and said I would do my best. The session ended and I left the room, having momentarily forgotten about the meek, cross-eyed girl waiting for me in the lobby.

Chapter 25 ❧ Sunny

Tiffany had the good sense not to ask me how I was feeling after the session. We drove without a word. Once home, she took my vitals again for some reason. My blood pressure was quite a bit higher than earlier. Then she asked me what I would be having for lunch as she looked through her notebook.

Give me a break, I don't need you monitoring my eating habits! "I'll figure it out later, don't worry. And please remove the air freshener from your car—I'm allergic to it." I didn't want to hurt her feelings, but my head was pounding.

"Oh, I'm sorry. Um…I guess I'll see you tomorrow then." She looked flustered, but at least she was compliant.

She said goodbye and shut the door softly behind her, which I immediately locked. I took some Excedrin and collapsed onto the couch. I was exhausted. By the time Joshua came home, I was on my third Lifetime movie, having digested a full dose of domestic violence, abduction, and drug addiction. I was lethargic, withdrawn, and unmotivated. I sat up on the couch when he came in, trying to look alert. He smelled of the outdoors.

"Hi, baby!" He kissed my cheek. "How did everything go today?"

"Fine." My speech was monotone. "Why did you hire a child to babysit me? A *cross-eyed* child, no less?" I spoke with irritation as I stared at the muted TV.

"She's actually twenty-six and came highly recommended. She's an excellent nurse, Sunny."

"How can she drive safely with a crossed eye? And I can drive myself, you know."

"She has a perfect driving record, so nothing about her vision is a problem."

I looked up at him, raising my voice, "Also, she counted my pills, Joshua. What is this, *One Flew Over the Cuckoo's Nest?*"

He sighed heavily as he walked toward the kitchen. "She's just temporary, honey. Until you feel better. Just go with it, okay?" He put down his keys and grabbed a beer. "Did you have lunch?"

"I ate a sandwich after she left." I lied. I had no energy to prepare anything.

"How's the new therapist?"

"She's nice, actually."

"That's awesome!" He was overly excited, seeking out any modicum of hope for his irremediable wife. "What's this?" he asked, picking up the Goal Form.

"Just some homework, I'll do it later."

We had takeout falafels for dinner and Joshua was asleep by 10:30, leaving me to finish my third movie. When I went to bed, I lay there for three hours unable to fall asleep. I tossed around, changed my nightgown, flipped my pillow, soaked my feet in hot water, and finally drank chamomile tea with honey. I must've dozed off around 3 a.m. Joshua woke me the next morning at 8:30, before he left for work—which I didn't appreciate, I was so very tired.

Tiffany was punctual, announcing her 11:00 arrival with her usual soft tapping. I had just gotten up and was drinking coffee when I let her in. Since we didn't have anywhere to go, her visit was all the more pointless. She took my vitals, checked my meds, and asked me how I was doing. I said I was fine and she asked me about lunch yet again.

"Look, I can see that you're well-meaning and just doing your job, but I actually don't have an eating disorder. My dad and husband feel better having you check on me, which is fine for the time being. But I'm going to have to ask you not to bother me about food. I'm an adult and can handle feeding myself on my own timeline."

"Okay, it's just that Mr…um…your father wanted me to check that you eat each day." She looked anxious, way out of her element.

"Well, just tell him what you need to, but I'm not eating in front of you every day." I didn't want to make her feel bad, so I spoke as kindly as I could. My program managers were crossing a line here and I wouldn't have it.

Tiffany didn't ask me about food again. She came over, completed her tasks, made meaningless small talk, and drove me to my appointments when I had them. When things became unbearably awkward, she cleaned the kitchen—which I'm sure wasn't in her job description. Hiring her was a colossal waste of money that was making me feel even more pathetic.

I attempted to do my homework on Wednesday evening, but ended up putting it off until fifteen minutes before my next appointment on Thursday. I was trying to come up with some socially acceptable responses when my babysitter tapped on the door. She was wearing basically the same outfit as before—didn't she have any other clothes? Her car smelled less toxic on that second drive to therapy, but her driving was no better and what little tolerance I had was waning.

Dr. Turner asked me about my delusions and whether I'd had any hallucinations. I'd only heard a single, fleeting "stupid bitch," during the night, but I wasn't sure if I was even awake at the time. I'd also had a few nightmares about my mother from which I awoke sitting straight up in bed. I didn't mention either of these. I was still anxious about the Germans, but denied that too. Then she brought up my homework and I told her four things that made me feel alive: nature, creativity, affection, and laughter.

"That's a good start, Sunny. Were you able to engage in any of them since Tuesday?"

I hadn't even tried. "I cuddled with Chester and saw some flowers outside when we drove here."

"Any affection with your husband?"

"A little."

"Any laughter, at all?"

"Um…maybe once or twice." *If I had laughed, it was not memorable.*

We talked more about my list, finding a few more things to add to it. Then we brainstormed realistic ways to engage in each of them, even if just a little bit. She wrote it all down for me. When she asked about the goal assignment, I realized I'd forgotten about it entirely. She gave me a new form and noted the importance of having goals and things to look forward to. She asked me to work on it when I got home today and then went into the usual depression questions.

"Sunny, I can see that you are moving and speaking slowly. And you seem unmotivated, is that true?"

"I guess. I don't feel like doing much of anything." I began feeling exceedingly self-conscious. Was I actually moving in slow motion?

She continued her questioning. I admitted that I was exhausted and hadn't been sleeping well. That I was on edge and couldn't concentrate on my books. And I had no appetite. But at least I didn't want to die.

"You're depressed, Sunny. I'm going to speak to Dr. Bensen about increasing your Prozac." She had me sign a form allowing the two to share information about me. "It's not uncommon to experience depression when receiving a difficult diagnosis, but I think we need to address these symptoms immediately."

She was right, I was depressed. She told me to contact her ASAP if things got worse or if I had suicidal thoughts. I agreed. She also said she would like to talk about the content of my delusions at some point when I was feeling better. *Ugh, no thanks.* And she said she wanted to start family therapy with me and my dad, and was in the process of scheduling with him. *Oh God, Dad, please be too busy for this.* Was there no end to her torture tactics?

Later that afternoon, Dr. Bensen's assistant called, telling me to increase the Prozac by 5 mg, getting it up to 30 mg, which was fine with me. I hated the lethargy, I had things to do. At least I thought I did.

For the rest of the day, I went through the motions—doing what was expected. Elizabeth showed up late in the afternoon, just after Tiffany left. I would do my best to seem alert.

She knocked twice and let herself in (I hadn't locked the door yet). Unlike Tiffany, Elizabeth had an entrance. "Halloooo!"

"Geez, are you loud," I said, entering the hallway.

"Some things never change." She gave me a big hug and handed me a smoothie. She was wearing black leggings and a pink Adidas T-shirt. Her red mane was French braided down her back and her face was pink from exertion. "What's with Blockbuster Girl?"

I chuckled despite myself. Elizabeth and I had always thought alike. "Oh, she's only the person in charge of keeping me alive."

She let out a laugh, then stopped herself, likely remembering she needed to be supportive of my treatment plan. "Is she a nurse or something?"

"Yeah, plus she drives me to appointments, though I don't know why. And, Lizzie, she drives less than 20 miles per hour *at all times!* I want to tell her to 'get the molasses out of her ass,' but I'm honestly afraid she'd cry."

"Oh damn! But at least she's safe." She slurped up the rest of her smoothie, making a grating sound.

"I mean, not if I kill her out of sheer irritation."

She smiled, set her purse on the coffee table, and took a seat on the couch. Chester immediately jumped on her lap and she scratched his back.

"And she also completely ignored Chester!"

"Well, now that's just diabolical!" She kissed him on the head. Then she looked at me more seriously. "So, how have you been, Sunny? Joshua didn't want me to visit you in the hospital. What happened?"

"Baba and Papa dying has messed me up. I just lost my mind for a bit there."

"Joshua said something about Nazis and that you were trying to hurt yourself?"

"I …um…I had this idea that the Gestapo was after me, must be from reading all of these books." I gestured toward the bookshelves. "Plus, being raised by Holocaust survivors. I thought they were going to kill me, so I decided to beat them to it." I could feel myself sinking as I explained the contents of my fucked up head. I was willing myself not to cry.

"Oh, Sunny, I'm so sorry."

God, did I hate her pity.

"Thanks, I'm better now." I tried to sound convincing, but I knew my pathetic, monotone voice was deceiving me. "And thank you for sending the food and flowers, that was really sweet." I was done with the conversation.

"Of course. Did the doctor say what was wrong, or give you a diagnosis?"

Oh hell, no—we aren't going there right now. "I don't really want to talk about this anymore, Lizzy. How are *you* doing?"

She went on to tell me about her new job at the *Times* of San Diego. She was a reporter, which suited her outgoing personality. And she was dating someone she met online and it seemed serious. I was happy for her, yet also envious. Why couldn't I just be a normal girl, enjoying normal things like she did?

She realized she needed to get to her mom's house. "Sunny, you're my best friend, my *sister*. You need to tell me when you aren't feeling well, psychologically or otherwise. Even today, you seem, I don't know. Off. Please don't shut me out."

Well, this is uncomfortable. "Okay. Love you."

"Love you more." She hugged me and flew out the door, emptying the room of its color and ebullience. I locked the door and flopped back down on the couch. I stared at nothing in particular as I listened to a lawnmower in the distance.

Tiffany arrived in true form on Friday—right on time and as passive as ever. There was a word I learned as an editor that fit her perfectly: *Milquetoast.* An ideal nickname for her. Tiffany didn't suit her anyway. I had no appointments, so she tried to talk me into going to the park. I had no energy to walk anywhere and sure as hell wouldn't ride with her unnecessarily—*are you fucking kidding?* So, she took my vitals, checked my pills, and then sat and watched me watch TV. *So ludicrous.* When she finally left, I went back to bed.

I was feeling ambivalent about the weekend. As I lay in bed next to Joshua on Friday night, I worried about being with him for two full days straight. This was a situation I normally adored, but the idea of keeping my madness within the lines had become a daunting prospect. And lately I felt less like a wife and more like a carnival freak that he was obligated to keep an eye on. I often saw him watching me. I wondered what was going through his head. Did he no longer recognize me? Was he wondering how to get rid of me? Where to dispose of the body? Twice I told him to stop looking at me, but I still caught him from time to time.

I didn't mention the Prozac increase to Joshua, figuring I'd get better and he wouldn't have to know. But I had a sense that he would find out anyway; one of the spies would fill him in. Fortunately, I had more energy on Saturday, so I did the laundry, vacuumed, and went to the grocery store down the street. Joshua was watching a game on TV and offered to help, but I told him to relax. I really just wanted him to leave me alone. Something about Joshua was getting under my skin. I managed to avoid him most of the evening, spending a long time in the shower, painting my nails, and doing various other grooming-related things in the bathroom. I pretended to be asleep when he came to bed, but I got up later and did crunches in the family room. I fell asleep well after midnight.

Sunday was a beautiful day and I decided to go for a long run. Normally able to run five miles, I could only do three—I was out of shape and it pissed me off. But at least I wasn't lethargic. I would keep running and get back to top form. My dad came over that evening, bringing dinner, which the three of us ate on the patio. The kids really wanted to see me, but I wasn't ready and my dad understood.

"You look good, sweetie. Your cheeks are nice and rosy!"

"I went for a run earlier."

"That's great! How's everything going with the new therapist and the home nurse?"

I told him about Dr. Turner, but laid into him about Milquetoast. Both he and Joshua emphasized that it was only for now, that I would be back on my feet in no time. Broken records.

After he left, we got ready for bed as usual, but I wasn't at all tired. And I was feeling increasingly distrustful, though of what, I wasn't sure. After Joshua fell asleep, I quietly went through my books, making sure each one was in the right place. I also leafed through every one of them, thinking there might be a note or something hidden inside. I just had a sinking feeling that *they* had sent me a message somewhere in those pages. I looked through all 411 books (yes, I counted), but found nothing. It was 4 a.m. when I finished and finally fell asleep. Fortunately, Joshua was a heavy sleeper.

"Wow, the bookshelves look great," he said as he came into the bedroom to take a shower the next morning. I guess not seeing them methodically piled throughout the condo was a sign of progress. He was always looking for such signs. He left for work and I went for a long run. I had forgotten about Milquetoast, who came at 1:00 on Mondays. She was driving up just as I returned. *Fuck, Fuck, Fuck!*

"Hello, did you go for a run?"

No, I always stand outside in my running shoes, panting, with sweat dripping down my face. I had zero tolerance for her today. "Yep."

"That's nice." We went inside and she completed her usual duties. After less than ten minutes, she asked if I was ready to go to my appointment. *What was with her? She must be the person who always shows up first at parties.*

"After I shower." We left at 1:40, which I could see was making Milquetoast anxious—but it sure as hell didn't make her drive any faster. Nonetheless, we arrived ten minutes early to Dr. Bensen's office, which was much closer than the hospital. It was in an old Tudor that had been turned into mental health offices. His was on the top floor, which required climbing four narrow staircases. There was a small waiting room at the top, with wooden floors and burgundy walls. It would have been dark if not for a large window pointing west which revealed a neighborhood with similar old houses and plenty of trees. There was a light green velvet loveseat and a few wooden chairs. Tiffany sat in one of the chairs as the doctor called me into his office.

The room was on the small side, with a wooden desk and tons of books on wall-to-wall shelves. There was a window over the desk beyond which a huge redwood stood guard. Hung on one wall were four square photographs—two on top and two on the bottom. Each portrayed a single bird, including a yellow-headed sparrow, an owl, a blue jay, and a small bird of many colors that I couldn't name. Apparently, Dr. Bensen was a bird enthusiast. There were four cushiony high-back chairs that were incongruous with the small space, and a rectangular coffee table made of distressed wood sat in the middle of them. There were numerous ivy-like plants both hanging and sitting on surfaces that softened the room's atmosphere. I declined his offer for coffee or tea and took a seat. I sat opposite the picture window which enabled me to watch the gently swaying branches and tiny birds fluttering about.

"Good afternoon, Sunny," he said, greeting me warmly with a handshake. He was wearing dark slacks and a pink checkered oxford shirt—a look Joshua could never pull off—and black high-end loafers I hadn't seen yet. He sat across from me in one of the high backs. "How is it being home?"

"It's better. I missed Chester."

"Chester seems like a quite the little fellow." He smiled, sounding sincere.

"He's the best."

"How's your mood after increasing the Prozac?" He opened his notebook.

"I guess I feel better," I lied. "I have more energy." That much was true. I was feeling increasingly antsy, but managed to control my foot from shaking. I was worried he could see right through me.

He asked me the rest of the standard mood questions. I told him the truth, that I wasn't suicidal and that I actually ate several complete meals over the weekend. Although my sleep had been minimal, I said it was fine. I told him I had more energy, although I downplayed just *how much more*. Maybe I was getting good at this.

"That's really fast for a medication-related effect. Maybe being home is helping. Have you had any feelings of euphoria in the past couple of days?"

I laughed sarcastically. "*Euphoria*, are you kidding? I wish."

He asked me about feeling especially irritable or angry. I had been more irritable the past two days than I could ever remember. I worried that he could sense it. So, with a forced expression of neutrality, I lied. This was probably one of those questions that could land me back in the hospital.

"I'm annoyed with my schedule and the home health nurse, but nothing out of the ordinary." Sounded believable enough to me. Then he asked me about *them*.

"Have you been hearing voices or seeing things others can't see?"

Why can't he just say "hallucinations?" I'm not an idiot. I hid my irritation. "Nope, no hallucinations."

"And your feelings of being hunted, are they still there in any capacity?"

Oh, they're still in there. Just because a desert is quiet, it doesn't mean it isn't crawling with life. "No, I feel much better." I couldn't tell if he was pleased or skeptical—he would kick ass at poker.

"How was your visit with Dr. Turner, do you think you'll be able to work with her?"

"Yeah, she seems competent. She doesn't look or sound like a Nazi, which is nice." More sarcasm. *I need to get out of here before the toxins start seeping out.*

"She's a wonderful psychologist and works especially well with women who are grieving."

"Well then, it's a match!" I said, a little too enthusiastically.

He looked at me strangely.

"Please make sure you do her homework assignments. You can only get as much out of therapy as you put in. And how are you feeling with the medications, any side effects?"

I had been feeling so lousy for so long now, I'd forgotten about side effects. I just thought I was supposed to feel the way I did. My muscles were constantly aching, but that wasn't surprising given my recent performance in the hospital bathroom. I was also really sweaty, but I'd just gone running. "Just a little dry mouth."

He told me to drink more water and listed various other side effects which, thankfully, I did not have. Then he checked my vitals and did what I guess was a neurological exam, having me touch my nose, move my eyes from side to side, etc. "I need you to contact me immediately if you have any side effects, particularly fever, rash, breathing issues or chest pain. Really, anything out of the ordinary. And, if you have any thoughts of death or hurting yourself, call me right away. Okay?"

"Okay." There was nothing left to say, so I told him I liked his photographs and that my babcia loved sparrows. His face lit up and he said his wife had taken the photos. Then he described the different species—although I didn't pay much attention.

And that was it—I'd survived another outpatient visit as a madwoman loose in the city.

Milquetoast and I rode in silence. When we got home, she sat in a chair until her obligatory time was up, and left. l loved it when she left. Still feeling energized, I organized my clothes and cleaned the kitchen. I saw my homework sheet and, remembering Dr. Bensen's badgering, decided to fill it out. I completed it quickly, hoping to add sufficient mollifying content. My goals mostly involved getting a job, exercising, learning how to paint, and having quality relationships with my family. In the long term, I had always wanted to travel and own a house, which I wrote down despite believing neither were in the cards for me anymore.

I was quickly bored with the exercise and decided to go for a walk to the outdoor market. I hadn't been alone in a crowded place since I started to unravel. There were way too many people and the sights and smells did not delight me as they used to. As I was feeling overstimulated and mistrustful, I heard my name.

"Sunshine!" It was Viktor.

"Hello, Viktor. How are you?"

"I'm great! You disappeared on me, I missed you!"

"Yeah, I've been busy with different ..." My words trailed off.

"I don't see you heading to work in the mornings. That's the highlight of my day, you know?"

"I'm working from home now." I didn't want to have this discussion and started backing away.

"Wait, Sunshine." He handed me a perfect pink rose. "A beauty for a beauty."

His words almost made me feel something. "Thank you so much, Viktor. I'll see you again soon."

He blew me a kiss as I quickly moved away. His kindness was suffocating. I purchased some fruit and vegetables at the market and jogged home, trying not to squish anything. That evening, I made mushroom stroganoff, Caesar salad, and strawberry shortcake (strictly for Joshua). He was thrilled by my monumental achievement of shopping *and* cooking—the bar was low. Dinner was delicious, but every time he complimented it—which was *way* too often, irritation surged through me like poison.

Afraid I would snap at Joshua, I retreated to my calming place—the bathtub. But, as I soaked under a sudsy layer of my favorite L'Occitane bubble bath, I couldn't relax. My mind was not at peace. I continued to worry about everything: my tormentors, my marriage, my career, my mental health, my dad, Chester, etc. Even worse was the undirected hostility that sat in my throat like a ball of tar. Despite the warm, almond-scented water, my mind and body would not be still. When I got out of the tub, I stubbed my toe on the bottom of the counter and barely contained the trail of obscenities flooding my mind. My pressure valves were fully cranked.

I stayed up late again—sleep was unnecessary. God knows what I was doing. I couldn't concentrate on books or TV, and the house had an OCD stamp of organization. But, at some point during that long night, I realized I hadn't taken my evening dose of Haldol after dinner—which Joshua failed to notice. Then I came to the conclusion that I didn't need either of the medications—they were making me hyper, anxious, angry, and defensive. Besides, weren't people always telling me how strong I was? I didn't need a crutch.

I hid my evening dose of Haldol in the bottom of the trash.

Chapter 26 ❧ Sunny

I awoke on Tuesday feeling a strong sense of trepidation. After Joshua left for work, I lay in bed staring up at the ceiling listening for clues as to what was happening around me. There was no sound at all—neither birds nor airplanes. I was done for, finished. I'd slept very little the night before and was both fatigued and restless. The atmosphere was eerie, like an invisible cloud was following me. It was *them*; they were zeroing in on me. I got up to go to the bathroom late in the night and, as I sat on the toilet, I saw that there was a light coating of blood on my hands. Then I remembered sitting up in bed for hours, unable to slow the rapid-fire thoughts streaming through my head. I was trying to devise a getaway plan as I chewed mercilessly on my cuticles. Several of them really hurt when run under water. When Joshua asked me what I was doing, I mumbled something about a bad dream and lay back down. But my planning continued.

As I drank my coffee, I saw that it was almost 10:00. Milquetoast was coming in an hour—shit! I darted around the condo like a squirrel as I considered my situation. I stopped every now and then to kiss Chester, who was sleeping on the couch. First, I went to the bedroom and removed my missed doses of medication from the bottles and crammed them into the bottom of the garbage. Then I pulled my backpack down from the closet. It still contained the clothes I'd added weeks earlier. There was also a bible, but no jewelry or pocketknife. Joshua was constantly nosing into my plans, putting me at increased danger. I loved him to death, but his interference was exasperating as hell. Just like the day before, I was running on a very short fuse.

Feeling energetic, I ran around the condo, gathering the items I would need. I added more clothing, several granola bars, three bottles of water, a banana, and a few carrots that I didn't have time to peel. I desperately needed a weapon, but good old Joshua had hidden away the sharp knives. Did he think I was going to kill him? Then I remembered Joshua's toolbox. I ran to the garage and dug through the various tools until I found a crowbar. I saw Joshua's tackle box on a high shelf and pulled it down. Bingo—a butterfly knife, which was really sharp. I ran to the bedroom where I shoved the knife and crowbar into my backpack. I looked through my wallet and saw that it contained all of $21—great. I placed my most valuable jewelry in a side pocket along with a tiny sewing kit. I'd sew them in my clothes later, no time now. I absently touched my neck, ensuring that Babcia's Star of David pendant was not there, still hidden away in the closet where it could not incriminate me.

I needed to get dressed. I chose comfortable nondescript clothing, including leggings, a T-shirt, and Nike running shoes—all in black. I put on a little makeup and brushed my teeth, then threw my cosmetic bag and other grooming items, along with my phone, into the backpack—which I shoved in the back of the bedroom closet. When I heard Milquetoast's telltale tap, I froze in place. I realized I was sweating from all of my activity and wiped my forehead with a towel. I took a couple big breaths and opened the door.

As we slowly headed toward Dr. Turner's office, I looked out the window and considered my surroundings. There was a bus stop four blocks from home. The SS would recognize my car, so the bus was a much better option. Plus, I was too keyed up to drive. As my anxiety increased, I heard it: *Stupid, crazy bitch.* I must've jumped because Milquetoast asked me if I was okay. I murmured something about a cat running across the street.

Okay, *they* were back—it was all happening again. But this time it would be different. *This time* I would escape. But first I would need to get through the next hour, an hour with someone who could see inside me.

As we got out of the car, I realized I'd forgotten my homework—*fuck!* I must've said it out loud, since Milquetoast asked what was wrong—God, she was annoying. I ignored her. Then *they* chanted as if on cue: *Stupid bitch. Fucking bitch.* I absolutely could not allow Dr. Turner to know *they* had returned. She had the power to put me in grave danger, to allow my murderers to find me. I would need to employ every bit of my acting skills and emotional restraint to fool this woman.

I sat in my usual chair and took a deep breath. I imagined hospital restraints around my ankles and wrists, thus prohibiting me from shaking. I would not respond to *them*. The doctors always seemed to know. I would not let her penetrate my skull or inspect my eye sockets.

"Good morning, Sunny. How are you today?" she asked with her usual affability as she sat across from me.

"I'm good." *Hold it down, don't act weird.*

"You're all in black, robbing a bank later?" she teased. At least, I think she was teasing—you never knew with these damn shrinks.

"Laundry day." *Nice play.*

"Ah, that makes sense. How are you feeling, how's your mood?"

"Great, I feel much better." *Oops, maybe that was too enthusiastic.* "I mean, better than last week," I lied. *Stupid Bitch. Stupid lying bitch.* I ignored *them*. She asked the usual depression questions and I only endorsed insomnia. I wanted to seem realistic.

"I'm sorry, I forgot to bring my homework, but I did do it." *This should distract her.*

"Great, what kinds of short-term goals did you come up with?"

Think, Sunny! You can remember them. "Um. Oh, fitness, getting a job, and…" That's all I had.

She talked a little about these goals, telling me fitness was great if I didn't overdo it and that thinking about future career plans was a good idea, but to be realistic about it. *No shit, like anyone would hire me now.* But I nodded agreeably. *Lazy bitch. Dumb bitch.*

We brainstormed additional short-term goals, like forging healthy relationships, having a creative outlet, and practicing mindfulness—*yeah right*. When she asked me about long-term objectives, my mind went blank. "I don't remember." *Stupid bitch. Fucking moron.* I needed a stall tactic. "May I please use the bathroom, too much coffee."

"Of course." I went to the bathroom, which was just off the waiting room. I saw Milquetoast sitting there reading a book. For once she didn't spot me. It was a one-person bathroom, thank God. I locked the door and paced in circles. *Stupid bitch. Crazy stupid bitch.* I needed an outlet. This was becoming too hard to suppress. I paced for five minutes, flushed the toilet, ran the water, paced a little more, and went back to her office.

"Are you okay? You look a little flushed."

I needed to get out of there—*immediately*. I remembered Elizabeth telling a cop she had diarrhea when she got pulled over for speeding. It worked like a charm. "Honestly, I don't feel well, it's my stomach. I have really bad diarrhea, must be the stomach flu. My dad was sick, likely caught it from him." *Good one!* I held my stomach as if in pain. *Disgusting stupid bitch.*

"You do look sweaty, do you have a fever?"

"Yes, I think I had one this morning." More lies.

Dr. Turner sent me home, telling me to rest. She said we would pick up where we left off on Thursday, but to call me if my depression symptoms worsened, if I heard voices, or if I felt paranoid. And she said to go to the doctor if I had a high fever.

"Okay," I said meekly, as I shuffled out of her office with my hand still over my stomach.

Milquetoast was surprised to see me, there were still fifteen minutes left in the session. I told her the same thing I said to Dr. Turner and she visibly took two steps back. *Brilliant!*

When we got home, Milquetoast advised me to go lie down—which I obediently did. As I was lying there, a thought pushed its way into my head: *The roundup is underway—they're coming for you! Go!* I waited until I heard my babysitter leave, then I shot out of bed like a rocket.

I looked out the bedroom window and watched Milquetoast slowly drive away. I was frantic to leave the condo. My body could sense *them* getting closer—my skin was itching and my feet were tingling. I threw on a black sweatshirt over my T-shirt and placed my backpack near the door. Then came the worst of it—my desperate heartache. I bent down over Chester as he slept on the sofa. I kissed him over and over again as tears rolled down my cheeks and landed on his head. "I love you so much, my sweet baby. Mama has to go away for a little while, I'll come get you when it's safe. You need to stay here with your daddy." Not registering the real meaning of my words, Chester purred at full speed.

I grabbed the softest blanket I could find and brought it to the master bathroom where I folded it into a large square. I ran to the kitchen and poured a huge bowl of cat food and filled an even bigger bowl with water. I placed them both in the bathroom. I moved the litter box into the far side of the bathroom and opened the little, screened-in window above the bathtub. Tears still streaming, I gently picked up Chester and placed him on the soft bed. Of course, he didn't stay there, but went straight to the food. I rubbed his back and kissed him several more times. "I love you so much, my baby." I needed to protect Chester as best I could. The bathroom was large and Joshua would be home later, but I still felt terrible leaving him in there.

I looked around to see if I'd forgotten anything and grabbed the two medication bottles from my nightstand. Then I picked up my keys and backpack, and headed out the door, locking the deadbolt behind me. I walked about half a block and tossed the pill bottles in the neighbor's trash. I decided to throw my phone in there too, since the Gestapo could use it to trace me. I then jogged to the SDSU bus station. When I finally arrived, I was covered in sweat and practically hyperventilating from fear and exertion.

There were several buses, but for some reason Anaheim seemed right, so I waited a little while for the bus and hopped on. I grabbed the closest seat to the door, which was two rows back. I placed my backpack next to me to deter anyone from sitting there—I just couldn't risk it. I pulled the knife from my backpack and placed it under my sleeve. As the bus driver closed the door and the bus began moving, I took a deep breath and looked around at the other passengers. There were a number of elderly people. Knowing their fate as nonessentials, I was glad to see them also on the run. None of the passengers seemed like collaborators, but I would remain vigilant.

Although there was reassurance in seeing the distance between myself and my persecutors expand, that bus ride was an excruciating exercise in self-restraint. It was hell. As sweat continued to trickle down my back and into my ass crack, I found that I couldn't sit still. Uncontrolled restlessness while confined to such a small space is insufferable. My every fiber was longing to pace or even run down the aisle, but of course I couldn't. I spent the three-hour trip alternating shaking each of my feet as I squirmed in my seat. *Stupid bitch. Disgusting bitch. Whore.* As I rocked back and forth, I noticed several people staring at me. I glared back and they quickly looked away.

Every time the bus stopped and more people got on, my agitation increased exponentially. Each person had to be closely examined. Several young women and at least five more old people boarded until we came to the fourth stop, where a young, blonde man stepped up to pay the driver. He was tall, at least 6'3," with broad shoulders. Pure Aryan. There weren't many seats left at that point and I saw him glancing my way. *Oh hell, no!* I moved the pocketknife into my hand and lunged forward onto my stomach, covering both seats with my body. The Aryan looked at me oddly and walked on by. I lifted my head and watched him. He found a seat three-quarters of the way back. Eventually, I sat back up and commenced rocking, as I kept an eye on him. The knife was just under my right-hand sleeve where I could easily access it. To appear less Jewish, I took out the bible and pretended to read it. *Bitch. Whore. Bitch. Whore.*

People were staring at me again, especially a nasty-looking middle-aged woman seated across the aisle. She had one of those zero-effort short haircuts

I detested. She wouldn't take her eyes off me and I couldn't stand it. "What the *fuck* are you looking at?" I yelled, louder than intended. Stunned, she immediately turned toward her window. "That's right, keep your fucking eyes to yourself!" I added for good measure. She hurried off at the next stop. The Aryan kept to himself, looking at his phone. I eyed him carefully.

As we got closer to Anaheim, I saw a sign for Disneyland and realized this was probably why I was drawn to this destination. Although I had not been there in years, as I was not attracted to rollercoasters or crowds, Disneyland had been a special place for me and my dad (my mom never had any interest in going). He would indulge me in all of my favorite things: cotton candy, kiddy rides, face paint, and anything involving pirates. I don't know that I even liked pirates, so much as my dad's impressions of them—which gave me belly laughs. And he always bought me a stuffed animal, my favorite being the battered Dumbo I still have today. But Disneyland was primarily a happy place for me because it was an escape from the chaos, disappointment and anxiety that had become a constant fixture in my life. We were just a father and daughter doing normal things, pushing our cares to the back burner.

After a few moments of bittersweet memories, I snapped back to reality. It had been over three hours and the bus was finally arriving in Anaheim. Early in the ride, I'd considered staying on longer, but I needed to get away from the Aryan and was starting to mistrust several other passengers as well. As soon as the bus came to a stop, I grabbed my backpack and flew to the door—which wasn't open yet. "Take it easy, miss," said the perturbed driver.

"Open the goddamned door!" What was his problem? As I pushed on the door, I was becoming increasingly hysterical.

"Are you okay? Can I call someone for you?"

I was ready to pry it open with my knife. I looked at him square in the eye, lowered my voice, and spoke slowly through gritted teeth. "Open. The. Fucking. Door. Now." His eyes widened as he pulled the lever. I flew out of the bus and ran at least eight blocks without looking back.

After stopping in an alley to catch my breath and drink some water, I started walking. I didn't know which way I was going; direction has never been my forte. But I speed-walked in the same direction, not stopping, for maybe three hours. I walked on sidewalks, and through alleys, fields, and private yards. I tried to stay as far away from people and cars as possible. My feet were hurting, but I had preternatural energy. I was like a sugar glider, flying around corners and trees—unreachable.

I started to notice more people around—maybe it was rush hour? I needed to hide. I headed toward a local park with a bathroom. My enemies hated bathrooms—too much disease. The bathroom, which consisted of only two stalls, was filthy. It smelled like urine and there were large spiderwebs in every corner. One of the toilets was clogged and there was a dirty sanitary pad on the floor. No, they would not find me here. I entered the least disgusting stall and locked the door. A few people came into the bathroom and tried to open my stall, but eventually things quieted down. I left the stall and paced around the bathroom until I thought I heard someone coming and went back in. Somehow my body shut down and I fell asleep hunched over on top of the dirty toilet lid.

I was awoken very early by a male voice asking if someone was there. I bolted upright, terror gripping me. I grabbed my pack, opened the stall, and startled an old man carrying a mop and other cleaning supplies. I ran across the park and stopped behind a tree. I tried to get my bearings, which was becoming increasingly difficult. I was now being relentlessly taunted. *Crazy stupid bitch. Dead bitch. Dead bitch. Dead bitch.* I held my ears, trying to shut them out, but to no avail. They chimed in even louder: *Crazy bitch. Dead bitch. Crazy bitch.* "Shut up, leave me alone!" I cried. It was no use. I'd forgotten my earbuds, so I couldn't try to drown them out. Maybe if I kept moving, I would lose them.

As I continued to walk, I realized that I desperately needed to go to the bathroom. *You were in a bathroom all night and didn't use it—idiot!* My stomach was churning, I needed to shit. *Oh no, this is terrible!* I wandered through a dingy neighborhood, clenching my butt cheeks together as sweat ran down my forehead. I was in someone's backyard and they didn't seem to be home. It was a tiny, rundown brown house with a yard surrounded by leafy bushes. I climbed inside a bush and pulled down my pants. I felt like bugs were crawling over me and eyes were watching, but I did what I had to do. I tried to wipe with a leaf, but it broke apart. *Disgusting stupid bitch. Stupid bitch. Nasty stupid bitch.* "Leave me alone!"

I pulled up my pants and fell out of the bush. I continued walking through the neighborhood until I came to the safety of a cemetery. I ducked behind the largest tombstone I could find and collapsed on the ground. It was a tall, two-person monument made of shiny granite with a huge white cross in the center. I felt protected next to Warren Edgar Smyth (1927-1996: Beloved Husband and Father) and Gladys Lynn Smyth (1926-2000: Beloved Wife and Mother). They likely had been someone else's babcia and papa. I felt sad that there were no flowers on their graves. I realized my grandparents had sent me here, to this gracious couple, and I whispered a "thank you" toward the sky. I leaned on the cold granite headstone and mumbled, trying to make sense of what was happening. Noticing I was lightheaded, I ate a granola bar and a few carrots. I took off my shoes and saw that my feet were bloody. On each of my big toes were open blisters that hurt like hell. I'd forgotten the first aid kit, so I wrapped my toes in toilet paper and put my shoes back on. I couldn't get too comfortable.

As I sat there, I received no warnings from comrades and, at one point, heard an Allied plane overhead. This was good—I was momentarily safe. I decided to secure my jewelry, taking out the diamond earrings, ruby ring, and diamond watch I'd grabbed on the way out the door. I also removed my wedding ring and added it to the pile. Making sure no one was watching, I sewed the jewelry into the hem of my sweatshirt and vowed only to remove it as a tradeoff for my life. When my task was completed and my body still, a piercing pain engulfed me. Being without Joshua was necessary; he would not have allowed me to escape and I couldn't put him in danger. But the sheer magnitude of leaving him crashed into me like a torrent. I bent forward and sobbed—keening over the loss of my beloved until emotionally spent.

I stayed in that cemetery, alternating between sitting and pacing—never venturing far from Warren and Gladys—until the next morning.

"Hello, ma'am?" I thought I was dreaming that an evil man was prodding me with a stick.

"Excuse me, ma'am, you can't sleep here."

I awoke to a gray-haired black man looking down at me. I sprang to my feet.

"I'm sorry, but you can't sleep here," he said, this time more kindly.

"I…I…I'm sorry. I will go now." I was disoriented, but picked up my stuff. I bent down and kissed each end of the headstones and took off.

This was my life now. I was hunted prey with nowhere to hide. I was running without direction or destination, alternating between unsafe and unwanted. I was bloody and soiled, my body aching without respite. As fear encircled me, I had but one objective: to flee. I considered the millions of Jews, including my ancestors, already murdered by the Nazis. I wondered how many would've survived had they known to act before the moment of exigency, had they not been systematically lied to, duped by Hitler's diabolical concealment of the Final Solution. I was lucky, I had been warned. There was nothing else for me to do except run.

Though my need to escape was obvious, my thoughts were convoluted—a scrambled mess of fear, confusion, and despair. There were occasional moments of relative clarity, like at the cemetery, where I felt some semblance of safety. But such moments eluded me, as I was continually harassed by forces inside and out. The demons had organized themselves into a belittling rhapsody that terrorized my every waking hour. They must've been implanted by the Gestapo, for their contempt was palpable, slowing down my escape. I would have to either ignore them and keep running, or lie down and die. This was the oppressive choice before me.

I wandered for a couple more hours. My superhuman energy depleted, I was growing weak. And the pain in my feet had become unbearable. As the sun started to go down, I knew I needed to stop. At this point, I was in an ugly part of the city, with rundown businesses and graffiti-sprayed walls. There were several check-cashing places, pawnbrokers, and liquor stores—with a mix of suspicious-looking and downtrodden people hanging out near their doors.

Garbage cans overflowed onto the sidewalks where disheveled homeless people sat with cardboard signs. The air was thick with cigarette smoke and smog. As I shuffled along, muttering to myself, I was struck by the dichotomy between that moment and those not so long ago when I thought I was normal. Men were not smiling at me here. No one was calling me beautiful or giving me roses. I was uncoveted. Worse, I was invisible. Yes, there was safety in invisibility, but it also came with astounding diminishment. I had become inconsequential, nothing. I found myself in an alley amongst other invisibles who sat around smoking or staring blankly. I collapsed there, consigned to the margins with my brethren, sitting with my backpack under my knees as I rocked back and forth. *At least here I would not be shunned.*

I don't know how long I was in that place, so blurry was my existence. There was one morning when my head had begun to pound—I needed coffee. I peeked around the alley corner and scurried toward the main street, with the knife under my sleeve. I came to a deli several blocks away where I bought a black coffee. I was considering buying some food when the store manager asked me to leave. *What had I become?* Ashamed, I hurried back to the alley.

The next day I found that a nearby tavern served coffee and had low standards when it came to clientele. As I was leaving with my cup, one of the patrons—an overweight man with thick lips and a red, swollen face reached out toward me. "Hey there, darlin,' I'll trade you a sandwich for a blow job?" He was missing a front tooth and his breath smelled like death. I pulled my arm back and was ready to punch him when the bartender told him to sit down and shut up. I flew out of there, reminding myself to be wary of that bloated bastard.

I quickly went through the little food I'd packed, as well as the money. I purchased a thick, scratchy blanket from an Army surplus store, and covered myself with it at night. Hunger began to gnaw at me. I could feel my shoulder and hip bones protruding sharply through my clothes, and my tailbone was aching from sitting on the pavement. I went to a grimy thrift store that smelled like BO and bought a used chair cushion. With no money left, I sat with my paltry possessions and contemplated how I might organize some food. I considered searching for a cash machine, but realized my wallet was gone. I'd likely be kicked out of stores anyway. At a loss, I filled my water bottle at a public bathroom and decided I could survive indefinitely on water alone. Or at least until the manhunt was called off.

Sitting under my blanket, my skin became irritated and itchy. The vermin had found me, abusing my skin and causing me to scratch until I bled. No amount of scratching helped, and I despaired succumbing to typhus. People in the alley mostly left me alone. If anyone came near, I scratched that much harder.

Once, when walking on the sidewalk, I saw a man with a yarmulke. He was about forty and had a slight limp. I was taken aback. "Hey," I said rather loudly, looking him dead in the face. "What are you doing out here? You need to hide! Or ride on the death cart. The pogrom is in effect. Defect. Defecate. Obliterate." He backed away, looking at me like I was garbage. How foolish he was!

I was constantly plagued by *them*—they were unremitting, bottomless. Seeing my latest level of depravity, they doubled their punishment. *Crazy, dirty bitch. Diseased bitch. Whore. Dead Whore. Dead. Dead. Dead.* I tried to drown them out by humming. Although somewhat muffled, they were still there, like a TV left on in another room. I rarely slept and, when I did, I saw my mother. She was always in red, and in constant movement—winding around my dreams with her huge, tortured eyes. I pleaded with her for some form of comfort, only to awaken confused and wanting. I often thought of Joshua, Chester, my dad, and my grandparents, which almost crippled me with grief. Like the demon chorus, I did my best to smother them out as well.

Twice, I saw Penterhaus when I left the alley. He was still on my tail. Both times, his yellow teeth flashed like traffic lights, as if to alert me of my impending doom. The second time, I screamed and turned the other way, smashing into a young Asian woman carrying a grocery bag. Onions, oranges, and frozen chicken legs hit the ground as she looked at me with disgust and yelled, "Watch it!" I grabbed an orange and ran. Later, as I devoured that orange, I felt such guilt—I'd never stolen anything before. *Stupid bitch. Stupid thieving bitch. Criminal. Bitch.* But that orange sustained me, keeping me alive for yet another day of abject misery—but alive, nevertheless.

Babcia came to me, only once, in a dream. I saw her there, with her Star of David necklace, pink lipstick, and blonde hair. She was watching me with tears rolling down her cheeks. She did not speak, but her love was omnipresent—in the air, on my skin, beneath my chest. She stayed with me for maybe an hour, consoling my afflicted mind. I crashed back into wakefulness with a distinct feeling she didn't want me to stay there. I looked at my bony arms and was reminded of the winding branches of a banyan tree. Soon I would be a Muselmann, and thus nothing more than fodder for the ovens. I needed to find food. Holding onto the wall, I stood up. After a few seconds of dizziness, I grabbed my pack and shuffled toward the street. I saw something bright in the distance and moved toward it. But then, heat permeated my body and my peripheral vision went black. As the darkness tunneled in, I succumbed to gravity. I felt the knife slip from my grasp just before my head hit the cement.

Chapter 27 ∽ Joshua

When Sunny returned from the hospital, I tiptoed around the condo like it was an active minefield. While she had regained her grasp of reality, Sunny was by no means herself. She wandered from room to room like a lost soul. I tried to comfort her, but she seemed too detached to receive it. I was a little relieved when she started to recover some energy. And, while I didn't want her to lose any more weight, I felt her renewed fitness was a good sign. She also cleaned extensively, organized all the drawers and cupboards, went shopping, and even cooked an amazing dinner. I did my best to show support and encouragement for each small accomplishment, but also found myself scrutinizing her as I waited for the next shoe to drop. I hated feeling such wariness, but it was beyond my control. My life had been hijacked by a mysterious assailant whom I could not see, yet who could ambush me at any moment. I wanted to better understand this invisible enemy and started reading up on mental illness. But when Sunny saw the small book I'd purchased about living with loved ones with schizophrenia, she became hostile.

"What's *this*?" she inquired, holding the book in front of my face.

"It's obviously a book about schizophrenia, I'm just—"

"Don't say that word!" she interrupted. "You think I'm crazy, you think I should be locked up." She tried to sound angry, but her face deceived her—revealing the shame that so viciously gnawed at her.

"Sweetheart, please don't be afraid of the word, it won't help. I want to understand schizophrenia, so I can be the best possible husband. And of course I don't want you locked up—that would break my heart." This elicited a flood of tears. Sunny couldn't accept her diagnosis and felt like a failure, which, based on the very book she was holding, was pretty typical among those first diagnosed. All I could do was hold her until she calmed down.

Even when she had more energy and was doing normal Sunny things, like exercising and organizing, something was off. It was as if she was only doing those things to present a healthy version of herself. There was no joy or satisfaction in any of it—she was just going through the motions. But I didn't comment on her increased activity, as I hoped it would become less feverish in time. Sunny had always been plagued by anxiety, and being hospitalized and stigmatized with a psychiatric label likely exacerbated it. She was keyed up and twitchy, and seemed to have an endless mental litany of what needed to be done next. Sometimes we watched TV together, but she seemed too distracted to follow even a basic plot. And she rarely smiled at anything funny—even Chester and me, her two favorite comedians.

By the end of her first weekend home, Sunny had become exceedingly cranky. But her irritability seemed to be masking something more sinister. Although she did her damnedest to suppress it, I could sense a red-hot current bubbling beneath the surface. One area where she was barely able to choke down those feelings was Tiffany. At first, Sunny refused to even acknowledge Tiffany's name, referring to her as "the babysitter." Then she came up with a strange nickname for her that made no sense to me. And any time she spoke of Tiffany, she did so with undisguised resentment and disgust, as if the poor girl was a festering sore that wouldn't go away.

I expected *some* backlash about hiring a home nurse—Sunny is a proud person after all. And I could understand her humiliation about receiving care from someone who appeared so young. But her degree of hostility was above and beyond. I knew the Tiffany situation was not sustainable— Sunny would eventually chew her up and spit her out—but, for now, it would have to do. For the most part though, Sunny didn't want to upset me and held her tongue about the various things pissing her off. But I could sense her igneous core and was careful not to enflame it. Like the excess energy, I figured it too would diminish with time, medication, and therapy.

And I was wrong. *Again.*

The Tuesday my wife disappeared was a hectic day at work. I'd been running from meeting to meeting and wasn't able to check my phone messages until around 2 p.m. When I heard Dr. Turner's message, my heart sank. She said Sunny was acting strangely during her therapy appointment earlier that day, that she was extremely distracted and restless, with a mask-like expression and eyes darting around the room. She said Sunny's responses were empty and vague, and that she left the appointment early because of an upset stomach.

Dr. Turner was worried that Sunny was decompensating and left a message with Dr. Bensen sharing the same information. My next message was indeed from Dr. Bensen, who said he'd been trying to get a hold of Sunny and she wasn't returning his calls. He too was worried about her recent behavior and wanted to see her right away. Tiffany had also left a message that Sunny had diarrhea, so they left therapy early. *This was just great.* Sunny had not complained of any stomach issues and was far too discreet to reveal a diarrhea issue to *anyone*—let alone Tiffany. At least not if she was in her right mind. No, her mind wasn't right at all. And I was an idiot for minimizing the signs.

I immediately called Sunny and it went straight to voicemail. She wasn't responding to texts either. *Shit.* I canceled my next meeting and headed home, apprehensive of what awaited me. When I got there, I was relieved to see Sunny's car in its usual spot. I opened the front door and called for her, no answer. I looked around the condo and everything seemed in its place, but Sunny was not there. Then I saw the closed bathroom door. I was immediately flooded with panic as I pictured Sunny submerged in a bath of bloodied water. Or sprawled out on the cold tiles with empty pill bottles strewn about.

I yelled for her as I approached the door, but the only voice I heard was Chester's. I threw open the door and saw that he had been shut in there with a soft bed, plenty of food and water, and a litter box. *What the fuck, Sunny?* My wife loved Chester beyond words. Sometimes I thought she loved him more than me. Her locking him in the bathroom was ominous at best. She seemed to be trying to protect him and, worse yet, was clearly not planning on being here to take care of him for a while. I ran around the rooms in a frenetic state, calling her name. As I looked more closely, I saw that her backpack was no longer in the closet. Her purse was on the dresser, but her phone and wallet were missing. And I didn't see her pill bottles anywhere.

Sunny was gone.

Hoping she hadn't ventured far, I ran outside to look for her. At first, I walked around the neighborhood, asking anyone who walked by if they'd seen her. When I realized I was getting nowhere, I went back home and got in the car. I drove everywhere I could think of—her favorite grocery store, a couple of local parks, and the beach. I also tried to follow her typical jogging route, but to no avail.

I went back home and called Peter, hoping desperately that she was at his house—although, deep down, I knew she wasn't. Peter had no idea where she was and became quickly alarmed. I also texted Elizabeth to see if she'd seen Sunny, but she hadn't. Elizabeth was also instantly concerned, calling me back right away and asking tons of questions. I didn't want to deal with her at that moment and, fortunately, she was at work so she couldn't come over. Just as I hung up, Peter rushed in. He must've dropped everything, because he was there in ten minutes.

He entered the place as if I hadn't already looked for her, walking from room to room.

"Peter, she isn't here. I've checked everywhere. And besides, she locked Chester in the bathroom and took her backpack and pills."

"Oh shit." He ran his fingers through his thick hair as he paced around, not sure what to do. "I called her four times, she's not answering."

"I know, I've called her repeatedly. I think her phone's off. Should we call the cops?" I asked.

"Well, she's an adult and it's only been a couple hours, so I doubt they'll do anything. But she's mentally ill, so maybe." He made the call. It must've been a slow day since two police officers were there in fifteen minutes.

Officers Brasko and Jones were both white men who looked to be in their 30s, but whose appearances were worlds apart. Brasko was at least 6'3" with thick, black hair and a bushy mustache. He also had a resounding beer belly that looked uncomfortable hanging over his gun belt. He was jovial and loud as he entered the condo, causing Chester to hide under the bed. Jones was only about 5'9" and had a wiry frame. He had dark blonde hair and glasses, and looked more like a college professor than a cop. We all sat down in the living room and Jones took out a pad of paper and pen.

"So, you say your wife's missing?" asked Brasko, looking at Peter.

"No, *my* wife," I interjected.

"And for how long?" he said, looking at me.

"Since noon or so."

Both cops looked at me like I was a moron. "Since *noon?* You mean today?" said Brasko, sounding incredulous. "How old is she?"

"She's twenty-three," answered Peter. "But you don't understand. Sunny is mentally ill. She was just in the psychiatric hospital on a 5250. She was psychotic and trying to hurt herself. So, her age is not really relevant, officers. She's a serious danger to herself."

"That may be, but it's only been a couple of hours. How do you know she hasn't gone for a walk or shopping or something?" responded Brasko. "Maybe, you know, meeting up with a friend?" His last point came with a sideways look in my direction. I could tell what he was insinuating and it filled me with rage.

"Look, you don't get it! My wife has disappeared with her backpack and medications after acting bizarrely at her therapist's appointment this morning. She's been extremely delusional and paranoid, and is likely running from some perceived enemies. She is not, I repeat, *not* at the mall or having a fucking affair. She is not safe and we need to locate her ASAP!" I was almost yelling and could feel my chest tighten as I was losing my breath.

Officer Jones looked at me with a softened expression. "Take it easy, Mr…"

"Fitzpatrick."

"Take a deep breath. We can fill out a report and, if she's still gone after three days, we can put her in the FBI database as a missing endangered adult." He sounded more compassionate than the other cop, but *three days? My God.* They asked a variety of questions about Sunny, including her description and what she'd been wearing. I went into the other room and called Tiffany for a description of Sunny's clothes that day while Peter answered their questions. I also gave them two recent photos of Sunny, which was gut-wrenching. I'd watched countless crime dramas where devastated parents provided photos of their missing children whom they rarely ever saw again. I never thought I'd be sharing Sunny's beautiful image to this end and it made me sick to my stomach.

When they finished their questioning, Officer Jones suggested we hang fliers with Sunny's photo, physical description, and contact information. He also said we should reach out to Sunny's friends, coworkers, and acquaintances, and regularly check in with local hospitals and shelters. Fortunately, he left out morgue, but I knew that too would be on the list if she didn't resurface soon. I also knew *that* was one phone call I couldn't make.

Once the cops left, Peter and I just looked at each other in disbelief. Neither of us had any words. We collapsed onto the couch and had a glass of Scotch, which I kept around only for Peter. But this time I needed it too.

"Well, looks like we've reached the next level of Dante's inferno," he said after polishing off his drink. "I guess we should drive around and look for her."

"I already did."

"Well, I can't just sit here. I'm going to go look for her. You stay here in case she comes home. And start calling her friends, okay?"

"I already did." Sunny only had one real friend. "But I'll work on the flier."

"Sounds good," he said, dropping his glass off in the sink before heading toward the door. "Joshua, we'll find her," he added on the way out, clearly attempting to make both of us feel better.

"I know."

Once he left, I felt an acute sense of the hollowness of my life without Sunny. I sat on the couch with Chester on my lap trying to brainstorm where she might have gone. I was struck with one idea and called Peter, who picked up in one ring.

"Is she there?" he asked, almost pleading. I hated to crush him.

"No, but I think you should check the cemetery."

"Oh yeah, good idea. Thanks."

Peter didn't call back for hours. He'd driven all over San Diego, asking everyone he passed if they'd seen her. I imagined him dragging his forlorn body back home only to sit staring at the wall just as I had. Understanding my and Peter's fragile emotional states, Linda ended up creating the fliers. She used a recent picture which showed Sunny standing on the beach with the ocean behind her. She was wearing a yellow sundress with spaghetti straps that accented her tanned shoulders. It was a windy day and her beautiful dark curls were flying all over the place. She was looking off in the distance with an expression that was both melancholy and nebulous—as if the secret behind the slight smirk on her face was hers alone. The way the light accentuated the green in her eyes took my breath away. *My beautiful girl with the broken smile—where are you?*

Linda came by with a stack of fliers. She gave me a warm hug, which I realized I needed. "We're going to find her, Joshua," she said, looking directly at me with her hands resting on my shoulders. She was more convincing than Peter. I just nodded my head; I didn't want to cry in front of her.

After she left, I grabbed a stapler and took off. I attached fliers all over the neighborhood and several miles beyond. I couldn't stand to look at the photo, so I attached them quickly—focusing only on the four corners. Then I went back home and sat some more. It turned out to be the longest night of my life thus far. I ate some cheese and crackers, watched the news apprehensively, and tossed and turned all night. I got no sleep whatsoever. The next morning my head was spinning and I was overwrought with panic. My mind was dragging me into the darkest circles of hell. I was consumed by "what ifs"—what if she'd been abducted? What if she was lying half dead in an alley somewhere? What if she was fruitlessly calling my name, desperate for me to come find her? I paced around the living room, totally nonfunctional. Eventually, I picked up the phone and called my boss.

"Hi, Julia, it's Joshua. Um…I'm so sorry, but I can't come in today." My voice broke, but I had to keep going. "My wife is missing."

"What, oh my God, Joshua! I'm *so* sorry. Is there anything I can do?" I could hear that I was no longer on speakerphone. Her voice took on a tone that was both compassionate and urgent.

"No, thank you, Julia. I just can't come in." I was crying, but doing my best to hide it.

"Well, of course you're not coming in! I *forbid* you to come in! You take all the time you need and don't worry about your job. We value you here so much, so please don't worry. You know, I went through something like this with my son a few years ago, so I understand and I'm here for you."

Somewhere beneath the deluge of despair that was trying to drown me, I felt relief. At least my job wasn't on the line. "Thank you so much, I really appreciate it."

She reemphasized her willingness to help me before we ended the call. It was a surprising conversation. Julia, who was in her early fifties, had always been nice, but was all business. When it came to marketing products, the woman knew her shit. But I'd always found her unapproachable. Or maybe I was just intimidated by her? Tragedy had a way of dissolving the layers we hide behind. In Julia's case, it revealed a kind and empathetic foundation.

Once I had coffee and my headache was under control, I got to work. I didn't want to see anyone, but there was no way around it. I called Peter and we decided to set up a meeting with the two of us, plus Linda, Elizabeth, and Randy. We met at the condo in the afternoon. Everyone showed up punctually, their expressions austere. Peter looked like hell. I imagined his night was similar to mine. Linda was all efficiency, bringing not only more fliers, but coffee and sandwiches. Elizabeth was full of energy, wanting to go look for her right away. And Randy, who'd never experienced anything like this before, was quiet but supportive.

We made a plan. Linda gave each of us more fliers and we assigned neighborhoods to each person. We also assigned bus and train stations. I'd been checking our bank account regularly to determine if Sunny had withdrawn any money. She hadn't, so I didn't think she could go far. Then we created a list of hospitals and shelters within a 200-mile radius and gave everyone a list of places to call each day. We promised each other to stay in constant communication, especially if we heard or thought of *anything* that might help. Peter and I would be contacting the police and if, God forbid, she wasn't found in three days, we would ensure that she was on the FBI registry of missing persons. And that was it. We had our mission and at least it gave us a purpose, a reason to carry on.

Once they left, I hopped in my car, driving ten miles outside of town to post fliers. Along the way, I saw Sunny's beautiful face in the most incongruous of places—on gas station windows, near supermarkets, and on posts near sleeping homeless people. There was a flier outside a bowling alley on which some lowlife piece of shit had drawn a cock near her mouth—*fuck!* I ripped the paper from the window, wadding it up and tossing it in the garbage. I was so enraged at that moment, I had to stop myself from punching my fist through the window. What had my life become? When I was done with the fliers, I went back home and made calls. I had five hospitals and shelters on my list, so I called each one. She was nowhere to be found.

On the third day, Peter called me in the morning and said Sunny would be placed in the missing person's database that afternoon. I didn't want it to come to this, but at least it might help. That day, just like the rest of them that week, I got up from a fitful sleep, slammed some coffee, drove around fixing and adding fliers, and making my calls. The front desk people I spoke with were generally nice, but were also starting to get sick of me. They had no idea of true sickness—the kind that annihilates the soul, burying you a little more each day. I fluctuated from being on autopilot and suppressing my pain, to being doubled over with grief at the thought of my Sunny out there alone and petrified. And the thought of living without her—this one was too much, it was incomprehensible.

The rare times I actually dreamt, I was plunged into my worst fears—Sunny lying dead, with bluish skin and wide, vacant eyes. Sunny being tortured by some sadistic fuck. Sunny jumping in front of a speeding car. Sometimes in those dreams I heard her calling my name, which was the most perverse kind of torture, as I awoke thinking she was right there, asking for me. That period was the most hellish twist on *Groundhog Day* imaginable.

Somewhere in that haze of despair, I knew I needed to call my parents. But I *so* didn't want to. Although I knew it was wrong, I'd been putting it off for days. I was dying inside and they were my parents, they deserved to know. I just kept postponing it, thinking we'd find her. But I also knew it had the potential to make things even worse. I finally talked myself into it one evening, downing two shots of bourbon before picking up the phone.

"Hi, Mom," I said, trying to sound normal.

"Hi, Joshy! We were just talking about you. How's everything going?

How's work?"

"It's okay, I mean work is good."

"Josh, what's wrong, you sound strange."

"Um, well, a couple days ago, or I guess three days ago, Sunny disappeared."

"*What?* What do you mean 'disappeared'?" I could hear her muffle the phone as she yelled, "Rick, come quick, Sunny's missing!" *Oh fuck, here comes the shitshow.* I poured myself another shot.

My dad got on another phone. "What's going on?" he asked calmly.

"When I came home from work on Tuesday, she was gone."

"*Tuesday?*" interrupted my mom. "And you're just *now* telling us?" *This is precisely why I didn't want to call them.*

"What do you mean?" asked my dad, ignoring her.

"Sunny has been having some psychological problems, really serious ones. She came back from the hospital and we thought she was better." I could hear my mom say, "Hospital?" But I just kept talking. "They think…" *No, I won't tell them that much.* "She's having a lot of depression and I thought she was much better. But then I came home and she was gone. Also, her therapist said she was acting weird that day, so…" *Okay, Mom, let me have it.*

"Oh, Joshua, why didn't you tell me. This is awful. I mean, I knew the girl had problems, but *this*? Are you sure she didn't leave town purposely?"

"What the fuck, Mom! No, she didn't leave *purposely*. She's mentally ill and terrified people are after her, so she fled. That's it. Don't *ever* say that again!" I was ready to hang up.

"Debbie, go get a glass of water," said my dad in an annoyed tone. "Josh, what's being done to find her?"

I explained everything and he listened quietly. I could hear my mom crying in the background and saying they needed to fly here immediately. *Hell no.*

"Dad, please get Mom to calm down. It's not helpful *at all*. In fact, it's really pissing me off! Sunny is the love of my life, *I have to find her.*" My voice broke yet again. "We're doing everything and I'll keep you posted. I just wanted you to know."

"I know, son. I understand. We will wait a little longer, but at some point, we will need to come help you. Can we at least send you some money, do you have enough? Are you eating?" I could hear my mom in the background. "Rick, what are you saying? He needs us there *now!*"

"Linda keeps dropping off food and I'm okay with money,

thanks though."

"We love you very much, and we love Sunny too. We're here for you, whatever you need."

"Okay, thanks, Dad." My dad had never been that mushy toward me, it felt strange.

Once we hung up, I rested my face in my hands and cried. Then I went to bed with Chester and tossed in and out of night terrors until morning.

On the sixth day, I dragged myself through the motions—driving, looking, and calling. I remember it was a rainy day and many of the fliers had become soggy and needed to be replaced. One of them was so wet, Sunny's face looked distorted, like she'd morphed into the demons within her. I just left it there, not able to touch it. Once I'd made my calls, I sat on the couch and drank a beer while I stared blankly at the sports channel. As I contemplated forcing myself to eat something, the phone rang. It was Officer Jones.

"Good evening, Joshua. I have some good news. A mentally ill street woman meeting your wife's description was brought to a hospital in Anaheim with a concussion. She refers to herself as "Sunny.""

Once I got more details and hung up, I let out a screech that must've sounded inhuman. I could feel the brick in my heart start to give way as I whispered to Chester, "They found her. They found our girl."

I called Peter and could almost feel his relief when he heard the news. He said he would be driving to the hospital straightaway. I also let Elizabeth and Randy know what was going on. Then I sprang from the couch, put on my shoes, and raced out the door.

Fortunately, it was after rush hour, so the traffic wasn't too bad. I listened to classical music in an effort to calm my mind. But, throughout the drive, the same line danced through my head in chorus with the music: "Please be her, please be her, please be her…" I drove like a madman, arriving in Anaheim in about ninety minutes. I located the hospital, which was a tall white building that looked more like a jail than a medical facility. I took the elevator to the third floor where I was directed to Sunny's room. I took several deep breaths before entering.

I'd never been a religious man, but when I saw my wife's battered body lying there, I whispered "thank you" to whatever omnipotent presence I hoped was protecting her. Then I approached her bed. Honestly, if I hadn't been told she might be here, I wouldn't have recognized the person sleeping before me as Sunny. Her dark hair was dirty and matted—well on its way toward dreadlocks, and she stank to high heaven. Her painfully thin arms were resting on her sides, each one being held by a restraint. *Just great.* Both of her arms were covered with horrible scratches, as though she'd literally tried to scrape her skin off. On the back of one of her hands was a hideous reddish-purple bruise; and, in the other hand, an IV was inserted, dripping fluids from a bag hanging off to the side. There was a pulse monitor gripping one index finger and several small tubes were attached to her chest. Her arms were covered in a light coating of dirt and her fingernails, on which only a spec of pink nail polish remained, were filthy and framed by mangled cuticles. She was sound asleep and would've appeared peaceful if not for the condition of her face. Her cheeks were sunken in, she had dark circles under her eyes, the parts of her skin not covered in dirt were ghostly white, and her lips were dry and cracked. There was also an ugly red knot on the left corner of her forehead.

She had the appearance of the hunted and brutalized Jew she believed herself to be.

Once I'd contacted Peter, Elizabeth, Randy, and my parents to let them know Sunny had indeed been found, I sat staring at her for about ten minutes when a woman appeared. She was young and pretty with blonde hair piled on her head in a bun and a pen behind one ear. She was wearing light blue scrubs and white sneakers.

"Hello, I'm Dr. Epstein," she said, shaking my hand firmly. Her high voice made her seem like an imposter rather than a real doctor. I introduced myself, but she already knew I was her patient's husband. I imagined myself with a stamp across my forehead: "Distraught husband of psychotic woman." I must've looked weathered and beaten well beyond my years. I gave her Sunny's full name and some basic demographic information and she filled me in on her situation.

"Your wife was picked up by an ambulance a couple of hours ago. She collapsed on a sidewalk downtown. She has a concussion, which we are watching closely. She was in and out of consciousness when she came in, and was extremely agitated. An IV drip was immediately inserted, given her emaciated appearance. We were able to run some tests and she's severely dehydrated, her electrolytes are way off—as is her hematocrit, and she's anemic. We're trying to pump her with fluids, but she's already managed to pull out her IV and jump out of bed—hence the restraints. We sedated her with a shot of Ativan." Despite her cartoon voice, Dr. Epstein appeared competent.

"She was recently diagnosed with schizophrenia, she's extremely paranoid—especially when it comes to hospitals," I said wearily. I considered how many times I'd be explaining this in my lifetime.

"That makes sense. Although we thought she was homeless."

"No, she ran off six days ago. Her father and I have been out of our minds looking for her. Even with the shape she's in, I can't tell you how relieved I am to see her. Doctor, what do you think happened to her arms—was she defending herself from an attack?"

"No, those are self-inflicted." *Thank God.* "We checked for lice, but she's clear. Does she use drugs?"

"No, not at all. Her lips look awful, can someone give her some balm or something?"

"Of course, I'll tell the nurse."

"What are the next steps for her treatment?"

"We need to get her stabilized before discharging or transferring her. We're monitoring her kidney function as we continue to administer fluids. She's also severely underweight. Has she ever been diagnosed with anorexia nervosa?"

"No, she's always been thin, but she hasn't been eating well because of her mental illness. Plus, I'm sure she's barely eaten anything while living on the streets over the past week."

"Well, we haven't weighed her yet, but I'm guessing her BMI is somewhere around fifteen, which is certainly not healthy. So, we'd like to slowly work on getting some meals in her. She will likely need to be here a few days. Do you have the name of her psychiatrist? Our resident psychiatrist would like to set up a call and get Sunny back on her meds."

I gave her Dr. Bensen's number and she said the psychiatrist, Dr. Haagen, would be by to chat with Sunny later. Before she left, she told me to press the nurse button if Sunny woke up or if I needed anything. Once alone, I sat back down and listened to the steady beep of the machines—dreading the moment she would wake up.

About two hours after I arrived at the hospital, all hell broke loose. I was surprised to see both Peter *and* Linda show up, waking me from a light sleep in yet another crappy hospital chair. They were both horrified by Sunny's appearance and stood there staring at her in disbelief for several minutes. I told them what the doctor said.

"My poor angel, she looks like a skeleton," whispered Peter, not taking his eyes off his daughter.

Linda came over and gave me a hug. Unlike her usual hippie chic look, she was wearing gray sweats and a pink T-shirt. Her blonde hair was pulled back in a tight ponytail, which exposed the gray strands around her face. It wasn't a flattering look. As she started to say something, we heard Sunny stir. The moments before Sunny woke up were like wind flurries before a tornado. In her case, we never knew if they foretold a light storm or one that could tear down walls. Our answer came soon enough.

Sunny's head started darting from right to left as she tried to pull herself out of the restraints. She opened her eyes and processed her surroundings.

"Oh no, no, no, no, no!" she lamented, looking around the room and at each of us. "Not *here*. This path of bloodied sand. Blood on your hands. Get me out, Daddy!" Linda went to get the doctor. Although panicked, with wide, terrorized eyes, the rest of Sunny's face was oddly expressionless. But she tossed herself around wildly, like a rabid beast.

"Sweetheart, please stop, it's okay," soothed Peter helplessly. He put his hand on her arm, which only caused Sunny to recoil and then intensify her struggling.

"Hide me, Daddy. They followed me, the Herrenvolk is here. Untie me, I'm scared. I'm nonessential. I'm going to die. Die, die, death, dead, dread. Say the Kaddish, Daddy. Say it! *Say it!*" At this point, she was screaming. I'd never seen her so hysterical. Tears rolled down her cheeks, she had spittle on both sides of her cracked lips, and her breath was repugnant. I was reminded of Linda Blaire in *The Exorcist* as I pictured Sunny's head spinning.

Peter and I were beside ourselves—there was no comforting her. Linda came back in the room with Dr. Epstein, which only fed Sunny's delusion.

"Stay back, murderer—you too Linda, *get the fuck out!*" The doctor started to speak, but she was interrupted by a scream of such shrillness it must've alarmed the other patients.

"Sunny, I'm Dr. Epstein and I'm not going to hurt you," responded the doctor ineffectually. "I'm going to give you something to help you relax." This only made Sunny scream louder. Dr. Epstein gave her an injection in one of her thighs, which I noticed was also restrained. "You'll be okay, Sunny," she said, backing away from the bed.

"No no no! I don't want to! It's genocide, it's the other line, the other side. *No!*" She continued her tirade, although her screams subsided after the shot. It seemed she'd given up and accepted her fate a bit more. She continued to pull at the restraints, but eventually closed her eyes and fell asleep.

In the sudden quiet after the storm, I looked at the other adults in the room. Dr. Epstein seemed flustered, and her brow was sweaty. Maybe this was her introduction to treating the grossly psychotic—schizophrenia 101. Peter was shaking and had tears in his eyes. And Linda was just standing there in shock as she stared at Sunny.

Dr. Epstein broke our communal stupor. "Okay, well, you weren't kidding about the paranoia," she said looking at me.

I wondered if I looked as shell-shocked as the others. I must've been holding my breath, as I let out an enormous sigh. "Sadly, no."

She introduced herself to Peter and Linda, then left the room to page Dr. Haagen. Peter sat down and put his head in his hands. I don't think he was actually crying. Maybe, like me, he was empty of tears and was too frustrated and sad to do anything other than collapse into himself. Linda sat next to him, rubbing his back as she wiped her teary eyes.

Such was our initiation into hospital number two. It wasn't that different from the first hospital, except that it was an older building with a dingy appearance. But this time we weren't in the psych ward—at least not yet. The three of us stayed in that room, not saying much of anything, for two hours. Sometimes one of us left to get coffee or go to the bathroom, but mostly we just sat there solemnly.

We saw nurses go in and out, checking Sunny's vitals and making notes. I had to ask again for lip balm and, after about an hour, a rather flamboyant male nurse coated Sunny's mouth with an excessive amount of Vaseline. Eventually, a short, overweight doctor with gray hair showed up. He introduced himself as Dr. Haagen, the resident psychiatrist. He was dressed in an ill-fitting blue button-up shirt that he'd likely been wearing since the 80s, along with cheap brown slacks. His coarse hair was wavy and in need of a trim, and his eyebrows were comical—sticking out in various directions. On a better day, those eyebrows would've made Sunny smile. His appearance contrasted sharply with that of Dr. Bensen, but he spoke with the warmth we so desperately needed.

He said he'd already consulted with Dr. Bensen, and we gave him the rest of Sunny's history. Since there was no psychiatric ward at this hospital, he wanted to transfer her back to San Diego. We readily agreed.

"I'd like to get Sunny back on antipsychotic medication as soon as possible. She should be waking shortly and I will assess her. However, based on my consultation with Dr. Epstein, it seems likely that she will not consent to medication. Do you agree?" he asked, looking at each of us.

"In her current condition, not likely," answered Peter. "But she trusts Dr. Bensen, so we need to get her back in his care immediately."

"I couldn't agree more." He looked at his notes, adding, "Sunny was acutely psychotic before being sedated. She's also medically compromised because of her mental illness. Therefore, I believe emergency antipsychotic treatment will be indicated here. Do the two of you agree that Sunny needs antipsychotic medication?" he asked, looking at me and Peter.

"Yes!" we said in unison.

"Okay, I'll chat with her when she wakes up and we'll take it from there."

Sunny woke up an hour later. She was in the same agitated state as before, except not as tumultuous thanks to the Ativan. She made more nonsensical statements pertaining to her impending murder and the SS, and pleaded with us to help her escape. When we stepped out so Dr. Haagen could meet with her, we could hear her profanity-riddled insults all the way down the hall. Mental illness had a way of making Sunny cuss like a sailor.

She of course refused treatment. Dr. Haagen performed emergency treatment as anticipated; however, he gave Sunny a shot of Risperidone rather than Haldol, believing the newer medication would have fewer side effects. The Risperidone and IV regimen continued for two days, with the three of us standing watch while Sunny alternated between sleeping, crying, screaming, and talking nonsense until she was finally transferred back to Dr. Bensen's care. At least then we were back to the hell we knew.

Chapter 28 ✣ Sunny

I awoke strapped to my deathbed. This was a new infirmary—the one where they would finally execute me. After all of my running and hiding, I was caught *yet again*. Joshua, my dad, and even stupid Linda were all there, watching the pathetic scene before them. Why wouldn't they hide me? Even I could see that I was now useless to the Germans. But my "loving" family just stood there studying me as I awaited my demise. *They* were there too, always by my side, reminding me who I was. *You're caught, stupid bitch. Dead bitch. Dead bitch. Dead bitch.*

A short, plump man came toward me with the poison. I screamed, "Get away from me, you fucker! Motherfucker, killer. Plump fucker of the motherland. Fat barrel of donkey spunk! Fucking collaborator!" I tried to scratch and claw, but those bastards had tied me down. I felt the shot in my thigh and realized it was all over for me. At least the pain would finally stop.

But the pain did not stop.

For endless blurry hours, or perhaps days, I was back and forth, in and out. Not so easy to kill, I gloated silently. There was a bag of poison dripping into my arm that I wanted desperately to pull out. But, since even *that* couldn't kill me, they'd decided to fatten me up—to prepare me for hard labor instead. This appeared to be a transit hospital—an intermediate step before the labor camp where I would be worked to death.

There was always food around me. Whether I awoke from mercifully dreamless sleep or sleep terrors either featuring my mother, Penterhaus, Nazi guards, or vicious German shepherds hungry for Jewish blood, the damned food was *always* there. Either my dad or Joshua would constantly beg me to eat, bringing muffins, crackers, bananas, pizza slices, and toast. But I was torn. Should I eat and go to the camps where I might survive, or should I just drift off into quiet oblivion? Plus, *they* were telling me the food was poisoned: *Eat it bitch. Die bitch. Eat the poison bitch.* Sometimes I ignored *them* and ate a little bit, especially after I awoke to see Babcia standing over me. She looked appropriately angelic, in a long white gown. She didn't say anything, but looked at me with a love so ferocious, it penetrated all the way through to my lucid mind. She wanted me to be okay—I could feel it in my bones. So, I tried my best to eat the food my family brought, not trusting the hospital food. But I could only digest small amounts.

There were constantly nurses checking on me, waking me up and asking questions. And my family was there too. I recall one particular moment when I awoke very late in the night and saw Joshua alone in the room. He was staring at me with a forlorn expression. He perked up and gave me a vacant smile.

"Hey, Slugger. How do you feel?"

"Let me die, Joshua. My Joshua, my gentile. You are not selected for the gas. The gas and the poison. This poison inside me."

I saw tears on his face, which should have touched me in some way.

"Sunny, *don't say that!* I will *never* let you die." His voice broke at the word "never" and he cried as he spoke, no longer trying to hold back. "You are *my life,* forever. You are sick, that's all. We *will* get you better, I promise." He stopped and blew his nose. I could see that he loved me dearly, though I hadn't a clue why.

Eventually, they put me in an ambulance. I didn't know if carbon monoxide would asphyxiate me or if I was going to a camp. They said something about another hospital, but I didn't believe them. I lay there, helplessly strapped down, as *they* abused me for the entire ride. *Death car, bitch. You're dead, whore. Bitch. Whore. Bitch.* When I was finally wheeled outside after that long, miserable ride, I saw the familiar building.

Okay, maybe I would not die today.

At some point, I realized I was back in the psych ward. My room was much the same as the last one, with its gray linoleum floor, four hideous green vinyl chairs—two on each side of the bed, small bathroom in the right corner, and framed print of a lemon tree hanging over the bed. All of the players were there too: Dr. Bensen, the Beautiful Beast, the skinny nurse with the zits, and the black male nurse whose hearty laugh echoed down the hallways. I eventually remembered that the Beautiful Beast was actually a kind woman named Maggie. And, just like last time, she removed my restraints after I promised to remain calm. It was a huge relief to be liberated from those straps. They made me feel panicky and claustrophobic. It seemed criminal to tie up such weak, rangy limbs.

Dr. Bensen came by a few times and, along with his ready supply of questions about my mood and twisted thoughts, he was constantly trying to talk me into taking some new medicine. I was drowsy and mostly ignored him, until one day when he caught me after my morning coffee kicked in.

"Good morning, Sunshine," he said as he sat his refined ass in the chair near my bed.

"That's what my dad calls me."

"Then I will reserve it for him," he said smiling. "How are you feeling? You sound much better."

"I feel nothing. Is this a transit hospital?"

"What do you mean?"

"A place in-between camps."

"No. This is a regular hospital where we are helping you to feel better."

"I don't feel." It was true, I was numb and apathetic—a deserted vessel.

"I understand. You have a psychiatric illness. It's affecting your ability to feel and understand reality. Plus, your meds haven't been consistent. But, when you first got here, your words made no sense and you were highly agitated. You're already doing better, even though you may not feel it."

This all sounded familiar. I was confused—as usual. "No camps?"

"No camps, I promise. At the prior hospital, they gave you injections of a medicine called Risperidone. You had been living on the streets and were at death's door. Do you remember this?"

"I was hiding. I was invisible. That plump doctor stabbed me with poison."

"Not poison, Sunny, *medicine*. Medicine that is already helping. You were likely having side effects from the Haldol, your face was expressionless and you were sweating profusely. So, Dr. Haagan gave you Risperidone instead. Do you remember when you were here before?"

I nodded. It was vague, but I did recall being there. Somehow, I'd survived it.

"Just like then, I'm going to ask you to trust me. I'd like your consent to continue the Risperidone, along with another medicine called Depakote. I believe you have psychosis as well as extreme mood fluctuations. The term for this is 'schizoaffective disorder.'"

"No, I'm schizophrenic," I said duly. *Crazy bitch. Lunatic. Whore. Whore.*

Crazy fucking whore. They were suddenly relentless.

"No, I believe you are *schizoaffective*. Which is similar, except that you also experience episodes of mania and depression."

I guess I was relieved. I didn't know anything about schizoaffective disorder, but I'd take anything over schizophrenia.

"I want to apologize for not catching this earlier." He was so void of arrogance, this doctor.

"That's okay, doesn't matter."

"It matters, but thank you. On a better note, I'm confident that these two medicines will be more effective for you. And they will help to stop the voices. Will you agree to take them?"

How I detested those *fucking murderous voices.* "You can make them stop?"

"Yes, the voices should subside after you're on the medicine a while longer."

He looked sad, maybe disappointed in himself. I wanted to please him. "Yeah, I guess that's okay."

"Terrific. We'd also like to keep you here for eleven more days, will you agree to that, too?"

"I don't know. I miss Chester, I want to go home." Then I thought about it for a moment. "But now they know where I live. Can you protect me here?"

"Absolutely."

"Will you hide me if they come for me? The last place refused to hide me."

"We will keep you safe here, you have my word."

And so I signed everything he wanted me to sign, not really caring one way or another. I would never truly be free.

My dad and Joshua were thrilled that I'd agreed to the doc's requests; it likely saved them a lot of hassle. I repeatedly told Joshua I wanted to go home, but all he said was, "Soon, my love, soon." My thoughts started to clear somewhat, but *they* still visited pretty regularly. It seems they were hard to kill too. Following Dr. Bensen's suggestion, Joshua brought me my iPod and earbuds. When the bastards chanted their insults, I would drown them out with music. They managed to worm their way into softer songs, like those by Nora Jones and, much to my disappointment, Jewel. So, I cranked Nine Inch Nails, Incubus, Nirvana, and Alice in Chains. If I was really desperate, I'd play AC/DC. It gave me satisfaction to know *they* couldn't get to me over the music, even if it did give me a headache. At some miniscule level, I felt I was winning.

I started to feel safe in the hospital, but I was getting bored. When I dared to leave my room, I sometimes came face-to-face with the other hopelessly befuddled. There was a gaunt teenage girl who resembled Karen Carpenter. She would often pace the hallways, talking to herself. But she never looked at me; she was alone in her misery. And then there was Phyllis. She was maybe seventy years old with enormous droopy boobs and a round body, almost no teeth, and long, straight platinum blonde hair. She always wore a lot of makeup and costume jewelry, along with brightly colored velour sweatsuits that accented her copious bulges. Every time she saw me, her face lit up. I guess I reminded her of someone.

"Hello, dear, ain't you a pretty one! Can I paint your nails?" she would say in her booming voice. I usually gave her a polite "no thank you," and went on my way. But I could always hear her—she talked to everyone who went by, especially the men. With them, she would flirt like her life depended on it, saying things like, "Hello, handsome. How 'bout a taste of this sweeeeet pussy? Want a romp in the hay? Or a little sucky sucky?" When she asked the last question, she would make grotesque sucking noises with her nearly toothless mouth. Once I caught her in the act of trying to seduce a timid young black patient. He looked like a trapped deer as she cornered him in the hall. She stuck her boobs in his face and was practically purring at him while gyrating her hips. "Hello, lover. Bet you ain't never fucked a *real* woman," she taunted garishly. Luckily for him, she was quickly admonished and sent to her room.

I remember initially thinking I was surrounded by freaks—that I didn't belong there. But later, as I was sitting in the sunroom trying not to stare at an obese bald man who was basically comatose, rocking back and forth as drool hung from his chin, I was hit by the alarming realization that *I was one of these people.* This was how normal people must've regarded me. That epiphany left me so depressed, I went back to bed for the rest of the day.

One particularly shitty day when I saw Phyllis in the hall, she stopped and stared at me. "Girl, you best wash that hair. No offense, honey, but you is ripe! You gonna scare away the mens!" At first, I thought she was speaking to someone else. Then I thought she was just crazy. I backed away from her, maybe telling her to fuck off, I'm not sure. Then I went to my room and looked in the mirror. That nasty old bitch was right; the person standing before me was unequivocally rancid. Like a monkey, I moved my limbs to make sure it was really me in the mirror. Unfortunately, it was. I vaguely remembered nurses trying to clean me days before, but I was still filthy. My hair was both matted and oily, my lips were cracked, I had acne on my chin, my nails were dirty, and—worst of all, I had deep scratch marks up and down my scrawny arms.

Dr. Bensen told me I'd inflicted the scratches myself—that I merely said, "One louse means death," when asked about them. The thought immediately made me feel itchy, but I didn't see any lice, thank God.

I considered how the rest of my body must have looked, not really wanting to know. I removed my clothes without looking in the mirror and took a long shower. I'll never forget the shitty water pooling around my feet as I washed away the grime. As I scrubbed back and forth, *they* taunted me. *Dirty, filthy whore. Nasty whore. Nasty whore.* This only made me scrub harder. When I emerged from the shower, my skin was sore and pink.

What the hell was happening to me? Hadn't I once been beautiful?

My dad and Joshua visited regularly, although Joshua only came in the evenings because he needed to work. He brought us dinner, which I did my best to eat. Somewhere along the way, my appetite had disappeared entirely. I could see that I was underweight, but my stomach wasn't cooperating. Joshua started bringing me vanilla milkshakes with protein powder. They were delicious and I drank a lot of them. Along with good coffee, my dad brought the less healthy things I couldn't resist as a kid: popcorn, chocolate muffins, saltine crackers and peanut butter, and Swedish fish. During rare moments when I could concentrate, I tried to read *Angela's Ashes.* But then I felt like an asshole for not eating when so many others had suffered *real* hunger. So, I nibbled on the treats, but there was no joy in it—not anymore.

After maybe six days in the hospital, Dr. Bensen came by when my dad was visiting. He was skunking me at cribbage, so I was glad for the interruption.

"Good afternoon, you two. How's the game?" he said, taking a seat on the other side of the bed.

"Sucks, I'm losing," I groaned.

"She was never a good loser," added my dad with a smile.

"Well, I'm glad you're both here. Sunny, you're responding well to the meds, which is wonderful news. I believe the next step in your treatment is family therapy."

I looked at my dad, trying to detect a note of trepidation. He gave nothing away. "Sounds like a good idea, doctor. When and where?" he said, trying to sound enthusiastic.

"I've been speaking with Dr. Turner and she's agreed to come here. She lives nearby and will occasionally meet with patients in the hospital. We have a private conference room on the fifth floor."

I wasn't sure how I felt about this. "Who will be attending?" I asked.

"Given your family history, I think we should start with the two of you, then Dr. Turner can take it from there. But I know she'll be wanting to meet with you and Joshua." He looked at my dad. "She'll be calling you to get it set up. Sound good?"

"Sure, thanks, doc," said my dad. Dr. Bensen left and he and I sat there quietly for a few seconds. He must've sensed my uneasiness. He reached over and touched my arm. "It will be fine, honey. I mean, you'll just be chatting with your dear old dad, how scary can it be?" He gave me a little wink.

No, *he* wasn't scary—not in the least. But there was *something* there, bubbling beneath the surface of our relationship. I couldn't place it, but it most certainly involved my mother. It was like a sleeping grenade that we had managed to avoid touching thus far. It was oppressive, pushing me further into myself. I began chewing on my thumb and my dad came closer, kissing me on the forehead.

"Oh, my *tournesol*, it will be okay. I love you to the moon."

I didn't say anything, but just sat there rigidly. I tried to forget about family therapy for the next couple of days, but I knew it was coming. I also knew that, once the box was opened, there would be no going back. My mother had been neatly tucked away for years. Yet I could feel her scratching at the surface—nipping at my consciousness and shaking my equilibrium. Did I really want to unleash the full weight of her?

Chapter 29 ❧ Sunny

By the time our first family therapy appointment came around, four of my fingers were bleeding. Feeling shaky, I put on my light blue Adidas sweatpants and a white T-shirt, combed my hair, and applied some light makeup. My dad had come from work and showed up wearing a black suit with a crisp white shirt and no tie. He looked dapper and his cologne smelled musky.

"Shall we?" he said. I took his arm as if he were escorting me to a fancy gala, as opposed to a lovely jaunt through the psych ward.

We almost made it to the elevator when I heard, "Woohoo, where *you* headed, Mr. Handsome? Ain't you a sexy one!"

"Oh shit, it's Phyllis, hurry up, Dad."

"Yes, I've had the pleasure." We practically ran to the elevator, barely escaping Phyllis' amorous advances. I could hear the click of her heels in the background along with more catcalls, "Slow down, darlin! Come taste my honey pot!" We both laughed with relief after the elevator door shut and, not having laughed in ages, it felt good.

The atmosphere of the meeting room was cold, with stark white walls and a large oval conference table in the middle. On the walls hung large oil portraits of old white men who must have been hospital founders or benefactors. *So nice to be represented,* I thought with mild disgust. There were two large windows overlooking a parking lot on one side and a courtyard on the other. Several patients stood around smoking in the courtyard. The room was clearly meant for hospital staff, which I actually preferred. It allowed me to pretend I was just a normal person in a work meeting—if only for an hour or two. Dr. Turner arrived right after us. She wore a knee-length yellow dress that flattered her tan skin, and low-heeled brown sandals. Her long hair was in a bun and silver hoop earrings dangled from her ears. As was her usual style, she looked both professional and approachable. She greeted us warmly and suggested we all sit together at one end of the long table. She didn't waste any time getting started. "Sunny, you look great today, how are you feeling?"

I sat in a hard wooden chair that would be hell on my tailbone. "I'm okay."

She asked me a little bit about my mood, then turned to my dad. "When a person is trying to manage a serious mental illness, as is the case with Sunny, I think it's important to surround her with as much support and love as possible. Sunny has had some serious trauma in her life, particularly in terms of her mother's mental illness, as well as the loss of her grandparents. You are the person most able to understand her past; the two of you have a shared trauma experience. I believe you can help Sunny to learn more about what happened, which will better equip her to navigate challenges in the future. Does that make sense?"

Oh God, here we go.

"If it helps her, I'll tell Sunny everything she needs to know," he said looking at me. His words were loving, yet also discomfiting. I wasn't sure I wanted to know *everything*.

"But I also want both of you to know that it's often the case with family therapy that things may get worse before they get better. Opening old wounds has a way of doing that. But you need to be patient and keep at it. If you do, things *will* improve."

Ugh. Just what I need, to feel worse. I stared at a finch fluttering outside and wished I could fly away to a better place. A better life.

During that first meeting, which was two hours long, we didn't go deep. Unpacking too much shit all at once could spill over and drown us. Dr. Turner was no dummy. We mostly talked about my mom—how beautiful and full of life she was. I learned more about how my parents met. That they had been deeply in love, even more so than I'd imagined. We talked about a couple of our favorite memories with her. Mine was when we played dress-up and danced around the house to French music. I remember her long, colorful skirts resembling flower petals as she twirled around and around. My dad recalled a trip they took to a lavish resort in Mexico. They watched the sunset every night from their patio and even skinny-dipped in the pool. He spoke of her as if she were a movie star. She *was* incredibly beautiful, my mother. Maybe that was the trade-off—beauty for the price of sanity?

We also talked about Babcia and Papa. I could see that it was still hard for my dad to speak of them, how profoundly he missed them. He shared what it was like having them as parents. To me, they were practically perfect. I always envied him for having them as parents. He described how different they were from other parents. Their overprotectiveness and odd behaviors. How Babcia was sometimes in another world for hours at a time, totally inaccessible. The peculiar way they were with food. How jumpy they were at loud noises, especially sirens. I had seen these things too; but, by the time I came around, they had acclimated somewhat. For my dad, however, their war experience was relatively raw—an irrepressible cloud hovering over the three of them.

My dad described an incident when he brought a German friend home to play after school and Babcia froze the second the boy opened his mouth. His accent propelled her to a different place—a horrific place. She started shaking violently and ran out of the room. The poor kid thought there was something wrong with him and started to cry. My dad must've been terribly embarrassed.

And he mentioned the nightmares—so very many of them. I knew about those too, but not to the extent my dad described—like hearing a thud when Papa flew from his night terrors to the floor. Or when Babcia started sleeping in a different room because Papa flailed his arms to such an extent, he accidentally gave her a black eye. There was so much I didn't fully understand. My father spoke of these things with such pain. I wish I'd been less selfish and realized how much he was impacted by intergenerational trauma. It also made me wonder about myself and why the Nazis had targeted me. Or, why I *believed* they had targeted me.

It was a good thing the session was over, since I couldn't handle the topic any longer. The familiar lump had formed in my throat and I was starting to pit out. And *they* knew it too, whispering "crazy bitch" just one time. Still, that session gave me a greater appreciation for my father and what he'd been through. When we stepped into the hall, I hugged him and told him, maybe for the first time in a while, how much I loved him. Then I went to my room and slept hard for two hours.

The next day my dad and I plodded off to our second family therapy session. Phyllis must have been sniffing after some other wretch since she wasn't around. My dad was casual this time, in jeans and a red short-sleeved Polo shirt, and I had on my usual sweats, which I had started calling "hospital chic." Dr. Turner was already seated when we arrived.

My mother had the starring role this time. My stunning, elusive, eccentric mother. The woman I loved immeasurably, yet resented for leaving me. We barely made any small talk before jumping right in.

"Sunny, we talked a bit about your mom yesterday, and today I'd like to explore that further. I'm wondering if there are things about your mother that confuse you? Things you'd like to ask your dad about?"

Everything about my mother was confusing. She was more of a shadowy entity than a real person. I thought for several moments as Dr. Turner waited patiently. "Um, why were you guys always fighting?"

My dad rested his hands on the table and let out a big sigh. "She was extremely sick. At first, I thought she was just quirky. You know, like an artist that I didn't understand. I didn't realize she was ill, so she pissed me off. She spent all of our money when I was working seventy hours a week and trying to pay the mortgage. At our lowest point, we had $30 in our checking account because she went on a $20,000 shopping spree. I had to borrow money from my parents." He stopped and sipped from one of the bottles of water Dr. Turner had set out for us.

"Wow, that's a shitload of money," I said. I couldn't imagine what she'd purchased.

"Yeah, it was." He paused for a moment and scratched his head. "And sometimes she would stay out extremely late after working at the gallery. I didn't know where she was and I was going out of my mind with worry. Then she would come in and act like *I* was the problem, like I should just *mellow out*. It was exasperating. Eventually, it became clear that she was mentally ill and couldn't control many of the things she did. I tried to be empathetic, but then, well, her behavior started to affect you. And that was too much."

I noticed Dr. Turner watching me, waiting for some sort of response. I didn't have one, I was just trying to appear calm as I took it all in. Of course, I was destroying my cuticles under the table.

"Sunny, she left you at school multiple times. Once until evening."

"I remember. I was so humiliated."

"I know. And she would forget to feed you, or not hear you crying because she was painting with the music at full blast." He stopped for a moment, then added as his voice cracked, "It made me so afraid for you." He gathered himself for a moment, then continued. "When we got her the help she needed, she would get better and then stop taking her meds. It happened over and over again. She just couldn't stay on track. It was the most frustrating experience I'd ever had."

"Why were you always sending her away?"

He winced ever so slightly at my question.

"She would become suicidal, I mean *really* wanting to die. So, I took her to the hospital—this very one in fact. If I hadn't, she'd have killed herself."

"Oh. I guess I knew she was going to the hospital, but not that she was suicidal." I felt the familiar swirl of pain, shame, and confusion as I thought of my mother leaving. An additional pang of guilt was added to the mix when I realized I'd thrown my poor father back into his worst nightmare—same hospital, same crazy bullshit. Not wanting to hurt my dad further, I considered whether or not I should finish my thought. I looked down, noticing scratch marks in the wooden table. The silence of that room was unbearable. I glanced over at Dr. Turner and perceived the slightest hint of a nod. Looking tentatively at my dad, I continued, "Sometimes, when I was little, I thought you were angry at her and wanted her gone. And once, when she left after I'd had a tantrum, I thought she needed to get away from me. That it was my fault."

I saw his eyes widen as he looked at me. He moved closer and took both of my hands in his. His breath smelled sweet. "Oh, sweetheart, that was *never* the case. None of this was your fault, you were only a child. And it wasn't your mom's fault either. I was frustrated with her when she didn't take her meds, but I drove her to the hospital because I didn't want her to die. Even with all of her odd and destructive behavior, I loved her more than I loved myself. I wanted her to *live*, and to be happy. I wanted our little family to be happy." He stopped, removed his glasses, and wiped his eyes. "And, as much as I loved her, I loved you more. I would've driven her to Timbuktu to protect you."

I sat there, frozen, as I looked into his pained eyes. He gently wiped my face with a tissue; I hadn't realized I was crying.

"I also want you to know how much she adored you. The only times she complied with treatment for any decent length of time were after we had you. She said you were the 'light of her life.' It's the reason she started calling you "Sunny."

I wiped my face. "I thought you gave me that name. So, why did she name me Sylvia, you know, after her batshit crazy mother?"

"Because, honey, just as you loved *your* mother—flaws and all, she loved hers. It was a gift she wanted to give her mom. When we told Sylvie, I'd never seen her so happy. She literally wept. No one can understand the relationship they had growing up. But there was always love." He paused for a few moments. "Later, both your mom and I realized that you were much more of a 'Sunny' than a 'Sylvia.' Although, to me, you're a beautiful sunflower."

I wished to God I could still be his sunflower, but I knew I had become something else entirely. Something more like oleander or poison oak. "Not anymore. You should probably start calling me Sylvia, seems much more fitting considering, well, you know…"

He shook his head emphatically. "No, please stop. Please don't say that."

Dr. Turner chimed in. "Sunny, what makes you say that?"

"Because I'm a nut job, just like Grandma Sylvie. Maybe my destiny is cat hoarding and funeral crashing." I could hear my dad sigh with exasperation.

"You are *here*, getting the best treatment. Your family is as supportive as any family I've seen. You're brilliant. Your destiny is not your grandmother's, or your mother's. It's *yours*. Your name doesn't define you, nor does your illness," said the doctor.

"Well, that's good, since I really hate the name Sylvia," I said with a slight smile while wiping my nose with the back of my hand.

"Well, your mom was adamant about the name. But you can always change it, you know. I won't be offended."

"Yeah, I guess. But, what was actually wrong with Mom?" It was a question that had always lurked in the corners of my mind. Yet it could never seem to make its way to my tongue.

"There were a lot of different diagnoses, but I think she was bipolar."

"But she could've been schizoaffective, like me."

"I suppose so."

"So, how does it make you feel to know that there is a family history of mental illness here?" asked Dr. Turner.

"Like I fit right in."

"I mean about the genetics."

"Oh, well, I guess I got some bad genes."

"Well, it seems you may have some genes that predispose you to mental illness. So, what does that tell you?"

"Like maybe I couldn't help being like…well, like this," I said, gesturing to my body.

"Like it's not your fault. Right?"

"Yeah, I guess it's not." I'd always blamed myself for my flaws. I'd have to think about this.

We talked a little bit more about my mom and her illness. As I thought about my own personal hell, I realized I was developing greater empathy for my mother and mentioned something to this effect.

"I think it's wonderful that you are empathizing with your mom. Understanding, firsthand, how ill she was may help to alleviate any resentment you may have toward her."

"Yeah, I think that's true," I said.

"You know, there's another person with a mental illness who also deserves your empathy, kindness and understanding," she said gently.

I wasn't sure what she meant. "Sylvie?"

"*You*, Sunny." She said it with such a mix of authority and kindness. I wanted to believe her.

"Oh yeah, maybe." I squirmed in my seat, feeling uncomfortable with the conversation.

"When you're hard on yourself, which I've noticed is quite often, I'd like you to remember that you have a medical diagnosis that's not your fault. Try to channel the empathy you feel for others and focus it on yourself too." I could sense my dad nodding his head, though I didn't look at him.

"Okay." What she said was logical, but less easy to practice. I'd been tough on myself my entire life. But I could see it wasn't serving me well.

I don't know if it was because time was up or because of how weary my father and I must have appeared, but Dr. Turner stopped the session and I shuffled back to my room, again exhausted.

I'd been in the hospital for ten days. Joshua continued his evening visits and had noticed my improvement. "You have your orneriness back," he said one evening after I teased him about his unmatching socks. If Phyllis was any indication, I'm not sure orneriness was a sign of healthy adjustment. But I did notice myself feeling like something had budged a little within my psyche. Maybe it was indignation or even anger toward my parents about things I hadn't understood. Either way, I felt slightly lighter, less burdened.

Joshua had informed other family members and friends about my situation, which I found incredibly humiliating. But I tried not to be pissed at him. He'd suffered enough because of me. Besides, they would've found out anyway. He told me his parents were concerned and that they loved me very much. *As if.* Debbie would remain on my shitlist.

Elizabeth called me almost every day. Well, every day after my meds kicked in. I was pretty reticent during those first calls, but eventually I opened up a little. She made me laugh, telling me funny stories about her job or how twitterpated she was over her nerdy, but apparently well-endowed, boyfriend. Elizabeth had a knack for oversharing. But I sorely needed those laughs. She didn't ask too many questions about my situation, which I appreciated. But she ended every conversation telling me she loved me. I found this both touching and embarrassing—I'd never been comfortable with intimacy between female friends. She wanted to visit me after I was discharged, which I almost looked forward to.

Dr. Bensen continued to meet with me every few days, always with his Spanish inquisition. Yes, I felt less depressed. No, I wasn't hearing voices most of the time. Maybe the Nazis weren't actually coming for me—I still wasn't sure about that one. I understood how illogical it was, but that belief was like words etched into a tree trunk—it might fade with time or be obscured by other forces of nature, but it was never fully gone. I wondered if it ever would be.

He also talked to me about the possible side effects of my new medications. Thus far, the only thing I noticed was constipation—which I didn't mention. I was also extremely tired, which he said was normal. He gave me a list of more serious symptoms to watch for and also insisted that I come to the hospital (or my primary physician) regularly to monitor my liver function. He emphasized that I *absolutely must not* become pregnant while on the meds. I told him that, along with having an IUD, there was *no way in hell* I'd be having a child given my defective genes. Cats would do just fine, thank you.

Dr. Bensen also described my new diagnosis in more detail. I did feel some solace in knowing that there was a reason, an *etiology*, for my extremely fucked up mood swings—especially the anger, which spewed out of me like acid, and then left me to wallow in contrition. At first, I was relieved to have a different diagnosis, but it didn't turn out to be any better. All of the familiar ingredients were still there: Delusions, hallucinations and thought problems. Except now there was an added bonus: bipolar disorder. *Yay.* In other words, I was still bonkers, or, as Papa would have said, "mashugana." I was mashugana alright. Hell, I was *Queen* Mashugana.

On a brighter side, the doctor said having the bipolar form of schizoaffective disorder *and* having a precipitating traumatic event, meant I had a better prognosis. That was at least something to hold onto. Dr. Bensen said he was pleased with my progress and that I would likely be discharged in a few days. This should have pleased me too, but, for once I was actually hesitant about going home—what if it started all over again? He said he wanted to speak with me, my dad and Joshua about next steps. And so, the following evening, the three of them showed up in my room.

"Thank you for meeting here tonight," said Dr. Bensen, looking at the two of them. He was wearing jeans and a beige cashmere sweater. Joshua moved one of the chairs to one side of the bed so they were facing each other and we each took a seat. Dr. Bensen said he wanted to talk to us about my living situation when I left the hospital. Apparently, he had already spoken to Peter and Joshua about this, which was news to me. "Sunny, I'm not sure that having you back at home is the best idea right now. Joshua will be working and it sounds like the home health nurse was a bust."

I let out an exasperated sigh. "Milquetoast was a disaster and fucking waste of money. Please don't ever do that to me again!"

Dr. Bensen smiled. "Like I said, the home health nurse was a bust. But, after speaking with Peter and Linda, they would like to have you stay with them. Just until you're feeling confident enough to be at home. What do you think?" *Okay, well, this sounds weird.*

"Um, well, I'm sure Linda doesn't want to deal with my shit."

"Actually, it was her idea," said my dad.

"Oh." *Interesting.* "Would I be in the cottage?"

"No, you'd stay in your old room. No one will be spying on you, we just want you to feel supported. The kids will be in school for a couple more weeks, so they won't bother you too much. Once school is out, we'll keep them busy. Please say 'yes,' sweetheart, please let us help you."

I looked at Joshua. "But I miss you so much! And I miss Chester—isn't he lonely without me?"

Joshua leaned toward me, touching my knees. "I miss you too, baby. I'm going to come to the house for dinner and maybe you can come home on the weekends. And Chester is fine. He misses you of course, but he sleeps with me every night and I come home for lunch on most days. He'll be okay. It's just temporary."

"Hmmm." I wasn't persuaded. "But are you sure?" I asked my dad.

"I'm positive. It's the best thing." He nodded as he said this, as if to seem more convincing.

So, I agreed to move back home with my dad and stepmother. There was comfort and security in the idea, but it was mixed with other feelings too— like embarrassment, a sense of failure, and anxiety over how things would go with Linda. But what could I do? I was basically an emotional invalid.

My dad and I had one more dreaded visit with Dr. Turner. It was scheduled on the day before my discharge. Every time I left those visits, I felt inexplicably fatigued. Even though I had gained some positive insights, they were an emotional drain that left me wilted.

On that final day of inpatient family therapy, the three of us sat in our usual spots wearing some variation of our usual outfits. As I looked from my dad to Dr. Turner, I was consumed with apprehension. I so wished I had my Xanax. What even happened to those magic pills? Dr. Turner got the ball rolling, "So, I hear you're being discharged tomorrow, how do you feel about that?"

"I have mixed feelings. I want to get out of here, but I'm scared of the world beyond these walls."

"That's perfectly understandable. This has been a safe place for you. Our goal is to expand those walls little by little, until you are comfortable fully joining the world. So, you will be staying with your dad and stepmother?"

"Yeah." I noticed the table bouncing and realized it was my foot. I stopped my foot and stared at the smokers outside. One was strapped to an oxygen tank. Humans were utterly ridiculous.

"Thoughts?"

"I don't know. Part of me is relieved since it's a familiar place and my dad will be close by. But I've never been sick there, not *like this*. And I'm not comfortable having Linda take care of me."

"You're dealing with a new illness in a place you've never done so before. Your anxiety makes sense. What is it about having Linda care for you that's troubling?"

"I'm not sure, I just have never felt close to her."

"Do you want to feel close to her?"

"I'm not sure." My foot was going again, I didn't try to stop it.

"Mind if I interject?" asked my dad. Dr. Turner nodded. "Sunny, Linda has always been so kind to you. She really cares about you. She's been devastated by all that's happened. Why do you push her away?"

I didn't know what to say. Linda had always been an annoying presence—a wort I couldn't get rid of. But I didn't really have a reason to dislike her. Several moments of silence passed, until I finally said, "I'm not sure, Dad. She's just always bothered me."

"Can you remember when she first started to bother you?" asked Dr. Turner.

I let out a big puff of air. "Yeah. It started right away, like when I was ten or eleven. It seemed like, all of a sudden, my dad perked up..."

"Sunny, please address your father."

I turned toward him. "I'd just never seen you so happy and relaxed. I mean, I wanted you to be happy, but I just didn't understand why me and Mom weren't enough. Why *we* couldn't make you happy."

"You always made me happy, honey. I was depressed when your mom died, and likely for quite some time before that too. Watching her just, well, waste away before my eyes made me feel totally helpless. And I walked on eggshells because I was so afraid of what she would do next. By the time I met Linda, I was starting to heal. But I was *so* lonely. Linda helped to pull me out of it, to find myself again." He spoke with such tenderness, his need for her was palpable.

"I understand. I guess I just felt like she was so, I don't know, different from Mom—like night and day. It made me wonder if you ever loved Mom at all." I was starting to feel like the spoiled, resentful child I once was.

He looked me in the eyes. "Sunny, your mom was my first real love; I was enraptured by her. Even with all of her chaos, I'd have done anything for her. I mean, she created you after all. I'll always love her—*always*. But, at that point in my life, I needed something, or someone, else. Another woman like your mother would've done me in," he said wryly. "They are very different types of people, that's true. But I have love for both of them."

I wasn't sure what to say. "What do you think of what your father just said?" asked Dr. Turner.

I was staring at a fly buzzing around inside the fluorescent light fixture in the ceiling. It found its way to the light only to be caught in a torrid death trap. I wanted to escape this place too. I focused my attention back to the discussion. "Well, it makes total sense. I guess I had those feelings when I was little and they've always just kind of stuck in my gut. I'm sorry for not understanding." It's true, I was sorry. My poor dad was so alone, why would I try to sabotage his happiness?

"This is why we're talking about these things now. Adults often carry around the pain they had as a child, even if they don't know how to express it. It's nothing to be sorry about, you were interpreting the world as a little girl who'd lost her mother. The fact that you are unwrapping those feelings now will help you and your dad to feel closer. And for you to be okay with Linda."

My dad smiled. "I love you so much, honey."

Then I thought of something. Something awful. With all of my worry and pessimism, how had this potential outcome not dawned on me before? "But Dad, you said another woman like mom would *do you in*. I'm just like her, will *I* do you in?" As I searched his eyes for a reaction, I felt sick with apprehension.

"But you aren't just like her. You both struggle with mental illness, but you're different people. For one thing, she lacked insight—never thought she was sick. Whereas you are far more introspective. And it's different dealing with a spouse versus your own child. I was the only adult she had in the world. It was an unbearable weight and I was naive about the whole thing. I'd like to think I'm stronger and perhaps more informed now. And neither of us is alone—you have Joshua, and I have Linda, not to mention our other friends and family. So, it's not the same. I'm fine, Sunny. Don't worry about me, okay?"

"Okay." I guess he had a point, but I'd always worry about him.

"But you know where you two are alike? Beauty, artistic talent, and intelligence. So, you did manage to inherit some of her best qualities." He gave me that warm and generous smile of his, the one he reserved for those he loved.

"Thank you, Dad."

"You're welcome. But I'm reminded of one other thing I'd like to say: Maddy and Spencer were *never* your replacements, as you used to call them. You are my first child, my *tournesol*. You could never be replaced. And don't tell them, but *you're my favorite*," he added with a mock whisper.

"It's okay, I got over that years ago. I love Winston and Churchill. And I know I'm your favorite." Both Dr. Turner and my dad chuckled.

"You two have a truly special bond," said the doctor. "I'm so impressed by both of you. Sunny, is there anything your dad can do to make it easier for you to live at home?"

"I guess it would help if I had my privacy. I mean, I don't want everyone staring at me all the time, waiting for me to do something crazy."

"We can handle that," he responded quickly, likely relieved by my simple request.

"And I don't want a thousand questions each day about my mood and other crap. That's for the therapists."

"Okay."

"Also, please don't push Linda down my throat. If I'm going to like her, I need to do it in my own time."

He looked a little less comfortable. "Okay."

"Anything else?" asked the doctor.

"That's it for now."

"Great. How do you feel about what Sunny is asking, Peter?"

"I understand. As a father, it may be hard for me not to watch her, to make sure she's okay. But I'll try to tone it down."

"When our children are hurting, allowing them the autonomy to move forward without constant vigilance can be a formidable challenge." She looked at me. "But it comes from a place of love."

I nodded my head.

"Okay, so let's go back to what we were discussing the other day." *Oh God.* Then she reiterated our past conversation about my mother and our flawed genes, and the chaos of living with a seriously ill parent. "Sunny, what was it like when your mom went away to the hospital?"

"Well, it started out terrible. I remember feeling angry at my dad…" I turned toward him again. "Angry at you, for taking her away from me. I didn't know… I'm sorry."

He shook his head. "It's okay, you were little. Please don't feel sorry."

"But then, as I stared out the window watching you both leave, Baba would show up. She would gently turn me toward her and hug me tight, kissing my cheeks the way she used to." I wiped my eyes. "Then we would go downstairs where Papa would greet me with his giant smile. They would make me comfort foods—always a lot of pierogi! Sometimes I took a bubble bath where I played and played. And Baba would tuck me into her big bed, which was always so soft and clean smelling."

"It sounds incredibly loving," said the doctor.

"It was. They spoiled me. I miss them so much." More infernal tears appeared—would they ever stop?

"Me too," said my dad softly.

"So, I always went downstairs with a heavy heart, but came back upstairs with a full one. That's how my grandparents were."

"They sound lovely," said Dr. Turner warmly.

"Yeah, I loved staying there with them. The last time it happened, before…they took me to the beach and I built the most enormous sandcastle with Papa…"

"Before?"

"Before my mom died."

"What do you remember about that day?"

I took a few deep breaths. "The beginning is hazy. I remember the house being quiet in the days before, except my dad talking on the phone with my mom's doctors, I believe. Mom was quiet. I tiptoed into her room once in a while, but she was either asleep or just uninterested in me. It hurt my feelings. Then I was at school and it was my favorite subject: art. I was covered in glue as I worked on a collage when Principal Murphy came to get me. She was a hopelessly cheerful person, but not on that day. Something wasn't right. I wanted to turn in the other direction when I saw my grandparents in her office. They looked broken. I didn't want to hear their words." I was fully crying at this buried memory. "I didn't want to know!" I put my head in my hands and my dad rubbed my back.

After a few moments, Dr. Turner gently asked, "What did your grandparents say to you?"

"That my mama had been in an accident, that she'd gone to heaven."

"Then what happened?"

"They took me to their apartment in the basement. I only remember crying and crying as one or both of them held me. We didn't really talk about what happened, you know, to my mom."

"Did you want to know?"

"When I was little, I didn't want any details. She was gone and that was that. What difference did it make *why* she was gone? But, as I got a little older, I wondered. I still wonder." I looked at my dad, who exhaled for several seconds before responding.

He held my hands again. "Honey, your mom was the most depressed she'd ever been. She wouldn't get out of bed or take care of herself in *any way*. She wouldn't even eat. Before, when she was depressed, there was always a hint of a spark in there somewhere—especially when she saw you. But this time she was unreachable. I was trying desperately to get her into longer-term care, but I couldn't find a bed. And the insurance company was not cooperating. After being on hold and about ready to throw the phone through the window, I went to the bedroom to check on her. She wasn't there. I ran outside and saw that her car was gone. I drove around looking for her, but there was no point—I had no idea where she'd driven. Sometime later, I got a call." He abruptly stopped speaking. I noticed he was breathing hard and his hands were shaking. He got up and walked across the room. He didn't seem to know what to do with himself. He stared out the window, wringing his hands.

"Peter, are you okay?" asked Dr. Turner.

"Yeah, I just…I need to catch my breath for a moment."

"Dad, it's okay. We don't have to do this," I said, my heart breaking for him.

"No, we do." He cleaned his glasses with his shirt and ran a hand through his hair—his typical stress response. Then he sat back down next to me. He held my hands, but didn't look at me. He was looking down at his feet. "Sunny, your mom jumped off the Pine Valley Creek Bridge. She killed herself." He paused for a moment. "I'm *so* sorry for not telling you before." And with that, he put his head in his hands and wept.

Those three words, "she killed herself," hit me like a punch in the face. I could feel myself physically recoil as he said them. But more than that, I felt a paralyzing sense of sadness—sadness both for my mother's desperation and for my poor dad who was left to deal with the mess. I also felt a vague sense of something else, maybe panic, that I too might be consumed by an irredeemable sense of futility.

I'll never forget the silence of those moments after my world was permanently altered. Aside from my dad's sniffles, there was nothing. Not a bird singing, not a noise from the hallway. The world stopped. My breathing stopped. Maybe my heart did too. I shouldn't have been surprised—my mother *was* mentally ill, after all. *Severely* mentally ill. Of course she killed herself. Yet, I did not know. I had not *allowed* myself to know.

At some point, my dad looked at me. "Sweetheart, are you okay? Say something."

I couldn't move my mouth. I was underwater, going down fast. I felt my dad's arm around my shoulder. I felt the vibration of his body against me as he trembled. Where was my voice? I tried again. "I uh, um. Why? I mean, why didn't you tell me?" The voice that came out of me was warped, amphibious. It could not have been mine.

"At first, you were too little. But in later years, I was selfish. It hurt me to even think about it. Then, when you were having problems, I didn't want to add to your burden. I'm so sorry. Please forgive me." He was looking at me with such anguish.

"I know, Daddy, it's okay." He wrapped me in his arms and we stayed like that for the rest of the session.

I fucking hated family therapy.

When I went back to my room, I was once again fatigued beyond reason. But my mind wouldn't let me rest. I paced around the room trying to process what I'd just learned. Suicide was of course part of my vernacular— we'd all known of people who chose death and the tragic consequences to their families. There were public service announcements and suicide hotlines posted on billboards. But now, the word took on a different meaning entirely. Suicide. *Su-i-cide.* That word, which rattled through my consciousness, had become personal. I was now collateral damage. And what did it say about my mother? Was she so desperate that death was her only option? I could perhaps understand that much of it. *But she had a child.* Her leaving me was something else now—not the car accident I'd always envisioned. It was purposeful, intentional. I was simply not enough to keep her around. This made me ache in the pit of my stomach. How could she do that to me? I was angry and disillusioned. I could reconcile having a mentally ill mother, but *this?* This was something else entirely.

I called Joshua and told him not to bring dinner. I said I was too tired and had leftover food from lunch. Besides, I would see him tomorrow at discharge. But I couldn't be around Joshua at that time. Small talk and playful banter would be an impossible feat. So, I instead continued to pace around the room as my thoughts moved in step with my feet. *They* also paid me a visit, saying *die bitch, die.* It was demoralizing. Since I hadn't heard them for days, I had a seed of hope that *just maybe* they would leave me alone for good. No such luck.

Eventually, I grew tired of pacing and tried to rest on my bed when Dr. Bensen showed up. "Hello, Sunny. How are you today?" He had on a sports jacket, khaki pants, and the brown Italian shoes I liked. He sat down by my bed.

"Not that great." I sat up in bed and tried to will myself not to cry.

"What's going on?"

"Turns out my mom killed herself." I could feel my insides start to tremble.

"Well, that's certainly a big piece of information to process."

"No kidding."

"How are you feeling about it?" He leaned closer with his chin resting on his hand.

"I'm angry, or maybe sad—I'm not sure which. She left me intentionally."

"I imagine this is an incredibly painful thing to learn. Do you remember her loving you when you were little?"

"Of course."

"Could it be that her love for you is the same regardless of this act?"

"I suppose. But she had a choice."

"Do you know what mental state she was in when she took her life?"

"I mean, she was really sick."

"Could she have been psychotic, meaning out of touch with reality?"

"Well, yeah. I'm sure she was."

"Then the love she felt for you would not have stopped her."

"I guess not."

"What could have stopped her would've been taking her medicine and going to therapy."

"Smooth, doc."

He gave me a slight smile. "I'm not trying to be smooth, Sunny. I'm trying to help you understand that her sickness was separate from her love for you. But had she complied with her treatment, things might have been very different. Also, please recognize that you are not her."

"I know, Dr. Turner went into that too. But I can't stop thinking about it. And, well, *they* came back today, just once. But still…I thought I was done with them." I hadn't planned to tell him this, but I wasn't even sure I wanted to be discharged anymore. So, I had nothing to lose.

"They? You mean the voices?"

"Yeah."

"Well, you've only been on the new medication for a couple of weeks, it's going to take longer to get the full effect. But, even then, you might have break-through symptoms from time to time—especially when you're stressed, like now."

That was disappointing to hear. "Great."

"I know. Over time, they may disappear entirely, we just don't know. But, when you do have them, use the coping mechanisms we've discussed, such as distraction and meditation. And remember, what they say has no truth. Their words neither describe nor represent you in any way. Have you been journaling your hallucinations?"

Ugh, not this again. Neither of my shrinks would give the journaling thing a rest. "I don't know, I keep being told to do this, but doesn't writing down their words give them more power?"

"That's a great question. But, by externalizing the voices, they may actually feel *less* oppressive. And, if you also write down the events that precede them, you can identify triggers."

I'd heard all of this before, but I wasn't convinced. "Okay, I'll think about it."

"Please do. Also, get plenty of sleep and continue with your art. And definitely contact me or Dr. Turner if you are feeling overwhelmed by the voices.

"Okay." He then asked me the usual questions, which I'd almost memorized at this point. He also emphasized, even more than usual, that I *absolutely must* contact him immediately if I had any suicidal thoughts. And I promised I would. Then he told me the medications were working well for me and that he was very encouraged about my progress. He shook my hand and said he was proud of me, that he had great faith that I would be just fine. Then he left me alone with my stupid thoughts.

That night I tried to distract myself with the TV. I didn't fall asleep until very late into the night. When I finally did, I was assaulted with visions of my mother falling. As she propelled toward the ground, she turned into me. Then I was falling. I would wake up sitting in bed with sweat dripping down my back. Then I would go back to sleep and it would start all over again. When the morning of my discharge finally came, I was depleted. I drank my coffee, ate a piece of toast, and packed my meager belongings. Then I sat and waited to be transported back to my father's basement where I could be a little girl again. I was okay with it. This adult thing wasn't exactly working out for me.

Chapter 30 ∾ Peter

The maelstrom of my life reached its peak when my beautiful daughter disappeared. Every day, no, every *minute*, she was gone was nothing less than torture. I took some time off from work since my mind could not process endless litigious bullshit when Sunny was missing. I continually envisioned the worst scenarios—was she lying dead somewhere without the dignity of a prayer or proper burial? Had she been sexually abused? Was she in pain? It was a father's nightmare. I also found myself thinking a lot about Gracie and her illness. But sometimes these thoughts became so interlaced with those of Sunny that I couldn't differentiate the two. After Gracie died, it took me years to find contentment again. I couldn't fathom being launched down that infernal hole again. Yet here I was. It was soul-shattering.

Those dark days consisted of a demoralizing dance of driving and walking mile upon mile in search of Sunny. She had become like a phantom—weaving in and out of sight, leaving me to question both my senses and my sanity. Eventually, as I was trespassing in the backyard of a large gray craftsman-style house in La Jolla, I heard a menacing male voice over my shoulder. "What the hell do you think you're doing?" I turned to see a giant of a man in his mid-30s. Given the size of his biceps and the veins protruding from his neck, he had to be a bodybuilder. He likely thought I was either a thief or a pervert—as I had been peering into the windows of an enclosed pool cabana. He glared at me indignantly while holding a cordless phone in one hand and a steel bat in the other. Okay, I thought, this is it. He's going to kill me.

Growing impatient, the man repeated his question and moved closer. I didn't know what to do, but my emotions took over. "I'm sorry, it's just that my daughter..." My voice cracked and my knees buckled. Leaning on the cabana, I wiped my nose and tried again. "My daughter is missing, I'm just looking for her. I'm very sorry." The next thing I knew, both the man and a tall blonde woman I presumed to be his wife were standing by my side, consoling me. They had seen the flier. They brought me into their kitchen and gave me Earl Grey tea as a golden retriever named Boomer gently licked my shins. Those two people, whom I thought would hurt me, spent the next two days searching for Sunny. That unexpected spark of humanity was just the catalyst I needed to keep going.

While much of that period is a blur of anxiety, I do remember being edgy and irascible, snapping at Linda and the kids—which added more guilt to my repertoire of emotional garbage. Sleep offered no escape. Mostly I tossed and turned, but when I actually slept, I was assaulted by a recurrent nightmare in which I was in the middle of the ocean on a small blue sailboat I'd owned years ago. While standing at the bow, I looked down to see the black water bubble up like hot lava and Sunny flailing and gasping for air. She was trying desperately to call for me. But when I reached down to take her hand, something abruptly pulled her under. That damned nightmare played again and again, each time plunging me back into reality drenched in sweat with the momentary belief that I'd jumped in after her.

It wasn't until I got the call from Joshua telling me they likely found Sunny that I could breathe again. Given my emotional state, Linda insisted on driving, so we got a babysitter and headed for Anaheim. We couldn't get there fast enough. I tapped my forehead on the window and tried to block out thoughts about where Sunny had been and what had been done to her.

When we finally entered the hospital room and I saw my daughter lying there, relief burst out of me as if from a broken pipe. I embraced my haggard-looking son-in-law and took a closer look at Sunny, who appeared to be asleep. I was astounded by the figure before me. My beautiful, brilliant little girl, the one who looked at me with trusting eyes as she took her first steps, was lost beneath a barely recognizable shell. The horror story of where she'd been was etched in her skin. She was dirty, battered, and bruised. And she was tied to her bed like a wild beast. I heard a quick intake of breath from Linda as we stood there paralyzed, unable to look away from my broken girl.

And then she woke up.

If there was ever a doubt that Sunny was severely mentally ill, it was forever obliterated in the moments that followed. She came to life like a demonic doll opening its eyes. Her words were both desperate and nonsensical, revealing a tortured mind. She was back *there* again—back in the nightmare that was her reality. Back in her role as the captured Jew who was soon to be murdered. All I wanted to do was calm her in some way, to ease her suffering. But she was an out-of-control steam train reeling toward calamity. My anguish and helplessness as a father twisted away at my insides as she asked me to hide her and say the Kaddish. Linda, who had not seen Sunny like this, was covering her mouth in disbelief. After a short period of psychotic belligerence, Sunny was sedated by the staff psychiatrist as she screamed abuses at him. We were greatly relieved when they transferred her back to the hospital in San Diego two days later.

There was one spark of hope shortly after Sunny's transfer. Dr. Bensen informed us that she had been misdiagnosed. And, while she was still desperately ill—not to mention incurable, at least now she would be taking the correct meds. Sunny's moods had vacillated to a staggering degree over the past months, so the diagnosis and treatment did seem more promising. And once her pharmaceutically-fueled metamorphosis began to take effect, I allowed myself to believe that she *just might* come back to us.

When I reflect on that second hospitalization, my mind always finds its way to yet another place of misery—the family therapy room. Both Sunny and I were terrified of what family therapy might uncover. But, needing to be strong for her, I swallowed my feelings and made a personal vow to confront the things I'd squirreled away long ago. Indeed, it was in that room that the mistakes and torment I'd tried so hard to suppress were laid out on the table like an ominous string of tarot cards. It was surreal to be faced with both Sunny and Gracie at the same time. I had pushed Gracie so far back in my mind that I had inadvertently hidden her from Sunny too. For this, I felt terrible. Sunny had a right to know her mother.

There were also some lovely moments in therapy, especially early on. Both Sunny and I had compartmentalized Gracie—keeping the beautiful parts of her off to the side, safe from memories that would tarnish them. As Sunny described her mother on the good days, I could picture the two of them twirling around the house in a mess of beautiful chaos. I was reminded of one particular evening when I arrived home after work. They must've made a hundred paper snowflakes in varying colors, which were then strung throughout the family room and kitchen. Frank Sinatra's "High Hopes" was playing and both Gracie and Sunny—whose face was painted like a rabbit—were singing along as they danced around the kitchen. It was a perfect moment.

And, while in the coming days I silently cursed Dr. Turner for forcing me to face the darkest parts of myself, I also recognized her role in reawakening cherished memories that had been lost in the mayhem. Learning that I didn't need to bury *all* of Gracie was a revelation. Those therapy sessions also reminded me of how much I missed my parents and the cavernous vacancy their deaths left within our family. The Nazis' abject failure to destroy Mama and Tata, to rid them of their humanity, is implicit in the tenderness and compassion that continued to pour from them until their dying breaths.

But then there were the other parts of family therapy, the parts that weighed me down with torrential guilt, threatening to shatter me entirely. I left those sessions ashamed of not talking to Sunny about her trauma. Dr. Bensen was right, she managed to fill in the blanks in her typical self-depreciating way. How could I have allowed my daughter to experience even the slightest bit of guilt over things her mother did? And Sunny's fear that I might see her in the same light as Gracie was especially troubling. Yes, they each inherited a mental illness I wouldn't wish on my worst enemy, but they were unique individuals. Still, the idea that Sunny could also give up on living left my mind reeling.

Of course, the ultimate heartache during our hours in that cursed room was having to reveal the worst of my secrets—the one I held so deeply within myself that even I couldn't look at it. I knew I'd have to tell Sunny about the suicide one day, but I kept putting it off both out of concern for her well-being, as well as due to my own weakness. I didn't realize the degree to which I had suppressed all aspects of Gracie's death until I heard the words "she killed herself" come out of my mouth. At that moment, along with the hours and days that followed, I was back there again—back in the darkness. I could hear the officer's words echo in my mind: "Are you the husband of Gracie Zielinski? There's been an incident." The immediate anguish of instantly knowing what the officer *didn't* say—that my Gracie was dead—also remained.

My anger toward Gracie for leaving us—for giving up, and for doing so in her typically dramatic fashion—also held strong over the years. And, as I learned in therapy, Sunny was harboring some resentment toward her mother as well. I could see that these unrelenting feelings would surely eat away at us if not addressed. Revisiting Gracie's death took me back to a place I desperately wanted to forget—the morgue. Before identifying her, I was informed that Gracie's body was badly mangled by the impact of the jump. I could've done without those details, as I was immediately assaulted by visions of Gracie's limbs lying all askew—disjointed and backwards like a broken doll. But, as they pulled back the body bag, I saw that her exquisite face had remained intact. As I looked over my dead wife, I realized it was my first time in knowing her, and possibly the first time in her adult life, that she appeared to be fully at peace. Gone were her crazed eyes and the pain and chaos forever lurking behind them. That realization, bitter though it was, at least left me with a momentary hint of solace.

I remember smoothing out Gracie's hair and pulling a few strands out of her face, and then admonishing myself for doing so. I mean, she was *dead*— what was the point? I remember the cool, clammy texture of her skin when I kissed her forehead. And, after leaving the morgue, I remember going to the Pine Valley Creek Bridge. I stood near the rail and imagined what it would feel like to see this as one's only option. Even thinking of it now, I'm struck by the degree of hopelessness it took Gracie to prefer such a horrific act over existing for another moment in her own skin. For weeks I went to that bridge, often setting lilies near the railing. But when going there became too much to bear, I avoided the area altogether—which wasn't always easy. That goddamn bridge was but another casualty of Gracie's madness.

As Sunny began to reemerge from her delusional haze, I worried about what to do with her after discharge. I wished I had some level of confidence that this would be her last hospitalization, that she would comply with treatment and stay well. But I'd been down this jagged road before. Like dealing with a drug addict, I knew relapses were typical and that Sunny would need extensive support and supervision. Dr. Bensen mentioned transitional homes for adults with severe mental illnesses like schizophrenia and schizoaffective disorder. This idea was unsettling, as, knowing my daughter, she would have fought it tooth and nail. And I wouldn't have blamed her. She was the most introverted, sensitive person I'd ever known. She was painfully self-conscious and she carried around a ready supply of self-doubt and shame wherever she went. No, she wouldn't thrive in such a setting, and would likely disappear again. But I also didn't think Sunny could handle going home— not yet. Along with Joshua being busy at work, that condo would represent a constant reminder of what happened before she became ill, of the person she used to be. It was also the location of her burgeoning mental illness and psychotic break. I wasn't sure she should stay there in her fragile state.

Around Sunny's eighth day in the hospital, I decided to discuss my concerns with Linda. The kids were in bed and we were sitting on the living room couch sipping hot cider.

"I don't know where Sunny should go when she gets out. I'm getting really worried about it," I said, running a hand through my hair.

"Have you talked to Joshua?"

"Yeah, he isn't sure either. He'll be working long hours over the next two months and doesn't feel comfortable leaving her home alone. And, of course, hiring another caregiver is out of the question."

"Why doesn't she stay here?" she asked casually, as if suggesting something for dinner.

I had lightly toyed with that idea, but didn't want to burden Linda. I was surprised to hear the suggestion. "That's incredibly kind, honey. But Sunny's a massive handful right now. She's getting stabilized, but continuing to comply with treatment at home is another story. It would be stressful for you, to say the least." I finished off my cider as Linda considered my words.

"I know that. But she needs her family to rally around her now. Plus, school's almost over, so I'll be home to keep an eye on her. I can take her to appointments and make sure she takes her meds. And, more than that, I can show her that I'm truly here for her, that I care." Her words sounded genuine. Clearly, she had given this idea some thought.

"You're an angel, you know that?" I said, kissing her hand.

"Yeah, I know," she said with a slight grin.

The decision was made, Sunny would be coming back home to her old room in the basement. The idea left me equal parts relieved and terrified. We did our best to prepare, as it enabled us to feel some semblance of control before venturing into the unknown. I moved boxes and extra furniture out of her room since we'd been using it for storage. We thoroughly cleaned it and I repainted the walls from dingy white to lavender. Linda purchased some exceptionally soft pink sheets and a white duvet covered in tiny yellow and red birds—totally Sunny's style. The room looked better than it ever had.

As the end of her hospital stay grew nearer, we had a chat with Spencer and Maddy about what was going on. They knew Sunny was having issues— issues that were affecting all of us. For the first time in their lives, they'd seen their father cry. And they couldn't have missed my edginess and petulance, especially when Sunny was missing. Of course, they were also aware of her disappearance and hospitalizations. When we said we wanted to talk about their sister, Maddy immediately asked what was wrong with Sunny and when she could come over and play. We told them their sister had an illness that she couldn't help, that it wasn't her fault. We described how this particular illness affects *behavior*, making people do and say unusual things. I'll never forget Maddy's response: "Is that why she's so wiggly squiggly?"

"Wiggly squiggly? What do you mean, sweetie?" asked Linda, bemused.

"Like how her legs and arms are always moving, and sometimes her eyeballs wiggle around." As she said this, she used her arms to pantomime a wiggly worm.

She was right, at times Sunny was in constant motion, unable to sit still. She'd always been restless and fidgety, but lately it had reached its peak. And, although I couldn't believe my little daughter noticed it, when Sunny was off her meds, her eyes did have a strange way of darting around.

As I contemplated this, Spencer chimed in. "Yeah, plus sometimes she talks to herself."

I'd heard that children notice a lot more than parents realize, and Spencer and Maddy were no exception. They already knew something was very wrong with Sunny. I was so glad we talked to them, especially since they were clearly worried about their cherished big sister. We answered their questions and also told them Sunny would be staying with us for a little while. Thinking they would have a daily playmate, they were thrilled with this plan. But we reminded them that Sunny would need plenty of rest and time to herself, that they needed to give her space. We also told them not to ask her a lot of questions about her illness, but to come to us instead. They listened patiently, asked great questions, and seemed to understand our expectations. I was proud of my children. They were developing into thoughtful, compassionate little people—traits no doubt cultivated by their equally amazing mother.

And so we readied our house and our children for Sunny's stay. The lingering question that remained was whether or not *we* were actually prepared. I couldn't help but wonder if Linda would have thick enough skin to handle Sunny's moods and acerbity. Or if she had the chutzpah to enforce treatment compliance with a mentally ill girl who had resented her very presence for years. And how would the four of us fare should Sunny become psychotic again? I pondered these and various other concerns in the days before Sunny came home. On the morning of her discharge, I was sick to my stomach and Linda had a light coating of hives covering her neck. The unpredictable and sometimes terrifying force of nature that was my daughter was racing toward us like a meteor. There was no putting it out of our minds for even a second, for reminders of the inevitability of her arrival and its potential upheaval to our family were always there, relentlessly gnawing at our insides and burrowing through our skin.

Chapter 31 ❧ Sunny

As my discharge time approached, I noticed I was feeling better. My thoughts were mostly clear and I was starting to believe that my paranoia about the Nazis had to be a product of my illness. Although still a little worried about it, I decided to trust Dr. Bensen this time. *They* were also on respite and, although numb, I didn't feel particularly depressed. I was extremely troubled by my mother's suicide, but at least the medication was doing its job.

Dr. Bensen went through his standard discharge rigmarole in the morning, reminding me to page him immediately if I felt suicidal or if my psychosis returned. He also reminded me that stress exacerbates my illness and to work on the relaxation techniques I learned from Dr. Turner. Afterward, I sat on my bed and waited for Joshua, who would be taking me home to pack and see Chester before going to my dad's house. I tried to read as I waited, but I couldn't concentrate as a constant stream of worries raced through my head. My mother's suicide was on the top of the pile, leaving me with nebulous feelings I didn't know how to process. Although it had been explained to me that her death was not my fault, guilt stuck inside me like a mass. I wondered if I could have done something to make her feel better. Or whether I was too much for her—too needy, sensitive or demanding. While a part of me knew I was being illogical, I simply couldn't intellectualize my way out of those feelings.

At least now I felt closer to my father. Therapy opened my eyes to his all-consuming love for my mother and how gutted her illness and suicide had left him. Amazingly, this realization caused the blame I'd directed at him since childhood to simply evaporate. Those feelings, however, now reared themselves in another, more unsettling direction. Although I understood why my dad needed to tell me about the suicide, I think I was better off not knowing. I preferred to remember her in my own childish way—keeping the good parts and squelching the rest. But now I saw her in a different, more inauspicious light. For now, I was not only consumed by macabre visions of her plummeting off the bridge and crashing hard into the dirt and rocks below, but I also couldn't shake the realization that her death was no accident. I think that was the worst part of knowing—that she *chose* a terrifying death to a life with me. If I had children, I'd like to think I'd never leave them—no matter what. But maybe this was naive or self-righteous of me; after all, *they* were enough to drive anyone to a violent and irreversible act. And maybe my poor mother's tormentors were even more malevolent than mine. Maybe she had no ability to fight back or to pull herself from her convoluted sense of reality. These were things I would never know.

I also thought a lot about going home again. While there was no way in hell I'd live in some sort of halfway house with fucked up people like myself, I also could see how leaving me alone in the condo concerned my family. Like a criminal, I'd lost their trust entirely. So, where else could I go? In any case, part of me wanted, or maybe *needed*, to be cared for like a child again. There was comfort in the security blanket of childhood, of knowing someone would be there to catch me. Perhaps my need to regress emerged from the chaos and inconsistency of my childhood. Perhaps I needed a do-over.

On the other hand, I questioned my ability to withstand even the slightest condescension—especially from Linda. I was a married woman after all. I also worried about confronting the endless reminders of my grandparents that inhabited the property. And so, just like pretty much everything else in my head during those days, the thought of going home left me confused by a conflicting barrage of thoughts firing in multiple directions. As I was contemplating the bliss of knowing one's own mind—of existing without a confusing stream of "what ifs" and "what abouts," the door opened. It was my handsome Joshua.

"Hi, gorgeous!" he said with exaggerated cheerfulness. He wore a light blue T-shirt and faded Levi's with holes in the knees. I could smell apple pectin shampoo from across the room. His wavy brown hair was still wet from the shower. One lock of hair formed a perfect curl that landed over his right eyebrow. He was sexy as hell and deserved better than having a wife in the psych ward.

"Hi, handsome," I answered as he leaned in for a kiss.

"So, are you ready?"

"Time will tell," I said, punctuating my words with a deep sigh. It was a pointless question. Yeah, I was ready to leave the sickening antiseptic/soup smell I woke up to every day. And I was ready to get away from the lunatics who had animated debates with invisible enemies, or who stared into space while drool dangled ungraciously from their open mouths, or who made lurid sexual advances toward my father. And I was more than ready to sleep through the night without hearing the plangent cries of my neighbors, especially the old guy across the hall who screamed, "Birds aren't real! Birds aren't real!" every night at around 3 a.m. But was I ready for the real world? I had no clue.

"It will be okay, honey." He looked around the room, picking up my sad plastic bag of clothes, toiletries, and sketch pad. "Is this everything?"

I stood up and grabbed my purse and a vase of orange sunflowers given to me by Maggie, who told me I was strong and beautiful just like them. I'll never forget the kindness of that gesture, especially after how I'd treated her.

"That's it. I travel light."

"No, actually you don't," he teased.

We headed out of the hospital yet again, with me leading at a quick pace in order to avoid awkward goodbyes. It felt strange to be in the car, like I'd been locked inside for ages. As Joshua held my hand and chatted away about some project at work, I stared out the window, watching the world going on around me—oblivious to my predicament. Endless highway construction caused traffic delays. Fast food restaurants with plastic play monstrosities littered the side of the freeway. Iridescent black birds rested on power lines. And Joshua drove too close to the car ahead of him. It was all just the same.

After stopping at the condo to grab some things and visit Chester, we headed toward my dad's house. I wondered how my family was feeling about having me home. Were they terrified of what I might do? Was my dad excited to have me home, while Linda just pretended to play along? When we walked through the front door, the house was spotless. The marbled foyer gleamed in the light and the formal dining and living room areas were immaculate. I felt an uncomfortable mix of appreciation for being welcomed back into this beautiful home, and guilt for not deserving it. It was strangely quiet until we heard Sparky bark a few times. Then he bolted down the hallway, crashing into my legs and covering my hands with kisses. He was followed by my dad and Linda. I set down my flowers on a side table and my dad gave me a big hug.

"I'm so glad to see you, sweetheart," he said, holding me at arm's length.

"We're so happy to have you home."

Linda followed his lead, giving me a kiss on the cheek. They both seemed genuinely pleased to have me there. I wondered how long that would last.

Joshua and I went downstairs to put my stuff away. I barely recognized my old room. The walls were newly painted and there was a beautiful duvet on the bed. There was also a white wicker dressing table with a mirror and chair that I'd never seen before, and someone had placed a vase of pink snapdragons on my nightstand. I couldn't deny how pretty the room looked and I knew exactly who was responsible. I made a mental note to thank Linda later.

Joshua and I lay on the bed next to each other, looking up at the ceiling with hands clasped. As I lay there quietly, breathing in the delicious scent of something cooking upstairs, I noticed the small blue spot near the light fixture where I once threw one of Maddy's rubber lizards. It stuck up there for hours before falling on me when I was asleep and scaring the shit out of me.

"I've missed you so much," Joshua said, breaking the silence in the room. "You have?"

"Of course, I have, you dork. I love you." He lifted my hand to his lips and kissed it repeatedly.

"I love you so much," I replied, leaning over and kissing his stubbly cheek. It felt strangely good to be there in my old room with the man I loved. I wanted to stay in the stillness of that moment forever, safely cocooned from the sleeping grenade within me.

When we headed upstairs for dinner, I found Spencer and Maddy playing quietly in the family room. When they rushed over to hug me, I realized I'd missed them. They smelled like fresh air and crayons. I desperately hoped they could continue to savor the best parts of life without falling to rack and ruin like I did. Thank God they didn't share my mother's genes.

Linda and my dad, who were busy setting out food and pouring drinks, asked us to sit down at the table and relax. Linda had prepared mushroom lasagna, which smelled heavenly and was still steaming as she set it on the table. There was also a salad, garlic bread, and tiramisu for dessert—an unusual feast for a weeknight. The dinner was pleasant in a plastic sort of way. We were more like acquaintances than family, making small talk and avoiding anything deep. I could see that the kids had been coached on how to act around the poor crazy girl, heaven forbid they should ruffle my feathers.

When dinner was finished and there was mention of dessert, I said I was stuffed, but that it looked amazing. Forgetting her instructions, Maddy blurted out, "You should eat it. Why are you so skinny anyway?" Reacting to

Maddy's apparent blasphemy, Spencer elbowed her, and both Linda and my dad immediately jumped in, saying it wasn't a nice question and to finish her food. Maddy lowered her head.

"Geez, it's okay," I said emphatically. "You all don't need to walk on eggshells around me, it just makes things worse. Please just be yourselves. And Maddy, you're right, I'm too thin and it's not healthy. I was sick for a while, but I'm feeling better now." I gave Maddy a big smile and she perked back up. I could see that having me live here was going to be an adjustment for everyone. Fortunately, Sparky lightened the mood by letting out a fart that caused both children (as well as Joshua) to laugh hysterically. If it took canine flatulence to get us through awkward dinners, I was all for it.

After dinner, Joshua and I went outside as he was preparing to leave. We stood on the front porch looking at each other. He had whipped cream on his cheek, which I wiped away.

"You look so beautiful right now," he said, touching my long hair.

I was taken aback. I had felt unattractive for weeks now and didn't believe him. But he was looking at me with such adoration that I let it go. "Thank you. I wish I could go home with you."

"Believe me, so do I."

We hugged for quite a while and then he left me there with my family who tiptoed around me as if I might shatter at any moment. Their wariness reminded me of Laura's unicorn in *The Glass Menagerie*. Like the treasured figurine, would I only be deemed safe if encased by walls shielding me from the outside world? Of course, unlike the unicorn, the forces from which I most needed protection lurked *within* me, lying in wait until summoned by some untouchable nemesis. Nevertheless, either my dad or Linda constantly stood sentry—separating me from anything that might knock me off balance.

My dad also insisted that I keep my meds in the kitchen, check in with him each day, and reach out anytime something was bothering me. He often mentioned that we should talk more about my mother's suicide—a prospect that both intrigued and repelled me. Although I had questions, I was afraid of reanimating the horrible visions I'd been trying so hard to suppress. Besides, I knew full well that he didn't actually *want* to talk about it; rather, one of my doctors must have suggested it. I decided to bring it up with Dr. Turner at our next meeting. I was scheduled to see her three times a week: Tuesdays, Thursdays and Fridays—a schedule I found excessive, especially when combined with my bimonthly Monday visits with Dr. Bensen. In the meantime though, since Dr. Turner was on vacation until the end of the following week, my family hovered over me like starved buzzards.

When I woke up the next morning, I was disoriented, thinking I was still in the hospital. Once I got my bearings, I looked around at my surroundings. With the bedside bouquet, the wicker and floral décor, and the window overlooking Linda's rose garden, the room had an aura of beauty and stillness. And maybe it was the sheets, but my bed had never felt so luxurious. As I lay there gazing out the window, I tried to allow my gratitude for being home to fill the emptiness within me. For the first time in my adult life, I lacked direction. At least when I was a hospital patient, my role was straightforward: take my meds and listen to my doctor. But here, in my old bedroom, my identity was ambiguous. I thought about productive ways to fill my time. I could sit by the pool and, despite my reservations, actually try some journaling. I thought about working on my resume, but decided making a list of goals would be less demoralizing. And, since I was feeling out of shape, I considered going on regular walks until I felt well enough to jog, and perhaps swim laps in the pool. I also wanted to get back into my art and maybe even teach Maddy and Spencer to draw—depending of course on my level of patience. Feeling slightly less astray, I dragged myself out of bed and found my way to the kitchen where Linda stood sipping tea as if waiting for me.

Over the next day or two, the kids started to act more like themselves, getting into one especially horrible fight culminating in Spencer throwing a soft clump of spaghetti at Maddy's face, which slid down her angry red cheek as she howled indignantly. It was the funniest thing I'd seen in ages. But it also reminded me of how annoying those two could be—making me all the more eager to be home with my husband. While the twins grew more comfortable with having me around, the adults, on the other hand, remained on high alert.

On Friday morning, I sat by the pool and drank my coffee. After texting with Elizabeth, who was in Mexico with her boyfriend, I decided to visit my grandparents' cottage. I hadn't been there since they died and felt a little sick as I walked up the little pathway to the door, which turned out to be locked. I wandered around the side and found the key exactly where it always had been, beneath the blue and white geranium-filled pot I painted in fourth grade. Once inside, I was immediately struck by the scent of the cottage. The combination of Papa's pipe tobacco, the bar soap in the bathroom, and something else I could not identify, activated my memories, making me catch my breath.

I looked at the bed with its frayed green and white quilt, and remembered the times I had lain there next to Baba when she was resting. She would tell me stories about her life growing up in Poland, which made me ache at the loss of my stolen family. I wandered around the cottage and took a seat in Papa's favorite spot on the loveseat, next to the reading lamp. The worn cushion still held the deep indentation of his body. I could see him there, with his pipe and newspaper—which he would immediately drop the second I came through the door. My grandparents always greeted me like I was the most special girl in the world.

I went to the little kitchen and envisioned Baba standing there, rolling out dough for pierogi. I looked in the cabinets and saw that everything was still there, my father hadn't changed a thing. I didn't blame him. I opened a drawer and found Baba's favorite apron. It was the type that had straps over the shoulders and tied in the back. I held it up, looking at the fabric's red rose pattern and two blue checked pockets in the front. Bringing it up to my face, I breathed in Baba's scent. I sat down on the kitchen floor and cried into that apron, begging my grandparents to give me a sign that they were still here— still with me somehow. But, of course, my wish was only answered with a bitter silence that echoed my longing and desolation.

My keepers granted me home visitation over the weekend, so Joshua came to get me on Saturday, telling me to wear my bathing suit. I was happy to see my husband and just wanted to go home and cuddle in our bed. I wanted to be surrounded by my books. And I wanted my kitty. But he seemed excited about the outing and I didn't want to dampen his spirit, so I went along with it. When we got to the beach, Joshua set up a beautiful picnic. He'd packed a blanket and a basket filled with strawberries, sparkling water, pistachios, and cheese calzones from my favorite pizza place. *God, I loved him.*

"Take off your shirt and I'll put some sunscreen on your back," he said, reaching into his bag.

While I didn't want to remove my clothes, I knew it would be strange not to. I was beginning to learn that being mentally ill involved constant hypervigilance aimed at keeping the ugly things inside me from creeping their way to the outside. How long could I possibly get away with dancing through life as a masquerader, a fraud? I sat there in my yellow bikini, hunched over with my arms covering my knees, trying not to expose my pale skin and protruding ribs, and the deep scratch marks on my arms that were turning into scars. Either Joshua didn't see me this way, or more likely, didn't want me to feel bad.

"You're so hot!" he said, rubbing lotion on my back.

"Yeah, well, since I have no career prospects, maybe I could become a stripper."

"I'd pay to watch you strip any day," he said laughing.

He didn't catch the desperation behind my statement.

For the rest of the weekend, Joshua made sure I took my meds and told me he loved me repeatedly. He tried to talk to me about my illness, telling me we were in it together, that I would be okay. But I didn't want to talk about my goddamned schizoaffective disorder. I didn't want it to be the center of my life—the undercurrent of every conversation. But rather than conveying the profound loss within me, I told him I felt fine. By the end of the weekend, Joshua had not tried to have sex with me. He kissed me, held me, and stroked my hair—but nothing more. This was unlike him; he had a strong libido. When he dropped me off at my dad's on Sunday, I felt like he didn't love me anymore. That he was just buying time until he could rid himself of me. He was young, handsome, and successful—why would he want to spend the rest of his life with someone like me?

Back at home, I felt awkward being there while my dad was at work. Linda's kindergarten class was already out for summer, but Spencer and Maddy stayed in school a bit longer—so it was just the two of us. I decided to start walking Sparky twice a day, both to get away from the awkwardness, but also to increase my fitness. When I came upstairs in the mornings, Linda was always in the kitchen either sipping from a mug or busying herself with something. She would ask me how I slept and tell me there was fresh coffee. Then, as I took my pills, I could sense her behind me, watching. Sometimes I would notice later in the day that the pills had been moved. She must have been counting them. After the Anaheim stunt, I guess I deserved as much.

I could see that she had stocked the kitchen with my go-to foods—wheat bread, granola, fruit, soy milk, and yogurt—which I appreciated. She offered to take me to the grocery store or even the mall, but I wasn't ready for that yet. Instead, I sat outside and tried to fill my time in meaningful ways. I tried to sketch my grandparents' cottage with its cobblestone path and vibrant flower garden, but I wasn't inspired. Or maybe it was still too raw. But I had trouble drawing more neutral things too, like birds. I also tried to come up with new goals for myself, but nothing beyond editing or writing seemed to fit for me. I considered writing a book, but it felt too daunting. Invariably, I would become discouraged and take Sparky for a walk around the neighborhood, which at least made him ecstatic.

In the early evenings when Linda prepared dinner and the kids played or drew at the table, I offered to help. Sometimes I unloaded the dishwasher or chopped vegetables. On one such occasion, Linda told me she was making Brussels sprouts the way her mother taught her. As she blanched the sprouts, I wondered about her family. I knew so very little about my stepmother.

"So, you grew up in Chicago, right?" I asked, sitting down at the kitchen table.

"Just outside Chicago in a town called Long Grove." She leaned on the counter near the stove, her face pink from the boiling water.

"And you have just one younger brother, right?" I'd met her brother, Frederick. He was quiet but sweet with an engaging smile.

"Yes, well, I had a younger sister too, but she died when she was four."

What? How did I not know this? "Oh my God, Linda! I'm so sorry. What, I mean—"

"It's okay," she interrupted. "I don't talk about it much. She choked on a piece of food. She got up early one morning and was eating a hotdog she found in the fridge, but it got lodged in her throat and, well, everyone was still asleep, so…" Her voice trailed off. She poured the sprouts in a colander as steam encircled her face.

I felt terrible for her, what an awful thing to endure. "I'm really sorry, I can't imagine what that was like for you and your family. How much older were you than your sister?"

"Thank you. I was twelve when CeCe died, so eight years older. I think she was a surprise baby." She was meticulously laying out the halved sprouts on paper towels, presumably to absorb the bitter liquid. "My dad died years before, so it was just the three of us. My mom didn't handle it so well. She couldn't forgive herself."

"Oh my gosh, that's so sad. But it was an accident, not her fault." I was watching Linda, but she showed no signs of distress. She just went about her work.

"Yeah, that's how it is being a parent. It doesn't matter how diligent or loving you are, when something happens to your children, you blame yourself. At least, that's been my experience." She looked at me pointedly when she said this and I got the message. "She tried to numb herself with alcohol, but of course that didn't work and it's ultimately what killed her," she added over the sound of butter on the frying pan.

What the fuck? "Wow, that must have been awful for you." I couldn't believe my ears.

"Let's just say it was character-building. And it's made me a better mother, more appreciative of my children—including *you*, by the way. But maybe also a bit overprotective. And, of course, I don't drink."

We chatted a little longer until I excused myself. I went outside to sit on the grass. My mind was reeling. I knew Linda didn't drink, but I just thought she was a goody-two-shoes. And I knew her parents were dead, but not *this*. To me, Linda had always been a soft-spoken little woman with no concept of the trauma I'd experienced in my life. I thought she was weak and vulnerable. As I gazed over at my grandfather's beautiful blue hydrangeas, I remembered him saying they were tough, hard to kill. Maybe Linda was like this too—seemingly delicate, but held together by formidable roots.

I was annoyed with myself for misjudging Linda, and even more so with my dad for not telling me more about her. Later that evening at dinner, when Maddy said, "Yuck—I hate brushy sprouts!" I told her she should appreciate her mom for working so hard to prepare healthy food for her and her brother. A few seconds of silence followed my comment, which was broken by Linda, who said, "Well, thank you, Sunny." I noticed my dad sitting there with a full mouth and a pleased look on his face.

While my newfound respect for Linda felt good, my sense of drifting aimlessly gnawed at me with increasing ferocity. Regardless of how I spent my time, without dreams and ambitions to steer me, I found myself on precarious ground that threatened to suck me under. On Thursday, as I thought about my future, I decided to go to the bookstore near my old office. I loved that store and had spent many hours there perusing the various titles and inhaling the delicious smell of coffee and old paper. I thought some books on novel writing or painting might give me some ideas. I also wanted an engrossing piece of literature that would offer some form of escape. Linda let me borrow her car with the requirement that I'd be home in less than two hours. I hadn't driven in a couple of months and it felt good to experience a bit of freedom again.

The bookstore was just as I remembered. I went to my favorite section, where all of the classics were stacked. There was a sense of comfort that came with being surrounded by Tolstoy, Eliot, Hawthorne, Steinbeck, Bronte, and the rest. I ran my fingers along their spines, looking for a novel I hadn't yet read—there weren't many. As I was pulling out a red-spined copy of *Anna Karenina*, I heard my name.

"Sunny, is that you?" It was a plasticky twang I immediately recognized. I turned to see Melody, the office manager from my old job. Her thick blonde hair was in a high ponytail and she wore her standard office attire of a knee-length black skirt, black pumps, and a silk blouse. She had on a ton of mascara that clumped her eyelashes together and she smelled like Giorgio perfume.

I put the book back on the shelf. "Oh, hi, Melody. How are you?"

"I'm well, thank you. Mr. Penterhaus is in town and I need a new style guide, but then I saw you here and…"

Oh holy fuck, Penterhaus. Just hearing the name of that beady-eyed bastard gave me a queasy feeling. I needed to get out of there.

"That's cool. Nice seeing you," I said dismissively, starting to move away.

"What's been going on with you? Where are you working now?" She tried to act interested in me, but I knew her—she was digging, ever on the hunt for fresh dirt.

"I'm uh, I'm looking for opportunities," I mumbled, feeling antsy and uncomfortable, my legs starting to wobble.

"I see. How are you feeling, are you doing better?" She was leaning too closely, I could smell her minty gum.

"I'm good. But I'm running late. So, I'll see you later," I muttered, backing away from her chubby, pompous face.

She muttered something in response, but I didn't hear it.

When I got back to Linda's car, I was shaking inside and out. I tried to steady my hands as I closed my eyes and took deep breaths. As I drove home, the familiar shame of that day—the day I peed my fucking pants at work—cycled through my mind. Clearly, she knew all about it. *They all knew.* Even worse, she reminded me of all that I'd lost. I'd never be a book publisher. Even if I got better, word was out and no one would hire me. As I drove past the condo, I lost it. Tears rolled down my face as I mourned my old life and my lack of a new one. Then *they* added their two cents, chanting *loser, loser, loser* as I pounded my hands on the steering wheel and pictured Penterhaus's pasty skin and amber teeth. I was back there again, sinking in the mud to the accompaniment of the death choir.

I pulled over at a park near my dad's house since it was too soon to go home, Linda might be suspicious. I wiped off my face and tried to calm myself. *They* quieted, but my thoughts continued to whirl around in rapid succession. I kept trying to remember who I was before a mountain of shit rained down on me, ruining my life. I was okay before all of this schizo crap started—before doctors decided to label and drug me. Why couldn't I just deal with life like other people? I thought of Linda with her soft voice and petite frame—even *she* was able to function like a normal person despite a traumatic childhood. Maybe I wasn't mentally ill, but just weak. What if that fucking diagnosis was just a charade—an attempt to confuse and control me? Since being branded with it, I'd never felt so flawed and off course. I knew what I needed to do—like Baba's sparrows, I would shed the damaged plumage that was holding me down, suppressing my spirit.

Chapter 32 ❧ Sunny

Once I'd calmed down, I drove back home. Linda was in the garden with the kids. They all yelled "hello" to me, with Linda adding, "How did it go?"

I rushed away from them, muttering something about it being fine, but that I needed to go to the bathroom. I headed down to my room and shut the door where I remained until dinner. I felt a strange mix of humiliation and anxiety, combined with relief at identifying the source of my problems. The epiphany I experienced in the car was the only thing propelling me forward. *Of course* I wasn't a lunatic—it was preposterous. How would I ever have graduated with honors or married such a wonderful man if I were crazy? I was an eccentric female—what more did the psychiatric community need to label and oppress me? They probably thought I was hysterical, with a wandering uterus—a woman who needed to be lobotomized and stifled.

I made myself presentable and headed upstairs for dinner just before Joshua arrived. He'd brought me red roses for no particular reason, reminding me of how desperately I needed to hold on to him. And of how precarious our relationship had become—teetering on the edge of my instability. That evening, my dad was in charge of dinner, which of course meant grilling. This made it easier for me fit in since there were a lot of distractions when eating outside, like birds, Sparky, people walking back and forth from the grill to the table, and the kids—who were especially wiggly and rambunctious when eating on the porch. I busied myself with my plate, going in the kitchen a few times for condiments. Fortunately, my dad was particularly chatty, discussing how one of the partners in his firm had invited our family to his Tahoe chalet in the fall, which delighted the kids. If it allowed me to stay home with Joshua for a few days, I loved the idea too.

When we were carrying everything back to the kitchen, I put my pills in my mouth and took a swig of water where the adults would notice. Then I went into the bathroom and spit them out. Joshua and I watched TV on my bed and made out a little before he left. He seemed relaxed, believing I was finally on the mend. That night I rolled around in bed, sitting straight up in a panic more than once. I dreamt about my parents. Although their words were warped, they were arguing animatedly as I stood between them, begging them to stop. I woke up feeling nauseated and trapped.

I gummed my pills again in the morning and sat outside, tossing the ball for Sparky. I felt the cool grass tickle against my bare legs, which had tanned a little over the past week. I was strangely drawn to my grandparents' cottage, unable to avert my eyes from it for more than a few seconds. I threw the ball until my arm started to ache. After about two hours, I could feel my skin burning, but I didn't much care. My compulsion to look at the cottage was getting stronger and I was having trouble looking anywhere else. I started having that familiar floating sensation—I was above myself looking down. And then it happened again. Like a robot, I was programmed, warned with the words: "Watch out, hide, they're coming for you." I wasn't sure if the warning was from the same comrades as before or, since it came from the cottage, if it was from my grandparents.

Realizing I'd been found again, panic infiltrated my insides, leaving me shaky and disoriented. But I still wasn't entirely convinced, since I remembered my doctors and the hospital nurses telling me the SS couldn't be after me—not here, not now. I was confused. I went into the house, grabbed an apple and a leftover sandwich from the fridge—all for Linda's sake, who would be asking me about lunch at any moment. I mumbled something about a headache and went downstairs where I paced in my room for an hour or two.

When the dinner hour approached, I texted Joshua that I had a migraine from sitting in the sun and that he didn't need to come to dinner. It wasn't a lie, my head hurt so badly I thought I might throw up. He wanted to come and take care of me, but I told him there was nothing he could do. He pushed back until finally agreeing to stay home.

I lay in the dark with my head pounding and my thoughts racing, it was a miserable combination that made me want to run and collapse at the same time. My dad brought me a prescription headache pill, which I pretended to take. I didn't trust pills anymore. Along with the belief that drugs were being used to control me, it had dawned on me that my mental illness diagnosis was merely a tool for the Nazis, giving them the perfect rationale for murdering my nonessential ass.

That night was one of the worst I can remember. It took hours before I slept and I threw up several times, once not even making it to the toilet. When I finally succumbed to sleep, it was fitful and disturbing. The warnings I'd received earlier in the day rolled through my head like picture film, "Watch out, hide, run …," over and over and over—leaving me startled and sweaty, convinced that the warnings were real and that I was in grave danger. I awoke in the morning, mercifully without the migraine, yet also feeling victimized and shattered by the constant admonitions.

I headed up to the kitchen where Linda appeared on cue, which struck a nerve. Didn't she have anything better to do than to constantly monitor me?

"Good morning, Sunny. How are you feeling?" she said in a cheerful voice that made me want to stab my eardrums with an ice pick.

"My head is so much better, I don't think I drank enough water yesterday. The sleep helped too," I lied. Then *they* started in on me with their usual stream of invectives: *Bitch. Stupid whore. Bitch.* It was hard to hear myself over them, so I spoke a little louder. "I'll take better care of myself today. I definitely need some coffee." I wondered if I was talking too much.

"Yes, help yourself," she said with a puzzled expression. "Remember, you have a session with Dr. Turner today. It's earlier now, 1:00. I have some errands to run with the kids, so I'll drop you off."

Oh fuck! Fuckity, fuck, fuck, fuck! I forgot about that stupid appointment! "Sure thing," I said with my best saccharin smile. I poured a cup of coffee and said I was going to take a shower. Then I put the meds in my mouth and took a drink of water straight from the faucet before going back downstairs.

I spit the pills in the toilet and tried to decide what to do next. My mind played like a disjointed orchestra, bombarding my head with a continuous stream of disorganized but urgent thoughts. The commotion was compounded by *them*, whose ridicule was gaining speed. *Psycho bitch. Whore. Stupid whore. Psycho bitch…* I didn't know what to do with my body. I wished I could go to sleep since it was the closest thing to a reprieve from the torture. But I was way too charged.

I paced around the room in circles, trying to work off the excess energy. This went on for quite a while, maybe hours, until I realized I needed to get out of there, to hide. What was wrong with me? Why was I wasting time in my room when the Gestapo had located me again? I needed to run. I put on some shorts and a T-shirt I found on the floor. I looked around for some socks, but could only find one. *Where the fuck was my other sock?* I was becoming incensed and wanted to scream. *Fuck!* I gave up, putting on only one sock and my running shoes, and left the room. The usual counting in my head when taking stairs was replaced by *them*, chanting in their typical staccato: *Bitch. Bitch. Stupid ugly bitch,* in rhythm with each step.

Once on the main floor, I peeked around the corner toward the kitchen; no one was there except Sparky, who was fast asleep on the living room couch. I glanced through the window above the kitchen sink and saw the kids on their wooden play structure and Linda doing whatever the hell it was she did in her garden for hours. I decided to go out the front where they wouldn't see me. As I reached for the door, I stopped in my tracks. A new warning landed hard on my brain: *Hide the children!* Oh God, that's right, I thought. They're half Jewish *and* nonessential, they would be exterminated without pause. Then I was hit by another alarming realization: Maddy and Spencer were *twins*. How could I not have thought of this before? If Mengele got a hold of them… Oh *fuck*, it was unthinkable. I needed to act quickly.

I went through the front door and closed it quietly. It was a gorgeous day outside and I could hear Maddy singing. I crept around the side of the house where I could watch them without being seen. I waited there for fifteen or twenty minutes as sweat dripped down my forehead. I could barely contain my body, I wanted to move so badly. And I felt rageful toward Linda for being there. When she finally went into the house, I made my move.

I walked as nonchalantly as I could toward the kids who immediately spotted me.

"Sunny, Sunny!" they yelled, thrilled to see me. Maddy jumped off her swing and grabbed my hand. "Come play with us, we can play restaurant," she said, pulling me toward a stump with plastic food on it.

"I have something even better," I said, trying to control the shakiness in my voice. "Let's go to the park! Your mom said it's okay."

"Yay!" exclaimed Maddy as Spencer headed toward us with equal enthusiasm. They loved going to the park and I felt like an asshole for deceiving them. But time was of the essence. There was no other way.

"Great, come on!" I looked toward the kitchen and didn't see Linda. Then I grabbed both of their hands and guided them out of the yard, away from the street, toward the neighbor's yard directly behind us. "We need to hurry," I said, forcing them into a light jog since their little legs couldn't walk fast enough.

"But that's the wong way," said Spencer, sounding impossibly young with his lingering baby accent.

"I know a shortcut, don't worry." This seemed to placate Maddy, but Spencer was dubious and I could feel him trying to pull away as we cut through one fenceless yard after another, sometimes pushing through thick shrubbery.

"I want to go home!" he yelled, now tugging even harder.

I could feel myself getting frantic, but also pissed. "Be quiet," I said through gritted teeth. "Do you want them to catch us?"

At this, both kids started to cry and attempt to get away. My blood was now at a rapid boil. What was wrong with these kids? "Shut up! Don't you know what happens to babies who cry?" I said with enough venom to quiet both of them for a moment. When they started back up again, I knew I needed to do something. I saw a battered green tool shed in the distance and dragged them toward it.

"In here," I said in a loud whisper. As I let go of my right hand to open the door, Spencer broke loose and took off running.

"Shit!" I said, as Maddy started to howl.

"Spencer, Spencer, nooooo!" she screeched.

Thinking I could at least save one of them, I pulled Maddy into the shed, which was filled with all sorts of yard equipment including shovels, a rake, gardening tools, and a lawnmower, along with bags of what looked like soil or fertilizer. The place smelled like rodent shit and gasoline. We hurried to the far back wall and crouched down below wall shelves holding rusted paint cans. I could feel cobwebs on my shins that made me shiver as I imagined spiders everywhere. I forced Maddy to crouch down in front of me and I held my arms tightly around her. She was still crying and I reminded her that she *had* to be quiet, otherwise they would find us. But she didn't stop.

"Maddy, you *need* to be quiet. There are *very bad* people after us. Hush!" I could hear myself speaking, but that menacing voice could not be mine. Then *they* reminded me how much I hated myself for this: *Nasty, horrible bitch. Nasty bitch. Nasty bitch.* But I loved Maddy and had to save her. She immediately quieted down, but I could feel her body tremble as silent sobs heaved through her.

We stayed like that for around fifteen minutes when I heard a commotion outside. I could hear Spencer say, "In there." The door creaked open flooding light into our dingy hiding place.

"Mommy, Mommy!" screamed Maddy, who jumped out of my grasp

and ran toward Linda. The three of them clung to each other as Spencer whimpered and Maddy choked through tears, almost hyperventilating. Then Linda looked at me hunkered there in the corner like a condemned rat. Her crimson cheeks were covered with tears that she didn't bother to wipe away. Her eyes, those lovely blue eyes, stared straight into me with a coldness I'd never seen in her before.

"How could you? How the fuck could you?" she spat, overemphasizing each word. Her hatred of me was palpable, permeating the dank air of the shed.

"I, I…I'm sorry," I said, jumping from the corner and flying out the door.

I ran from that cursed place, all the while sobbing hysterically. Linda's words kept replaying, "How could you? How could you? How could you?" I knew *they* were after me, but I had hurt Maddy and Spencer. Linda's venomous expression was scorched in my mind. I was finally starting to see that she loved me, truly cared about me. And now, even this gentle, ridiculously kind woman detested me. I was nothing, pure garbage, shit. I wasn't even sure whom I was running from anymore, but I kept on going. I moved with the conviction that I was done, that I'd had enough. But still, I would not let the Nazis win; they would not choose my destiny.

I continued to run until I came to a dead end. I ventured toward the street where I saw a six-story apartment complex. It was made of dark wood and I could see that each apartment had a square deck that jutted out from the building. I opened the front door of the building and entered a lobby containing rows of metal mailboxes built into the wall. I saw a dingy white door and opened it to the stairs, which I ran up until there were no more. I opened the door to a long hallway with maroon carpeting and newly painted beige walls. As I moved along the hallway, I checked each door until the fourth or fifth one finally opened.

I entered an apartment and rushed down a carpeted hall. I approached a small kitchen that opened to a dining area on the other side. There was a round wooden table cluttered with books and papers. The place smelled like cooked meat and I could hear a TV. I saw the door to the deck directly in front of me and raced toward it. I heard a man say, "Hey, what the hell!" I ignored him and opened the sliding door.

There was a small table on the deck which I pushed toward one of the wooden side railings. As I stepped on the table and began climbing up, I heard the man say, "Hey, what are you doing? Get down from there!"

"Leave me alone!" I muttered as I stood unsteadily on the side railing, still holding onto the building. I heard the man say, "Oh my God!" I didn't care. I finally understood my mother, she was right. I couldn't be here with normal people. I hurt the people I loved and I had no future. And I was constantly, endlessly tormented and chased. But I wouldn't be caught—I would die by my own hand. My plans were reinforced by the demented cheerleaders who repeated *Die bitch. Die stupid bitch. Jump. Jump. Jump.* I would silence those relentless bastards too.

Still holding onto the wall, I looked down and realized how high up I was. Seeing grass directly below me, I knew I'd need to jump from the farthest railing in order to land on concrete. To be trapped in the body of a quadriplegic with my demented mind was my worst nightmare. I couldn't let that happen.

I sat down and straddled the railing. Then, using my hands and hips, I shimmied away from the apartment inch by inch. Eventually, I came to the end of the side railing and carefully eased my way around the corner until I was in the middle of the outer railing. Now I was perfectly placed over the cement below. This would do the trick.

As I looked down, I was suddenly horrified by what I was about to do. I thought about how much it would hurt to splat against the ground. And the sensation of falling was horrifying, unfathomable. I sat there for several minutes, sweating and shaking profusely as I tried to garner enough strength to lift one leg over the rail and jump. I knew I had to do it, but I was terrified. *God, I was such a coward.* I whispered to my mother, "Mom, wherever you are, please help me. Please give me strength, help me leave this place." But my pleas were only answered by *them*, goading me on with their abuse. *Jump bitch. Jump bitch. Jump bitch.* When I heard a siren, I knew I was running out of time and needed to make my move.

People started to gather below, staring up at the crazy, suicidal girl. I wished they would mind their own business. I heard a woman yell, "Please get down, honey. It will be okay." What the hell did she know about anything being okay? Did she have violent forces tormenting and trying to destroy her every second of every day? Did she get locked in the psych hospital where doctors labeled and deceived her? Did she hurt everyone she cared about? She had no fucking idea.

I sat there for several more minutes as the crowd grew. I really didn't want my death to be a spectator event, but nothing, not even my last act, ever seemed to go my way. Maybe it was my final punishment for being a hopeless introvert who never much liked people. I closed my eyes and softly recited the Kaddish to the best of my memory. I didn't even know if I was allowed to say it, especially considering what I was about to do. Then I chastised myself for being such a lousy Jew. As I sat there straddling the wood, consumed by a calamitous stanza of terror and self-hatred, I heard my name.

"Sunny, sweetheart, please come down from there." It was my dad. His voice was both soft and vehement—insistent yet pleading. He was standing on the deck, just outside the sliding door, in a dark blue suit. I must have interrupted an important meeting. He moved toward me very slowly.

"No, Daddy," I said through tears, which made the ground look blurry, less intimidating. Continuing to straddle the rail, I reached up and quickly wiped my eyes and looked at him. His big brown eyes welled up with tears and he looked as if he could crumble at any moment. "I'm sorry, Daddy. But I can't be here anymore, it hurts too much."

He seemed to feel the intensity of that statement like an internal blow. "I know you're in pain, honey, but you can't…you can't do this," he said, fully crying now. Then, in a more commanding voice, he added, "This cycle has to stop *now!*"

My beautiful father whom I loved more than life, stood there reaching out to me with both arms. His face was wet with tears and he held an expression so wretched and utterly decimated that I couldn't do it. I couldn't jump to my death right here in front of him, leaving my bones and blood littered about the street. I couldn't do to him what my mother did. I leaned toward him and reached out with one arm and he grabbed hold of me, pulling me down from the railing. The two of us collapsed there, an intertwined heap of tears and arms holding on for dear life. I could feel him rocking me back and forth like when I was an infant, softly whispering, "Shhhh, don't cry. Don't cry."

At some point later, he was still by my side, holding my hand as I was strapped down in an ambulance. The straps were unnecessary, for I was weighed down, paralyzed, by the ranting voices, terror, and anguish that spiraled around and around inside me. Yet, somewhere buried beneath those layers of sickness and despair, lay an awareness that I did not want to die. It was a crippling revelation for a body that didn't know how to live.

Chapter 33 ❧ Sunny

The next few days were punctuated by the haze of sedation. The first time I woke up, I saw my mother standing over me with an almost pleading expression that I didn't understand. I thought for sure that I was dead. When I awoke later, I recall momentarily feeling dead and, with that feeling, came a flash of relief at no longer being hunted; yet also a guttural sense of loss at losing my family. But of course I was not dead. Rather, I was back in the hospital *yet again*. The hospital had become a revolving door for me—like some sick version of a carnival whirligig ride, its ceaseless momentum sucking in my bewildered body and spitting it back out on the other side. I wanted off that ride.

In my less lucid states, I didn't know if I was being hunted or whether I had actually decided to die. There was one particularly disturbing moment when I thought I was in a medical experimentation infirmary. "Take my uterus, I don't need it!" I recall screaming at the hospital staff, as if a guinea pig ever had any choice. And of course, *they* were there, harassing me with their standard diatribe of insults. But mostly I felt paranoid and trapped, both within plaster walls and, worse still, within my own disturbed mind. It was the most hellish confusion I'd known thus far in my anguished existence.

Once the meds did their thing and I was hurled back into reality, I wanted to drown it all out and slip back into sedation. There's an old song by the Ramones that ran through my mind during those first days in the hospital. Regardless of my state of consciousness, "I wanna be sedated..." serenaded my addled mind again and again. It would've driven me crazy if I wasn't already there. The song attached itself shortly after my Nazi delusion had mostly diminished, only to be replaced by the sickening awareness of what I'd done to my siblings. Of all of the people in my life, *why did it have to be them?* Guilt and self-reproach were nothing new for me, but this shame sat at the base of my throat like a malignancy, choking any possibility of solace. For whatever reason, *they* continued to hang on beyond the waning of my delusion, mocking me at random intervals: *Bitch. Loser. Stupid bitch. Loser. Bitch.* And, as an added bonus, I found myself locked in a barren cell with only regret, self-loathing and the infernal voices to keep me company. So I desperately yearned for the nothingness of sedation.

Although many aspects of the hospital were the same this time around, I was now a different sort of patient—I was a suicide attempter, a jumper. This meant a smaller room, with no art and almost no furniture—just a bed and a small side table that was bolted to the ground. There was a bathroom, but it was only unlocked with permission. The food came in paper containers and consisted of things like tapioca pudding, apple juice, and microwavable soup. I actually didn't mind this as much as the regular hospital food, which generally smelled like vomit or dirty socks. But eating with disposable utensils, which were actually more like scoops, felt infantile. And most annoyingly, the coffee was never hot enough. Did they actually think I'd squander the one thing I looked forward to by trying to scald myself to death? There was no logic in this place.

I also soon realized that any modicum of privacy did not exist here. I wondered if I was being watched when I jiggled the bathroom door handle and a nurse appeared out of nowhere. Then, purely out of boredom, I put my palm against the room's tiny window and, sure enough, there she was again. Looking around the ceiling, I saw the tiny camera monitoring me. Kind of a sick joke for the paranoid psychotic, I thought indignantly. And, unlike my prior hospitalizations, I was only allowed to leave my room for an hour a day and the TV room was totally off-limits. I remember thinking how all of these safeguards designed to keep me alive created an environment that was decidedly unlivable.

Sometimes I saw either my dad or Joshua as I wove in and out of lucidity. When I awoke early one morning to a glorious stack of magazines and books on the bedside table, I knew Joshua had been there. When some of the pages fell out, I realized every single staple had been removed. So, apparently taking myself out with a staple was also off the table. But I was grateful for Joshua's thoughtfulness. I missed him to my core, a feeling accentuated by an unspeakable fear that I'd finally lost him for good. Joshua was a devoted husband, but how much could he possibly take? I tried to push those thoughts out of my mind by leafing through one of the trashier magazines when Dr. Bensen showed up on the morning of around my fifth day.

"You're awake, I'm so glad," he said. He brought in a chair from the hall and sat down. He wasn't wearing glasses for once, but was otherwise donning his usual business casual look. He crossed his legs and brushed a piece of lint from his khaki pants. "Doing a little reading?"

"Oh, just contemplating fall fashion accessories for the hopelessly bewildered," I remarked dryly.

He let out a little laugh, but his expression quickly turned somber. "So, how are you doing, Sunny?"

"I'm alive," I muttered, setting the magazine off to the side.

"Well, yes, I can see that. But you were pretty close to *not* being alive."

"I know," I said softly, eyes downcast. I knew I'd fucked up royally this time, so I sat back and braced myself for the dreaded conversation.

"Why did you do that?" He leaned toward me, his intelligent eyes locked on mine.

"It was just…*everything*. I'm just so tired of…" I started to cry. And not just a little bit, it was like something broke open inside me. He went into the hall and brought back a box of tissues, not even bothering with one of his pretentious hankies. I cried for a couple of minutes, blew my nose, and started again as he sat there patiently. "I'm so tired of being afraid, of being chased. And the voices—*oh my God*, I hate them so much! They say the most horrible, cruel things… But really, it's what I did." I blew my nose again, for once not bothering with any sense of decorum or self-restraint.

"What you did?" He scratched his chin without averting his eyes from mine.

"I…I hurt Maddy. Spencer too, but especially Maddy. I'm so ashamed!" I blurted. I'd never been this emotional in front of Dr. Bensen and couldn't seem to get a grip. But he didn't flinch.

"How did you hurt them?" He uncrossed his legs and leaned back, watching me closely.

I described the whole sordid tale, stopping to cry or blow my nose multiple times. "God, I scared the hell out of them. I'm such a piece of shit," I added, looking down at my lap as shame consumed me. Then *they* started barking at me: *Loser. Garbage. Worthless bitch.* I held both hands against my ears, rocking slightly.

"Are you hearing voices?"

"Yes," I muttered miserably.

"I've upped your dose, but it will still take a little more time for the medicine to work. Try to calm down, take some deep breaths."

I did so and he began again. "I certainly don't agree with your self-assessment—you are *not* a piece of shit. You are ill. Remind me, Sunny, what was your reason for hiding the children?"

"I, um…well, I thought they would be murdered. I was warned again and, you know, with them being half Jewish *and* children—not to mention being *twins* for God's sake. I thought their deaths were imminent. So I panicked." A few tears rolled down my cheeks which I wiped away with a soggy tissue."

"So, were you trying to hurt them?"

"*What?* No! I wanted to protect them. I *love* them," I retorted, suddenly incensed. Why wasn't he listening?

"Exactly. Please remember this when you come down on yourself."

I guess he had a point. In my own thoroughly twisted way, I *was* trying to save them. But I was still a world-class loser. "Okay. But you should've seen Linda's face. She *hates* me now." It was surprising how much it hurt to say those words.

"Did she *say* she hates you?"

"No, but her face…" *I hated myself for what I did—surely she did too.*

"She's a protective mother, she was likely scared and upset. But you don't actually *know* if she hates you." He paused a moment, then asked, "Why did you stop taking your meds?"

"I just felt like the diagnosis didn't seem real. And if it was, that I should be strong enough to control it, without leaning on meds."

"When did these feelings start?"

"I guess after I saw a stupid woman I used to work with. She looked at me like I was pure garbage. She reminded me of my worst humiliation. And of what I've lost." Envisioning Melody's fleshy, pompous face made me want to scream. Instead, I let out a huge exhale and chewed on my thumb.

"Okay, so you experienced a stressor that made you start to question yourself. Did you also hear voices?"

"Oh, of course, *they* never disappoint." Those damned voices were like clockwork, always there to beat me further into the ground, to drive me deeper into the darkness. The thought of never being free of them was beyond demoralizing.

"Well, we know that anything related to your old job is a trigger and it sounds like this was a big one. So, not wanting to believe the severity of your diagnosis, you turned it around in your head, deciding you could overpower it, right?"

I nodded. He was right, as usual.

"This is not uncommon, Sunny. People with mental illnesses often believe that having to rely on medication is a sign of weakness, which leads to treatment noncompliance. What you need to remember is, just like any medical diagnosis, weakness has nothing to do with it. Like multiple sclerosis, diabetes, or asthma, schizoaffective disorder is a *medical* condition that will always require management. Does that make sense?"

"Yes, I know that logically, but I don't understand what happened to my brain."

"Well, you experienced a trigger, which caused you a great deal of stress and even breakthrough symptoms. It's the reason we need to identify your triggers and act immediately when you get upset."

"Okay," I said wearily, wondering just how many triggers I might have.

"After a few days, you became acutely psychotic and wanted to save your siblings from your perceived tormentors. But Sunny, I'm not going to minimize or rationalize your behavior with Maddy and Spencer, I'm sure it was terrible for them. But you need also to realize that they *will* get past it. They have a close, supportive family and they will be okay. I imagine they know you have an illness that sometimes causes you to act strangely, is that right?"

"Yes." I felt myself squirming at the humiliation of it all. Even little children thought I was a nut job.

"Okay, so for now, let's let your dad and Linda worry about the kids. But I'm confident that they will be okay."

"But you didn't *see* them, they were just so horrified..." And still more tears ran down my face.

"No, I didn't. But you've described it very well and your dad mentioned it to me."

What the hell? I sat up abruptly, knocking a book onto the floor. "He did?"

"Yes, and the kids are okay, Sunny."

I sat there dumbstruck, not knowing what to say. If only I could believe him.

"What does this experience tell you about taking your medication?"

"*Oh my God.* I can't let anything like that *ever* happen again. I'd rather die."

"And do you still want to die?" He leaned forward, his eyebrows furrowed.

"Not really. I can't hurt my dad like that." This was true. When I saw his face on the deck, there was no way I could add to his burden.

"Then what are your options?"

"Well, I mean, I need to take my meds no matter what."

"Bingo. And remember, each time you relapse, you put yourself at risk for greater psychological harm."

"Oh yeah." I hadn't actually remembered this, but it was a grim predicament. He told me I'd signed the papers allowing another fourteen-day hold, which I didn't recall doing. But it was fine, I needed to be contained for a while. I didn't trust myself.

Meeting with Dr. Bensen was like taking a quick-acting opioid that provided relief, but wore off far too soon. I tried to read after he left, but my mind wouldn't allow it. I was also distracted by the noise in the hallway. I could hear the medical staff moving around and chatting, but there was also a shuffling sound that went on for long intervals, multiple times a day. The noise was grating on me, so, one evening, I peeked out the door. I saw a 30-something-year-old patient in green pajamas and worn slippers shuffling down the hallway just outside my room. He was pale and scrawny with a shaved head. As he came closer, I noticed his pock-marked face and unfocussed eyes, which darted around like bouncing marbles. He radiated nervous energy. Once he passed by me, I saw that he had a large eye tattooed on the back of his head. Just one long-lashed, oval eye maybe six inches long etched in his skin like a backwards cyclops. It was creepy as hell. Worse yet, it was another grim reminder of my own mental state—I was no better than this odd, jittery man whose madness would not spare him a moment of rest.

My delusions dissipated relatively quickly this time around, presumably because I wasn't off my meds for very long. Nonetheless, my situation was considered serious, and I remained confused and mildly psychotic. Dr. Bensen visited every day, and the nurses were constantly in and out of my room. I wasn't suicidal anymore, but no one seemed to believe me. I'd been branded with a scarlet letter that would ensure my sentence for God knows how long.

Joshua and my dad must've worked out a schedule since each seemed to show up on alternate days. My dad was the first person I recall visiting once I was lucid. It was evening of the same day I'd sobbed in front of Dr. Bensen. He opened the door tentatively, as if some vile beast might snap at him from the other side. But of course he only saw his pathetic daughter staring blankly at a book—the monster inside her on pause.

He placed a chair next to me, kissed my forehead, and sat down with a slight grunt. He's getting older, I thought glumly. "Hi, sweetheart," he said with a hollow smile. He must've taken the day off, since he was wearing brown cargo shorts and the Rolling Stones T-shirt I gave him a few years ago. He smelled like aftershave.

"Hi, Dad," I said, barely able to look at him. He placed a bag of baked goods on the nightstand and we made small talk before my words burst out.

"Dad, I'm *so* ashamed about Maddy and Spencer. Do you hate me?" I covered my face with my hands and, as if watching a horror movie, peered through a spec of light between my fingers.

He let out a big breath as he shook his head from side to side. "You're my daughter, I love you unconditionally. I could never hate you, honey," he said sadly, as if resigned to repeat this phrase for the rest of his daughter's wretched life.

"But, I—"

"I know what you did and I've thought a lot about it," he interrupted, handing me the box of tissues as a tear landed on my book, forming a little pool around the letters. "There are a few things I want to say. First, yes, the kids were very upset about what happened. But the first thing Maddy said once she calmed down was, 'Is Sunny okay?' She was *really* worried about you. We had a long talk with them and they understand that you have an illness. I know you will beat yourself up relentlessly about this, but I want to reiterate that *they are doing fine.* Are you hearing me?" He spoke sternly, like I was a bratty teenager again.

"Yes, I just...yes, I hear you," I stammered, wiping my eyes.

He moved a little closer to me, resting his hand on my forearm. "The second thing you need to know is that I'm not pissed at *you*, I'm pissed at *the illness*—at the goddamned schizoaffective disorder. It's not your fault that you have this thing—not your fault *at all*. But here's the third thing: you simply cannot stop taking your meds, honey. It's no way for you, or any of us, to live. I want you to live with your husband, to pursue your dreams, and to watch Maddy and Spencer grow—to teach them things." He squeezed my arm and then added, "I want my daughter back."

"Daddy, I know. I'm so sorry, I will take my meds, I promise," I pleaded. "Nothing like this can happen again. I love Maddy and Spencer, I won't hurt them, I..." I meant what I said, this *had* to be the last time.

"Sweetheart, you nearly jumped off a balcony—you were going to *kill yourself.* Of course I don't want the twins to get hurt, but *you* are the one I'm most worried about here. You are the number one victim of this illness. I simply cannot have you..." He stopped and took a breath, then repeated, "I cannot lose you. I barely survived the loss of your mother, I just don't think I could take it," he said with an anguished expression, running a hand through his dark hair.

"I'm *so* sorry I put you through that. I don't want to die anymore, it won't happen again." I was holding his hand in both of mine, pleading. I knew I could never make him suffer like that again, but I needed to convince him.

"I know, honey. It's okay, I love you. The important thing is that you have the best treatment so we can manage your illness better, do our best to see any warning signs. And I need you to talk to me when things are bothering you."

"I will." I sat up straighter in the bed and started picking a cuticle. "But Dad, how much does Linda hate me?" I wasn't sure I really wanted to know.

"Sunny, Linda hates your illness, not you. Just like I said before. She will be extra protective with the kids around you, of course. And, given her standard overprotectiveness, that's a little scary," he added wryly. "But you need to stay on a steady treatment course so that we don't have to constantly monitor you."

I missed most of what he'd just said. "She really doesn't hate me?"

"She really doesn't. Not even one tiny bit." He smiled and I could see the little crow's feet at the corners of his eyes.

"Wow, you really should hang onto her." He laughed and gave me a hug. I felt so much better after my dad's visit that I was hardly bothered when I heard Cyclops shuffle by as he tried to outpace whatever was assailing him.

The guilt over what I'd done still lingered in the coming days, but not like before when I believed I'd damaged the twins irreparably. I started to think that I *just might* be able to live with myself, that I wasn't totally irredeemable. But the white cell in which I was trapped wasn't helping and I wanted out. Later that day, I reminded Nurse Maggie that I wasn't suicidal and asked if she would move me to another room. She just looked at me sympathetically and shook her head. I guess a hysterical girl offering up her uterus didn't exactly inspire confidence. So, I sat around with my books and innocuous food as the hospital staff busied about the madhouse.

Joshua came to see me the day after my dad's visit. He was wearing white shorts and a blue Nike T-shirt. I'd almost forgotten how much I loved his muscular legs. His face was a little red as if he'd just exercised, but his soft brown hair was perfectly coiffed. *God, he was beautiful.*

"Hi, baby," he said, kissing me on the cheek. "You look so much better than when I was here before," he added, standing back to look at me.

"You mean neither a raving lunatic nor comatose?"

He smiled. "Damn, I've missed you." He stood next to the bed, gently grasping one of my hands.

"I've missed you, too, I want to come home. I love you," I said, holding both of his hands, feeling needy and pathetic.

"I love you, too, sweetie. But Sunny, you…" He stopped speaking and looked out the window for a moment. When he turned back to me, I saw he was crying. Joshua rarely cried and it startled me. He wiped his eyes and continued, "You tried to kill yourself. *Why would you do that?*" He spit the question out like bitter fruit.

Feeling humiliated, I explained it all again—not taking my meds, the voices, the torment over what I'd done to Maddy and Spencer—all of it.

"Honey, when shitty things happen—*and they will*—you need to talk to me. Don't just stop taking your meds and think you'll be okay. I'm your husband, I'm always here for you. *Always.*"

Now *my* eyes were tearing up. "But I'm so… I'm just such a pain in the ass. Aren't you sick of me?"

"Scooch over," he said, climbing onto the bed and placing an arm around my shoulder. "Well, you've always been a pain in the ass, it's part of your charm," he teased, squeezing my shoulder. In a more serious tone, he added, "But you have an illness and I want to be here for you. Remember, for better or worse." He kissed one of my hands, then said, "You aren't getting rid of me, so stop trying."

It was odd, in recent days I'd gone psychotic, nearly jumped from a six-story building, and found myself locked in the hospital under suicide watch; and yet, those few minutes with Joshua felt better than any I'd had in months. I tried to stay motionless, as if to tiptoe around the sleeping beast within me—lest it should awaken, sinking its greedy teeth into that elusive moment of stillness.

Chapter 34 ✀ Sunny

The next day I had a brief check-in with Dr. Bensen in the morning. Fortunately, as I told him, the voices hadn't made an appearance since the morning of the prior day. He finally talked me into attending art therapy, which met every afternoon at 3:00. In all honesty, I was bored out of my mind and would have attended an appliance repair workshop if it got me out of my room.

After I nibbled on my crackers and rubbery cheese, I decided to go for a walk. Like the criminal I was, I had to ask permission from the front desk *and* have a staff member accompany me—which I found almost as offensive as my time with Milquetoast. Fortunately, the sweet young nurse who was instructed to watch me stayed a good ten feet behind me, so I barely noticed her. I had timed my walk according to the shuffle schedule and, sure enough, just as I turned toward the hall, I saw Cyclops in the distance. I stood near my room and watched him move toward me. He was staring forward blankly as one arm flittered about on his side. He was wearing a gray sweatsuit that made him look less diminutive than the last time I saw him. When he was about twenty feet from me I said, "Hello." This wasn't like me, but I couldn't stop thinking about him.

When he heard me, it was as if he woke from a trance. His eyes focused and his face softened. "Hello," he said, his voice surprisingly baritone. "My name's Eddy," he added without interrupting his pace.

"I'm Sunny. Um. Nice to meet you."

"Likewise." He was missing one front tooth, but it didn't stop him from smiling all the way to his cheeks. There was a kindness about him I didn't quite understand. He kept moving, going right past me, but he looked over his shoulder and said, "Have a wonderful day, Ms. Sunny."

"You too," I called to him as I watched his inked eye grow smaller.

I went back to my room and waited for Joshua. It was my seventh day in the hospital and we finally had our first counseling appointment with Dr. Turner. Joshua greeted me cheerfully and we found our way to that cold conference room where white-haired men in silver frames presided over us. I hated that room. The aftermath of the bombshell—my father's agony and my own perturbation—comingled in the air like a stale cloud. It was ground zero and I didn't want to be there.

Dr. Turner greeted us warmly and we sat together at one end of the large table. Although she'd gotten a haircut, her dark hair, which almost looked iridescent in the light, still hung several inches below her shoulders. She had on a white sweater that flattered her shiny hair and tan skin.

"So, you've had quite a week, Sunny," she said, looking at me intently with her hands clasped on the table. She wore a simple gold wedding band on her left hand and a large silver ring with an aquamarine stone on the other hand. She wore no nail polish, but her short nails were neatly manicured.

Considering my recent deck antics, I thought about making a joke about being up and down, but I knew it was too soon. It would always be too soon. "Yeah, it's been rough."

"Can you tell me what led up to you nearly jumping from a building?" She rested her chin on one hand, eyebrows furrowed.

I explained the meeting with Melody, my sense of having no purpose in life, and the incident with the kids. I'd pretty much memorized the whole spiel by now.

"Okay, I'd like to back up a bit. Why did you stop taking your medication?"

God, I was tired of explaining this! "I felt like a loser in front of Melody." *Awful Melody, I hate to even say her name.* "Plus, I was feeling alone and thought I could control my behavior without medication." I looked up at the light fixture, which was littered with more fly corpses than the last time I was here.

"So, as far as feeling like a loser, do you mean in terms of your career?" She was scribbling notes on her pad, which likely contained a litany of unflattering adjectives.

"Yes. Melody reminded me of who I was before."

"And who were you before?"

I started pulling at a thread in my sweatpants; Dr. Turner's gaze was unnerving.

"I was an editor at a good publishing company. I was, you know, on track with my plans until…" My voice trailed off.

"Until?"

"Until I went nuts." *Why do I need to explain this shit again? You know what happened.*

"Until you got sick, you mean?" She looked at me sternly, eyebrows raised.

"Yes." I must've rolled my eyes or something because she got even more serious.

"Language matters, Sunny. You have an *illness.*" Her tone was adamant, unyielding.

I nodded. I'd heard this a lot in the past few days. A car alarm went off outside and she waited for it to stop before speaking.

"I want to talk to you more about your goals in our one-on-one sessions, but for now you need to understand that schizoaffective disorder does not preclude your career plans. I've seen clients with psychotic disorders who are college professors, lawyers and even physicians. You may have lost your job, but it doesn't mean you lost your career."

Her words were reassuring, but hard to imagine. "But how does a medical doctor manage psychosis? What if something happens while seeing a patient?" I was genuinely curious. I sensed Joshua nodding in agreement. He was likely wondering how someone like me could possibly manage a serious career.

She took a sip of water and continued. "The physician I work with knows his triggers. When he gets stressed or upset, he contacts me immediately. It's taken some time, but he's learned that he can't function without his medication and, when he starts to question whether or not he needs it, he pages me. This is something I'd like to work on with you. What do you think?"

"Oh, I never want to go through that again. I'm so ashamed of what happened…of hurting the twins. So, yeah, I'll do anything," I said, wiping a tear from my eye.

"That's really great to hear." She leaned back and smiled. I noticed Joshua looking pleased with my response too.

"I'd like to ask you about another thing you just mentioned: feeling alone. I see your devoted husband here next to you and I'm wondering where he fits in with that feeling."

I wasn't expecting that question, shit. I stared into the haughty, lined eyes of the wall voyeurs, then turned toward Joshua. "I have just sort of felt like you don't want me around anymore." *Please don't say you're done with me, I will die inside.*

Joshua's face instantly morphed into an expression of incredulity. "Sunny, why would you say that? I love you more than anything on this planet." He was facing me now. His breath smelled stale, like he needed to eat. There was an eyelash stuck to his cheek and I wanted to touch it, to blow it away.

"But you wanted me to live with my dad after my last hospitalization." I hadn't mentioned this feeling to anyone and could feel a shakiness in my stomach.

"No, that's not true *at all.* All I wanted…all I *want* is for you to be home with me and Chester," he said, sounding insulted. "I hated the whole idea. But, honey, I was terrified at having you home. Your illness is new to me, I don't know how to handle it. And I was working all the time. So, while I didn't want you at your dad's, I just felt you'd be safer there."

"Oh, well, I guess that makes me feel better. Except, sometimes—well, a lot of the time—I'm afraid for you to see how messed up I really am. I know this is all very bizarre for you and I'm so worried about being too much. Of scaring you away." *Phew, I said it.* As the tremble in my stomach made its way to my voice, I knew it was something I'd held in far too long. I looked down at my lap, awaiting his response.

When Joshua cleared his throat, I glanced over at him. His expression had softened and he looked at me with more love than I could handle. "Sweetheart, I'm here with you at the psych hospital for the third time and I've seen you fully psychotic. You nearly killed yourself, for God's sake. But don't you see—I'm *still here.*" He removed a strand of hair from my face before caressing my left hand, which was resting on the table.

Tears welled up in my eyes. "I guess I just wonder how much more you can take before you hit the limit." I stopped and sniffled a couple of times before continuing. "And when I'm medicated and functioning my best, I'm still odd—I know that. I mean, we can at least blame the worst of my behavior on the illness. But what if me being stabilized is *still* too much? I mean, you're an amazing catch, why do you even want to be with someone like me?" I raised a shaking hand to my face, wiping away a fresh stream of tears.

The incredulity was back. Joshua let out a sigh and squeezed my hand. "*Oh my God*, Sunny. First of all, I adore your quirkiness—and it's *always* been there. I'm fully aware of your anxiety and self-consciousness. The fact that you have no idea how beautiful and incredible you are is, I don't know, endearing. Your love of books and animals, your ridiculous artistic talent, your dry sense of humor, the way you so carefully measure every word you say, the way you see beauty in things I barely notice… Hell, even the way you pick at your fingers…it's all just part of what makes you, *you*." He gently wiped a tear from my cheek. "I married you because I want to spend the rest of my life with you. Your illness is something we will deal with together, as a team. No, as a *family*. It doesn't make me love you any less."

His earnest, youthful face reminded me of when I first met him on the lawn in college. Only, back then, I just thought he was handsome. I had no idea of the depth and overwhelming kindness below the surface. I didn't know what to say, I was choked up, inarticulate. Or, as Baba would have said, verklempt. I wiped my eyes again and blew my nose with a tissue Dr. Turner handed me.

"Sunny, how do you feel knowing that you don't have to hide parts of yourself from Joshua, that he already sees you and hasn't gone anywhere?"

I took a big breath and tried to compose myself. The room was dead silent except for the low hum of the air conditioner. Turning to Joshua, I said, "I've been just so exhausted trying to hold back, to keep certain things in. The thought of letting down my guard feels like one less burden to carry. It's just so…" I was overcome with emotion and not sure what to say. I looked at his hand and the white gold wedding band encircling his ring finger, then turned back to his eyes, taking in their tenderness. "I just love you *so much*, Joshua." I couldn't believe I was talking like this in front of Dr. Turner, but I was overcome with such love for this man who was truly seeing me—yet loving me anyway.

"I love you, too, so much," he said, kissing my hand and then holding it against his lips for a moment.

Taking my hand back, I looked down at my lap, then back at Joshua. "One other thing though. When I was back at the condo with you over the weekend, why didn't you want to have sex with me?" *Might as well just put it all on the table.*

He momentarily held his hands out in front of him, palms up—as if I'd said something preposterous. "What? Are you kidding? I *definitely* wanted to. I mean, not only do I love you immensely, but I find you so damn sexy. But you seemed so frail, and I didn't want you to think I only wanted you home for one thing. I guess I just didn't want to break you."

My beautiful husband didn't see me as already broken. I wanted to laugh and cry at the same time.

"Sunny, do you see now that Joshua was holding back from touching you out of love and protectiveness?"

"Yes, I had no idea. I feel relieved, but I also don't want you to do that."

"Okay," he said softly, squeezing my hand.

"What Sunny is saying here is important," added Dr. Turner, looking directly at Joshua. "Intimacy is incredible medicine. Sunny has an illness, but she's not fragile. Don't be afraid to love her with everything you have."

"Of course, there's nothing in this world I'd rather do," he said, giving me one of his irresistible smiles.

That therapy session redeemed the dreaded conference room. There was a large part of me that felt I was losing, or had already lost, Joshua. The words spoken there revealed how deeply affected I was by that perceived loss. It diminished any incentive to keep going, to get better. Joshua was my best friend and the love of my life, I needed him. But what I hadn't realized until that session was the mutuality of these feelings—that my beloved husband needed me too.

I slept better after that session and was even able to concentrate on a book the next morning. *They* were also on reprieve. After lunch, I waited for Joshua to show up for another therapy session. He arrived with a gorgeous bouquet of pink dahlias. Just moments before, I had been overthinking my diagnosis and how I might learn to live with it, so the flowers were a needed boost. However, when I looked at the card, I saw that it was signed, "To Sunny, with love, Debbie and Rick." My mood immediately plummeted—any reminder of Debbie had a way of knocking me down. "They're beautiful," I mumbled coldly.

"Hey," said Joshua, gently placing his hand under my chin. "They care about you, they really do."

"Okay," I answered, slipping on my sneakers. "Let's go."

When we arrived at the conference room, we took the same seats as the day before. Dr. Turner was already there, looking through a stack of papers.

"Good afternoon, you two."

Once we'd greeted each other, she asked how I was feeling after yesterday's session.

"Honestly, I felt so much better—like I could breathe again." Somehow my words didn't fit with my mood, which she of course noticed.

"You seem a little down, Sunny. What's going on?" she asked, removing her reading glasses.

"Well, I woke up feeling okay and definitely better about me and Joshua, although I've been ruminating about the future—you know, how to live with this disorder. But nothing unmanageable. Then he showed up with flowers from his parents and I immediately felt, I don't know, angry." I could feel my foot shaking the table, but didn't bother to stop it.

"That's an interesting response to receiving flowers. Can you tell me where the anger comes from?"

I could hear a barely perceptible sigh from Joshua. I knew he hated the topic. "I know it was a nice gesture, I just, I guess I don't trust them."

"Joshua, I noticed your jaw clench just now. How do you feel about what Sunny just said?"

He exhaled loudly. "She winces at any mention of my parents. They really do care about her and she refuses to believe it. She won't let them come for a visit and actually leaves the house when I have them on the phone. Plus, my mom sent a huge basket of Sunny's favorite foods a couple of months ago and she was convinced my mom was trying to poison her. She literally vomited after eating something from it."

Why the hell is he bringing that up!

"Wasn't that during a psychotic episode?"

"Well, yeah, but she doesn't like my parents—psychotic or not."

"I understand. But let's focus on Sunny's behaviors when she's stable—when she has some control over them."

Thank you, doctor.

"Sunny, why don't you trust Joshua's parents? Did something happen?"

"Honestly, it's not really his *parents*, it's Debbie. I feel judged by her. I know she disapproves of me, especially after the wedding. I see how she looks at me and she's always making passive-aggressive comments. It's not just me, you know? Elizabeth, my best friend, has noticed it too."

"What do you think about what Sunny just said? Does your mother disapprove of her?"

Joshua was visibly uncomfortable, squirming in his chair and biting his lip. "My mom was a little bothered by the wedding, yes. I mean, Sunny did throw cake across the room and puke on the lawn, so…"

"She was judgy *before* the wedding, Joshua. You don't see how she looks at me. You don't hear the snide comments."

Joshua was quiet for a moment, as if he didn't know what to say.

"Have you noticed your mother being judgmental toward Sunny besides regarding the wedding?"

He paused for another interminable moment before speaking. "Yeah, she can be judgmental and overbearing at times. And she doesn't understand Sunny at all."

"What do you mean?"

"After the wedding, she was really concerned about her."

"Please speak directly to your wife."

He turned toward me, his expression somber. "She was concerned about you, she knew something was terribly wrong. But she does tend to say the wrong things, to make things worse. I know that and so does my dad."

"Can you give an example?" asked the doctor.

He stopped for a moment, either trying to think of an example or to avoid the more hurtful ones. "She just has this mentality that a person with looks, education, and other advantages shouldn't be unhappy, or have problems. And when Sunny was missing—when I felt like I was falling totally apart—she questioned whether Sunny left on purpose."

I could feel rage bubbling up, but I managed to hold my tongue just long enough for the doctor to speak.

"Well, that's a lot to unpack. It sounds like she doesn't understand mental illness—that there's no choice involved and that it doesn't discriminate based on appearance and socioeconomic status. Does that sound right?"

"That's exactly right, although she has come around quite a bit since then."

"But can you see that Sunny was picking up on your mom's attitude, and how hurtful that must've been for her?"

"Yeah, I can see that," he said softly, barely looking at me with his hands fidgeting under the table.

"And how did you respond when your mom made these comments about your wife?"

He suddenly livened up, speaking more animatedly. "It fucking— I'm sorry, it *really* pissed me off! We argued a lot after the wedding and I ended up telling her to back off. And I was ready to hang up on her when Sunny was missing. In fact, I pretty much avoided her during the worst periods even though I could tell it hurt her. She wanted to help, but she didn't know how."

Wow! All this time I thought Joshua was incapable of standing up to Debbie.

"Sunny, did you hear what Joshua said, how he took your side with his mom and established some boundaries?"

"Yes, and it means so much to me. I had no idea." I took his hand under the table.

"I think we've made some great progress here. But we do have more work to do in terms of boundaries," she said, looking pointedly at Joshua, "and compromise," she said, turning to me. "It's simply not reasonable for Joshua's parents to never visit their son and daughter-in-law. In fact, not allowing this will likely make Debbie resentful of you. And how can she possibly ever know how amazing and lovely you are if you never let her in?"

I could feel a light blush cover my skin as I nodded in agreement. Much as I hated the idea of spending time with Debbie, I knew it wasn't fair to alienate Joshua from his parents. And it was true that she didn't know me at all.

"So, here's your homework: Talk to each other about when Debbie and Rick might visit over the next few months and how that visit will be the most manageable for Sunny. In-laws can be a tricky topic and clients often compromise in terms of where they stay and for how long. If the economic means are there, I generally suggest a nearby hotel. And a visit should not entail a full day for Sunny, she will still need plenty of time to herself. Boundaries surrounding acceptable language are also important. This is where communication comes in—Sunny, you need to tell Joshua when something his mom does offends you; and Joshua, you need to be prepared to speak up should that happen. And I also suggest you find a tactful way to help your mom to learn more about Sunny's disorder."

"I actually sent them a bunch of books last week and my mom says they've already started reading them."

"Well, there you go—progress!" said Dr. Turner grinning.

I couldn't believe it. Debbie had been a jagged thorn in my side since the beginning. I had felt alone in my frustration with her and had no idea Joshua had stood up for me. And I *never* thought she cared enough about me to read multiple books. I must've had a stunned look on my face as Joshua gently poked me in the shoulder, saying, "Did you hear the doctor—*progress!*" Joshua and I sat there smiling at each other like idiots until Dr. Turner broke the silence.

"I think that's the perfect way to end the session," she said cheerfully as she closed her notebook.

Outside the conference room, I gave Joshua a huge hug. He squeezed me back, lifting me off the floor. I told him I loved him, but words were not enough to convey my adoration at that moment. When I got back to my room, I arranged the dahlias and gave them more water. As I looked at them, I saw no evil symbolism or cruel intentions. Rather, etched within their delicate fibers was a message of forgiveness. And with it, a reawakening of the optimism that had deserted me so long ago.

Chapter 35 ❧ Sunny

Over the next week, my dad and Joshua visited regularly and I met with both Dr. Bensen and Dr. Turner multiple times. I was getting antsy and asked Dr. Bensen when I could go home, telling him I was no longer suicidal or psychotic. He reminded me that I signed myself in, but agreed that I was doing much better. Since the hospital had a bed for me, he suggested I stay just a few more days. He wanted to ensure that I was stable on my meds and didn't want to see me back in the ER in two weeks. He was probably right, so I didn't push the issue. Plus, I didn't know where I'd be going when I left and was afraid to ask.

This hospitalization was different from the others—something had shifted inside me. Even when I'd obediently taken my meds in the past, I still harbored a seed of belief that the diagnosis wasn't real, or that I could beat it. And when anything challenging happened, that seed sprouted, blossoming into a full-blown delusion. But my suicidal behavior and what I'd done to the kids was like an addict's rock bottom. In a sense, the diagnosis was the only thing that allowed me to live with myself—if I wasn't mentally ill, then I was a colossal piece of shit. So I guess I preferred the mental disorder. And knowing that Joshua accepted me was like the removal of a veneer of bullshit I'd been hiding beneath since this whole thing started.

Art therapy was better than expected. Yeah, there were several patients engrossed in the art of gluing glitter and pompoms to popsicle sticks, or weaving together flimsy faux leather wallets; but the art teacher—a plump, middle-aged woman named Ginny, pretty much let me do what I wanted, which was to draw. Holding a simple pencil over a blank piece of paper felt inexplicably healing. As I captured the images in my mind on paper, some of the deep ache within me seemed to recede, if at least for a little while. I was reminded of how I used to get lost in my artwork as a little girl. When my mother's madness knocked the household out of orbit, drawing pictures helped me to focus on something else. It was like a temporary elixir for my troubled mind.

With few exceptions, the same general cast of six or seven characters showed up at art therapy each day. Among them was Agnus—a 30-something black woman who was almost expressionless as she wove piles and piles of flimsy, multicolored potholders. There was Trevor, who was around 40 and wore such a blatantly terrible black toupee that I could barely look at him. He always showed up in camo as if preparing for a hunting trip, which made me immediately dislike him. I don't think he cared about art, since he mostly just sat there pretending to draw. As he did so, he rambled on and on with a pronounced lisp, sometimes at hyper speed, about professional sports. Those of us most in touch with reality found him intolerable.

There was a child-like elderly woman named Fern whose lips smacked at random intervals as she colored in pictures of farm animals. She often hummed a series of disjointed melodies I could not place. Sometimes Fern's mouth moved in synchrony with her hand and she frequently drooled on her artwork, causing the ink colors to meld together. I think she liked this effect, since more than once I saw her purposely spit and rub the colors together when she thought no one was looking. And then there was Bob—a young, skinny guy with multiple facial piercings who blatantly stared at me while drawing impressively realistic purple penises all over his coloring pages. Bob wasn't invited back to art therapy.

Heidi made the biggest impression on me. She was in her 20s with dark, wavy hair like mine. Painfully thin and soft-spoken, she was like a ghost within herself. I often noticed her staring at me. One day, as she was studying my drawing of a small bouquet of daisies Ginny had provided, I gestured for her to come sit by me. When she sat down, she seemed embarrassed and covered her work. When I told her I was not judging her, she showed me what she was hiding. Heidi had sketched *me*. And, in doing so, she had managed to capture, not only my overall facial characteristics, but also the anxiety and sense of inadequacy I carried within me. It was an eerie likeness, which she said I could keep. Later, once the other patients had left, she showed me the rest of her work. She had drawn every female patient who'd come to therapy, masterfully revealing each woman's unique form of insanity. This timid girl who had cut marks all up and down both of her arms, was like a quiet storm contained by cardboard scaffolds.

In the days that followed, Heidi and I always sat together. We were two insecure misfits who were more comfortable expressing ourselves with a canvas than with words. Eventually I learned that this was her sixth hospitalization for borderline personality disorder and her fourth suicide attempt. For her latest attempt, she used a pair of tights to hang herself from her closet, but the rail came crashing out of the wall before she lost consciousness. Instead of pitying her, Heidi's dad was pissed about the mess and generally "sick of her crazy bullshit." Although she wasn't psychotic, Heidi was decidedly fragile. Something within her had been broken long ago and, although she didn't share the details, I presumed it had to do with men. I didn't press her on what happened to her, but instead tried to take her under my own barely functional wing. No one ever visited Heidi and it wasn't lost on me that, without my unflinching support system, my own agony and crushing hollowness would be similarly etched within the membranes of my skin.

After art therapy, I attended individual therapy sessions with Dr. Turner. When I sat down in the cold conference room for our first session, my apprehension about attending therapy was far less than usual. Dr. Turner noticed the difference.

"Sunny, this the first time I've seen you walk into a therapy session without your head down. You even greeted me with a smile—a little one, but I'll take it." I thanked her as I got situated in the chair. "To what do you attribute this change?"

"I suppose I've stopped fighting it. Fighting the diagnosis." At some point over the past couple of days, I had basically surrendered. I could no longer reject the diagnosis's existence or gravity. Nor could I fight it alone. Without medication and an army of advocates, I simply wasn't a formidable opponent.

"That's wonderful to hear. Another way to put it is that familiar word I've been driving into you for some time now…?" She looked at me like a strict schoolmarm expecting a correct answer.

"Acceptance," I said, watching a fat fly buzz around the room until finally landing on a window.

"Exactly. You tried rejecting or ignoring your diagnosis and, like ignoring a wound, it just became worse, infected. *Acceptance*, on the other hand, allows you to take control, to be in the driver's seat. How does that feel?" She crossed her legs and smoothed a strand of hair from her forehead.

"It's the first time I've had any real hope for myself since I went crazy." *Oh shit, wrong word again.*

"Hope is a powerful thing. But Sunny, remember what I said about language? You didn't go *crazy*, you became *ill*," she said, overemphasizing the last word.

"Oh yes, sorry," I said, disappointed in myself for not pleasing her.

"No need to apologize to me. But there are several key areas I'd like us to work on together. The first is your self-esteem. You have a unique acerbic wit, but you often aim it at yourself in a non-flattering way. Believing that ticker tape of negative self-talk you have rolling through your head isn't healthy. I'd like to help you to break that cycle."

I nodded. My self-ridicule was so automatic, I wasn't sure it could ever be stopped. I picked at my thumb, discretely wiping blood on my pants.

"Where do you think it comes from?"

I squirmed in my chair, unable to relax. "Since I was little, I haven't felt comfortable in my own skin—like there's something inherently wrong with me." I don't think I'd ever said those words out loud; yet they so accurately described the catalyst for so much of my pain.

She nodded her head and spoke softly. "It's not uncommon for children who've been traumatized to internalize what happened, to believe it's their own fault. The fear and anxiety you experienced due to your mom's illness, as well as the intergenerational trauma of what your grandparents went through during the war, may have also informed the content of your delusions and hallucinations."

Much of that sounded right. My mother's illness and death had left a gaping hole within me that I hadn't begun to deal with. My Holocaust-driven delusions had perplexed me since all of this started. I wasn't in the Holocaust, so what right did I have to suffer the effects of it now? But, even as a little girl, I knew horrible things happened to two of my most loved people, so maybe the delusions were my way of empathizing with them. Or maybe they were a way of punishing me for not being a better person. Or maybe they had no meaning at all?

"Yeah, for a very long time, there's been a part of me that just wants to disappear so I don't have to feel the guilt and pain anymore," I said softly, almost feeling myself shrink down in the chair. I could imagine myself sliding all the way under the table.

"Can you think of the earliest time you felt that way?" She wrote in her notebook.

I thought for a moment, tapping my fingers on the table nervously. Then I remembered something. "When Mama was out of control, pacing and talking to herself or screaming at my dad, I would sometimes make myself really small. There was a tiny cabinet under the stairs that I would squeeze myself into for what felt like hours. I wanted to escape the chaos, but I also felt like my absence would make things better for everyone." I had forgotten about the cabinet until that moment; it felt heavy in my chest. "One time I somehow fell asleep in there all day and no one noticed until my dad came home in the evening. She didn't even miss me." Moments like these made me angry with my mother for not trying harder—if not for herself, then at least for me. I was starting to feel agitated.

Dr. Turner looked at me with intense compassion. "That's a devastating image, Sunny. And it must have felt like a betrayal to be left in there for so long. Let's just sit with that for a moment. Think about that scared little girl, hiding from the chaos surrounding her with no one coming to find her for hours. How do you think she felt?"

Ugh, shouldn't the session be over by now? This was too much. I sighed heavily. "Abandoned. Why doesn't someone look for me? I think that particular day reinforced the sense that I should just disappear." I began chewing on one of my fingers, which tasted vaguely of grapefruit.

"I can see a child making that conclusion. But it's important to remember that your father was at work, I'm assuming, and your mother was dealing with her own illness. So, when they didn't come to find you, it's because neither was fully aware of your absence. It wasn't due to lack of love. What would you say to that little girl now?"

I thought for a moment, feeling one side of my head start to throb. "That it's not your fault. That being quiet and invisible won't make it go away. And that Daddy did come for you as soon as he could." I started rubbing my temple. I wanted to leave.

"And when you feel that familiar urge to blame yourself for things over which you have no control, like your disorder, or to disappear into yourself rather than stand up to that which hurts you, what might you say to your grown self?"

I exhaled loudly. "That it's not my fault. And that hiding or trying to disappear won't help."

"What are some of the ways you try to disappear now?"

Please let this end soon. "Oh, I don't know. I guess I stay quiet. And small."

"In terms of staying small, is this one of the reasons you're so thin?" she asked gently.

I didn't want to go there, but I couldn't disagree. "Yeah maybe."

"So, how about instead of trying to get smaller, that you focus on nourishing your body because you *deserve to be healthy*. And with that, standing tall instead of shrinking down, because you also *deserve to be seen?*"

What she said made sense. I didn't want to be that powerless little girl under the stairs anymore. But Dr. Turner must've sensed that I was exhausted and in pain, since she ended the session soon thereafter. Wanting only to get back to my bed, I shuffled through the halls toward my room. As I approached Cyclops walking in the opposite direction right next to me, I didn't even look up and neither did he. Perhaps he'd had a rough day too. As we crossed paths, I imagined some sort of bizarre, backwards square dance—*do-si-do, don't look up as he shuffles by, then faces you with his faceless eye…*

The remainder of my individual sessions primarily focused on self-esteem, including a new annoying twist: Dr. Turner started each session with a meditation exercise. Meditation had always seemed like a waste of time for me. On the few occasions I'd tried it, I spent the whole time admonishing myself for not being able to stop the noise in my head. Relaxing had always seemed unattainable to me. She told me to allow my thoughts to pass on by without judgment, which I found very difficult. When I told her I was stuck on certain things I couldn't stand about myself, she made me visualize those things and then say the mantra, "I am not perfect and that's okay." She also gave me homework, which basically involved writing down any negative self-thoughts, questioning them, and turning them around. I had little faith in these touchy-feely exercises, but, embracing my new attitude of surrender, I did what I was told.

I arrived at my next therapy session downcast and fatigued. I'd had a nightmare about my mother in which she was falling and pulling me down with her like a drowning victim. The dream was narrated by the voices chanting their hateful insults and directives. I awoke thinking *they* had returned, which, fortunately, was not true. I told Dr. Turner what happened and we spent some time discussing the symptom of my disorder I most despised—the damned voices. I was petrified I'd never be rid of them, even if I took my meds. She reminded me that the voices are liars and can't hurt me. We talked about ways to avoid stress, which often brought them out. She also suggested treating the voices as a friend, maybe even giving them a name. She said it would make them feel less powerful and frightening. I rejected the friend part of her suggestion, but I liked the idea of giving them a name. I wanted it to be something befitting, a name that would always remind me of their sheer malice and stupidity.

That same evening, as I was playing cribbage with Joshua, it came to me. "That's it!" I said abruptly. Joshua looked a little alarmed, probably thinking I was losing my mind again.

"Huh?"

"I know what I'll call the voices," I said, pleased with my epiphany.

From that day forward, those bastards who always made an appearance at the worst possible moment, ever ready to trample my fragile ego and obliterate my stability, would be known simply as "the Wankers."

Chapter 36 ✑ Joshua

Since she first became ill, Sunny's disorder knocked me around like a tsunami. When she was in the hospital or staying with Peter, I wandered around numbly, as if in a trance. As I told her when we first met, my wife had the perfect name; without her, my world was overcast and chilly, without comfort. Once allowed into her light, I couldn't be without her. And I'd been without her a lot lately. When Sunny was living with Peter, loneliness descended upon me like a black cloud. It felt different than when she was hospitalized, more permanent. I was terrified that she'd never come back to me, but I didn't see any other choice at the time. I knew I couldn't keep up my work schedule while taking care of someone who hid meat cleavers and wandered a hundred miles away, living like a rabbit amongst wolves.

I'd been functioning like an automaton for months—my life consisting of little more than going to work, running to and from the hospital, and sleeping (although not nearly enough). I rarely ate a healthy meal, instead grabbing whatever was available. Dinner often consisted of a slice of pizza near my office or a crappy sandwich from the hospital. I was worn out and haggard, dragging myself through each day as the weight of my fears and obligations tried to break me.

Plus, I could never get ahead of my workload. Like Sisyphus and his cursed boulder, every time I made any progress, a new stack of work knocked me back down to the bottom again. I was terrified of getting fired and losing both my salary and, perhaps even more important, our health insurance—so I did my best to stay on task and meet the demands of my job. Yet, regardless of what I was doing, something always seemed to be pulling me in another direction. When I was home or at the hospital, I felt guilty for not being at work; when I was at work, I felt I should be with my wife. Chester also needed my attention, which added to the pile. The constant tension of never doing or being enough frazzled my nerves, leaving me distracted and edgy. I wondered how much more I could take before something within me finally cracked. But, knowing my marriage couldn't withstand two fractured psyches, losing it simply wasn't an option for me. So I trudged along, placing one leaden foot in front of the other, trying to detach myself from the feverish turmoil of my mind.

In the evenings, when I had neither work nor Sunny to distract me, I was besieged by loneliness. In high school, I was voted "social butterfly," so isolation went against my very nature. But I had little time to socialize and doing so would've only added to my guilt. Outside of family, the only people I saw regularly were my coworkers, but I wasn't close to any of them. They had *some* idea of what I was dealing with, but no one, aside from my boss, ever broached the topic. It reminded me of a close friend who had cancer as a teen. I remember how she sobbed when I visited her, telling me how even her closest friends were afraid to talk to her about her disease, as if it might be contagious.

While I knew mental illness was also a tough subject for people, I began to learn the extent of this when I tried to confide in a coworker named Marc. I was especially stressed one morning and screwed up an urgent press release. When Marc asked me what was going on, I told him my wife had schizoaffective disorder and was in the hospital. This guy, whom I thought was a friend, looked flummoxed and uncomfortable. He said he hoped she'd be okay, then never brought it up again. I also felt like several of my coworkers were talking about me. It was disconcerting to sense their eyes on me and hushed voices when I entered a room. Of course I was aware of the stigma of mental illness, but, now being the office leper myself, it truly sank in. It gave me a new level of empathy for my brilliant wife, who would be forever branded as mentally unbalanced.

Though I tried to appear capable and enthusiastic at work, there was no hiding my beleaguered state once I got the dreaded call. I was in an all-company staff meeting, though barely concentrating due to the gnawing sense of foreboding I'd had all morning. When the receptionist told me I had an urgent call, I panicked—spilling coffee all over the long rectangular table. The room fell silent for one terrible moment as nineteen pairs of eyes rested on me. Once the woman next to me grabbed some napkins and told me not to worry, I apologized and ran to my office. When I heard Peter's anguished voice on the phone, I could feel stomach acid rising in my throat.

My beautiful girl was dead, I just knew it.

But, as Peter spoke, I was seized with such relief that I slid down the wall, practically collapsing on the rug. When my boss, Julia, tapped on my door a few minutes later, I quickly sprang up from the carpet and tried to collect myself.

"Come in," I said, feeling as if my words came from someone else.

She opened the door and stepped forward gingerly, as if she might set something off. "Joshua, are you okay?" She stood there in her pink Chanel suit and perfect makeup looking as if someone died. She was pretty damn close.

I was flustered and out of breath, but tried to answer, "I, um, Sunny's not well…" I looked aimlessly around my office; where were my damn keys?

She moved a little closer. "I'm *so* sorry. I think you need to sit and catch your breath for a moment, you're hyperventilating," she said softly. She was a kind person who, in any other situation, would probably have put an arm around me and guided me to my chair.

I didn't know what to do. I felt an urgency to run out the door, but I was trembling and nauseous. I sat down at my desk and she went to get some water.

"Drink this and take some deep breaths before you leave," she said, handing me a cup. I remembered Sunny describing the ridiculousness of people always giving her water when she was at her lowest, as if something so simple could even touch her smoldering madness. She was right, it was stupid. Nonetheless, I took a few sips and tried to calm down.

"Can I give you a ride?" She stood at the side of the desk. I could smell her perfume.

"That's very kind, thank you, Julia. But I'm okay, I can drive. It's not far." I drank a little more water and stood up, then located my keys on a side table.

"Please call me if you need anything, Joshua. And don't stress about work right now, you're doing a terrific job even with all that's happening. It's okay if you need to take some time off, just let HR know what's going on. We're here to support you."

I felt a surge of relief run through me. I thought I was heading toward unemployment, which had been eating away at me for some time now. But maybe I didn't need to beat myself up every second of the workday, thinking I was a failure and a disgrace. And maybe I could have some degree of faith that at least this one aspect of my life was actually secure. I wished I had more time to express my gratitude, but I needed to get out of there. "That means so much to me, thank you," I said before hurrying out of the office and running down the stairs toward the parking garage.

Traffic was lousy that day. I sat in a row of cars on the freeway for a solid ten minutes without moving. As exasperation and despair swirled around in my chest, I could feel myself coming unhinged. Like a first-rate asshole, I pounded on the steering wheel, honked the horn, and spewed a string of expletives toward anyone who got in my way. I was an idiot for not taking a cab. When I finally made it to the hospital ER, I ran through the front door where I found Peter, distraught and disheveled, pacing in the waiting room. I hugged him longer than I'd ever hugged a man, repeating words of gratitude for saving Sunny as both of us cried. I truly loved Peter in that moment. The two of us had become brothers-in-arms in an all-consuming battle to save the girl we loved.

When I first saw Sunny, she was lying in bed asleep with four-point restraints. Her thin arms were bruised and scratched, but her face was peaceful. It was an almost laughable façade. I kissed her forehead and whispered, "I love you" before leaving the room. Peter and I got coffee and sat in the waiting room where he told me what happened with the kids. Later, as I sat next to Sunny's bed, I dreaded her waking up to the crushing awareness of what she'd done. It was a scenario with only two possible outcomes: she would either successfully kill herself the next time around or fully commit to getting better. I pleaded with God, the universe, or any entity that might be listening for the latter.

She could not die.

As Sunny's psychosis waxed and waned over her first week in the hospital, I wandered around in a daze, barely functional. I still went to work, though I accomplished very little. One particularly difficult morning, as I was standing in the staff kitchen waiting for the coffee to brew, I heard a booming laugh. I looked up and saw Brad—the office douchebag, staring at my feet. "Dude, you're wearing two different shoes!" I looked down and, although both of the leather shoes were brown, one had a tassel and one didn't. "Jesus. It's been a rough few days," I mumbled, embarrassed. I wondered if my socks matched. I poured a cup of coffee and hightailed it out of there, hearing Brad laughing in the background. He could fuck right off.

Every corner of my mind was preoccupied with Sunny and her demons. My superficial awareness was fuzzy, causing me to wear unmatched shoes and make stupid mistakes at work, while my deeper consciousness was infiltrated with a swarm of morbid visualizations. Sunny's near death was the key player, hijacking my mind with images of her beautiful bones snapping apart and lying mangled on the cement. Like a detective, I had begun scrutinizing the days leading up to her near suicide for clues I may have missed. I remembered her detachment during our weekend together—how she floated around the condo like a shadow person, my words of love rolling right off of her. I remembered how unusually vague, confused, and irritable she was the day before it happened. And, when we said goodbye on the porch that same evening, I remembered the ghostly impenetrability of her green eyes, as if there was something dark lurking behind them that I could not reach. As I went through the motions of my life, I mentally recorded every sign I'd either missed or shrugged off, berating myself for the innumerable ways I had failed as a husband.

I should have known.

A part of me also was angry at Sunny for stopping her meds *yet again.* I believe she was lucid at the time, so after everything she'd learned, why come to that decision? The last time this happened, when she was living in Anaheim amongst thieves and drug addicts, was terrible enough. But this time, she was inches away from death. I knew she was very sick, that it wasn't her fault. But still, *why couldn't she just take her fucking medicine?* I couldn't seem to disentangle her sickness from her responsibility as a patient. Even when she started to come back to herself, I had a level of resentment I couldn't suppress. I decided to contact Dr. Turner, who squeezed me in during her lunch hour the following day. As a welcome change from driving to the hospital, we would be meeting in her office.

When I entered the waiting room, Dr. Turner was making tea. She said hello and offered me a cup. I declined, as my stomach had been in knots all morning. She invited me into her office, which was comfortable, with Native American art and light green, velvet chairs. The window behind her desk was open, allowing a soft breeze to lightly ruffle the papers on her desk. I could smell a hint of jasmine tea.

Rather than sitting behind her desk, she sat in the velvet chair across from me, setting her steaming tea on a side table. She smiled and said, "It's nice to see you, Joshua." She had such warmth about her that I was immediately put at ease.

"Thanks, you too," I said, trying to situate myself in the chair. I had a kink in my neck, so I turned my body in her direction.

"Aside from the obvious, what's going on?" She placed a pen behind her ear and leaned forward.

I cleared my throat, which was hoarse for some reason. "I love my wife immensely, but I'm having trouble dealing with a few things. I guess my main issue is that I'm sort of angry at her for not taking her meds again. And I feel terrible for being mad, I know it's not her fault, but still…" My voice trailed off as I stared at some fluttering leaves outside the window.

She had her hands clasped in her lap as she locked on my eyes, never looking away. "I'm so glad you came to talk with me. You need to know that your feelings are absolutely valid and chastising yourself for having them won't help you or Sunny. You've been plunged into a caregiving role you likely never prepared for nor saw yourself in, am I right?"

"Oh yeah, I never would have imagined this for myself." *That's an understatement.* "I didn't even think I'd be married at this point, much less, well, *this*." Worried I sounded like a jerk, I added, "Not that I regret it." It was true, I had no regrets. But I was miles out of my element.

"I understand. Having a loved one with a serious psychiatric illness can be extremely stressful and frustrating, especially when they don't comply with treatment—which is common I'm afraid. It might help you to remember that, even when she's stabilized, Sunny *still* has a serious mental disorder. This can affect her memory and decision-making when it comes to meds, especially if she experiences a trigger." She blew on her tea then set it back down.

I nodded, although her words weren't very encouraging. "I'm just not sure what to do with my feelings. Or how to keep her from relapsing."

"Well, you're doing the first part already. When you have resentment toward her, which is not unexpected, don't beat yourself up about it. Talk to someone to help you process and normalize those feelings, just as you are today. I'm also going to recommend a support group for families of people with psychotic disorders. It's close by and I know the facilitator. He's an excellent psychologist and has a daughter with schizophrenia. It would allow you to talk about your feelings without judgment among people who truly understand what you're going through." She wrote something in the spiral notebook that was resting on her lap.

I wasn't sure about the support group, sitting in some dank church basement comparing psychotic war stories just didn't do it for me. Uncomfortable with the doctor's penetrating gaze, I looked at her desk. It was tidy except for a mug of tea that had left a mark on the yellow legal pad beneath it. There were several upright pictures facing the window. I wondered who was within those frames.

"And while you can't exactly *keep* her from relapsing, you can lovingly

322

encourage her to take her medication as directed. You can work with her on strategies that will help her remember, like calendars and phone reminders. Whatever the two of you come up with." She crossed her legs. She was wearing a low, black heel with gray pants. I noticed a small black tattoo of a turtle on one ankle.

"Okay, I like those ideas. The other thing is, I'm really upset with myself for missing the signs. I could see the day before this happened that she wasn't herself. I should have *done* something." A shooting pain ran through my neck, which I briefly rubbed with one hand. I desperately needed a massage, but that was a low priority these days.

"You know, I often wish I could erase the word 'should' from the English language," she said with a slight smile. "It's a blaming word that keeps people in the past. You did your best at the time with what you knew. Sunny hasn't been ill for very long—you, along with the rest of us, are still learning her triggers."

Her words were comforting, but I knew it would take time for me to let myself off the hook. "Yeah, I see what you're saying. Next time she's acting weird, what should I do?"

"Talk to her and see what's going on, and ensure that she's taking her meds. Then page me and Dr. Bensen." She took a few sips of tea and set it back on the table.

"Okay, I'll definitely do that."

"Excellent. Is there anything else you'd like to discuss?"

"I think that's everything, at least for now," I said as I tried to suppress a yawn. "Excuse me, I'm just really tired." I ran my hand through my hair and tried to look alert.

"Well, that's a perfect segue for something else I'd like to mention," she said, removing the pen from behind her ear. "One of the best things you can do to help Sunny is to take care of yourself. I can't help but notice the puffy circles under your eyes, Joshua. Being rundown and sick won't get you anywhere. So, here's what I'd like you to do, and I'm going to write it down." She began writing in her notebook as she spoke. "Talk to people, whether it's the group I mentioned or family and friends, social interaction is essential for stress alleviation. And learn as much as you can about schizoaffective disorder, including advice for caretakers. Take care of your body—eat healthy and exercise, even if it's just a walk outside. Get plenty of sleep and do whatever you can to relax. Be careful about maintaining a good work-life balance." She looked out the window for a moment. "And what was that last one...oh yeah." She commenced writing. "You need to do things you enjoy, either with Sunny or not. Even while she's in the hospital, don't feel guilty about going to a movie or spending time with a friend. Think of it as your own medicine—without it, you won't be functional either. That's my prescription," she added with a smile as she ripped the paper from the tablet and handed it to me. I saw a phone number for the support group written at the top of the page.

I left Dr. Turner's office feeling better. While I knew I wasn't taking care of myself, I felt guilty exercising or doing anything enjoyable while Sunny suffered. I vowed to do better, for both of us.

Over the next couple of days, I mostly worked, visited Sunny, ate, and slept. But I also started jogging during my lunch hour and made a concerted effort to eat healthier and drink more water. The exercise helped me sleep, so I was a little less worn out. But I remained tense and lonelier than ever.

I knew people had been trying to contact me, especially my parents. I'd been ignoring them mainly because, during one recent conversation, my mom said, "When is Sunny going to get this mess under control?" *God, my mother could be so clueless.* Lately I'd also come to the realization that she was fair-weathered—considerate and helpful when things were good, but generally useless when things turned to shit. It was as if she'd never built up any resilience.

My dad was pretty repressed about most things involving feelings, but he at least lacked my mother's penchant for saying idiotic, hurtful things. After that conversation, I decided to send my parents some books—if they were going to be a part of our lives, they needed some general understanding of mental illness. They had seemed agreeable enough, so I sent them a pile and hoped for the best.

The day after my meeting with Dr. Turner, I had just sat down to relax after work when my phone rang. When I saw that it was my mom, I really wanted to ignore it. But Dr. Turner told me to talk to people and I couldn't avoid her forever, so I picked it up.

My mom immediately laid into me. "Josh, I've been trying to reach you for *ages!* Don't you know how worried we've been? You need to call me back!" Then she yelled for my dad to pick up the other phone.

"I know, I'm sorry, Mom." *Oh fuck, I need a drink.*

"What's going on, are you okay? What's happening with Sunny?" she asked impatiently. I heard my dad pick up the phone and say hello.

I leaned back on the couch, took a deep breath, and got on with what I needed to say. "Sunny is in the hospital." There was an audible sigh on the other end.

"Tell us what happened, son," said my dad calmly.

As I described the situation with the kids and the horror that took place on the deck, I could feel my voice shaking. I hated hearing it all out loud and of course I dreaded how my mom would react. I thought I heard sniffling on the other end of the phone when I spoke of the intended suicide.

"I'm sorry, Josh. That's terrible. How's she doing now?" asked my dad.

"She's better, getting stabilized." I got up and started pacing the living room.

"Oh my goodness, it can be so hard for schizophrenics to take their medicine. But it sounds like she has a supportive team of doctors, right?" said my mom.

My jaw nearly hit the floor.

Okay, so she didn't get the disorder quite right, but still… "Mom, you're reading the books I sent!"

"Oh yes, I've read four so far and your dad's read three, right dear?" My dad muttered something that sounded affirmative.

I wanted to hug them. "Thank you, Mom and Dad. I love Sunny so much…" And my voice broke. I took a deep breath. "I just love her so much and have felt so alone." I collapsed back on the couch.

Then, through a cacophony of sniffles from all three of us, my mom said, "We love you too, honey. We love *both* of you and want to help."

I ended the conversation before she inevitably found a way to blow it. After I hung up, I sat in stunned silence for a few moments. Having only Chester to talk to, I said, "Well, it looks like there's hope for your grandma yet!" He stretched his front legs and yawned, clearly not impressed. While my mother could be unfiltered and abrasive, I knew she was genuinely worried about us. I would tread carefully with her, but I had come to realize during my darkest days that I still needed her. She was my mother after all, and I was suffering too.

Later that week, Sunny and I were finally meeting with Dr. Turner for therapy, which I didn't look forward to. When I met Sunny in her room, her hair was pulled back in a high ponytail and she was wearing mascara and lipstick. She was starting to look like herself again. We held hands as we slowly walked the linoleum halls, buying our time until having to face whatever festering daggers Dr. Turner pulled out of us.

As expected, the session was a bit of a rollercoaster ride. And I hated rollercoasters. Just when my mood started to lift, some new feeling or piece of information would knock it back down again. I knew Sunny had serious confidence issues, but her level of self-reproach perplexed me. She had this asinine idea that I could do better than her, and that I would eventually leave. Wouldn't she ever understand that she had always been out of my league—even now? And hearing how alone she'd felt made me feel like a failure as a husband. By holding back on my desires in order not to hurt her, I had actually added to her pain. I needed to do better.

It pained me to see Sunny cry as she talked about hiding parts of herself from me—masquerading as someone she thought I could tolerate. It was so unnecessary. How could I possibly convince her that I would never leave her? That I loved *all* of her? But in a way, that revelation was reassuring since, before the near suicide, I'd sensed that something was off with her. It was as if I couldn't quite reach her. Maybe I wasn't such an idiot after all. Maybe I could actually learn her triggers.

Our second day in therapy started out rough. Sunny's chilly response to receiving flowers from my parents really annoyed me. She could at least have recognized that they were extending an olive branch. I felt like Sunny was trying to push my parents out of my life. It wasn't fair; we were all going through hell right now. She had her father, but who did I have? But during therapy, when Sunny realized I had her back and that my parents were really trying—even educating themselves—her body language relaxed and her facial expression softened. I could almost see the weight of resentment she'd been dragging around slide off of her, releasing some of the burden from her weary shoulders.

There were several moments in therapy when I saw a change in Sunny that hadn't been there since we lounged by the pool last summer, innocently dreaming about our future. Her words had regained some of their emotion and sincerity. And she was starting to trust me enough to emerge from her hiding place, revealing what she deemed the most vile parts of herself. Just as I'd hoped, her behavior during her last psychosis seemed to have shaken her up to the point where she simply *had to* accept her illness. Plus, based on the pile of sketches in her room, her passion for art had been reignited. They were beautiful and haunting drawings of what I assumed were other patients, as well as birds, trees, and various other things in the hospital. As I watched her creativity, honesty, and humor reemerge from the dark recesses of madness, I felt choked up. *My girl was still in there.*

Chapter 37 ❧ Sunny

After well over a week in the hospital, my head had cleared enough to fully drop the charade that I was perfectly normal, that my symptoms were transient and controllable. Surrendering to my diagnosis was no easy task. It required me to trust my doctors, as well as the collective wisdom surrounding schizoaffective disorder. I kept picturing the wicked witch from The Wizard of Oz and her message to Dorothy in the clouds, except with my name: 'Surrender Sunny.' I even sketched the scene as a way to remind me of its message, adding a field of bourgeoning lilies on the ground below.

Accepting my illness and its prognosis also meant that, no matter how lucid and normal I might feel, the absence of my disorder was only illusory—the demons were merely asleep. It would be up to me to keep them tranquilized by fully recognizing the gravity and incurability of my disorder. There was no way around it—I would be taking meds for the rest of my life. But if being medicated meant no longer believing myself to be hunted and condemned to certain death, I suppose it was a small price. Nevertheless, it was one hell of a lot to swallow and I often found myself grieving my old life and the person I thought I was.

While Dr. Bensen assured me that a mourning process was to be expected, it didn't make it any easier. How I envied those who would never experience the emotional bedlam of being taunted by forces from within, or of not knowing the veracity of their own perceptions and beliefs. While I would never again be one of the privileged who took their sanity for granted, I was ready to live amongst them again. And so, each day I tried to relax, taking deep breaths and attempting to ignore my nagging doubts and self-recriminations. Following Dr. Turner's advice, I questioned the familiar insult I'd always thrown at myself: 'You're pathetic, a loser,' listing all of the ways in which I wasn't a failure in my life, especially given my mental health challenges. I changed the statement to: "You are resilient, a fighter." I liked the way this sounded, though I didn't entirely believe it. Maybe one day.

This hospitalization was beginning to feel like an eternity. I was done being prodded and questioned, picking at barely edible food, listening to random intervals of screeching outside my door, and just being a mental patient—I wanted to be more than that again. And I was desperate for my home, my kitty, and, most of all, my husband. As my lucidity increased, so too did my longing for Joshua. I often reached for him during the night only to be slapped with the grim reality of my predicament. I'd never loved anyone the way I loved Joshua, but now that love seemed somehow lacking, insignificant. Throughout the entire nightmare of the past five months—when my affliction had me running and hiding like some hysterical, rabid animal; speaking with the twisted tongue of the deranged; and sabotaging my recovery—*throughout it all*, his commitment never faltered. Even with my affinity for language, my love and respect for Joshua had become as ineffable as the beauty of a lotus flower—it could not be articulated. I wanted to immerse him with kisses and adoration—to inoculate him with enough love that nothing could ever hurt him. And to never disappoint him again.

Fortunately, the eagle watch portion of my hospital stay was lifted, so I could now walk around the floor unsupervised, go to the bathroom without permission, and use pencils in my room. On the morning of my eleventh day, I had a brief chat with Dr. Bensen, who confirmed that I would be discharged in two days. I wanted to sketch after our meeting and wandered around the ward seeking inspiration. I ended up in the sunroom which, fortunately, was empty. On one side of the room, there was a TV and family room area with a couch and several cushiony chairs. I sat on the opposite side, at a round table next to a large window. I placed my supplies on the table and gazed outside.

It was a gorgeous day, the sky was cloudless and I could hear birds singing. There wasn't much on the ground that excited me, just a parking lot and a few medical buildings. But there was a black cable connecting two posts to the left of the window where three crows perched. One was a bit larger than the others and had slick, iridescent feathers that looked almost purple in the sunlight. The other two, who looked young, had scruffy feathers and seemed to be cawing impatiently at their parent. As I watched them, I considered the bizarre juxtaposition of that little bird family basking in the sun only feet away from the pathetic human trapped behind the glass. I tried to envision myself also on the outside—liberated from oppressive walls designed to keep me safe, and managing to survive despite myself.

I sketched the crows for around fifteen minutes, completely lost in thought, when a sudden sound made me jump. I looked over and saw Eddy, aka Cyclops, sitting on the couch with a large book. I was immediately uncomfortable.

"Hello, Ms. Sunny, I'm sorry for scaring you. I have that effect on people," he said in a jovial manner, as if we were old friends. He had a Southern accent I hadn't noticed before.

I felt bad for him, since my nervousness had nothing to do with his odd appearance. "Oh, that's okay. I was just lost in my sketching," I said, feeling shy.

"You're an artist? That's so cool," he said, closing his book. He was wearing blue and white plaid pajama bottoms and a gray T-shirt that said, "Ski Tahoe" on the front, and his usual worn-out navy blue slippers. I noticed several small tattoos on his knuckles, though I couldn't see them clearly.

"Thank you," I said, trying to sound friendly, but feeling awkward. "It helps me relax, sort of calms my mind."

"I sure could use that! I wish I could draw, but I ain't got the knack for it." He was less edgy than I'd seen him, pretty much sitting still except for one shaking knee. "Can I take a look?"

I wasn't thrilled about being close to him, but I didn't want to hurt his feelings. "Sure, but I just started a little while ago." I'd only sketched two of the crows thus far. I crossed my legs and leaned back, bracing myself for his approach.

He set his book down and came over, not dragging his feet this time. He stood to my left, keeping at least two feet between us. He smelled like cigarettes. He looked down at my pad and said, "Well, damn, girl—you're good! I see your models out there," he said looking out the window.

"Oh, well, thank you. Hopefully I'll get to all three of them." I said, staring at the crows.

"Do you have more?"

I met his eyes when he said this and saw that they were a stunning cornflower blue with enviable long black lashes. I tried to focus on his eyes rather than his pock-marked cheeks.

"Yeah, I've been bored here, so I just started sketching everything." I leafed through my sketchbook to some of the drawings I did earlier in the week. There were sketches of Ginny, the bouquet from Joshua's parents, my sneakers lying on the floor, Heidi, Chester, and my plastic lunch from two days ago.

"These are amazing! And *that* one, holy smokes," he said, pointing to Heidi and her melancholy expression. "That's intense." I flipped to the next page and he said, "Who's the cat?"

"That's Chester, my baby." It pained me to talk about Chester; I'd failed him.

"He's really cute! I love orange kitties. Me and my brother have two tabbies, Fred and Igor." His voice became softer. "I ain't seen them little guys in months," he said sadly as he gazed down at the drawing.

"I'm sorry, I definitely know how that feels." Closing my sketch pad, I decided to change the subject to something less depressing. "You have some really cool tattoos, especially the one on the back of your head."

"Oh yeah, well, that one's special." He leaned on one of the chairs next to me. "When I'm manic, my paranoia kicks in and I become convinced people are after me, trying to kidnap me and steal my organs."

"How awful!" I offered a sympathetic frown, though nothing shocked me anymore.

"I know, it sucks. It got real bad around five years back. The men were on my tail for weeks. I didn't get no sleep since I'd have to close my eyes. I was always looking over my shoulder and hiding behind cars, buildings, trees, anything I could find. Then I got this idea to ink an eye back there." He gestured toward the back of his head. "That way I could see who was after me, you know, keep an eye on them from behind." He rubbed one hand across the back of his nearly bald head as he spoke.

Okay, so this is interesting and actually sort of genius.

"I know it's stupid. But when I'm at my worst, it becomes a *real* eye. Then I think they can't never catch me. Nobody gets it though. My parents fucking—excuse me, they hate it, won't be seen with me unless I wear a hat," he said while continuing to lean toward me with both hands on the chair. His cigarette smell was starting to give me a headache.

"I get it," I said softly, and I really did.

"Thank you," he said with a smile that belied the resignation in his eyes. "When I feel better, I start growing my hair to cover it. But then comes another episode and I shave it all off again." Then he added with sing-song inflection, spinning one hand in circles, "And around and around in circles I go…" He stopped for a moment, gazed out the window, and then looked back at me with a forlorn expression. "On days like today, near someone so pretty,

I sure wish it wasn't there." He rubbed the back of his head again.

Now I was totally embarrassed, likely blushing. "Thank you," I said, looking down at the table. "But, there's no judgment here."

"That's kind of you, Ms. Sunny." He took a deep breath. "Well, I won't bother you no more, but nice chatting with you." He smiled, fully displaying his missing front tooth.

"You, too." I smiled back.

I watched him as he headed back to the couch. I imagined that his protective marking likely did keep people at a distance, although not in the way he intended.

I went back to my sketching, but couldn't concentrate and just stared out the window. I wondered how I appeared to this poor, tormented guy. Of course he could see that I, too, was in the psych ward; but still, he likely thought I was some sweet, demure girl who didn't belong there.

He had no idea.

Eddy had such a startling appearance, I'd have been afraid to speak to him only a short time ago. But here he was, complimenting me and looking downcast when speaking of himself and his illness. We weren't so different, he and I. When I was running from the SS—hiding in public restrooms and cemeteries, I could imagine myself wishing for a third eye. With that eye, I could've watched the Aryan on the bus or the Gestapo as they trailed behind. I could have kept an eye on Mengele or Penterhaus as they tried to murder me. Mental illness was the great equalizer. I was no better than this tenderhearted man who loved his kitties and felt ashamed in front of a girl he thought was pretty.

After lunch, I headed over to art therapy. I was looking forward to finishing my drawing of Ginny and also wanted to see if Fern would allow me to sketch her. I sat down as usual, getting my supplies ready. Along with Ginny, today's cast of characters included Travis—who was wearing a NY Giants sweatshirt and his usual camo baseball hat; Agnus—who was sorting her potholders into piles based on some category I couldn't discern; and Fern—who was coloring so hard, she'd ripped the paper. There was also a new woman I'd never seen before whom Ginny introduced as Becky. She was around forty and had long, stringy brown hair and a mustache. Heidi had mentioned a mustached woman who, like a chimpanzee, was known to throw her own shit against walls. I sincerely hoped Becky was not this person. She didn't say anything, just nodded her head without smiling. When she placed a thick clump of hair in her mouth and chewed it hungrily, I nearly lost my lunch. So I focused on my drawing of Ginny instead, adding more details to her hair and clothing. After ten or fifteen minutes, I started getting worried about Heidi—she never missed art therapy.

"Excuse me, Ginny, do you know where Heidi is?"

She was organizing a box of pens and looked up at me, hesitating for a moment before speaking. "Oh, I'm not sure, dear." Her expression deceived her; she knew something.

I set my pencil down. "What do you mean? Isn't she coming today?"

"I'm not really at liberty to say. I'm sorry, Sunny." Her voice was soft, almost consoling. Something was up.

I closed my sketchbook and gathered my pencils. "I need to go." I almost ran toward my room, stopping at the nurse's station where I saw Maggie sitting behind a computer. When I got to the counter, I abruptly blurted out, "Where's Heidi," causing her to jump.

"Hello, Sunny. Let's go chat in your room." She grabbed something and came out from behind the counter. She was holding a manilla folder under one arm. Dread swirled around my brain before lodging in my throat like an omen. I wanted to run in the other direction, but followed along obediently. Once we were both inside, she closed the door most of the way and stood before me. I was getting queasy. "Heidi isn't here anymore, she snuck out of the hospital last night and never came back," she said, gently touching my arm.

"What? Why did she do that? Where is she now?" I moved away from her, I didn't want to be touched. I was getting frantic.

"I'm afraid I don't know. Her family hasn't been able to locate her." Then her voice got softer. "Sunny, please sit down." She gestured toward the bed.

"I don't understand, how did she get out? Why wasn't she being watched?" I was getting increasingly upset, but allowed myself to be guided to the bed where I took a seat.

"Sunny, she left something in her room for you." She handed me the folder, which had "Please Give to Sunny" written in red ink on the cover with a little red heart drawn beneath it. I set the folder in my lap. I felt panicky and was afraid to look inside. I took a couple deep breaths and slowly opened it, finding her sketches. I saw my face on the top of the stack, but there were at least twenty other drawings, mostly of people. As I was leafing through them, something fell into my lap. It was the blue and yellow macramé bracelet Heidi always wore—the one her little sister gave her. I picked it up and immediately started shaking.

"Oh no! No, no, no, no, no," I said, my voice quivering. "She's giving her stuff away—even the bracelet she loved." Then I added in a hushed tone, "She's dead." When tears started to roll down my face, I moved the drawings to the side so they wouldn't get ruined.

"We don't know that. All we know is that she took off without being discharged. Please don't jump to conclusions." She sat down next to me and handed me the box of tissues. Then she gently patted my back. "Take a few deep breaths."

I didn't need to take any goddamn breaths! I maneuvered myself to the head of my bed and leaned against the wall. I curled my knees up to my chin, wrapping my arms around them and rocked back and forth.

"I'm sorry you're so upset. I can see you really care about her."

I stared into space, but I could feel her eyes on me as she spouted her useless words.

I curled up in the fetal position as Maggie sat with me for a while, saying whatever consoling things she could think of. I was relieved when she finally left. I wanted to be alone so I could sob freely. By the time Dr. Bensen showed up twenty minutes later, my pillow was wet with tears and smudged mascara. I had a headache and was just lying on my side numbly staring at the wall. He pulled in a chair and sat down.

"Hi, Sunny," he said softly. He looked at me with such a fatherly expression that I almost wanted to hug him. I missed my dad.

"Hi," I mumbled very quietly.

"I'm sorry you're so upset about Heidi, I know you two had become friends." He crossed his legs.

"Yeah, it just makes me wonder…you know, like, why even bother." My voice sounded nasal, I turned away from him and blew my nose, then sat up straight.

"Bother with what?" His voice was still soft, but his eyes were peering into me.

"You know, taking my meds. Going to therapy."

"Well, you need to do those things because you have a serious mental illness and will become very sick otherwise, as we've seen. Right?"

"Yeah," I mumbled, not really feeling it though.

"I'm not understanding why Heidi's situation makes you feel so resigned. Can you please tell me more?"

I let out a big sigh. "I guess because she was doing what she was supposed to, you know, going to art therapy and everything else, and this *still* happened," I said with an exasperated tone, picking at one of my middle fingers.

He just looked at me and seemed to shake his head with such subtly, I wasn't sure if I imagined it.

"She left against medical advice, didn't she?"

"I can't give you that information," he said. But I knew the answer. "And do you really know what was going on with her in terms of treatment?" His hands were clasped together, resting on a knee of his crossed legs. He wore a shiny platinum wedding band with an ornate pattern of some sort.

"I guess not," I mumbled.

"You and Heidi are unique individuals with different backgrounds, diagnoses, and family dynamics. Her situation is totally separate from yours."

"Yeah, I guess. But I just feel like, if bad things are going to keep happening, why even bother?" I pulled my hair out of its ponytail, which was starting to hurt.

"Because difficult things will *always* happen, that's just life. But, by taking care of your mental health, you will get through them."

"But what if I don't?" I didn't realize how afraid I was of failing until I said those words. Feeling antsy, I started pulling at a thread in my shirt.

"And what if you *do?*" He paused for a moment, giving me a slight smile. "I'm not big on 'what if's,' Sunny. But we've talked a lot about triggers and how they can exacerbate your illness if you don't manage them. This situation with Heidi appears to be one such thing. But it's also an opportunity to put your coping strategies to use and minimize the likelihood of a recurrence of symptoms. Do you remember the things we talked about in terms of coping?"

I listed the various strategies we'd gone over as he nodded in approval.

"And how about confiding in your family? Do you have someone coming to visit this evening?"

"Yes, Joshua." I'd been looking forward to it all day, until *this* happened.

"Excellent. Please don't be afraid to show him you need him. Allow him to comfort you."

"Okay. But what if I do all of these things and the Wankers still show up?"

"Excuse me?" he asked, furrowing his eyebrows.

"Oh, the voices—it's what I'm calling them now." I was a little nervous about his response, he seemed so proper.

But he laughed out loud. It was a merry laugh that softened his whole face and made him appear younger. He shook his head back and forth, saying, "Oh, Sunny, that humor of yours is going to benefit you in so many ways. Did you know that a sense of humor actually promotes recovery?" He took off his glasses and cleaned them with his hanky.

"No, but whatever helps…" I couldn't help but smile. I loved seeing Dr. Bensen laugh.

"Well, I think it's a fitting name for the voices, but maybe just don't use it in England." He chuckled, putting his glasses back on. "So, if the Wankers show up, use the coping skills you've learned, including talking back or disputing them, if that helps. And remember that you're safe, regardless of what they say. Then page me. We'll handle that situation without allowing it to get worse."

"Okay, but I'm also upset because I feel like I should've *done* something. I shouldn't have let this happen to her." A few tears leaked out, which I quickly wiped away with the back of my hand.

He uncrossed his legs and raised his eyebrows, speaking a little bit louder. "Sunny, you're talking about a young woman on the psychiatric ward whom you only met a short time ago. And yet, considering what you know about her and her struggles, you somehow believe you could rescue her? You must be very powerful indeed!" His words were facetious, but not unkind.

"Well, when you put it that way." He was right, *again*. Heidi was the most tortured soul I'd ever known. She'd sliced the insides of her forearms to such an extent that there was virtually no healthy skin left. When I first met her, her wounds were so fresh and deeply etched that her arms resembled raw meat. Plus, she was a repeat suicide attempter with abusive parents.

Now I was starting to feel like an idiot.

He smiled very softly. "You have a way of taking on the world's problems as your own. You have no control over another patient's recovery, so how about if you take that one off your list?"

I was silent for a moment. I liked the idea of scraping some of the emotional garbage from my plate. Though it sounded easier said than done. "Okay, I'll try."

"Good," he said, glancing at his watch. "I need to run to an appointment, but I'm on call tonight if you need me. In the meantime, remember what I've said about taking care of yourself and leaning on your husband."

"I will."

He stood up and smoothed the creases out of his slacks. "You know, Sunny, I'm really proud of you for befriending Heidi."

I was surprised by his words. "Why?"

"Because, by allowing her into your closely protected circle, you took a risk. I know that's not easy for you. And, in doing so, you gave her the privilege of knowing you."

I wished I could take Dr. Bensen home with me, just keep him in the spare bedroom for emergencies. Maybe I was experiencing some sort of transference, but I was starting to feel very attached to him. After we said goodbye and he was almost out the door, I said, "Um…"

He turned back. "Yes?"

I paused for a moment, feeling embarrassed. "Thank you for being my doctor."

He flashed me his Hollywood smile. "My pleasure, Sunny."

Although I was still terribly sad, since I knew my friend was dead, Dr. Bensen's visit had left me less frantic and hopeless. I put the little bracelet on my wrist and glanced through the rest of Heidi's drawings. When Joshua arrived a couple of hours later, I was trying to take my mind off of Heidi by reading a book, though my brain kept circling back to her. He had come from work and was wearing black jeans and a white button-up shirt with a black T-shirt underneath. His wavy hair was getting long and he had quite a bit of beard stubble, but he was unforgivingly handsome. He was my Joshua.

"Hi, gorgeous," he said, kissing me on the lips.

"Hi, honey, I've missed you."

"Me, too, baby. I brought you a couple things." He handed me a brown lunch bag. I glanced inside. "Oatmeal raisin, my favorite." I breathed in the sweet scent.

"Yup, and they're *very* soft. I tested them just to make sure," he teased.

"They look delicious, thank you. I'll save them for later." I set the bag aside, not feeling in the mood for sweets.

"You're welcome. And I found this in the back of the closet, thought you might want it." He handed me a tiny white box.

When I opened the lid, I saw Babcia's Star of David necklace. "Oh, Joshua, thank you." I gently pulled it out of the box and unclasped the gold chain. "Can you please move my hair?"

He lifted my hair and I put on the necklace, resting my hand on the pendant as if it held powers. He allowed my hair to fall and whispered, "Beautiful."

"You're beautiful," I said, kissing his hand. "Thank you for finding my necklace."

"Of course. You know I'd do anything for you."

"I know," I said softly.

Joshua sat next to me on my bed and I told him what happened with Heidi. He listened quietly, keeping an arm around me and never once trying to diminish my feelings or fix things. He told me how sorry he was, which was exactly what I needed. As I emptied my heart all over his shoulder, this time I didn't try to appear strong or to hide the ugliness of my pain. Instead, feeling Baba over my heart and my precious husband beside me, I allowed myself to wilt into them. And, as Joshua tried to comfort me with the full weight of his patience and innate goodness—this time, I let him.

Chapter 38 ❧ Sunny

I must've been emotionally exhausted since I fell asleep on Joshua's chest and didn't even awaken when he left my room. I had a fitful sleep and woke up in a panic, sweat dripping down my back. The stillness of the night always seemed to magnify my anxieties, leaving me defenseless as they loomed around me in the darkness. Although I wanted to go home, I was also terrified of leaving the protective cocoon of the hospital. I had a dream in which I was running from the psych ward, feeling a sense of freedom as I left my doctors and fellow patients behind. Eventually, I was running outside and Heidi was standing in front of me, trying to block my path, but I pushed past her only to fall into a rabbit hole reminiscent of that in *Alice in Wonderland.* Although I could feel the weight of my skin pulling me down, I never hit the bottom. Instead, I awakened sitting straight up in bed. I didn't know the time, but it felt like those hours of deafening calm when even crickets and bullfrogs are silent.

As I tried to get my bearings, the Wankers reminded me of their presence: *Psycho. Pathetic loser. Loser. Loser. Loser.* Their reappearance infuriated me. "Not this time," I said out loud, followed by, "Shut up, Wankers! You aren't real and I don't believe you!" I tried to sound confident and even a bit threatening as I scolded the enemy. I heard, *Fucking loser,* and answered with, "Shut up, Wankers! Just get lost." Then I sat in the darkness and listened, desperately hoping they'd gone back to sleep.

Hearing the usual beeping and humming noises of the hospital, and nothing more, I relaxed my body and lay back down. The retreat of the voices back to their sleeping den was an Elysian reprieve only the chronically psychotic could appreciate. Lulled by that exquisite nothingness, I dozed off until morning.

Once fully awake, I remembered what happened and felt a mix of disappointment at the return of the Wankers, and pride for having finally stood up to them. As I sat in bed drinking coffee, I thought about how the voices might never leave me entirely. They were sort of like Grandma Sylvie, whose presence could turn any situation into a shit storm. I decided to picture the voices like a drunken uncle who stumbled in late to family gatherings, bringing only his offensive breath and latest string of insults. I would continue to stand my ground when that old uncle appeared, dismissing his bibulous words and maintaining some semblance of control over my mind. I was in charge now and refused to let him break me. Not this time.

As I was organizing my stuff and getting ready to leave the next day, I found myself thinking a lot about Heidi and how she'd wormed her way into a small corner of my heart. I didn't know her well, but something about Heidi touched me. I got the sense that she'd never known contentment or solace in her life. And, like me, everything was far too difficult for her. I wondered how she'd done it—pills, bullets, or my family's preferred method: jumping. And although I felt in my gut that she had left this world, I hoped to God I was wrong. Even more, I hoped her soul would find comfort. I whispered a thank you to Heidi for giving me a brief glimpse into her kindness and astounding talent, and for reminding me that, unlike her, I was not alone in my battle.

I was lost in thought when Maggie stopped by. She was wearing pink scrubs and her blonde hair was piled up so high, it must've raised her height to over six feet. She was wearing pink lipstick that matched her scrubs.

"Good afternoon, Sunny. How are you doing today?" she asked, standing over me like a giant as I was organizing my clothes on the bed.

"I'm sad about Heidi, but at least I'm leaving the hospital soon."

"Yes, I heard. How do you feel about it?"

"Oh, I'm ready, just a little anxious."

"I've seen so much growth in you during this hospitalization, Sunny. I'm really optimistic about your recovery," she said, grinning. She had a bit of lipstick on her front teeth.

"Thank you, that means a lot." Maggie had become a steady fixture during my hospital stays; I would miss her.

"I have a little something for you. It's nothing big, but…" She handed me a pink satin gift bag and a card. "You can open it later," she added, looking a little embarrassed.

"Okay. Thank you so much, Maggie—for everything."

"You're welcome. Please keep drawing, your work is so lovely. And follow Dr. Bensen's orders—I don't want to see you back here again!"

"No offense, but me neither." She gave me a little hug and left the room.

I sat down on the bed with the gift, which felt like a bag of gravel. When I opened it, I saw that it was a large packet of sunflower seeds for planting. On the cover, it said "Ring of Fire" along with a photo of several large sunflowers with dark red centers that bled onto yellow petals. I opened the card, which had three adorable orange kittens on the cover. Written in flowy, feminine cursive, Maggie left the following message on the inside:

Sunny, I'm giving you these seeds so you can grow and cultivate your own sunflower garden. These flowers especially remind me of you. They are soft and beautiful around the edges, but hold a ring of fire within their center. I hope that when you look upon them in the future, and perhaps draw them, they will remind you of the passion and resilience you hold within yourself. When you see them standing tall and withstanding the elements, imagine yourself doing the same. You are stronger than you know. Love, Maggie.

It was a good thing Maggie left the room. I would've been at a loss for words. It was one of the loveliest gestures I'd ever known. And yet it came from a woman I'd insulted repeatedly, convinced she was the *Beautiful Beast* of Auschwitz. As I examined the bag, I vowed never to allow my mind to return to that infernal place, but to make her proud of me. I thought of the exact location to plant the flowers: just outside the kitchen window where I could see them each morning as I drank my coffee. It also would be an ideal place to sketch them. As I placed the bag in my small suitcase, I felt moved by this small but monumental act of kindness.

After lunch, I realized there was something I needed to do. I grabbed my sketch pad and pencils, and went for a walk around the ward. I looked in the sunroom, as well as another smaller sitting room, and wandered down multiple halls. The floor was oddly quiet and I decided to head back to my room when I heard the familiar shuffle. I turned back and found Eddy heading toward me, eyes downcast. "Hello, Eddy," I said softly, trying not to startle him.

He looked up and smiled halfheartedly. "Hello, Ms. Sunny."

He kept on walking and had barely passed me when I said, "Excuse me, I don't mean to bother you. I was just wondering if you'd allow me to sketch you. It's okay if you feel uncomfortable, I just thought…"

He stopped and turned back toward me. I was afraid I'd offended him and, given the pace of his shuffling, that he was decompensating. He looked at me with teary eyes, and said, "You want to draw *me?*"

"Yes, if you'll let me, I'd be honored."

His face softened a bit more. "That's the kindest thing I've heard in years. But, can you please just draw the back of me? I don't want them to see my face."

He sounded paranoid, which made me sad. "Of course."

And so we stayed right there in the hall as I stood behind him and sketched. I don't think I'd ever drawn anything so quickly, but I could see that he was restless and uncomfortable. When I was done, he didn't even take the time to look at the drawing. He just said, "Thank you, beautiful Ms. Sunny," and took off at full speed. I watched him shuffle away, wishing the doctors could find a way to alleviate his suffering.

Back in my room, I tried to read as I waited for my dad to show up with dinner. It had been a couple of days since he'd visited and I was eager to see him. Joshua would also be showing up later since we had a family meeting with Dr. Turner at 6:00.

Shortly after 5:00, I heard talking in the hall as my door opened. Both my dad and Linda entered the room causing me to freeze as that familiar shame burned through my body. I hadn't seen Linda since being hospitalized and was trying to push her out of my mind. I was sure that somewhere deep down, beneath her ultra-tolerant, tree-hugging exterior, she hated me.

"Hi, sweetheart," said my dad with forced enthusiasm. I could tell he was trying to lighten the atmosphere given that it was my first encounter with Linda since the incident. He was wearing jeans and a white, short-sleeved golf shirt. His arms and neck looked tan, maybe from working in the yard or playing tennis. His dark hair appeared to have just been cut, which always made him look younger despite the gray strands framing the sides of his face. He was carrying a grocery bag, which he set on the bed before giving me a hug.

"Hi, Dad, I missed you."

"I missed you, too, honey."

Then it was her turn. Linda stood before me, also carrying a brown bag. She was wearing a plain white cotton shirt and a long, flowy skirt in multiple pastel colors. Her hair was pulled back in a bun and her skin looked pink and freckly. As always, I was surprised by her diminutive stature and overall lightness—as if a storm could blow her away. "Hi, Sunny," she said with a smile that seemed genuine.

"Hello." I stood up, feeling uncomfortable sitting on my bed with two visitors. She came over and hugged me tightly. At first, I stiffened, then I allowed one of my hands to rest softly on her back for a moment.

"You look well. It's so nice to see you," she said, looking at me.

"You too," I said meekly. She actually looked the same as always—as small and wispy as a dandelion flower. But I knew there was far more to her than that—I'd seen rage within those blue eyes and the prospect of facing them now made me jittery and nauseous. I wormed away from her and straightened up my bed, for lack of anything better to do.

My dad went into the hall to get a couple of chairs as Linda started pulling food out of the bags. "We stopped at your favorite Mexican place," she said, as she started setting containers on the bed.

"You can put that stuff here." I began moving books, pencils and other crap from my nightstand. "Not much room in this place."

"That's for sure. You must be thrilled to be getting out of here." She was cramming everything on the small nightstand.

"I am." *God, this is awkward.* As I pondered what else I might say, my dad returned with two chairs. He faced them toward the bed, where I took a seat on the edge. I was certainly tired of feeling chained to that stupid little bed. Although it wouldn't fit in this room, I wanted to merit an actual chair like a normal person—or at least like an adult.

The three of us were quiet for several moments, as my dad crunched on fish tacos while Linda and I ate beans and rice. We made a little small talk as we ate, then cleaned up the mess and sat staring at each other. I tried to steel myself, as I knew there were things that needed to be said. I took a breath and looked over at Linda, who was sitting with her back perfectly straight and her legs crossed. She was wearing her horrible granola sandals.

"Linda, I'm *so* sorry!" And I was crying again, *dammit.* Then an avalanche of words spilled out of me. "I would never want to hurt Maddy and Spencer, I thought I was saving them. I know it's totally absurd. I will never do anything like that again. I won't stop my meds, I promise. I'm so sorry, I wouldn't blame you for hating me." I wiped my eyes with my shirt as I nervously awaited her response.

Linda's face visibly softened. "Of course I don't hate you, Sunny." She handed me the tissue box. "It's not your fault that you have a serious mental illness. I know you love your brother and sister, and would not intentionally hurt them."

"But I *did* hurt them, even if not intentionally," I said, sniffling.

"The kids are okay, please don't worry about them."

"Linda's right," added my dad, "the kids are fine."

"I should've been watching them more closely. I could see that you were acting a bit off that day. In fact, we all should've been paying closer attention to you. I feel bad about that."

Huh? *She* feels bad? I didn't know what to say.

"So do I," said my dad. "From now on, we're going to do a better job of watching for your triggers."

"But the kids, what I did…" I said, nervously twisting my damp tissue.

Linda came over and gave me a hug, then held me at arm's length as I continued to sit on the edge of the bed. "Of course the incident with the children was terrible and scared me to death. We will need to be more careful with you around them. And you need to do your part. That means telling us how you feel, especially if you start questioning your need for meds. It's imperative that you keep taking them."

"Oh, I know, I never want anything like that to happen again."

"Good. I know we're going to talk about this with Dr. Turner, but I want to be here for you. I want you to lean on me and trust me. I love you, Sunny."

Oh holy hell. What could I possibly say to that? I saw my dad staring at me with a pleasant, yet surprised, expression. "I…um…thank you."

"No need to thank me," she said as she softly patted my arm.

"But why are you so goddamn nice?" I blurted through tears, which broke the tension in the room, causing them both to laugh.

My dad got up and walked over to us. "I *told you* she was nice," he said smiling. He gave me a hug as Linda placed an arm on his back.

We were so caught up in the moment that we didn't hear Joshua come in. "Hey, I hate to break up this beautiful kumbaya moment, but…" He had a smile on his face and was dressed for work, wearing a wrinkled blue and white striped shirt and brown pants.

"Joshua!" I said happily before wiping my nose with the mangled tissue.

"Hi, honey, are you okay?"

"I'm great," I said while still slightly crying for some reason, which made everyone laugh. I composed myself. "No really, I'm okay." I smiled.

"I'm glad to hear that. We have our meeting in a few minutes. Are you guys ready?"

My dad looked at his watch. "Oops, we'd better get moving."

And so, I walked along with the three of them—my father and husband whom I loved beyond description, and this extraordinary woman who, after all of the mayhem and pain I'd brought to her life, was somehow still here for me—toward the conference room where we would plan my reentry into the free world.

Chapter 39 ✤ Sunny

As the conference room loomed ahead, I felt my usual sense of trepidation. But I was less nervous this time around since my family was there to support me. And besides, hadn't we already covered my impressive litany of psychiatric symptoms and traumas? As I pondered over what Dr. Turner had in store for me, Eddy shuffled past us. I was immediately struck by his gray countenance and hollow eyes—his spark was gone, fully extinguished. He didn't look over as we passed by, perhaps because there were too many of us and it made him anxious. As I moved within the cocoon of the people who loved me most, I was saddened by how isolated and lost inside himself he appeared.

"Hi, Eddy," I said, just as he passed us.

"Hello, Ms. Sunny," I heard over my shoulder. But his voice was monotone, void of any pretense of affability. He was like a Warhol painting that had been drenched in darkness.

I saw Joshua look back at him. Noticing the tattoo, he looked at me and whispered, "Holy shit, what's up with him?"

I just shook my head, refusing to indulge him. Joshua didn't lack compassion, but there were some things regular people would never understand.

When we arrived at the conference room, Dr. Turner was in her usual seat at the far end of the large table. There was a stack of papers on the table in front of her, along with a hot beverage in a disposable cup. She was wearing dark pants and a sage-colored sweater. Her hair was in a bun and a heart pendant made of some type of green stone hung from her neck. She stood up and greeted each of us. My dad and Linda sat to her left, across from Joshua and me. Once we were situated, she got started.

"Good evening, everyone, it's nice to see you all," she said, as she held her warm drink with both hands and looked around at each of us. "Sunny, I imagine you've had about enough of this room," she said, smiling.

"You can say that again," I answered dryly. The room felt less oppressive than during prior meetings, but only because this was, as I desperately hoped, my last visit. I suppressed the urge to raise a middle finger toward the pasty old farts on the wall and say, "So long, bastards!"

"I totally understand, but this shouldn't be too painful. Given your discharge tomorrow, there are several things we need to discuss. But first, Sunny, I just want you to know that I'm proud of your growth during this hospitalization. You've been following your treatment recommendations and it shows—you have a clarity about you that I hadn't seen until now." Her praise was a little embarrassing, particularly since everyone was nodding in agreement.

"Thank you," I said softly.

"What do you think is different about this hospitalization?" She set her drink down and folded her hands together on the table as she looked at me.

God, I hated being on the spot. I sighed and thought for a moment, then said, "Well, I suppose dragging my brother and sister into my Holocaust delusion and nearly jumping to my death was a bit of a wake-up call." Sounding snarkier than intended, I softened my tone and added, "I don't ever want anything like that to happen again. But it showed me how sick I am, that I can't function without medication."

"I know you went through an awful lot to reach that realization. But I'm so glad you did. And I'm truly impressed with each of you," she said, looking around at Joshua, my dad and Linda. Then her gaze came back to me. "You are fortunate to have such a supportive family."

"Oh, I know." I immediately thought of Heidi and how her external scars and lacerations seemed to mirror the damaged soul beneath them. And I pictured the desolation and fear that never left Eddy's lovely blue eyes. I imagined how much different their lives would've been if they had a family like mine. Yeah, I was lucky as hell.

She sipped her drink, then continued. "Just like any serious illness—psychiatric or otherwise—supporting Sunny in her recovery is a family affair. So, what I'd like to do now is work as a united team to make some plans that will best support Sunny after discharge." She looked down at her papers and then back toward Joshua. "I know you want Sunny to come home again, right?"

"Oh, definitely," he answered assuredly. "The condo is her place of comfort." Then he turned toward me. "It's not just that I miss you—*and believe me*, I do—but you have everything you love there: Chester, your books, your art...*me*. Plus, I've talked to my boss and she's agreed to let me work at home several times a week, so I'll be there quite a bit." He moved a strand of hair from my eye.

I felt a sharp surge of love for this man, my husband. I'd been harboring a seed of hope somewhere deep inside me that I'd be allowed to go home again. But I was so terrified of being disappointed that I never even raised the question. My greatest fear was that they'd put me in some sort of transitional house because I could neither live independently nor with my father. I'd heard about such places from Heidi and was appalled by the idea of continuing to live amongst strangers. But now, as my almost painful longing for home rose to the surface, I felt elated by Joshua's words. I gazed at his trusting face and promised myself not to let him down—*not this time*. "Oh my God, Joshua, that's *exactly* what I want. Being away from you and our home has been so painful for me. I need to be there with you and Chester. I've missed you so much." He held my hand under the table. "It's going to be different this time. I won't mess up, I promise," I added, almost pleading.

"I know," he said softly.

"I can see how dedicated you both are to each other and it's really beautiful," said Dr. Turner, smiling warmly along with both my dad and Linda. "I'm good with this plan provided there are a few caveats, which we'll go over. The goal is to keep you stabilized," she was speaking directly to me now, "so you don't have a return of symptoms. The term 'mess up' confers blame—you have a disorder, there is no blame here." She was peering into me again, making me squirm in my seat.

"Okay." I was so pleased about going home, I was barely bothered by my poor word choice.

My dad cleared his throat and chimed in. "While I agree that home is the most comforting place for Sunny, I also want her to have plenty of people around her—like a village, as they say. Linda and I have discussed this with Joshua, and one of us can come over three times a week for lunch or a walk or whatever."

So they were going to monitor me 24/7, sort of like transplanting my hospital cell into the condo. And they'd been talking about it without telling me. I felt a twinge of irritation as I looked from my dad to Joshua, but decided to let it go. In the recent past, this scenario would've pissed me off, but I could see that it beat any of the alternatives. At least this time there would be no Milquetoast—so how could I complain?

"That's wonderful," said Dr. Turner, scribbling something on her notepad.

"I just want to mention that Elizabeth is also part of this team," said Joshua. "She's been out of town, but will be back in a few days." He looked at me, adding, "She really wants to help, honey. She feels shut out."

The twinge was back; why was my best friend talking about me with my husband? I looked out the window at a distant pine tree, watching its needly branches sway in the breeze. "When did you talk to Elizabeth?"

"She called a couple of days ago. She thinks you sometimes, um…you don't rely on her as much as you can. She feels left out and sad about not being able to help. She loves you so much, honey," he added tenderly.

Damn, it was true, I had shut her out. And hearing that I'd hurt her gave me a familiar pang of guilt. "Oh," I said, picking at my thumb.

"Sunny, how do you feel about what Joshua just said?" asked Dr. Turner.

"At first, it irritated me, like they were talking behind my back. But I have sort of pushed Lizzie away from the worst of this. I'm embarrassed, you know?" I could see my dad shaking his head.

"Sweetheart, no one is talking behind your back—we are all allies here. We love you and want only to help you," he said with an almost pleading expression.

I nodded at him, not really sure what to say. Trying to balance my obvious inability to function autonomously with my fragile ego was a precarious place for me. I picked at my thumb, which was starting to ache and looked disgusting. I held both of my thumbs beneath my other fingers and tried to control myself. I would be out in the world soon and didn't want totally mangled hands. I stared down at the wooden table and noticed a spot just to my left where someone had penciled the word "anus" in very small letters. I wondered who would sit in this giant, suffocating room overlooked by pedantic old men, and write such a word. Then I decided it was the perfect word.

"I understand how difficult this is for you," said the doctor. "How long have you known Elizabeth?"

"Oh wow, since second grade, I think." I had a sudden image of Elizabeth and I riding skateboards through an apartment complex near our school. I was always the fast one and could hear her lagging behind, yelling at me to slow down. And I remembered the countless times I slept over at her house—not wanting to subject her to the storm forever brewing within mine. I think her mom had an idea of my dysfunctional homelife, she would always greet me with a warm hug and a sympathetic smile.

"That's a *really* long time, I imagine even longer than you've known Joshua. Have you been close this whole time?"

"Yes, she's my best friend, I mean, besides him." I nudged Joshua with my elbow. I could barely remember a time in my life without Elizabeth by my side. Despite everything, I always tried to act tough around her, like none of the chaos in my life could knock me down. She would often tell me how strong I was. I guess I didn't want her to see me fall apart, to dispel her image of me.

"Kind of like *family?*" Dr. Turner's eyebrows went up. She was messing with my head again.

"Yes, she's family." There was that particularly terrible time when my mom was really sick and my parents were constantly fighting. It was Elizabeth who got me through it. I'd cried on her shoulder more times than I could recall. She was absolutely family.

"Soooo, she's family *and* she wants to be here for you. Seems like a no-brainer to me. The only question is, will you let her in?"

"Yeah, you're right. I didn't want to burden her, that's all."

"It's not a burden if she doesn't see it that way, those are *your* words." She paused, looking out the window for a second, then back at me. "Seems that you have plenty of people who really love you."

"I do," I said softly, feeling Joshua squeeze my hand.

She smiled and then looked down at her papers. "Now I'd like to work out a schedule in order to keep everything as clear and consistent as possible." She gave each of us a sheet of paper with a chart that had a column for each day of the week. She'd written her own name on Mondays, Wednesdays, and Fridays at 2:00.

"So, each week, we're going to fill in this form for the following week. Sunny, I know we discussed this briefly, but you will be seeing me three times a week, which I've already added. You will also see Dr. Bensen twice a month, though I don't know the exact days yet. This can be added once we know. But, for each of you, I'd like you to write in the days and times you can spend with Sunny at the start of each week, ideally on Sunday."

"I won't know my weekly schedule until Mondays," said Joshua.

"How about if I take Sunny to lunch every Monday, so that day is always covered?" asked my dad.

I felt like a new puppy who had to be watched around the clock or she'd piss on the couch and eat the pillows.

"Perfect," said Joshua.

"Excellent. So, every Monday, Peter will have lunch with Sunny, and Joshua will fill in the days he can work at home for the rest of the week. And Linda and Peter will cover the rest. How does that sound? Sunny?"

"I mean, I feel like an infant. But I guess it's okay." I picked at another finger.

"I know it feels strange, perhaps overprotective. Maybe just think of it as people who love you and want to spend time with you, because that's honestly what it is. And once you've established a routine for a decent period of time, we can loosen up the schedule."

"Plus, it's a lot of free lunches," said my dad smiling.

"That's true." They could've sent me to a halfway house where I would sleep amongst people who dodged invisible adversaries and chucked their own shit against the wall. No thanks. I had no right to complain.

"And you can always join me for yoga twice a week," offered Linda.

"Ugh, yoga," I said with a sigh. Everyone chuckled—my disdain for yoga was no mystery. "I'll think about it."

"Yoga is wonderful for anxiety, it can really help to clear your mind and make you feel more grounded. Not to mention the added flexibility. I hope you'll keep an open mind," lectured Dr. Turner.

I just nodded my head. They were starting to push it.

"Okay, the next thing I'd like to discuss is triggers. The Cherokee have a saying: *"Pay attention to the whispers, so you won't have to hear the screams."* Triggers are much like whispers, and recognizing them is essential for preventing relapse. This is *really* important, since each relapse can cause increased harm, worsening a person's prognosis—this is called a kindling effect. So, noticing and acting on triggers is absolutely vital for Sunny's recovery." She handed out another paper to each of us, which was entitled, Relapse Plan. "This form is very important, please keep it in a central location at all times."

We all looked over the form. It contained a list of the warning signs I'd heard so many times, including changes in mood, irritability, isolating from others, anxiety, sleep changes, hallucinations, delusions, paranoia, inappropriate reactions, depressed mood, lack of enjoyment in pleasurable activities, lack of motivation, agitation, lack of hygiene (e.g., not showering or grooming), disordered speaking, lack of speech output, questioning the diagnosis, and questioning the need for meds.

There was also a list of preventative measures, which included keeping medication reminders, spending time with loved ones, attending group therapy, engaging in creative activities, eating healthily, avoiding alcohol and recreational drugs, exercising, meditating, getting plenty of sleep, and avoiding stressors.

Below these lists, there was a list of names and numbers, including Dr. Turner, Dr. Bensen, Joshua, my dad, Linda, and Elizabeth. There were also phone numbers for two ERs, a crisis hotline, Joshua's parents, Randy, and Joshua's boss. Lastly, there was a list of steps to take if relapse was suspected.

Once we'd looked over the paper, Dr. Turner said, "Of course, each person is unique, but these are the most common warning signs I'd like you to look for. And please let me know if I missed any. Sunny, you're the expert here. Does this list seem accurate to you?"

"Yeah. I tend to get really irritable and can't sleep. Nothing is fun or interesting and of course I start thinking I'm not really sick, that everyone else is the problem. And then there are the Nazi delusions, can't forget those."

I could see her head nodding as I spoke. "That's a great description. Importantly, the mood aspect of Sunny's disorder tends to be one of *dysphoria*, including irritability or anger, rather than *euphoria*, which often occurs among people with schizoaffective and bipolar disorders. So those kinds of mood symptoms are important indicators for Sunny."

"Just my luck, rather than getting the happy mood swings, I inherited the nasty ones," I said wryly.

Dr. Turner smiled. "I know, it seems unfair. But there are additional risk factors associated with euphoric mania. And compliance is especially challenging."

"Well, at least there's that." I looked over at my dad, who seemed lost in thought. He removed his glasses and cleaned them with something in his lap before putting them back on. Lately, I'd been ruminating on the physical and emotional toll of my disorder on him. But, at the very least, he was still handsome and fit. I noticed Linda's left arm angled toward him and thought they must've been holding hands under the table. Given all that I'd put him through lately, I was thankful that he had her.

"I've also noticed that when she starts to decline, Sunny really isolates herself and you can barely get a sentence out of her," said Joshua, startling me out of my thoughts. Everyone nodded in agreement, likely envisioning me in my most irascible, nearly mute state.

"That's a good point, Joshua. I've actually noticed that too. And what about preventive measures, what else can we add?" said Dr. Turner, looking at me.

I looked down at the paper. "I see a lot of good ones. Spending time in nature or with animals also helps me. Along with cooking and reading," I said.

"Great, I'll add those to the list. Also, you will see that I've added group therapy to this list. Sunny, I *strongly* encourage you to attend group therapy for people with psychotic disorders. There's an excellent one near the hospital that meets on Sundays. I've also encouraged Joshua to attend a support group for family members. Of course, it would be beneficial for you two as well," she said, looking at my dad and Linda who nodded their heads. "I'm going to add those two groups and their contact information on the bottom of the page." Group therapy sounded perfectly horrible to me and I didn't see Joshua wanting to go either. It would be a last resort.

"I have a couple of questions," said Joshua looking at me. "I've noticed that when you're not doing well, you start exercising *like crazy*. Just disappearing on long runs or walks. And you get extremely thin. So, I'm not sure that exercise in and of itself is such a great preventative measure for you."

"I've noticed that too," added my dad. I could see Linda nodding her head as well. Nice that there was such a consensus regarding my peculiarities.

"So, maybe the long walks or runs are a way to self-isolate?" asked Dr. Turner looking at me.

"Hmm. Well, I guess I do tend to take off when I get really anxious. It's almost as if I'm trying to outrun my thoughts…and people, I suppose." I immediately regretted my words, worrying that exercise would be removed from my list of approved activities. On top of everything else, there was no way I'd allow myself to get out of shape.

"Okay, so for the time being, do you think you can limit your exercise to thirty minutes outside the home? It would also be really great if you could go on your walks with someone. Or come up with some other types of exercise, like attending a class."

"Yeah, I can do those things." Okay, this was manageable. *But no fucking yoga.*

"Great. I'm going to add lengthy solitary walks/runs to the list of warning signs."

"Also, isn't it kind of unhealthy to have several shelves full of Holocaust books, you know, considering…?" asked Joshua, looking at the doctor. My dad was nodding in enthusiastic agreement. If I was feeling paranoid, this meeting would've done me in.

"Sunny, what are your thoughts about the books?"

"Well, I guess I don't need *all* of them—okay, most of them. I just felt like, given what Baba and Papa went through in *real life*, the least I could do is learn as much about the Holocaust as possible. And also keep the books near, just out of respect." I paused for a moment, "I guess it sounds kind of stupid when I say it out loud."

"Sweetheart, you aren't honoring Babcia and Papa by submerging yourself in that hell. Do you really think they would want that?" asked my dad gently.

I started getting a little teary. "No, they wouldn't."

"And you've already educated yourself more on the topic than the vast majority of people. So why do you need the books, what purpose do they serve?" he asked before running a hand through his hair.

"I'm not really sure." I wiped the tears from my face. I could feel Joshua caressing my hand.

"Sunny, would you be willing to save some of the books, those that are most important to you—maybe five and no more than ten, and get rid of the rest?" asked Dr. Turner.

I sighed and thought for a moment. "Well, actually, I could give them to a Jewish school or charity, maybe help others to be more informed. I like that idea." I really did. It would appease my family while also making me feel like the books were serving an honorable purpose.

Everyone nodded in agreement. I would give away the books that felt like bricks pulling me further into the mud. And I would keep only those that had touched me the deepest, such as Primo Levi's memoir. I felt ready, even somewhat relieved, to let go of the rest. And I knew it would've made my grandparents happy, which was everything.

Dr. Turner wrote some notes. "Okay, we're making great progress here. You will keep a weekly schedule, watch for warning signs, practice prevention, and contact me and Dr. Bensen when any of you notice signs of a recurrence. If you can't get a hold of us immediately, call the ER. If you feel the situation is urgent, go to the ER. And remove the majority of the Holocaust books." She looked at me and Joshua. "By the way, when you empty out the bookshelf, it will leave room for other things—like art or keepsakes that are special to the two of you. It can become a very positive and loving space for your family."

Joshua smiled. "I love that."

I loved the idea too. But I was tired of the meeting. We'd been in that room for over an hour and I was getting antsy. I could feel crusted blood around my thumbnail and I had to go to the bathroom. I wanted out of there.

Dr. Turner glanced at the large round wall clock. "We're just about done. I'd just like to go over a couple of things about medication. Importantly, you cannot constantly remind someone to take their medication. It's ultimately up to that person and pushing too hard can create conflict. So instead, I'd like you to set up a plan to help Sunny remember on her own. I suggest that you thoughtfully place the medicine in a location where you can't miss it each day. For some, this is next to a toothbrush or the coffee pot—whatever makes the most sense to you. And then set up daily medication phone reminders. Does that make sense?" she asked, looking at me.

I nodded. "Yes, I've already thought about that. I feed Chester in the morning and before bed, so I can keep my medication next to his food. He nudges and yells at me when he's hungry, so he's a perfect little alarm clock." I missed that kitty so much.

"I think that's a great idea. But just make sure you're the one feeding him and that your medication is in a place where it can't be missed."

"Okay." My foot was shaking, causing the table to move. I really needed the bathroom.

Dr. Turner leafed through her papers and pulled out yet another one. "My clients often find it helpful to think of medication like an insurance policy for wellness. Along these lines, a compliance contract is good way to remind people of their responsibility to follow the treatment plan." She passed the paper to me. "By signing this, you are agreeing to take your medication as prescribed. There are more details here of course, but that's the gist of it. Think of it as any type of formal agreement, such as a lease or business contract. Except this one is far more important than those because this one is about your life. Please read it over and, if you agree, sign it and I'll do the same. Then I'd like you to tape it somewhere with high visibility."

I glanced at it, that was enough. There was no way in hell I'd be plunged back into the snake pit without a fight. I signed it immediately. Dr. Turner added her signature and gave it to Joshua to take home. I imagined it prominently displayed along with our college diplomas and other certificates. Only, instead of an accomplishment, this document felt more like a warning notice, forever reminding us that I was not a normal person. And that, without meds, sickness would commandeer my body, leaving me at its mercy. The lack of trust stung a little, but I knew I'd earned it.

Dr. Turner looked at the clock again and said, "Well, I don't know about all of you, but I'm ready for dinner. I think we've covered everything, unless you have any questions?"

We looked around at each other, but no one spoke. I think we were all pretty overwhelmed by everything. And Joshua's stomach had been growling angrily for the past ten minutes.

"Great. Well, if you think of anything, give me a call. Remember to follow a routine and to practice plenty of self-care—and I don't just mean Sunny, this goes for each of you," she said somewhat sternly, looking at everyone but me. "And Sunny, none of us can watch you all of the time, nor should we. And we can't read your mind. It is *your* responsibility to confide in someone on the team if you start to experience any warning signs. Will you do that?"

"Yes, absolutely." I was done holding it all in. And I was starting to believe that my family would always be here, despite the sickness idling inside me. I no longer wanted to bear this burden alone, it was too much for one person.

"Excellent." She put both of her palms down on the table, gesturing that we were finally done. Everyone pushed back their chairs and thanked the doctor. She shook each of our hands and reminded us to contact her if anything came up. As we left the room, I thought about Dr. Turner. She had somehow materialized out of the rubble that nearly buried me; I felt indebted to her.

The four of us walked quietly toward my room, stopping in front of it. "Well, that was a lot of information. How do you feel, sweetheart?" asked my dad.

"I feel...optimistic and, I guess more than anything, I feel loved."

His eyes grew watery as he gave me a gentle smile. "Well, that's one thing you can always count on."

"Also, I really need to pee." My bladder was starting to ache.

Both he and Linda quickly hugged me and said goodbye. Joshua hung out in my room, eating the leftover Mexican food. He didn't stay long, though, as he had some cleaning to do back at home. Before he left, we stood in the middle of the room holding each other for several minutes.

"I love you, Joshua."

"I love you, too, Slugger."

I held him at arm's length, looking at the face I loved so dearly. His trusting eyes overwhelmed me with a sense of contrition for what it had cost him to be with me. "Every time something awful has happened over the past year, I kept thinking, 'how much more can he take? When will he finally leave?' But here you are, still loving me anyway," I said, gently caressing the back of his head.

He kissed me softly behind my ear and whispered, "Wild horses."

That night I slept like the dead. It was as if the culmination of my entire hospital stay hit me all at once, knocking me out. I woke up disoriented and, once I got my bearings, I saw a little gift on my nightstand. It was flat and rectangular, wrapped in pretty lavender paper with a purple organza bow tied in the middle. There was a small card with a picture of a flower garden on the outside. Inside, the card read: "Sunny, this prayer, which I believe transcends all religious and spiritual beliefs, is a beautiful reminder of the power of acceptance. I hope you will allow it to guide you in finding the comfort and peace you so deserve. Yours truly, Dr. Turner." I opened the gift and found a black wooden frame containing several lines of calligraphy. It read:

> *God, grant me the serenity*
> *to accept the things I cannot change,*
> *the courage to change the things I can,*
> *and the wisdom to know the difference*

Of course I'd heard this before, it was the *Serenity Prayer*. I knew it was typically associated with recovery from alcoholism; but as I reread it multiple times, I could see that it applied to so much more. And it most certainly applied to me, as acceptance had been one of my biggest obstacles in getting better. It was a touching gesture from someone who knew me so well. I had never achieved serenity in my life—even before the madness, but at least now I could believe it was within my grasp.

After I drank my coffee and organized my stuff, I sat on my bed and waited for Joshua to pick me up. I heard footsteps in the hall and a light tap on the door. When I said, "Come in," Dr. Bensen entered. He must have just come from home, his blue suit and white shirt looked freshly pressed and he smelled like men's cologne or fancy soap.

"Good morning, Sunny. How are you doing today?" he asked cheerfully.

I paused for a moment, and said, "You know, I'm actually okay."

He looked at me a bit strangely. "I think that may be the most honest response you've ever given me to that question," he said with a light smile.

"Gee, thanks," I said sarcastically. But I knew what he meant.

He asked me the standard questions about side effects, my mood, and various other symptoms. I was feeling better than I had in a long time. The Wankers were slumbering and, while thinking about the Nazis still gave me a pang of anxiety, this was mostly due to my fear of relapse. At least at this moment in time, I knew they couldn't hurt me.

"You look really nice today," I said.

"Oh, this old thing!" he said, looking down at his suit. "It's my wedding anniversary today, so I thought I'd get extra spruced up. We're going out after work."

"That's awesome, congratulations!"

"Thank you. She's put up with me for fifteen years, so I can't complain."

"Yeah, right, she's lucky to have you." She most definitely was.

"That's kind of you to say. Thank you," he smiled.

He gave me all of the usual reminders and shook my hand warmly. "You're going to be okay, Sunny. I'm honored to know you."

I sure would miss him.

A short time later, Joshua arrived. He picked up my bag and I carried the folder of sketches. As we left the room, I thought again of Heidi and how she'd succumbed to her illness. And of gentle Eddy, who was still at war with his. And there were so many other similarly tormented people who'd touched my life—they would never be forgotten.

I wrapped my arm through Joshua's and headed down the hospital corridor, hearing the usual beeps and chatter, and inhaling the oppressive stench that would always be linked to this place. When Joshua pushed open the door to the outside, I stepped out and paused for a moment, closing my eyes. Feeling the sun on my face, I could hear birds, cars, and an airplane flying overhead.

"Are you good?" asked Joshua.

I looked into my beautiful husband's eyes, which the sunlight cast in hues of copper and green, and saw the unwavering love behind them. I softly kissed his cheek, and said, "I am. Let's go home."

Chapter 40 ❧ Sunny

There's nothing like being locked away in the psych ward to make you appreciate home. I felt like I'd been gone for weeks and had never been so grateful for comfort, quiet and privacy. But Chester was by far the best part. After I kissed the mezuzah, I dropped my bag and immediately went to look for him. I woke him from a deep sleep on our bed, hugging and kissing him until he'd finally had enough and squirmed out of my hands. I was worried that he didn't love me anymore, but, on that first night home, he couldn't get enough of me. He walked all over me for more than an hour, going around in circles and kneading my stomach to the tune of that raspy motor I'd so missed. It was well worth the disruption. That sweet kitty eased my battered spirit, reassuring me I was loved.

Joshua took a couple of days off to help me get acclimated. At first, everything felt surreal—as if I belonged in neither the hospital nor the outside world. I floated around the condo like a spirit untethered, noticing reminders of my mental collapse around every corner—each threatening to pull me back into the muck. I was especially repelled by the family room couch, as it was a place where I suffered, plotted, and sobbed in desperation as the sickness took over. Plus, I kept picturing Milquetoast on the other side of the room, silently judging me with her non-wonky eye as I sat fuming with indignation. I also noticed that our entire knife set had disappeared. So, I guess if I wanted cucumbers or carrots in my salad, I was shit out of luck. Although, given my track record, I wouldn't have trusted me with knives either.

And then there were the books. Joshua was right; they symbolized something profoundly disturbing at a personal level. Not only did they connect me to the heart of my delusions, but I kept picturing the ethereal image of my mother in the hallway, commanding me to stack them in piles.

Afraid of succumbing to my triggers, I decided to make some immediate changes to my surroundings. First, as the couch continued to quietly mock me, I threw a quilt over it. But that wasn't enough. Then I managed to drag it to the other side of the room, rearranging the other furniture along with it. As I stood back admiring my work, I decided I liked the room's new look. But, more importantly, when I sat on the couch, I wasn't immediately slapped in the face with visions of myself slipping into the abyss.

I most dreaded my next task, which was to remove the bulk of my Holocaust books. As I stood in front of rows and rows of memoirs, I considered their authors. These people—*my people*—had experienced and witnessed an earthly Gehenna only they could comprehend. Had I done them sufficient justice by learning their stories? Could they sense my profound need to understand? I had to think so; it was my only way forward.

As I sat cross-legged on the floor, I pulled each book from the shelves, reading the inside covers and flipping through the pages almost as a way of saying goodbye. Then, as I determined whether each one belonged in the pile on the right (those I would keep) versus the pile on the left (those I would get rid of), I had a haunting visualization of Mengele and his indifference as he alone decided the fate of countless innocents. As I tried to shake the ghastly image from my mind, I heard Joshua come back from a run. I looked over my shoulder and saw him standing in the hall staring at me, his face ashen.

"Um, Sunny, what are you doing?" He spoke slowly before wiping his sweaty forehead with his T-shirt.

"I'm just organizing my books, you know, so we can get rid of most of them." Trying to appear as composed and coherent as possible, I smiled, adding, "Don't worry, I'm still here, amongst the living."

He looked somewhat relieved. "And the furniture?" he asked, looking around the room.

"I wanted to try something new—make a fresh start." He continued to stand there blankly. "Geez, everything's fine. I just didn't want reminders of what happened. I'm okay, truly." I went over and gave him a hug, kissing each of his salty cheeks. I could feel his body loosen up as he let out a huge breath. "There's no crime in rearranging the furniture, you know?"

"I know, I just…"

"I promise I'm okay. But I need to get back to work. Can you please find me some boxes?"

"Sure." He went into the kitchen and drank some water, then headed out to the garage.

So this would be my life—each of my behaviors held under a microscope in order to gauge whether I was normal, actively psychotic, or just Sunny—which often fell somewhere in between. I thought I should make myself a sign which I could flip depending upon my condition, sort of like those on store windows: "Lucid: Come on In" versus "Crazy as Fuck: Come Back Next Month."

I hated seeing my husband's alarmed expression and knew it would take time for him to believe I'd be okay. But, at least for now, I would walk on tiptoes, tempering any behaviors that might appear to tip the psychogenic scale.

While Joshua took a shower and worked in the study, I continued my sorting until I had twelve boxes ready to go, and just seven books remaining on the shelf. We immediately dropped the boxes off at the Jewish Cultural Center before I changed my mind. I experienced a moment of sadness when I let them go, but it was quickly replaced with an affirming sense of lightness. I realized there was something more to those books that had been tugging at me for some time. Even beyond reminding me of man's bottomless capacity for cruelty, they forced me to repeatedly visualize the horrors experienced by those I loved most. I hoped their removal would help me to envision Baba and Papa as I knew them rather than as they were during the nightmare years.

That evening, as I put away the rest of my stuff from the hospital, I came across the framed Serenity Prayer. After reading it a few times, I propped it up in the middle of the empty bookshelf, allowing the poignant words to replace the burden of the books on my conscience. Following doctors' orders, I also hung both my treatment plan and medication contract in the kitchen just above the cat food. Seeing them at least twice a day reminded me of my commitment to wellness, not to mention the miseries that would befall me if I didn't comply. Chester obediently did his part, yelling for his food morning and evening (and often in between), never allowing me to slip up. Sometimes his meows sounded like "Now!"—which Joshua found hilarious, but I took as a sure sign of brilliance.

My treatment team performed their roles like star employees. Each day someone was around, watching my every move. After the constant clamor and activity of the hospital, I relished the idea of being alone. But my family remained steadfast. Even when Joshua was home during that first week, my dad or Linda showed up around mealtime, often with dinner in hand. And, while he tried to be subtle, I could see my dad peering around the rooms—making sure my medication was where it belonged, and that nothing suggested my unraveling. I tolerated my family's constant presence by taking regular rest breaks in my room and reminding myself that the surveillance wouldn't last forever. But there also was a part of me that appreciated being distracted from my own thoughts, as well as the levity provided by the goofy banter between my dad and Joshua.

On my second Saturday home, both Linda and my dad showed up, leaving the kids at a birthday party. Linda handed me a bag of homemade molasses cookies and a fragrant bouquet of yellow Charlotte roses from her garden. As I thanked her and put the flowers in a vase, I heard my dad pushing for Mexican takeout. I yelled to the other room that we could actually *go out* to a restaurant, like regular people. That I wasn't triggered by sombreros and chimichangas. We walked to a favorite place of ours, but, after about thirty minutes, the noise and commotion started to get to me.

Although keyed up and anxious, I tried to ignore my feelings as long as possible. Aside from not wanting to ruin dinner, I felt stubbornly committed to being well enough to go to a damn restaurant. But I wasn't there yet. As utensils rattled against plates thanks to my shaking foot, I finally said I was uncomfortable and needed to leave.

I don't think my family could've finished their food and paid the bill any faster than if the restaurant was on fire. Perhaps they thought I was moments away from sliding under the table or warning the unsuspecting diners of an imminent aktion by the SS? The scene might've been comical had it not been so fresh. Although I did chuckle to myself when I imagined how useful this new dynamic could be for getting out of holiday parties.

Elizabeth came over the following week while Joshua was at work. She stood in the doorway like a massive burst of fresh air. Her long red hair hung in perfectly messy spirals, her face was pink and freckled from the sun, and she was carrying a brown paper bag. Seeing her felt as if nothing had changed in our friendships, we were still the same little girls who wandered through neighborhoods in search of lost cats, built elaborate forts out of blankets, and stayed up all night giggling.

"Hello, Ms. Sunshine!" she beamed before going in for a hug.

"Hello, Pinky Tuscadero," I said, using my old nickname for her. "Looks like you've gotten some sun." I guided her toward the family room.

"Yeah, Brandon and I were in Palm Springs hanging out with his parents." Brandon was Elizabeth's boyfriend. I hadn't met him yet, but she was clearly crazy about him.

"Oh, that must've been interesting," I said as we sat on the couch.

"It was fine until his dad got out the good Scotch. Then we had the joy of watching the old jackass get louder and more obnoxious with every sip. But his mom is really sweet. And, as you can see, I enjoyed sitting by the pool." She looked down at her pink arms.

"Ever heard of sunscreen?"

"Yeah, I missed a few spots." She reached for the bag and said, "I brought you a few things." She handed me two thick, hardback books and a plastic bag of candies with a pink bow. "It's nothing big. These are from Oprah's book club, so I hope they're up to your level," she said, smiling.

"Oh geez, I'm sure they are." I looked over the two books and they seemed interesting.

"And I know how you love your sour gummies!"

"I definitely do. That's really thoughtful, thank you so much," I said, setting the books and candy on the coffee table.

We talked a little more about nothing important as Chester curled up in her lap, purring raucously. "So, how are you doing?" she asked, almost alarming me with her sudden seriousness.

"I'm doing well. It was strange being at home at first. I felt like I was in the hospital forever, so it was sort of an adjustment."

She furrowed her auburn eyebrows, "What's it like in there, you know, in the hospital?"

I leaned back on the cushions and thought for a moment. How could I possibly explain my hospital experience to someone who'd never even stepped foot in a psych ward? That it was like being nestled under a protective blanket in the middle of a circus. She wouldn't get it. So I just mentioned the obvious aspects of it such as lack of privacy, noise, and boredom.

"What about the other patients? Were you around them much? What were they like?" Her voice was soft, almost conspiratorial.

I understood her curiosity. Before I became ill, I would've pictured a psych ward like something from a horror movie—its hallway floors littered with any manner of deranged bodies twitching and screeching obscenities. "Yeah, I saw other patients from time to time, especially when I started going to art therapy. I guess, like everybody, some were nice and others were more…um, noncommunicative." I wasn't ready to tell her about the patients, especially Heidi and Eddy, whom I needed to keep to myself for a while.

She chewed on her nail for a couple of seconds. "Were you scared? I mean, was anyone violent?" She leaned back and crossed her leg. She was wearing a light green sundress and four-inch brown wedges. Her legs were sunburnt, but not as bad as her arms.

I knew it was a common misperception that mentally ill people were dangerous and told her as much, adding, "Honestly, the people I met were only dangerous to themselves. Kind of like me. Actually, the people in the hospital were *exactly* like me, just…different, if that makes any sense." Chester switched to my lap and I scratched under his chin.

Her face softened and she touched my arm briefly. "I think it does. I'm *so* sorry about what you went through, with the deck and everything." She paused for a moment, seeming to weigh whether or not to ask the next question. "So, were you really planning to jump?"

Okay, she's really going here. "Yes, if my dad hadn't shown up, I'd have been splattered all over the street."

She flinched at my word choice.

"Sorry, yes, I would have jumped, I was done." I went into the kitchen and brought us each a glass of lemonade.

She took a few sips. "It's okay if you don't want to answer this, but why were you willing to do that?"

I exhaled loudly. I didn't like the line of questioning, but I knew it was inevitable. And necessary. I explained the hellish shitstorm that was my life at that time—the paranoia, the voices, and the aching shame over what I did to my siblings. And how I just didn't see any way out. As I recalled some of the worst moments of my life, I started feeling agitated. I pulled Chester closer and sank deeper into the couch.

With tears in her eyes, she said, "I'm *so* sorry, that sounds just horrible. Thank God you didn't go through with it. Not to sound selfish, but you're my best friend—it would have destroyed me." She sipped her drink and set it back down. "Do you think…I mean, could it happen again?"

I explained that I was no longer suicidal and hoped to never be again, that it would hurt my family too much. And that I would be okay as long as I took my meds, which I fully intended to do.

She was visibly relieved. "I'm so glad to hear that, otherwise I'll be shadowing you night and day, keeping your ass in check!"

"Ugh, just what I need, another watcher," I said dryly.

I took a deep breath and looked her in the eye. "Lizzie, I want you to know how sorry I am for shutting you out. I didn't want you to see me as a psychotic person, it's so humiliating. But I shouldn't have done that to you, I'm really sorry."

"Well, that's okay. But you don't need to be humiliated about it. I mean, it's a *disorder*, not a choice. You shouldn't be ashamed of what you can't help. Plus, I'm your friend, I'm not here to judge you. You can swing naked from a chandelier and I'll still love you," she said, smiling.

"Well, I'd be more inclined to straddle deck railings, but I appreciate the sentiment."

"Yeah, don't do that again."

"Yes, ma'am."

"What's it like having schizo…" She paused, forgetting the name of my illness.

"Schizoaffective disorder," I interjected. Oddly, no one had ever asked me this. I thought for a moment and said, "Well, when unmedicated, it's sort of like being trapped inside yourself. You're still in there somewhere, but never really alone. Your brain is not under your control—you are at the mercy of ideas you have no choice but to believe wholeheartedly, no matter how absurd. And the voices, which are just as real as the two of us talking, never let up. If I'm upset or scared, they feed off my feelings, punishing me without pause. And there's the mood swings and overwhelming paranoia that propels me to run and hide. Unfortunately, in my case, my tormentors were always Nazis, which was truly terrible. Think of your worst nightmare and multiply it by a hundred, then imagine no ability to wake up from it. That's the hell of this disorder." I drank the rest of my lemonade while my words sank in.

Elizabeth appeared transfixed. "Holy shit, Sunny, that's just absolutely dreadful. So, when you're delusional, can't you look around and see that it's the 21st century? I mean, how do you resolve knowing when and where WWII happened with being here in 2002?"

"It's sort of hard to explain, but even when I know logically that my beliefs are totally irrational and, well, crazy, every aspect of my perceptions and beliefs say otherwise. And if you say it's impossible for the SS to be after me, I'll just tell myself you don't have all of the facts, that you're misinformed. Or even that you're a collaborator. It's like my mind has been hijacked and no matter what sane people tell me, my beliefs will always land in support of the delusion. It's a dead end."

"Wow, I can't imagine that." She was leaning toward me, her eyebrows again furrowed.

We talked a little longer before she left to meet her boyfriend for dinner. It was such a relief to confide in her about everything. I admonished myself for pushing her away, then I admonished myself for admonishing myself. I still had much work to do.

I met with Dr. Turner three times per week, with someone, usually Joshua, driving me there until I put my foot down and insisted on driving myself. I was continuing to experience unrelenting guilt and shame, not only because of what happened with the kids, but also regarding the impact of my disorder on Joshua and my dad, the way I'd treated Linda over the years, my mortifying behavior at my old job, and whatever other transgressions my brain latched onto at the moment. Dr. Turner helped me identify the ways in which my excessive guilt actually aided me in avoiding or masking the feelings beneath it. Her theory made sense. I'd never been great at voicing feelings of anger; I hated to feel out of control and didn't want to hurt others. Yet, I was pissed at my mom for leaving me, at my dad for not telling me everything, and, most of all, at the goddamn Nazi murderers. She explained how, when I turned my anger inward—resulting in guilt—it was less terrifying than dealing with the true villains. But it was an ineffective strategy since it precluded me from dealing with my actual feelings. Through therapy, I would continue to chip away at my layers of guilt while also working on self-forgiveness.

If there were any silver linings to my illness, my relationship with Linda was the most obvious example. She eased her way into my life so unobtrusively during those summer weeks that I wasn't even annoyed by her increasing presence. She was like a phantom that quietly flitted about while gradually transforming into a more tangible, corporeal entity. At first, my dad came by multiple days a week, but eventually his work responsibilities only enabled him to reserve Mondays for me. Linda, who shared a babysitter with the neighbors, took over Thursdays and Fridays—always arriving promptly at noon, and rarely doing so empty-handed. She often brought flowers, baked goods, or drawings from the kids—which I hung in the kitchen.

Linda was patient and without judgment, even on days when I was sick to death of being around people. At some point during mid-July, I found myself opening up to her. We talked about my chaotic childhood, my anxiety, and my psychosis. I even confided in her about my feelings toward Debbie. Being a mother herself, she helped me to empathize with the experience of having a son who lived thousands of miles away with a mentally ill wife. She said this would be upsetting for her too. I even told her about my chronic constipation thanks to the Risperidone, which resulted in her bringing an endless array of organic fruits, vegetables, and even prunes—which made me laugh as I hunched over and said, "Thank you, Missy," in my best old lady voice.

When I discussed my illness with Linda—including some of my most embarrassing delusional beliefs—I didn't feel like a sideshow freak. She was consistently compassionate and nonplussed, and seemed to have endless kernels of wisdom when it came to relationships. The more Linda did for me, the more contrition I felt for how I'd treated her in the past. One afternoon, after she showed up with flowers for me and toys for Chester, I couldn't contain my guilt anymore. "Why are you always so kind to me?"

As she stood in the kitchen arranging blue hydrangeas in a crystal vase, she stopped moving for a moment and looked at me. "What do you mean?"

"Well, you're always bringing gifts, you take me shopping, you give me great advice—you know, just *everything*."

"That's how I treat the people I love."

She answered as if it were the most obvious thing in the world. I wasn't sure how to respond. But I remembered what Dr. Turner told me about guilt and wondered if something else was lurking underneath. I needed to clear the air. I set Chester's toys on the counter and leaned back against the refrigerator. "Linda, I'm so sorry for how I treated you as a teenager and even over the past five years. You're just so nice, I don't even know why I acted that way. But I really am sorry." It was a relief to finally get those words out.

She set the flowers down and smiled lovingly. "Sunny, you were a young girl with a severely mentally ill mother who died. I expected you to be sensitive about some new woman coming into your life and stealing time with your father. I knew I was no replacement for your mom and never could be, so I understood your resentment. And honestly, you weren't *that* bad."

"I don't know, I was kind of a brat."

She smiled. "Okay, you were a little bratty from time to time, but I never took it personally. And I fully accept your apology. But more than that, you need to forgive *yourself*. You acted that way because you were hurting. I've let it go and it's important that you do the same. Do you think you can do that?"

My God—this woman, was there no end to her goodness? Embarrassingly, I teared up a little bit. "Yeah, I'll try," I answered in a soft voice.

She came closer to me and pulled me in for a hug. As always, her hugs made me uncomfortable as hell, but I leaned into her as best I could. As I stood there, smelling her wispy blonde hair, I suddenly recognized the unconditional love and astounding kindness I was receiving—I'd felt this way with Baba too. Maybe these two slight women with their irrepressible strength and benevolence weren't so different? I hugged Linda back, subtly wiping a tear from my eye. I wasn't ready to say it yet, but I loved her too.

One particularly memorable day in late July, Linda surprised me by showing up with Maddy and Spencer. It was the first time I'd seen them since…well, since *it* happened, and I felt a confusing mix of shame, gratitude, and happiness. As I stood in the hallway, feeling frozen and dumbstruck, Maddy yelled, "Sunny, Sunny!" and both of them ran to me, putting their little arms around my legs.

I wiped the tears from my eyes and bent down on one knee as I squeezed both of them. "I missed you two monsters so much," I said, looking from one to the other.

"Me too!" said Maddy. Her blonde hair was in ponytails and she had chocolate or something smeared across her cheek.

"Me free!" added Spencer, who was wearing a Spiderman T-shirt.

I glanced over at Linda and saw that she was smiling as she put something away in the pantry.

Before I let go of the kids, I needed to say a few things—my apology tour wasn't over quite yet. "You know when I dragged you guys through the neighbors' yards and," looking at Maddy, "pulled you into that creepy shed?"

They both nodded their heads. "Daddy said not to bring it up with you," said Maddy. I could sense Linda no longer moving as she watched the scene closely.

"Daddy was just worried about me. But I'm okay now, you can talk to me about it. Do you have any questions?"

The kids looked at each other, not sure if it was okay to speak up. They glanced toward their mother who nodded her head ever so slightly.

"Who was the bad man?" asked Spencer with a worried expression.

I was taken aback as I felt the sting of his question. "Do you mean who was I running from?"

"Yeah," said both kids in unison.

"The thing is, there was no bad man. I have a disorder that made me *think* someone was after me. It's very important that the two of you know that there was *absolutely no bad man*, so please don't be afraid."

They both looked relieved. I knew my dad and Linda had gone over this with them, but I guess they weren't convinced.

"There are two more things I need you to know: First, I'm much better now because I have medicine and people who help me. And second, I'm so very sorry for scaring you like that. I hope you can forgive me."

Almost at the same time, they said, "That's okay." I felt a tear roll down my cheek, but before I could wipe it way, Maddy's little hand reached over and did it for me. "Don't cwy," said Spencer.

"I'm okay," I said, trying to get a hold of myself.

"Sunny?" asked Maddy, pulling back a little from me. I wiped my eyes and tried to brace myself for the next question.

"Where's Chester?"

"I think he's asleep on my bed," I said, laughing at the abrupt change of subject.

As the two of them took off for the bedroom, I could see that they really were okay. And despite everything, they still loved me. In that one beautiful moment, the shame that had been constricting my chest released its hold and allowed me to breathe again.

That evening when Joshua came home, I was doing the dishes with the music cranked. I felt more at peace than I had in months. As I danced around the kitchen to "I Am a Rock" by Simon and Garfunkel—a song I had always loved—it dawned on me that I was, in fact, not a rock or an island, as I had always believed. I had people who loved me and would do whatever it took to keep me from drowning. As Joshua saw me dancing around like a fool, I ran to him and he spun me around, lifting my feet off the floor. No, I was not alone. And although it took me twenty-three years to realize it, I never had been.

I continued to improve over the following weeks, taking my doctors' orders very seriously. I never missed a dose of medicine and Chester never tired of reminding me. I went on walks every day and started running again. Still uncomfortable being in crowds, I found private places on the beach where I would draw or read a book. And, once I'd planted my sunflower seeds, I sketched from the deck as the little buds eventually broke through the ground.

I thought of Heidi a lot during that time, especially when I was sketching. Although she was gone—of this I was now certain—I often felt her presence. Whether it was something beautiful in nature or a sad movie, reminders of my lost friend were around every corner. But her memory had a way of inspiring me, making me want to stay healthy and to experience the joys in life that had so eluded her.

One afternoon as I was organizing my studio, I came across Heidi's stack of drawings. As I looked through them, I was once again haunted by their realness, their brutal rendering of Heidi's considerable torment. This, I remembered, was the reason I'd pushed the drawings into the corner. But there was one sketch that only made me smile. It was supposed to be of a fruit bowl Ginny brought from home. The dish consisted of several ancient-looking bruised apples, two oranges, and one half-rotten lemon. The sight of that sad fruit bowl made Heidi and I laugh so hysterically that we were excused from art therapy. We decided to find ourselves a new object of inspiration—perhaps something that wasn't decomposing. As we walked by the nurses' station, I saw Dr. Bensen's coffee mug on the counter. It was white with a blue Rorschach inkblot in the middle. I remember joking with Dr. Bensen that the inkblot was obviously a pair of rabid demons having sex, which made him laugh heartily. "Fortunately for you, I don't use projective tests," he said smiling. The mug was sitting on a white plate along with the remains of a mostly eaten blueberry muffin.

"Let's draw this!" I said, gesturing to the cup. Heidi and I looked around conspiratorially before I grabbed the mug and saucer, and headed toward the sunroom. Once we found some paper and pencils, we sat on the sofa and sketched for about an hour. I wasn't happy with my work, but Heidi managed to bring those simple objects to life—you could almost smell the mustiness of the stale coffee and the sweetness of the crumbs. She used a colored pencil for the blue inkblot, which made it pop against the white paper. Sitting on the floor of my studio, that drawing reminded me of a rare and fleeting moment when Heidi was almost happy. It also reminded me that I played a part in bringing about that sacred moment. And it reminded me of Dr. Bensen— who held a special place in my heart. I decided to frame the drawing, adding periwinkle matting that accentuated the inkblot. I hung it in the kitchen above the coffee pot so that each morning I could sense both Heidi and Dr. Bensen there with me, pushing me to keep moving forward, and to believe in the worthiness they saw in me.

When my birthday rolled around on August 10th, my family had a party for me at my dad's house. It was a sizzling hot day which I spent floating in the pool and playing with the kids until they exhausted me. There seemed to be no residual effect of what I did to them. They were just as silly, energetic and annoying as ever. Elizabeth showed up too, just in time for dinner. For dessert, my dad presented my favorite homemade peppermint candy ice cream. As he placed one big candle in my bowl, Maddy said, "Hey, where's the cake?"

"Yeah, where's the cake, Slugger?" teased Joshua as he mimicked a baseball pitcher.

"Ha, ha, you're so funny. But who needs cake when you have *ice cream!*" I said, causing the kids to start chanting, "Ice cream, ice cream, ice cream!"

As Joshua and I lay in bed that evening, something that had been in the back of my mind for a while was tugging at me. Lying on my side, I propped myself up on one elbow and looked at my handsome husband. He was shirtless and his tanned chest contrasted with the white sheets. He looked more relaxed than he had in months—something I hoped would not be crushed by the conversation I needed to have.

"Honey?"

"Yes, my love." He turned on his side to face me.

"It was fun playing with the kids today."

"It was, but also exhausting! Don't those two ever slow down?"

"Yeah, they're a handful. But I love them so much."

"I know. Me too."

"So, I guess, I mean…" I couldn't find the right words. "I don't think I should have any biological children, not with my genes." There, it was out. While I'd never been gung ho about having children, there was a time not long ago when one seemed okay; but now even that was beyond imagining. Besides, I was perfectly fine with pets. I held my breath as I waited for his response.

"Oh, I know," he said nonchalantly, moving his index finger lightly along my arm.

I propped myself up a bit higher. "But, aren't you upset or disappointed? I mean, don't you want to, you know, sire your own offspring?"

He laughed. "I'm not all that interested in breeding. The world's overpopulated enough."

I'd never heard him say this and was a little stunned. I could've sworn he wanted at least two kids and hoped this wasn't only for my benefit. "You're *really* okay without having kids? Or at least biological ones. We could always adopt one day—I mean, once I'm stabilized for a while."

With Chester plunked down between us, Joshua petted his head then reached over to touch my hair. "This is more than enough."

Chapter 41 ❧ Sunny

Before leaving the hospital, both of my doctors had reminded me that a hospitalization is not a cure. I would still have challenges and need to continually monitor and manage my symptoms. That summer, as I became stronger and gradually rejoined the world, I did indeed experience setbacks. A few days after my birthday, Joshua and I were invited to dinner with several executives from his company. I dreaded the idea and didn't want to go, especially since at least some of Joshua's coworkers knew I'd been in the psych ward. I felt incredibly self-conscious as I imagined them whispering about Joshua's poor, loony wife. Or picturing me strapped to a gurney with an electrode secured to each temple. But I'd already wormed out of multiple invitations, so I knew it was time.

Although I dressed up and made sure my hair and makeup were perfect, I felt like an outcast amongst the three couples seated with us at a pretentious French restaurant. Everyone, especially the women, was almost sickeningly sweet toward me—as if I were a puppy or decrepit old granny. And despite its presence looming overhead, no one actually brought up my illness, but only danced around it. Although awkward and uncomfortable, I tried to smile and contribute to the banal conversation. But by the end of dinner, my head was throbbing and two of my fingers were bloodied.

I was disappointed that my social awkwardness had shown limited improvement despite my meds and psychotherapy, and discussed this with Dr. Turner at our appointment the following day. She reminded me that, along with schizoaffective disorder, I also had the comorbid diagnosis of social anxiety disorder. It was true that I had battled social anxiety to the point of avoiding parties, meetings, presentations, and even small gatherings my entire life. Hell, I had to take Xanax to get through staff meetings at my old job. Over the coming sessions, she focused more on my social anxiety, using a cognitive-behavioral approach to help me combat my feelings of inadequacy and fear of looking like an idiot. But I knew I'd always be uncomfortable around new people, so another aspect of my growth was to accept that part of myself instead of evaluating and beating myself up after each and every social interaction.

My first major challenge that summer occurred in mid-August, not long after that dreadful dinner. It was a Sunday morning and I was planning a romantic dinner for Joshua. I made a list and drove to a large grocery store downtown. Things were going well—I'd added almost everything and found my way over to the wine section. I wasn't used to buying wine and couldn't remember the name of Joshua's favorite Syrah. As I stared at the endless rows of bottles, I started to feel overwhelmed. I told myself to get a grip and grabbed the nearest bottle. As I tried to make myself put it in the cart, I glanced up toward the champagne rack and froze. Although his back was to me, I saw a tall, thin figure with orange-blonde hair perusing the champagne. Even without seeing his face, my mind somehow determined that it was indeed that priggish old bastard, Penterhaus.

My head clouded over, leaving me confused as to whether he was a pompous old guy or an Aryan who'd come to find me. As I closed my eyes and tried to convince myself that he couldn't possibly be an Aryan and that my thoughts were grossly irrational, *they* interjected with their usual abuse: *Crazy bitch. Stupid whore. Crazy stupid bitch.*

Oh no! I thought helplessly. I hadn't hallucinated since the hospital and was distraught and confused by the voices. But this time I wasn't having it! After another long string of *crazy stupid bitch*, I said, "Shut up, Wankers!" My words must've been loud, since several people began to stare in my direction. Using a softer voice, I said, "Go away, you stupid Wankers! I don't believe anything you say! Get lost!"

As people continued to stare, I began shaking so badly that the wine bottle slipped from my hand and shattered all over the floor. "Oh holy fuck!" I exclaimed without thinking. Now numerous people were blatantly watching and not one offered to help as broken glass and red wine spilled all over the floor, the wine display, and my pink sneakers. As I backed away from the awful scene, I apologized to an approaching store clerk and ran out of the store leaving my full grocery cart behind.

As I ran toward my car, the Wankers continued their assault: *Stupid pathetic bitch. Stupid bitch. Whore. Whore. Whore.* Once in the driver's seat, I yelled at them for several minutes. Eventually, I calmed down just enough to call Joshua.

"Hello, my love, what's up?" I heard music in the background.

Breathing hard, I said, "Joshua, I don't feel good. I, I…I saw someone, Penterhaus, at the store." I tried to catch my breath. "The Wankers came back. I'm scared," I said, holding the phone in my trembling hand.

"Sunny, where are you?"

I gave him my location.

"Hold tight—do *not* go anywhere. I'll be right there. I love you."

He was there in less than ten minutes. He sat in the passenger seat and held me as I continued to shake.

"It's okay, honey. They told us there would be triggers, but we can handle this," he soothed. He had left messages with both of my docs before leaving the house and his phone started to buzz. It was Dr. Turner. She reiterated Joshua's words, telling me that break-through symptoms were typical and not to catastrophize. I told her about seeing someone I thought was Penterhaus.

"So, you say you *thought* you saw Penterhaus? You aren't sure?" she asked.

"I only saw the back of his head, but it sure looked like him."

"Okay, let's think about this. You don't actually *know* if it was him since you didn't see his face. *But*, even if it *was* him—which seems unlikely—then you basically saw an old man you used to work with. He's not a Nazi, he's just a man going shopping. Right?"

I could feel my breathing slow down as she spoke. "Yeah, I guess so."

"Please remember that. He can't hurt you and neither can the voices."

We talked a little longer before Joshua took me home where I rested on the couch until my nerves steadied. I thought more about what Dr. Turner had said. Penterhaus's face had somehow become linked to the most horrible parts of my delusions. Even if he was pompous and snooty, he was still just an old man who worked in publishing—nothing more. It almost made me feel sorry for him.

Dr. Bensen also called not long after the incident, asking me several questions and offering reassurance that I would be okay. We would discuss things further during my appointment the following week. That evening Joshua made dinner while I lounged around. After taking my meds, I went to bed early, holding Chester close to my heart.

When I went to see Dr. Bensen on Monday morning, I was well rested with a better frame of mind. Mostly I was embarrassed and worried that it would happen again. As I sat in his office staring at the bird photographs, Dr. Bensen took a seat across from me, holding a large mug of coffee. He was wearing black jeans and a beige cashmere sweater. He asked me more about what happened, which I described in detail.

"So, you had a trigger, immediately called your husband, and spoke to your doctors. And you also talked back to the voices. What did you do when you got home?"

"Nothing much, just rested."

"And you took your meds?"

"Of course."

"Then I'd say you did what you were supposed to. We've always known this won't be easy and that you will need to manage your disorder. It seems to me that you managed it quite well."

I hadn't thought about it like this. "Oh yeah, I guess so."

"This being said, I'm going to increase your Risperidone a little bit, which should help to minimize breakthrough symptoms."

I liked that idea. He talked about the medication and side effects as he wrote a prescription. "How are you feeling about everything we've discussed?"

"I guess I feel better. You say it's normal—and I use that term lightly—to have occasional symptoms even though I'm taking my meds?"

"Yes, it can happen, particularly after experiencing a stressor. But I've noticed over the years that the less a patient resists treatment, the more minimal the relapse. I believe that's what happened here, which enabled you to nip it in the bud." He sipped his coffee, which smelled delicious.

"Yeah, but now I'm scared to go to the store again. I'm so embarrassed! I can't believe I broke a bottle of red wine all over the floor—it's horrible!" I could feel myself getting amped up. How many damn times would I have to mortify myself?

He smiled patiently. "It's not the first time there's been a spill at a grocery store, nor will it be the last. When my sister was five, she vomited all over the frozen food in the only store in town. So, it could be worse."

"Yikes, that's disgusting." I gazed out the window. Angry, dark clouds suggested rain, maybe even thunder.

"It certainly was. So, wait a couple of weeks, wear a hat, and go back. No one will know, trust me. And, in the grand scheme of things, being embarrassed at the grocery store is something you can move beyond. Truly."

He was making me feel so much better. The wine mess had germinated into something far worse in my head, but he brought it back into reality. "I'm also afraid of seeing Penterhaus. Although Dr. Turner has reminded me that he's just an old man."

"That sounds like a good reminder. He's not the person you think he is when you are delusional. Have you ever looked him up? I bet he's not even German."

"Oh, I don't know why I hadn't thought of that. He's actually British." Now I felt stupid.

"Just a sec," he said, walking over to his desk and sitting down in front of his computer. I spelled Penterhaus's name along with that of my old company as he typed. "Okay, is this him?"

I walked over and looked at the screen. With a deep sense of revulsion, I stared at that ancient, yellow-toothed geezer. Dr. Turner was right, he was just an old man. "That's definitely him," I said.

"He doesn't look all that powerful to me. But he's well accomplished in the publishing world, there's a lot written about him. And there are several photos too. Hey, check this out," he said, enlarging one of the pictures.

As I looked at that withered old face, something immediately jumped out at me. "Holy shit," I whispered. "He's wearing a yarmulka."

"Yes, he is." He swiveled his chair in my direction, looking me in the eye. "So now what will you do if you see him at the store?"

Stupefied by this new discovery, I let out a huge exhale and shrugged my shoulders, "Say, Shalom Aleichem?"

I had a meeting with Dr. Turner the following day. She also gave me kudos for managing my symptoms, but we spent most of our time discussing the Wankers. I told her how I'd argued with them, which may have helped, but that I was discouraged about their return. I wanted them to completely disappear. I wanted them *dead*. Dr. Turner described a strategy called reattribution. In doing so, she asked me to go into more detail about the experience, with emphasis on how I was feeling at the time. I reiterated that I thought I saw someone who wanted to hurt me, and how upsetting and terrifying that was. I also told her that I was still feeling a little off that day because of the dinner with Joshua's colleagues, which had battered my self-confidence.

Taking in all of my information, Dr. Turner showed me how my hallucination could be attributed to my response to the stress of both the dinner and the possible Penterhaus sighting. She explained how attributing my reaction as a rational response to stress would help to normalize my behavior. In other words, if it was a *stress reaction*, then maybe it wasn't so bizarre or insane after all. It was a perspective I hadn't considered, but completely welcomed.

And so my first relapse since being hospitalized came and went that August; but it did so without my landing in the ER, hiding in sheds, vomiting up "poisoned" food, climbing on deck railings, or taking orders from cemetery ghosts. There was empowerment in the realization that, even during a relapse, I still had some control over just how far down the rat hole my disorder could take me.

During the hotter days that summer, I often sketched at the beach or next to my dad's pool. When he had a break from work, my dad would sit next to me and chat. I knew he was there to check in on me; but, after a while, it seemed that he simply enjoyed my company. If I was sketching, he always offered words of encouragement. He especially loved my animal drawings and often pointed out new birds for me to sketch. When he mentioned that the sketches needed color, I told him I had signed up for a watercolor class in September. I had little experience with paint and was excited about bringing some vibrancy to my work. He was thrilled about the idea, complimenting me on my talent and saying I'd have no problem picking up the new skill.

We also talked about my mom. Although discussing her sometimes made him uncomfortable, there were questions that had continued to gnaw at me. One afternoon in late August, as we were quietly lounging about, I decided to take advantage of his attention.

"When mom wasn't totally out of it, what was she like as a mother? I mean, did she like being my mom?" I glanced over at him, using my hand to shade my eyes. The air was heavy and smelled like sunblock.

He immediately sprang up, saying, "Oh gosh, yes! Your mother did everything within her power to be a good mother to you, but of course, she was limited by her disorder. When she was her most calm and lucid, she read to you constantly—or made up stories of her own. Sometimes she fell asleep with you and I'd have to peel the books out of her hand and escort her to bed." He sounded animated, even a little proud of his former wife. He wiped his forehead with a towel, then applied more sunscreen.

"I remember that. I loved hearing her stories. She read a lot of nursery rhymes too, like the one about the little girl who was either very good or horrid. I always thought she was talking about me, that I was horrid."

He removed his sunglasses, revealing a perplexed expression. "What? Of course she didn't think that. She had a thing for Longfellow and I think maybe her mom read her the same poem; it wasn't about you, honey. In fact, she thought you were the most beautiful, perfect little girl in the world. She often dressed you up and took you out shopping, relishing the compliments about her beautiful baby. She was so proud of you."

I pictured my elegant mother pushing me around in a stroller as onlookers smiled. I liked the way it made me feel.

"Even when your mom wasn't doing well, she still spent hours playing with you, dancing, doing art, playing games, making cookies, and on and on. She made me feel like a schmuck for being too tired at the end of the day to join in the fun. You were always her first priority."

I could feel my pulse quicken. "But then why did she leave me?"

He leaned over and briefly touched my arm. "Sweetheart, she saw no other way out. Her life became agonizing. Her depressions were like the darkest, most torturous hell—they left her incapacitated. And during those times, she reproached herself endlessly about being a terrible mother, about not being good enough for you." Sweat was dripping off his chin, which he wiped with a towel. "She believed herself to be a failure when it came to motherhood and, toward the very end, was convinced you'd be better off without her. But *God,* did she love you, honey." He sipped from his water bottle and continued to look at me through blotchy sunglasses.

As I took in his words, I felt a pressure within myself start to give way. For as long as I could remember, I believed myself to be a burden to my mother—an annoying child who got in the way of her desire to be a famous artist. I did remember some fun times with her and, now that I thought about it, she played with a level of creativity and energy on par with that of a kindergarten teacher. And she was always smiling, laughing and singing during those times, so she must've enjoyed being with me. I could feel my confusion and sadness about my mother switch to something else, something more like a painful yearning to see her again. To be held by her and smell her perfume. And to tell her how much I miss her. "Dad, I wish I could put lilies on her grave. Why doesn't she have one?" I watched a black and orange butterfly land gracefully on a nearby table.

He leaned back in his chair, but continued to look at me. "She told me many times that, when she died, she didn't want people fussing over a hole in the ground. She thought she'd already burdened us enough in life and didn't want to add to it. But she also believed her soul would be all around us, *within us*—not buried in dirt. She wanted to be cremated and, perhaps knowing at some level that her life would not be a long one, she made that clear to me many times."

"Wow, she sounds just like me. I don't plan on dying any time soon, but when I do, I'd like my ashes scattered somewhere beautiful with a lot of animals."

He sighed and patted my arm with his hand. "Okay, but let's please not go there, my heart can't take it," he said sadly.

"Oh, I'm sorry Dad! I don't want to die. In fact, I feel better than I have in ages." I got up and kissed his warm cheek, which made him smile.

Those moments in the sun with my father brought us closer together and left me even more grateful for my family. These feelings were further bolstered as Joshua and I attended our first Shabbos at my dad's house since losing my grandparents. This dinner, which was held on a blistering hot day toward the end of August, was especially important since it occurred on what would've been Babcia and Papa's 56th wedding anniversary.

The dinner was bittersweet since it was Baba who had always prepared most of the food and lit the Shabbos candles, the latter eventually becoming my honored job. The meal was less formal than in the past, consisting of a mix of Jewish (kosher) and non-Jewish food. And since we lived near a fantastic bakery, Joshua and I brought the challah. My dad served a vegetarian cholent he'd recently learned how to make. It was a lot spicier than Baba's, but still delicious. I tried my hand at kugel for the first time and, while everyone was polite, it was a runny, overcooked disaster. I needed *a lot* more practice.

We went around the table and shared stories about my grandparents, some of which were pretty hilarious. Like when Baba sent my dad to school with a lunchbox full of cabbage pierogi that stunk up his entire classroom and earned him the nickname "Stinkybutt." When he came home upset and told her what happened, she replied, "What this means, 'Stinkybutt?' You go to school with dirty underwear?" My poor dad. But we couldn't help but laugh at his misfortune.

That Shabbos meal was also extraordinary because my father had invited Sam, the old guy who fought with Papa in the Polish resistance. Sam's body was disturbingly withered and he walked gingerly, using a cane. His thick hair was stark white and he had deeply etched smile lines around his mouth and pale blue eyes—which lit up whenever he spoke of my grandparents. He told us how his experiences during the war impacted his children, particularly his daughter, who couldn't speak of the Holocaust without crying. He described how both he and his late wife had wanted their children to understand what happened during the war, but to not be defined or consumed by it. They wanted the cycle of pain to stop.

Sam said I had a beautiful heart like both of my grandparents, who would want me to think of them as they were *after* the war: two loving and generous people who adored their first grandchild. When he said, "They did not survive the worst hell only to have their most beloved relive it, no?" I felt choked up. I knew my dad had filled Sam in on my illness, but I didn't mind. That sweet old man made me feel closer to my baba and papa.

After being home from the hospital for several weeks, I started getting antsy about not having a job. Along with the boredom, I hated that Joshua was the sole breadwinner. When I mentioned this to Dr. Turner, she had me create a vision board using magazine cutouts and my own drawings to illustrate where I'd like to see myself in the future. Along with art, a key theme on the board was language—particularly in the form of books. I covered the board with my favorite book titles and words, with punctuation marks scattered about. The vision board clearly revealed how much I missed my career. When I discussed this with Dr. Turner, she suggested I call my old boss, Emily. Of course, I told her there was no way in hell I'd go back to work there again after humiliating myself. Not that they'd even want me. But Dr. Turner thought Emily would have some good connections and, even if she didn't, what did I have to lose?

That therapy meeting was on a Monday, but I couldn't stop thinking about it for the rest of the week. Of course Dr. Turner was right, Emily knew tons of people in publishing. And, while she was likely appalled by what happened, I didn't think she actually *hated* me. For several days in a row, I tried to gather enough courage to make the call. I would go in my bedroom and shut the door, go over exactly what I wanted to say, and take several deep breaths. On the third day, I also drank a glass of wine. But I only dialed her number once, then immediately hung up when I heard the familiar voice. I was just too ashamed.

A couple of days later, I decided to email Emily instead. I told her how sorry I was for what happened and that I was much better now. I mentioned how much I loved my job there and missed the publishing world. I asked her if she had any suggestions for finding part-time editorial work. I also thanked her for mentoring me and being such a great manager (not entirely true, she was only a decent manager, but I was doing my best to butter her up). I obsessed over the message for a day or two and finally sent it.

I was shocked to see her reply within an hour. As I fidgeted and chewed my thumb, I opened her message. Emily, who had always seemed bookish and cold, said she was thrilled to hear from me, that she had been worried about me. *Huh?* She mentioned having a sister with mental illness and was so glad I was doing better. And best of all, she said I was the most skilled junior editor she'd ever had! I jumped from my chair and squealed with delight before reading the rest of the message. It got even better; she suggested working freelance. That way I could work from home and design my own schedule. She offered to send my resume to several of her friends who often hired freelancers. After writing her back and expressing my gratitude for her help, I danced around the condo. It seemed that I really could retain my identity as an editor—something I hadn't quite believed. That I wasn't just a girl with a mental disorder.

I'd been sketching a great deal since being discharged, varying my routine from parks, the beach, the desert, and my dad's backyard. My first priority was a new self-portrait, which I drew from a recent photo of myself standing in front of my burgeoning sunflower garden. When it was complete, I was pleased with what I saw. I had only a slight grin, but my eyes were dancing. I appeared coy and mischievous, like I had a secret. More than anything, I looked fully present—my mind belonging only to me. I wrapped the drawing in pink floral paper, tied a red satin ribbon around it and hid it under the bed.

It was the last Friday in August—the day before our one-year wedding anniversary, which was a huge milestone for us since I wasn't even sure I'd be alive at this point. I awoke feeling strangely calm snuggled there in my warm bed as Chester made biscuits on my belly. Feeling braver than I had all summer, I decided to try cooking again. I wanted to make something special for our anniversary and needed to go to the store. I would avoid the location of my recent humiliation and go to my favorite outdoor market instead. I took my meds, ate a light breakfast, fixed my hair and makeup, and put on my old cutoff Levi's with a pretty pink camisole.

I parked my car and walked to the farmer's market, which was particularly crowded that day. I took a deep breath and reminded myself that I was strong and that nothing there could hurt me. I'd kept my shopping list short this time and had already collected most of the produce when I heard my name. For only the briefest second, I worried that it was the fucking Wankers again. But then I heard it again and turned around. It was Viktor. I walked over to his flower stand for the first time in quite a while and he greeted me with a warm handshake.

"Beautiful Sunshine! It's been a long time, no? How gorgeous you look! Where have you been, I missed you!" His voice was animated and he smelled sweet, like pipe tobacco.

"Thank you, Viktor, I missed you too. I've been sick, but I'm better now."

"Oh no, I hope nothing serious." He appeared genuinely concerned.

"Well, yes, I guess it is. I have a mental illness similar to schizophrenia. But I'm managing it. I'm okay now." I'd never said those words out loud, not like this. It felt empowering to be so honest, but also terrifying. I chewed my cuticles as I awaited Viktor's awkward response, but he didn't flinch.

As both his face and voice softened, he said, "I'm sorry to hear that, but so glad you are better. You come see me any time you are having a bad day, yes?"

I felt like hugging him. "Yes, I will. Thank you, Viktor."

"You are welcome, Sunshine. One more thing," he said, as he reached under the flower stand. "A beauty for a beauty," he smiled, handing me a pink rose.

As I left Viktor, I felt so alive and invigorated that I lost track of where I was going. As if on autopilot, I found myself near my old office. Everything was exactly the same—the clocktower was still stuck at 2:47 and well-tended flower boxes decorated the top floors of the familiar brick building. Butterflies fluttered in my stomach as I glanced up toward the seventh floor. I pictured myself bounding up those stairs, counting all nighty-eight of them, with a sense of either optimism or despair, depending on the day. And I pictured myself running down them in a frenzied state before slipping and scraping my arm against the wall. I shook my head as if it would dispel the disturbing image and focused on the ground instead.

As I was about to turn around and head home, I saw the homeless girl on the corner. She was seated on dirty cardboard, holding a sign that simply said, "Please help." As I approached her, I saw how very young she was—no older than twenty. She was bone thin and had frizzy brown hair in desperate need of a wash. Her fingernails were dirty with only specs of black nail polish remaining. And, while her face was covered with large sores, I could see that she would have been quite pretty if fate had treated her differently. She didn't look at me as I came closer, only mumbled to herself as her dull eyes looked right through me. I took a breath and crouched down toward her.

"Hello, my name is Sunny," I said in a soft voice, not wanting to startle her. She smelled strongly of cigarettes and dirty hair.

She barely acknowledged me, only nodding her head slightly.

"What's your name?" This question seemed to snap her out of wherever she'd gone. As she looked up at me, I saw that her large brown eyes were bloodshot and there was a deep scar under one of them.

"Grace," she whispered.

My throat immediately constricted and I didn't know if I should laugh or cry. I paused briefly, gathering myself. "That's a beautiful name. What are your favorite foods, Grace?"

She looked shocked by my simple question. Perhaps no one had asked her name, much less any details about herself, in a very long time. But she would not be invisible to me.

Not sure what to say, she just shrugged.

"Okay, what's your favorite sandwich?"

She seemed to consider the question carefully before responding. "Grilled cheese."

"Hey, me too! I'll be right back." I went to a nearby deli and bought two grilled cheese sandwiches, several pickles, orange juice, water, apples, and a big cookie. I went back to the corner and handed her the bag. "Here, please take this."

She took the bag hesitantly and peered inside. "Oh, thank you. God bless you," she said a little louder this time, her voice hoarse.

"You're welcome. Oh, one more thing," I said, handing her the rose. "I'll see you again soon, Grace."

On Saturday, I prepared a pasta dinner and strawberry shortcake. Afterward, we gave each other our anniversary gifts. Mine was an easel, an incredible paint set and brushes. I'd been pining over the paints and brushes for a while, thinking they were too expensive. I gave Joshua a big hug and several kisses, thanking him profusely.

"Okay, now your turn," I said as I placed Joshua's gift on the table. After he unwrapped it, he sat staring at it for several seconds. I was worried that he hated it, but he seemed to be at a loss for words.

"This…" He stopped and wiped his eyes. "I'm sorry, it's just that," he said, looking at the drawing, "it's *you*, it's really you."

He didn't need to say anything more. I knew what he meant.

That evening, we held each other, dancing slowly to the songs we had fallen in love to. As we listened to "The Luckiest" by Ben Folds, Joshua whispered in my ear, "I really am the luckiest." *God, I loved my husband.* Without words, we found our way to the bedroom where we fell into bed, rediscovering and tasting every inch of each other. It had been quite a while since we'd made love in this way—slowly and rapturously; yet, when he was inside me, it was as though no time had passed, our souls remained interwoven, indivisible.

The following Thursday, my dad took the day off and picked me up in the morning. I wore a long yellow sundress with tie straps and a slit up the side—it was a gift from Baba that also happened to be my mother's favorite color. My wavy hair, which had grown quite a bit over the summer, cascaded halfway down my back. We were quiet as my dad drove toward one of San Diego's most beautiful beaches.

We parked the car and, as we walked toward Mission Bay Marina, he said, "How are you feeling, *tournesol?*" His white shirt fluttered gently in the wind, but his yarmulke remained securely fastened atop his head.

"I'm okay, Dad." I paused for a moment. "No, I'm more than okay."

He said nothing, but I saw his smile.

We were greeted by an old friend of my dad's, who was standing near the shore. As we approached him, I inhaled the familiar briny air which had always seemed pure and restorative. He guided us toward the marina's docks, which were crowded with all manner of recreational boats, from small fishing vessels to catamarans and luxury yachts. To my delight, one of the piers was inhabited by a group of seals languidly sunning their rubbery skin. An especially large one was sitting upright pointing his or her whiskery nose straight up as if to snub passersby. Several gray and white seagulls stood amongst the seals, releasing a few caws as we came nearer. I stopped for a moment to enjoy the scene, wishing I'd brought my sketchbook or at least something to feed the gulls. But, making a mental note to come back another day, I pulled myself away and was guided onto a large white and blue cabin cruiser with the word 'Clementine' along its side. Although the boat's living quarters appeared plush and inviting, it was a beautiful day, so we stood at the bow drinking hot chai tea as the boat left the marina. After around thirty minutes, the boat stopped moving.

As we idled there, surrounded by shimmering blue water, I removed the pink velvet bag from my backpack. As I held it, I wondered how a person with such vivaciousness and complexity could be reduced to only a couple of kilograms.

I closed my eyes and took several deep breaths before speaking. "Mama, I understand now. Thank you for loving me the best you could. I love you so much." After my father wispered, "Rest in peace, sweet Gracie," I opened the bag of ashes and gently tossed all that remained of my beautiful mother into the sea.

As my dad and I both sniffled, the boat turned around and we headed back to the marina where we thanked my dad's friend and got back in the car. We remained quiet and contemplative as we passed the usual landmarks. Less than an hour later, we arrived at the Jewish cemetery. Arm in arm, we walked amongst those whose corpses were laid to rest, but whose spirits remained tied to the living in a thousand different ways. The grounds were well maintained, with lovely eucalyptus and flowering jacaranda trees standing sentry over the deceased. It was a hot day, but there was a pleasant breeze and the air smelled of mowed grass. We walked past endless graves that ranged from small granite markers to ornate headstones that stood nearly as tall as me. Some had rocks on top of them, others did not, but most bore the Star of David. As I looked at the names, I imagined what their lives were like. What were their dreams? What had they endured?

When we reached the southern edge of the grounds, just beyond a weeping willow tree, I saw my grandparents' double monument. During my last visit to the cemetery, I was far too lost to really look at the gravestone, but today I saw it clearly. On Papa's side of the stone, below a Star of David, were several Hebrew words translated as: "Here Lies Aron, Son of Akiva and Miriam Zielinski." The remaining epitaph was in English and included the dates of his birth and death, along with "Beloved Husband, Father, Grandfather, Son and Brother. Courageous Polish Resistance Fighter." Atop Babcia's side of the tombstone was a menorah, followed by the Hebrew words for "Here Lies Chana, Daughter of Dvora & Benyamin Weiss." Again in English, this was followed by the dates of her birth and death, along with "Beloved Wife, Mother, Grandmother, Daughter and Sister."

As I stared at the gravestone I realized how rich, beautiful, complex, and agonizingly painful their lives had been. Born in the early 1920s, my time with each of them was but a fragment in their lives' tapestries. As I envisioned them as children in their native Poland, I saw them laughing, dancing, and playing amongst the beloved family members I had never known. I desperately hoped their early lives were abundant with joy, and that peace and contentment did not fully elude them after the war. I also thought about how fate had brought them to each other, with their physical bodies now resting side by side for all of eternity. And for this I was grateful.

My father spoke some words in Polish then removed his glasses and wiped his eyes. Then it was my turn. I had a thousand things I wanted to say to them, all of which were jumbled together in my head. So, I thought about what I really wanted them to know and simply said, "Baba and Papa, thank you for teaching me about love and for always being that soft place I needed. Please don't worry about me anymore. Your love has strengthened me and I know I will be alright. I will love you forever." After I blew my nose, my father and I placed rocks on each side of the gravestone. And this time, as we stood there beside my beloved grandparents, it was quiet. There were no warnings or admonitions, and no airplanes flying overhead—and that was okay. There was only the birdsong of a distant sparrow.

The End

Acknowledgements

I am deeply grateful to those who have guided, supported and encouraged me throughout the writing of this novel. To my top-notch editor: Kitty Bucholtz, thank you for your guidance in elevating and polishing this manuscript down to the last word. Your knowledge of publishing, eye for detail, and general positivity and enthusiasm are unparalleled.

Much appreciation also goes to Dr. Katherine Skillestad Winans who, as a licensed clinical psychologist with extensive experience treating individuals with serious mental illness, provided her expertise on schizoaffective disorder. Thank you, Katherine, for ensuring that I have portrayed the presentation and treatment of this illness in the most accurate, realistic, and sensitive way possible.

To my husband, Andrea, who motivated and inspired me from the moment I expressed the idea of writing a novel: Grazie, amore mio! I cannot imagine a more encouraging, generous, and loving partner. Thank you to my children, Ivy and Julian, and my stepdad, Don, for their constant love and support as I embarked on this challenge. And, most of all, I am blessed to have had a mom whose fierce love and encouragement has equipped me with the determination and resilience to fulfill my dreams. And thank you, Mom, for teaching me to adore books. I know your beautiful spirit is somewhere smiling at the publication of this work.

Sources Cited

Byron, G.G., (1975). The poetical works of Byron. Houghton Mifflin Company.

JewishGen.org (n.d.). Retrieved February 2, 2023 from https://www.jewishgen.org/Yizkor/Dabrowa/dab023.html

Longfellow, H.W. (1918). The little mother goose. Dodd, Mead & Company.

Nabokov, V. (1955). Lolita. Olympia Press.

Plath, S. (1953). Mad girl's love song. Mademoiselle. Retrieved April 15, 2023 from https://allpoetry.com/Mad-Girl%27s-Love-Song

Wilson, B., & Smith, B. (1939). Alcoholics anonymous: The big book. Ixia Press, an Imprint of Dover Publications, Inc.

Yad Vashem (n.d.). The Holocaust. Retrieved January 10, 2023 from https://www.yadvashem.org/holocaust.html

Printed in Great Britain
by Amazon